BETWEEN HEAVEN & HELL

GENESIS

BETWEEN HEAVEN & HELL
BOOK ONE

BRANDON M DAVIS

For Pamela Ann Davis

Thank You For Everything

INTRODUCTION

Heaven and Hell, demons and angels, God and the Devil. These are ideas that we choose to believe in. But whether we choose to believe in them or not, they are real. But what causes us to be assumed into Heaven or fall into hell? The answer is simply the choices we make but, I ask you, which choices in life matter most?

Is it the simple actions we take by natural reflex or the difficult choices that require much more thought? Do the choices that make *your* life better matter, or do the choices that make a stranger's life better? Is every decision you make being judged by God, or is he waiting for that one choice in your life to decide your eternity?

No one knows. So before you choose not to help someone in need; before you choose to lie and cheat; before you choose to pick on someone smaller than you, and before you choose to pull the trigger. Remember that demons and angels are watching everything you do and simply choosing whether to believe in them or not may affect whether you see the smile of God at the end of your days or the grimace of the Devil.

Welcome to Between Heaven and Hell.

SECTION I

Footsteps.

Faint, sluggish, and weak but footsteps undeniably.

This was the only sound to be heard, traveling like the ghost of a whisper on the cold midnight air. The next audible sound was that of breath, hurried and irregular, then the sharp slap of a wet hand against hard brick.

A dark figure limped down the pitch-black street, a single hand against a stone wall for support. She was beautiful once, beyond human comprehension. Now, barely a vestige of her former glory, beaten and broken she turned and stumbled down an alley.

As if dipped in ink, her hand left a trail of black prints across the brick wall. Her body trembled as she struggled down the damp cave, knocking over the half-full trashcans in her path.

Her clothes were tattered. The black overcoat that once fit her perfectly was now in shreds and hung loosely off her body. Her long black hair was matted and dirty. Patches of her scalp could be seen where her hair had been torn out.

She pushed herself from the brick alley wall for a moment, attempting to regain her balance. Like a newborn calf daring its first crucial steps, she hesitated, not fully trusting her own feet.

Her caution was justified.

She barely traveled a foot before slipping in a puddle of water and falling painfully onto her side. Her teeth clenched as once indolent pain receptors lit up her nervous system.

Cursing loudly, she pulled herself up against a dumpster for support. Her legs wobbled beneath her. Her vision, a spotted mess of points of light smeared with shades of darkness. Her hearing, eroded and irritating like a broken pair of headphones with only a single working side.

Her sense of smell?

Still functional, but what good would one sense do alone? And it too would soon be gone.

She was too far gone, pushed too hard too fast and this was the outcome of it. Forced to do the unthinkable, her brothers and sisters would be ashamed. She was surprised the transformation came without added pain. Or did it?

Ripples of agony spread throughout her body at regular intervals, so she couldn't tell even if she tried. Her lips trembled and her eyes twitched.

Was it supposed to hurt this much?

She couldn't fight back a smile. For all her grace and power she sounded just like one of them.

Like a human.

She took three solid steps before her legs buckled, pitching her face first into a puddle of slime. Pain shot up and down her body, reintroducing itself to her nerve receptors as she clutched her wound. Her blood dripped between her fingers, and her breathing became heavier.

She gazed at her muddled reflection in the puddle for what

seemed like an eternity; she looked at the blood on her hand. It had been so long since she'd seen her own. She had almost forgotten how black it was.

As she lay lamenting her circumstances, five men dressed in black came upon her. Their faces and bodies were splayed with fresh scars that dripped black blood and their clothes were almost as worn as hers. Though they were riddled with grievous injuries, all five men's faces remained stoic.

The frontman addressed her first.

"Hello." His words floated from his mouth laced with dole and uncertainty.

The soft peal of his voice made her eyes flutter. His short black hair matched his thin beard and trimmed mustache, which sat under a bruised and blood-stuffed nose.

The woman looked up and set a long gaze upon the frontman. She leaned up and put her back against the dumpster, facing the men.

"Hey." Her voice was weak and struggled when she spoke.

He wiped the sweat from his forehead as he approached her. "You're a hard one to keep up with. For a moment I didn't think we'd catch you, sister."

A puckish smirk crept its way across her lips. "You never were able to keep up with me."

"Yeah, but you know I always had to try." The man smiled back.

"I keep thinking about the time we first fought *him*. When he was trying to convince me to come to his side. He told me, *your brothers await your return with great anxiety.*"

"He was trying to make you like him, preying on the weakness inside you."

"Yeah, and you jumped in out of nowhere and flung him into his followers screaming, *you are no longer a brother of ours!*"

Her smile grew to a laugh which made her cringe at the pain it caused.

"I was always proud of you for standing up to him like that," he said as he walked nearer to her.

"Well, I have a confession. If you hadn't shown up when you did I would have joined him. He was *that* convincing."

"I know."

The woman looked at his right arm and saw a stream of black liquid rolling down his hand and dripping from his fingers.

"Did I do that?"

He clutched at his arm. "You got me pretty good."

"Looks like you got me better." She held up her blood-soaked hand.

She squeezed the open wound in her chest, trying to stop the blood flow. Silence fell over them both as they stared at each other. Then the woman's smile disappeared.

"Why, brother?"

The smile that spread across his face faded, and he could no longer make eye contact with the woman. His gaze found the floor as he answered her.

"I just wanted her to love us. That's all I wanted."

"And she does. She loves us second. Isn't that enough?"

"No. Second will never be enough. I will not let us be second to them. Not them."

"She made them in her likeness. Are you so much like Lu—"

"I AM NOTHING LIKE HIM!" The man shouted, his voice so powerful, the brick walls in the alley cracked under his breath. "Don't...*ever* compare me to him." His eyes found hers again, this time edged with malice.

"I can see there is no convincing you, brother. So finish it."

The woman lifted her chest toward the man and struggled to remove her torn coat.

"Leave us," he spoke to his men without turning, kneeling in front of her.

As his soldiers left the alley, he assisted the injured woman in removing her coat. He held her wounded body as she winced in pain, sliding her arms from the sleeves. Once finished with the methodic task, he tossed the stained jacket aside. A loud exhale escaped her mouth in celebration; a declaration of the minor victory against the torn garment.

His eyebrows furrowed, and his voice reached a somber tone as he spoke. "Will you not reconsider? Please...for me, Gabriel?"

This time, it was *her* eyes that met the floor of the alley.

He swallowed hard. "I see. Very well then." He took the woman's black-stained hand in his and kissed her forehead softly. "I love you, sister."

"I love you as well, Michael, but..." She pulled her hand from his grasp. "...you are no longer a brother of mine."

The wounded man stared at his sister, his face one of surprise mottled with points of boiling anger. He quickly forced his emotions back down into the pit of his stomach. He knew the rage he felt was unnecessary.

"Goodbye, sister." seraph

Michael slowly curled his hand into a tight fist and punched into Gabriel's chest, tearing open her previous wound even further. An agonizing expression shot threw her face as she screamed, making the walls buckle around them.

The piercing howl steadily increased in intensity and pitch until it became an elongated din, palpable but impossible for human ears to hear. The dumpster rolled away from the two as the concrete floor of the alley trembled and cracked, and just as the clangor built to an impossible fusillade, it was over.

"...forgive me," she whimpered, her body falling limp.

Michael stood over his sister's still corpse for a moment, staring at it blankly as the high-pitched ringing was followed shortly by hundreds of dogs barking in the distance. As he watched, tiny flames the same color as the cold moonlit night lit across Gabriel's hands and feet and slowly spread up her body. He knitted his brow as the minuscule fire consumed his sister at an arduously slow pace, almost as if to torture him more with his transgression.

"Is this what happens when seraphim die?" One of the men at his back questioned.

Michael shook his head. "I don't know." He turned and walked out of the alley with blood-red tears sliding down his cheeks. "It's never happened until now."

The beaten and worn company followed their commander out of the alleyway and disappeared into the darkness. Though they had just won a hard-fought victory, a thick melancholy hung in the atmosphere like charcoal-laden smoke. This was no ordinary victory. This victory was great and terrible.

Several quiet and undisturbed minutes passed before a jolly and slightly unharmonious song pierced the silence.

"*When you're hot you're hot, you really shoot your shot. You're Dyn-o-mite, child, yeah.*"

The off-kilter tune heralded the entrance of a new figure into the alleyway. He was dressed in a black hooded long coat and wore a thick shaved goatee upon his face. He stepped lightly, his feet twirling and flashing, pitching him rhythmically across hard concrete without a sound but the tune he bellowed as he danced.

"*Well, I can tell by your game, you're gonna start a flame love, baby, baby.*" His feet slid across the ground in step with the melody and carried him up the brick wall in defiance of gravity. "*Got me burnin, burnin, burnin.*"

He spun on his toe and moonwalked across the cracks in the wall before leaping back to the ground in front of Gabriel's burning corpse.

"Hiya, Gabes." He pulled a pack of cigarettes from his pocket, tapping the case against his palm and sliding a single between his fingers. "Got a light?"

Laughing to himself, he spun the white stick into his mouth. He arched his head to the sky and exhaled a cloud of smoke into the night air. Somehow the cigarette had lit on its own.

The hooded man removed the cancer stick from his mouth and shook the ash from it. In a single breath, he had half finished it.

"I never thought it would happen here. In all the worlds in all the universe, I never thought the first of us would die here. In the back alley of a shitty coffee shop." He returned his gaze to the burning woman. "Not saying you deserve it, but I would've given you better."

He leaned himself against the brick wall next to her, being infinitely cautious not to touch the black fire.

"For you, I would've erased an entire species, crashed planets together, tore stars apart, cannons and fanfare and all culminating in an epic battle atop a giant red sun, where I would have ripped your chest open for all life to see. It would have been spectacular."

The man took a second drag on the cigarette and flicked it away, finishing it.

"Oh well, I suppose you'll have to settle for the stench of a hobo's piss water and rat feces instead."

Just as he pushed himself from the wall, the dark fire engulfing Gabriel went out, leaving a half-burnt and smoking corpse lying on the alley floor. The hooded man paused for a moment, his face twisting into a mask of confusion. She was nearly char black bones now, patches of flesh sizzling where they remained.

His curiosity had gotten the best of him. He would never claim to be an expert here, but something about her death seemed off. He reached out his hand and pressed two fingers into her cheek, wiping away the char. Unmistakably, under the black crust was bubbling red blood. The goatee on his face pulled back his lips into a smile.

"Why, you little minx! I never once thought you had the *balls* to do this, much less the inclination." He wiped his hand across his mouth in disbelief. "And Michael didn't notice. Oh, this is too good. You are just full of surprises aren't you, Gabriel?" The man stood to his feet and smiled at her. "I'll keep your secret for now, Gabriel. If only to see their faces when everyone realizes what you've done."

The dark man placed his index and middle digits to his lips and with a snap of his fingers, Gabriel burst into flames again. This time it was the hot and reddish orange variety. He turned and strolled a whimsical two-step back down the alleyway he came, singing the chorus to the song in his head as the flames quickly turned her body into ash.

"*Fiiiiire! Uh, uh. Fiiiiire!*"

A man, clad in black, ran down an empty street. His body was racked with pain as black liquid dripped from the side of his head and torso. He looked back and forth down the empty street as he ran. His face pervaded his anxiety, almost as if he had lost something of irreplaceable importance. He grew more anxious, running faster down the street, and in his desperation, he cried out.

"Gabriel, where are you!?"

Another man, uniformly dressed, stepped out of a nearby alley and signaled to the injured man. Immediately, he changed course, dashing into the alley.

As he entered he saw dozens of men and women standing in the alleyway, all garbed in black. They turned to look at the injured man; he could see their eyebrows rise and eyes widen as they recognized him and formed a pathway. He stopped in his tracks and the alley became deathly silent.

The dim glow of moonlight cascaded into the brick hallway and was the only light for which there was to see. Even by the light of the moon, the alley remained a dark cave through which no human eyes could penetrate. Like the mouth of hell, the dreary backstreet opened to him and invited him inward, begging him to come with unspoken words. He knew the work of evil stained this place, and he knew what it contained would be blacker than the devil's soul.

He wiped his long brown hair from his face and the sweat off his brow. He fixed his clothes and tucked his hair behind his ears as he walked down the path created for him.

Passing the men and women on either side, he gave them each a cursory glance. Their faces were riddled with reminisces of battle. All of them were hurt and many had grievous injuries, yet they all stood silently.

"Where is she?" He asked the crowd. "Where?"

He looked around at the quiet gathering. No one would make eye contact with him. No one would dare.

"Where is my sister?"

The desperation in his throat made his voice tremble. Tears began to form in his eyes, but before they could fall, someone called out.

"Here. She is here, Raphael."

He turned around and walked to the one who had spoken out. The man was standing in front of a dumpster in the corner of the alley, holding a dirty black coat over a pile of ashes on the alley floor. Raphael slowly walked up to the man and looked at the ashes.

"Is this...?" He couldn't bring himself to finish the question.

"Yes, it is."

Tears welled up in Raphael's eyes as he stared. He gently placed his knees to the alley floor, taking both hands full of his sister's ashes. Holding the remains close to his face, he sniffed them, breathing in the overwhelming burnt stench.

"Her scent is still strong."

Raphael clutched the ashes to his face and wept over them. His tears fell into the ashes, wetting them in his hands. The heartbroken sibling knelt there, weeping for his lost sister, and after a while lifted his head. His face was bathed in anger even more than the ash that now covered it.

"Who?" Raphael stood to his feet.

"We're not entirely sure, but we believe Michael killed her himself," one of the men replied.

"No, who else was with her?"

Everyone looked quizzically at one another. The answer was clear. No one was.

Raphael turned around, eyes beaming at them all, his face overflowing with rage. "So, not one of my siblings found the time to defend my sister!? Where were you? Where were you!?"

Raphael darted from one person to the other, grabbing them, and pulling them close enough to his face to scream at each of them personally.

"Where were you, my brothers and sisters!? How dare you show your faces here when you were not here to defend her!"

The ground underneath the black-clad figures rolled under Raphael's breath. He grabbed one of them by the head with both hands and pulled him to his face, pressing their foreheads together.

"Where were you, my brother!? Where were you when the one we needed most..." The anger on Raphael's face faded suddenly and only sadness remained. "...needed us the most?"

He pulled his hands from his sibling's face, resting them on his shoulders and hanging his head low.

"I cannot blame you. I can only blame myself. I failed her as well."

Raphael fell to both knees once again in the middle of the alley, his upturned arms resting on his legs as he stared toward the night sky. Red tears flowed down his face, soaking his collar and staining it crimson.

"Nonetheless my brother, you are now our leader," a woman spoke out. "For better or worse, until the lord says otherwise, we follow you."

And with that said, all of the battle-weary men and women circled their leader and knelt before him. Raphael beheld his new army with apprehension filling his stomach and doubt filling his heart.

"Lead us well, Lord Raphael."

The newly appointed leader closed his eyes for a moment, searching for a modicum of clarity, the faintest sign or proof that he was on the correct path and that everything would be all right. After finding none, his eyes again found the moonlit sky.

"Lord help us."

CHAPTER
TWO

T *he Guardians*

SECTION I

A man lies on his back in a king-size bed. His eyes are tightly closed as cool air from an open vent spills into the room and washes over his tan skin. His narrow eyelids flutter slightly above his thin nose and strong cheekbones. He takes his right hand, combs it through his long straight black hair, and sighs deeply through his thick lips. His mouth barely moves as he mumbles an inaudible prayer to himself.

"Dear Lord, so far I have done all right. I haven't gossiped, haven't lost my temper. I haven't been greedy, grumpy, selfish, nasty, or overindulgent. I'm really glad about that. But in a few minutes, God, I'm going to get out of bed and from then on I'm going to need a lot more help." He took a breath, inhaling the hope and joy of a new day. "Saint Thomas, pray for me. Saint Sebastian, fight for me. Saint Monica, wait for me. Saint Jude, believe in me. Amen."

The thin-eyed man opened his eyes, and at the foot of his bed stood at least eight men dressed in black. The man at the forefront of the group was an average-height bald man with eyes the deepest blue he had ever seen. His nearly pale white skin held a scowl that sat triumphantly on his face.

"Daniel."

The man sat up in his bed, surprised that his room was occupied by so many people without him knowing. "What is this? What are you doing here?"

All of the men in black stared silently at the startled man.

"Raphael has ordered a conference with you and your men, Daniel." The bald man spat his words.

Daniel inspected each of his intruders as his eyes traced the room. Suspicion was overflowing his mind.

"Where is she?"

The pale man reached into his pocket, pulled out a piece of paper, and threw it on the edge of the bed as if in reply. "Gather your forces and meet us here in one hour."

He shifted his eyes toward his men, nodding his head slightly. Immediately, they all began making their way out of the room. After the last man exited the room, the bald man turned and began walking toward the door.

"She's dead isn't she?" Daniel's words spilled from his mouth sounding more like a statement than a question.

The man stopped abruptly before he reached the door as if hearing those words had paralyzed him. He turned his head slightly to the right and glanced off as if he were staring into a distant realm, arcane thoughts mulling over his mind.

"One hour," he repeated as he walked out the door.

Daniel opened the piece of paper on the edge of his bed and memorized its contents before balling it up and swallowing it whole. He then snatched his cell phone from the nightstand, punched in a few numbers, and waited for a ring. After two rings, a voice answered in a deep baritone.

"Yeah?"

"Call everyone you can and tell them to meet me at the old abandoned church on Forest Road in 30 minutes."

"Uh, everyone? You do know that half of them are in the middle of an operation—"

"I know," Daniel cut off the voice. "Call whoever you can get a hold of. Something is happening, something big."

"Where the hell is he?" Daniel fumed from inside the car. "He doesn't have any assignments, so why hasn't he shown up yet?"

He was sitting in the back seat of a parked black Charger, but he was not alone. In the driver's seat sat a large muscular black man, bald with a squared chin that wore a thick black beard. His heavy voice made his words seem to echo from inside his mouth.

"Hey, I called him. He said he'd be here. Just give him a little more time. I know it doesn't seem like it sometimes, but he's trying."

"You're right, Prophet." Daniel raised an eyebrow at him before looking out the tinted window. "It *doesn't* seem like it."

Prophet gave a slight chortle in reply and Daniel shook his head as he continued.

"I just don't understand him. He gets more chances than anyone else and he just refuses to correct himself."

"Try looking at it from his point of view. He's the youngest member of the Guardians. He has to constantly train to keep up with the rest of us. Every day he's learning something new that probably makes little to no sense to him *and* he has to deal with a tight ass, smart mouth, know-it-all breathing down his neck every second of the day."

Daniel shot the muscular man an accusing stare. "I'm assuming those last few comments were about me?"

Prophet shrugged his shoulders. "Hey, you're the genius."

"I suppose this is your lackadaisical way of telling me I'm being too hard on him?"

Prophet glanced up at Daniel through the rearview mirror. "Is a pig's pussy pork?"

Daniel couldn't hold back laughter at his old friend's comment. He had known Prophet for years and probably knew more about him than any other person, with the possible exception of his brother.

He was the one person he didn't have to think about trusting because it came so naturally. They had the kind of friendship that allowed them to understand what the other was thinking without them having to say a word.

Though, Prophet was infinitely better at telling jokes.

Daniel coughed out the last bits of laughter. "Fair enough, so what do you suggest?"

"Simplicity, patience, compassion. These three are your greatest treasures. Lao Tzu."

Daniel raised an eyebrow. "And that means?"

"Just ease up some, and acknowledge when he does something right for a change. Paying him a compliment wouldn't hurt either."

"Is that what you did with *your* brother?"

Prophet smirked before he spoke. "I tried something a little different."

"What's that?"

His half-smile grew into a proud grin. "Left him in a room with Sera for five minutes."

Daniel rolled with laughter again. "So much for compassion." He checked his watch and then tapped the back of the seat Prophet sat in. "Time to go, Superman."

Daniel opened the door and stepped outside the car. He wore a black suit with a long black leather coat.

The driver's side door opened, and a mountain of a man stepped out. Prophet was about 6'4, of muscular build, and was wearing a striped black, button-down shirt and slacks, covered by a black trench coat. The coat, which came down to his knees, covered him awkwardly. He wore it with only the right arm in its proper sleeve. His left arm hung inside the coat, hidden from view.

Prophet stepped around the car and took in his new surroundings. He scanned over the old abandoned building in slight confusion as to why a meeting was being called here of all places.

The church was boarded up and vacant; there had been no life here for years. The stone staircase leading to the broken double doors was cracked and worn. Even the streets near the church were barely inhabited. The only sign of life was the pigeons that made a nest in the split church wall.

"Why are we meeting here? They coulda picked a better place than this, right?" Prophet queried.

"You got me. We're begging for trouble meeting at this dump."

The roar of an engine interrupted them as a black and red motorcycle careened down the street and pulled onto the curb. Daniel looked at the rider and let out a disappointed sigh. He felt a heavy hand grasp his shoulder.

"Take it easy," Prophet spoke as if sensing Daniel's frustration.

He was correct in his assumption. Underneath his long-time friend's calm demeanor churned an ocean of suppressed irritation. Daniel was not good at hiding his emotions when it came to Adam. Just as with most siblings, his brother had a knack for pushing his buttons. Most times he didn't even have to try.

Daniel, a scowl glued to his face, watched the rider step off the bike and walk toward him. "You're late."

The rider took off his helmet and revealed his pecan brown skin and black straightened hair styled into a sleek pompadour. He had accentuated cheekbones with a small nose and thick perfectly sized lips.

"I know, sorry."

"Sorry? You say sorry when you forget to take out the trash, or when you accidentally eat one of Prophet's snacks. This, you don't say sorry about, Adam."

The sleek-haired young man wiped his hand down his face and huffed at Daniel's reply. "Well, what do you want me to say?"

"I don't want you to *say* anything, I want you to be on time. I know that you didn't have any assignments today, so you should have been the first one here. Instead, you're ten minutes late."

"I lost track of the time, all right? It's not like I didn't show up, so chill out."

Daniel stepped up close to his brother, his seriousness radiated from his body as he glared into Adam's eyes. "This is not a game, Adam. You're one of us now, a Guardian, and people's lives are at stake. What if this had been a trap? You would be our only help and our survival would hinge on you being here, *on time*."

"If this was a trap then my being late would probably save all our lives."

Daniel stared frozen daggers into Adam's skin. The younger sibling decided to change his reply.

"Okay, I'm sorry. I'll be early next time."

"I'm sure you will be."

He could nearly taste the sarcasm in Daniel's words.

"We'll finish this afterward."

Adam released a long irritated breath as Daniel turned and walked up the aged stairs. One of the doors swung open, and a figure stepped onto the concrete staircase. The high-pitched squeal of rusty hinges, deep guttural moan of dry wood, and growling scratch of the dragging door heralded his exit in a chorus of racket.

He was an old man, long since removed from his Scottish ancestry, with a thick grey beard and mustache hanging from his chin. Robed in an ankle-length priest's cassock with rosary beads hanging at his waist, he wore a large brown bag strung across his shoulder and silver framed glasses hanging from the tip of his nose. His thick, uncompromisingly grey, hair blew in the wind without fear of showing his age. The old man lifted his hand and placed a black, wide-brim hat on his head.

"Father." Daniel's voice was one of complete reverence.

"Daniel. I hoped you were going to cut this hair of yours." The old man pushed his glasses up with one hand and ruffled the hair on Daniel's head with the other.

"Tomorrow," Daniel replied.

"You said that yesterday." The priest smiled. "Are you ready?"

"Yes."

"Then bow your heads, Guardians."

Daniel and his brother dropped their heads. All of the playfulness, trepidation, and doubt vanished in an instant.

Father removed his hat and gave the bearded black man a glance and a nod. "Prophet."

The dark-skinned man stepped to the front of the group, shut his eyes, and bowed his head. "May the Lord watch over and protect us in all of our travels. May she keep us in her sight when the demons of hell bare down upon us, and may we all fight with valor and dignity until the end of our days."

Father called out to his men, "Saint Thomas."

"Pray for us," the Guardians responded in unison.

"Saint Sebastian," the priest called.

"Fight for us," they answered.

"Saint Monica."

"Wait for us."

"Saint Jude."

"Believe in us."

"May the Lord God make our days long and our end swift." Father pulled from his bag a metal flask and sprinkled droplets of its contents upon the group. "Amen. Now—"

The old priest returned his hat to his head, placed the flask to his lips, and took a swallow of the liquid, offering a slight cringe as it burned its way down his throat. He then snatched a cigarette from his pocket, lit it, and took a long drag on its tip, expelling the smoke out through his nostrils.

"—let's go see what these angels want."

THREE

A *Meeting of Powers*

SECTION I

Father forced open one of the wooden double doors, allowing access to the inside. There was a large wooden beam nailed across the entrance to prevent anyone from entering the church. The board was half broken at the bottom, which meant that the wood was either rotted or someone had previously broken their way into the church. Father ducked under the aged wooden beam and stepped into the church, the rest of the men following after.

The inside of the church easily showed more age than the exterior. The old concrete floor and walls were brittle and covered in dust and sand. The windows were boarded up so that only trickles of sunlight pierced the gloomy sepulcher. Not only were the pews broken and carelessly thrown into a corner in the church but the marble columns throughout the building were cracked and barely standing.

It wasn't hard to imagine that, many years ago, this church was the shining jewel of its neighborhood, with polished marble columns, a soft thick carpet covering the hard stone floor, and hundreds of the faithful pressing into the packed pews.

Daniel was less preoccupied with the deprecation of the church and more concerned with the men and women dressed in black suits and coats littering its center. He recognized the ones from his room immediately but with them stood many others he had not seen before.

"You're early," Daniel spoke, stepping to the forefront of the group.

A brown-haired man stepped forward in response. His hair was wrapped into a single ponytail that flowed down his back.

"So are you. But I expected as much from you, Daniel."

"And I of you, Raphael. It's an honor to finally meet you. I've heard a lot about you."

"From my sister's mouth, no doubt. I wonder, what else has she shared with you?"

"Enough to know that this is extremely out of character for you. You wouldn't normally bother yourself with the business of humans. Not unless it was something of grave importance."

Raphael huffed at Daniel's remark haughtily. "You need not feign ignorance, Daniel. I'm well aware of your quick-witted nature. From the moment you saw my angels in your room, you guessed exactly what had happened. So, if you haven't already, now is the time to fill your comrades in on the most important piece of information."

Daniel's jaws tightened as he turned slightly toward the men behind him. "Gabriel...is dead."

There was a slight pause before anyone answered. The words took their time to sink in.

"Bullshit," Adam snapped at the suggestion in utter disbelief.

"Are you serious, D? Is this for real?" Prophet asked softly as if gentle words would make it untrue.

Father remained silent, his words caught in his throat, his stoic face masking the swirling emotion behind his eyes and his hand over his heart as if it had suddenly stopped.

"It is interesting reading your responses to this," Raphael interjected. "You seem to have become quite attached to her."

Prophet placed his right hand on Adam's shoulder in a mild attempt to assuage his anger. "Yeah, you have to understand, Gabriel was like a big sister to us all."

"Coincidentally, she was my *actual* sister, so I believe I can more than understand. Though, I still find it odd that she spent so much time with you. She always had a soft spot for humans, but I didn't think she would fraternize so rigorously."

"Maybe we knew Gabriel better than you did."

The words sprang from Adam's mouth matter-of-factly and everyone knew it was meant to be an insult. Daniel gritted his teeth and Raphael cut his eyes at the young man.

"You would be wise, young Guardian, to never assume you know *anything* better than a seraph. Not even yourself," Raphael spoke slowly, inferring his seriousness with each word.

"Perhaps we should get back on topic." Daniel intervened before the subject could go any further. "How did it happen? I think we deserve to know at least that much."

Raphael cleared his throat and took a deep breath. The expression on his face was a lugubrious one as if merely repeating the events was equally as horrible as the act itself.

"As you know, there is a war going on between the angels in heaven. Between those who accept that humans are loved above all others and those who reject this notion. There was a crucial battle in heaven recently. Our side was ambushed. From what I understand, there were thousands of them."

"From what you understand?" Daniel interrupted.

"I was not there at the time. I was on Earth. Michael kept

me preoccupied with a group of his strongest angels, and I could not get there in time."

"So what did you do?" Daniel asked.

"Do you mean before or after I ripped out their hearts?" A puckish smile played on Raphael's lips.

Daniel stared at the angel with a stone face, refusing to acknowledge his sarcasm until he continued.

"I received word from one of my sister's lieutenants that the battle was over and that Gabriel was nowhere to be found. I knew she would've escaped to Earth so I ordered a search for her, but by the time we found her it was too late. Her entire army had been decimated and she was left severely weakened and alone. Michael got to her first."

Adam slammed his fist into the palm of his hand and cursed loudly. "Why weren't any of you there?! She's your sister, you should've been—"

Daniel snatched his brother tightly by the arm before he could finish. He could tell from the look on Raphael's face that the last remark touched a nerve, and it was his job to nip his younger sibling's rant in the bud before an angel did it for him.

"Go home. Now."

"Go home!? Gabriel's dead, Daniel, and they weren't even there to—"

Daniel tightened his grip, making sure to cause discomfort as he repeated his words. "Now."

Adam stared at Daniel with a blank look on his face, struggling to find the correct emotional anchor to vent his frustration. His hands clutched into tight trembling fists at his sides and Prophet's hand fell onto his shoulder once again.

"He's right, kid. Save it for another time."

Adam huffed in dissatisfaction and jerked his arm free of his brother. "We're useless in this stupid war."

The young Guardian stepped back through the boarded church doors, cursing again under his breath.

"Sorry, Raphael. Please continue," Daniel said ignoring his brother's outburst.

"Michael has crippled us badly and he knows it, so he will move quickly to finish this war. I have a feeling that this is the beginning of a large-scale plan he has been working on. Michael has always been a tactician, but his recent maneuvers have been different...more convoluted and aggressive."

"That's fine, but what does this have to do with us? We can't help either side in this war."

Raphael stepped closer toward Daniel as he spoke. "I fear Michael did not act alone in this. And if it is whom I suspect then there is more at risk than ever before. Even for you."

"Are you implying that Michael would move against us? Why? What would he have to gain?"

"Just be on guard. I don't think Michael would be so brazen, but I'm warning you regardless. Now that Gabriel is gone, things are changing and no one is safe anymore."

"And what are you going to do?" Father's voice reached across the room, surprising everyone with his abruptness.

Raphael paused a moment, his face taking a petulant form at the thoughts in his head. "I have someone to talk to before I decide. For now, this meeting is over."

Raphael snapped his fingers, and the angels behind him began leaping into the air. One after the other they catapulted through an opening in the ceiling at least 20 feet from the ground. As his angels flighted away, Raphael addressed Daniel and his men again.

"In case there is any uncertainty, let me be absolutely clear. I don't trust any of you. Her death is the only reason I warn you. I don't know why, but for some reason, Gabriel had a remarkable amount of faith in you. I, on the other hand, am less than convinced. I see nothing special about you Guardians. Maybe she saw something that I don't. More likely, there is nothing more to see than a huddled mass of trembling humans who are in over their heads. I'll be waiting for you to prove me wrong, but I won't be holding my breath."

With that, Raphael followed his men through the opening in the ceiling. The Guardians were left in silence amid the rising dust covering the church floor. It was Prophet who first chose to break the silence.

"Kind of an asshole, ain't he?"

The remainder of the Guardians eyed the giant blankly.

"I mean, as far as divine angels go." He smirked innocently. "I don't see what good we are in this whole civil war thing, though. As crazy as the kid is, he's got a point. And a pair of cast iron balls to boot. Fact is, we're trained to fight demons, not angels."

"Point and testicles aside, that doesn't justify the surplus of empty space between his ears," Daniel spat. "That was completely reckless and immature, insulting Raphael like that. Not only was it rude, but it's stupid to offend someone who could literally put you through a wall."

Father stepped in between both men. "Gentlemen, perhaps we could continue this gripping exchange of dialog elsewhere? Unless you've forgotten, this place is not safe."

Both men bit their tongues. Father was right, and even if he wasn't, neither of them would question his word. The old man was wise beyond even his own years, and both Daniel and Prophet owed him their lives and respect several times over.

"You're right, Father. We'll finish this later, with Adam present." Daniel nodded.

As the three men moved toward the exit, the double doors blew off their hinges, shattering to pieces as they were thrown into the church.

Father's throat tightened and his hand went to his chest. "Too little, too late."

Inside the church stepped four figures. Two of them were dressed in sleek stealth commando-like suits with black vests and boots. Their faces were completely hidden by thin black cloths which fit snugly and outlined the shape of each of their heads.

They glided with the ease and appearance of ninjas, not making a sound as they entered the church. Abstruse as they were, they were not the most menacing of the four.

There was one much taller figure with them. He wore long tattered, dark purple robes concealing his face and body. He was by far the noisiest of the four. Each step he took into the church was followed with grunts, snorts, and growls. His entire body was concealed, giving no hint as to what hid under the cloak, but the pluming smoke that fissured from his mouth as he breathed presaged a malicious intent.

The final figure stood in front of the licentious group. He paced steadily toward the Guardians, his arms folded behind his back in an urbane manner. His face was the only one completely uncovered.

He was a tall black man with his hair cut short, two tiny gold hooped earrings in each ear, and deep brown eyes. He wore a long black coat trimmed with red at its corners with same colored pants and shoes.

"The Guardians, I presume?" The lead man asked with a gentle smile.

"Who wants to know?" Daniel replied at the back of the group.

"Ahhh, that must be the infamous, Daniel. Your reputation far precedes you; I've heard so much about you. And of course, the legend himself, Father. You've aged well."

Father scowled at his addresser. "You're a familiar beast. I don't, however, recall your name, Mr..." He let his voice trail off.

"Forgive my rudeness, I didn't even introduce myself. My name is Obsidion and had I known you'd become such an iconic figure, I'd have followed you more closely and killed you years ago." He gave a short bow without dropping his equivocal stare.

Prophet almost laughed at the man's words. He glanced at each of his teammates with a derisive grin smeared to his face and scratched his head in disbelief. "And I thought *Adam* had balls. Listen, buddy, trust me when I tell you this ain't a fight you want. Now, I'm sure your men ain't too shabby in a brawl. Not that they could fight very well with pantyhose on their heads but—"

"Silence, human!"

Obsidion shouted in a heavy voice so loud that dust rattled from the church ceiling. The Guardians stared in quiet surprise at the suddenly furious man. He glared angrily at Prophet and, in the next moment, his rage peeled away leaving a smile spread across his face.

"You know, I was a bit skeptical when an *angel*, of all beings, told me Daniel of the Guardians would be at an abandoned church this morning." Obsidion kicked a small piece of debris across the church floor. "Naturally, I assumed this would be a trap. I almost dismissed it altogether, but luckily one of my scouts noticed this little meeting of yours." He patted the head of one of the concealed ninja figures at his side.

"Are you saying an *angel* gave us up?" Father demanded more than he asked the question.

"Indeed," Obsidion replied. "Most peculiar isn't it? It seems angels aren't just betraying each other, but even their human allies as well, leaving us demons to our own devices. I tell you I couldn't be happier than I am right now to be of the latter group."

Daniel stepped to the forefront of his team once again. "It's a catharsis that won't last. Enjoy it while it does."

"Oh, I intend to in a few moments, most rigorously." A vulpine grin slowly slid across the demon's face as he stared down his intended prey.

Daniel's face returned the slightest smirk as he replied. "That's a powerful voice you have, Obi. I'm surprised a second-class demon like yourself could do that."

Obsidion's face immediately twisted from delightful to livid as the words fell from Daniel's mouth. It was shameful for a human to know a demon's class and was downright disrespectful to discuss a demon's class in public. To do so would be the equivalent of prodding a sleeping lion with a stick, dangerous and nearly suicidal. The demon would almost have no choice but to disembowel you where you stood.

Obsidion clenched his teeth as Daniel's verbal assault continued.

"I mean, only a low-class fire demon would be in charge of so few half-breeds, right?"

Almost as if it caused some irretrievable discomfort, Obsidion forced a genteel smile across his face. "How astute of you, Guardian. Even with their bodies concealed, you were still able to glean the half-breeds from the true demons. You even noticed I'm a fire demon. Talk of your skills has not been over-stated. Very impressive indeed."

"It's not very difficult," Daniel said sharply. "Rephaim don't have the *odor* that full-blood demons do."

Obsidion began to slowly pace back and forth in front of the group. "But what kind of Guardians hold secret meetings in an abandoned church?" The demon bent forward, wiping the church floor with his fingertips. "Especially, when said

Guardians know that when a church is abandoned by the faithful..." He rubbed his fingers together and then blew the dry dust into the air. "...it is no longer considered holy."

"You're correct, Obi. I suppose we'll have to work on where we hold our meetings in the future. Or maybe this was just an elaborate plan to lure spies like yourselves out into the open?"

Obsidion chortled at Daniel's words. "Now *that*, my sagacious friend, I find hard to believe."

As Daniel and Obsidion exchanged words, Prophet slowly moved his body next to the old priest, Father, tilting himself slightly over the much shorter man as if no one would notice. "So, old man, did Adam really eat my snacks?"

Father smiled lightly, his eyes staying focused on the interlopers. "Possibly, but doubtful." The priest could see the wave of relief flow across Prophet's face as his fears were allayed. "I would think you'd have more to worry about at the moment than the loss of chocolate cakes."

Prophet motioned toward the group of intruders to his front. "These guys? Two rephaim and an ogre? Losing snacks is way more important."

"So, you could tell which ones were the half-breeds?" Father queried.

"Hell no. I don't know how the hell Daniel does it with their bodies fully covered. Never met another person in my life that could tell a half-breed from a real demon without at least seeing their face."

"You pointed out the ogre." Father ended his statement with an upward inflection as if posing a question.

"That's different." Prophet rubbed his hand across his bearded chin. "I've fought my fair share of ogres and I know what they sound like, but I still couldn't say one way or the other based on sight alone."

Father kicked a tiny piece of broken marble across the floor. "So, how sure are you about that creature being an ogre?"

"Pretty sure."

"Sure enough to wager a box of your beloved chocolate cakes?" The old priest could hear the air leave Prophet's chest.

"I would never do something as reckless as bet in the middle of a life or death situation."

Both men stood stoically as an awkward silence passed between them.

"Make it two, old man."

Father's smile spread to both sides of his face.

"Well done, human. You are correct." Obsidion abruptly jumped into their conversation, startling both men momentarily and leaving them wondering if he had been listening to their exchange the entire time.

Obsidion snapped his fingers and the cloaked figure tore the robes from his body in earnest.

Underneath was a giant purple-skinned creature with throbbing green eyes and a completely bald head except for three small white bones protruding from his forehead. The demon's incisors were massive, hanging outside its mouth even when closed. The most daunting feature of the ogre, however, was his muscular physique. The beast's body was so ripped, it could have been chiseled from stone.

"Since we're showing off now," Prophet spoke stepping forward, "you won't mind if I go next."

He grabbed his black trench coat and tossed it from his shoulders to the floor. Under the covering was a shining silver-metallic limb in place of a flesh and blood arm. Giant steel coils and copper wires ran through the metal attachment connecting to the veins in his natural body.

Gears spun tirelessly in his joints, issuing soft clicks with each movement. The abnormal appendage squealed joyously as Prophet balled up his fist and extended his gleaming arm through the sunlight at the ogre.

"Quite an interesting group of humans, aren't you?" Obsidion spoke as the ogre locked eyes with Prophet and drew its tongue across its lips. "I must admit I was hoping to meet your little brother, Daniel. Suffice it to say, in the demon realm, we have high expectations of him. I was quite anxious to see what he is capable of."

"Sorry to disappoint you," Daniel replied icily. "You just missed him."

"The next time I see him, I'll be sure to say hello." A cold grin slid across the demon's face."Some even expect your sibling to surpass you. Unlikely, but nevertheless, you won't live to see the day."

As he spoke, the ogre began to growl and snort even louder, as if growing restless. The figures in the black vests began to unsheathe their weapons for battle. Obsidion gave a cursory glance over his belligerent warriors, smiling as he did so, then rested his eyes on Daniel.

"Why don't you and I adjourn to a less crowded space and allow our ancillaries to get to know each other better? I'm sure they have much to discuss."

"Fine." Daniel nodded. "The church basement a suitable arena?"

"That'll be heavenly."

Daniel turned to walk away and Father grabbed him by the arm.

"Be careful, Daniel. This demon is not to be underestimated."

Daniel nodded slowly, his stare locked onto the priest. "Worry about your own fight. I'll be done before you know it."

"May the Lord be with you."

The young Guardian winked at his mentor. "Where else would she be?"

Daniel walked past the old man toward the back of the church with his demon opponent in tow. Obsidion strolled in between the two Guardians, hands still behind his back. As he headed toward the basement, he stopped suddenly, turning to face the church entrance.

"Oh, I almost forgot."

He looked at his minions fidgeting anxiously, waiting for the signal from their master. An evil grimace spread across his face as he gave the command.

"Kill them."

CHAPTER
FOUR

D *aniel*

SECTION I

He woke up screaming.

Fiery tongues licking the skin from his body had suddenly become soft white bed sheets. Crass mammalian claws scratching at his flesh transformed into warm compassionate hands assuaging his nightmares. He felt his body pulled from the floor and lifted into soft loving arms. He was bleeding a little from his forehead from thrashing so wildly underneath the bed.

"Not again. I think it's getting worse."

"The doctor said the pills were supposed to help with this."

His mother petted his head gently. His father rocked him back and forth in his arms.

"Maybe we should call the doctor again." He suggested.

"So they can give us more pills to drug him up with?" She asked cynically.

"Well, what else can we do?"

"We need to talk to him. Find out what's going on in his head."

"That's what his psychiatrist is for."

His brother stood in the doorway watching. The whites of his eyes hung in the darkness. He had been standing there for a while now.

"Adam." The woman turned, noticing him. "What are you doing out of bed?"

His mother lifted him from his feet and carried him off to his room. His father stayed, rubbing his brother's back and wiping the blood from his face.

"You know that you're safe here, right? You understand that don't you, Daniel?"

Tears ran down the boy's face as he answered.

"No."

His father raced back and forth in the kitchen grabbing his coffee and breakfast, a thick piece of sausage, and a bagel.

"You know you need to eat more than that. And drink your orange juice for once," the woman said as she placed two plates of food in front of Daniel and Adam.

The man eyed her irritatingly, his slightly narrow eyes one of the many features Daniel had inherited from his Asian father. "Fine."

The two brothers watched their father swallow down the eight-ounce glass in two swift gulps and place it back on the table.

"Happy?"

"You're taking Daniel to school, right?" She asked, ignoring his gibe.

"No time. I need to get to work early."

The woman shot the man a cutting glare, her pecan brown skin showing just a hint of red.

"What?" He threw his hands dismissively.

Daniel and Adam already knew an argument was imminent. They decided to keep their heads down and finish breakfast. It was what they usually did.

Her next words had a touch of warning to them. "We need to talk."

The woman wiped her hands on a kitchen towel and headed into the living room, her husband huffing behind her. Once they believed they were out of earshot, she spoke.

"Didn't we talk about this? You need to bring him to school so you can talk to him."

"Listen, I need to get to work early today. I've got a ton of work to do, and you're already bringing Adam to school, so why don't you take Daniel and talk to him?"

"Because this is supposed to be *your* son confiding in *his* father. Maybe he can talk to you about things he can't talk to me about."

The man folded his arms over his chest, his temperature rising in his face. "Look, we've tried this already, remember?"

"Yeah, months ago when he wasn't saying a word at all." The woman folded her arms as if to match him.

"And he's talking now. He's getting better."

"No thanks to you."

"Don't do that."

"Do what?" Her hands were on her hips now and her mini afro shook above her rolling neck.

"Don't make it seem like I'm not doing anything. Like *I'm* the problem." His face was beginning to flush. "I took a job out here to get him away from anything that might trigger an episode. Less pay, more work. I'm doing my best here!"

"And it's still like you're not even here! You weren't even here the night I had to move Daniel into his own room because his nightmares were getting so bad, they were scaring Adam. And he *still* sleeps under his bed every night."

"What do you want me to do, quit the job I just got? We can barely pay for the medication and therapy now."

"I *want* you to be there for your son!"

Their voices had slowly gone from a slight whisper to now, almost shouting. This was usually how their fights began. Closed in a separate room, talking and then screaming at one another. The two brothers sat quietly at the kitchen table. They could hear every word.

Adam ate his food slowly as he watched his older brother stare blankly at his plate. "Was it bad?"

Daniel glanced at him for a moment, then nodded his head.

"They want you to talk more. You don't talk enough," his younger brother said as if it would solve all their problems.

Daniel dragged his spoon through the scrambled eggs on his plate and stirred them into his grits. He didn't reply to his brother. He couldn't explain how distant he felt from him now. He felt far away from everyone, including himself. As hard as he tried, he just couldn't seem to get comfortable in his body.

It was so different from the one he had grown accustomed to. His arms were short and stringy now. His legs, limp and weak. His lungs lacked the stamina to carry him very far, and his heart struggled to keep up with any strenuous activity he was performing.

He hated everything about his body now, except his tolerance for pain.

It was the one silver lining he could find throughout his ordeal. Pain was as disconnected from him as a good night's sleep. He could no longer be punished physically because he didn't feel pain like everyone else.

He once cut himself at the dinner table with his knife and didn't notice until his mother started screaming. She thought he had done it on purpose and just didn't tell anyone. The truth was, he hadn't felt anything until she brought it to his attention.

Needless to say, his plates were devoid of sharp kitchenware from then on.

"Was it shoal?"

Daniel almost smiled at his brother's mispronunciation of the word, then decided to scowl instead because it sounded like he didn't take it seriously.

He couldn't even get his six-year-old brother to believe him. If he couldn't pronounce the word, how could he even begin to believe him?

"Sheol," Daniel said it slowly so that he could catch on.

"I believe you, you know."

Daniel felt his eyes roll in his head. "No, you don't."

"I do. Really!"

Daniel leaned in close over the table. "And what's that?"

His brother cowered away, putting his head down and playing with his food.

Daniel sat back down in his chair, satisfied. "Yeah, that's what I thought."

"I believe that you woke up surrounded by monsters. And that they hurt you and burned you and wouldn't let you go."

Daniel stared at his brother in surprise. He didn't expect him to actually pay attention to his story. He allowed himself a subtle internal smile.

"*Maybe there's hope for me yet.*"

In the car with his father, Daniel didn't say a word. He could sense his dad wasn't very eager to start the conversation. Being that he had lost the battle with his wife, he wasn't in a particularly gregarious mood.

That was perfectly fine with him. He never enjoyed their talks anyway. His father had the uncanny ability to make him feel completely and undoubtedly insane.

It was a feeling he could do without this morning.

"So, you wanna talk about that dream?" His dad struggled to say.

Daniel dropped his eyes to the floor and shook his head in silence.

"It might make you feel better if you talk to me about it." The man prodded again.

"That's what the psychiatrist is for, isn't it?"

The man bit his tongue at his own words being used against him. Daniel had a unique ability to make his father feel utterly useless.

"Well...um, yeah. But I'd still like to talk to you. You're still my son, aren't you?"

"*Only by blood.*" Daniel thought. "We've tried this before, remember? You don't believe me."

His father sighed dispassionately. "It's a little hard, son. In fact, it's more than hard."

"It's impossible." Daniel spat almost angrily.

There was a short silence between them before the man spoke again.

"Imagine if someone came up to you and told you they went to Hell, spent years there, and came back. Now imagine that someone was an eleven-year-old boy. Would you believe it?"

"Depends."

"On what?"

"Is that eleven-year-old boy my son?"

Daniel had effectively ended the conversation. His father was now too irritable to continue and Daniel was done long before they had begun.

Truth be told, he could understand his father's situation, but that didn't mean he held sympathy for him. And the fact that he *didn't* have sympathy for him didn't mean he *shouldn't* have sympathy for him. He suddenly felt the need to say something more but decided to wait until they arrived at his school.

They pulled up in front of his school building and Daniel jumped out of his seat. He knew his father wanted to say more, but his guilt wouldn't allow him to. Daniel decided that this was his moment.

"I know this must be frustrating for you. I know you were proud of me once. I was doing well. I was in Mensa until..." He cleared his throat. "I want you to know that I'm trying. I'm trying to get things back to how they used to be, but it's no longer fair for everyone to keep making sacrifices on my part."

Daniel paused for a moment to take in the look of surprise on his father's face before continuing.

"No more compromises. I'll figure this out, I just need time." With that, he closed the car door and strolled into class.

The pills helped with his nightmares by a small amount, but beggars couldn't be choosers. Last night was the first really bad one he'd had in a few days.

He noticed a slight decrease in the frequency of his dreams since beginning the medication, but what they seemed to have no effect on were the terrors that hid within his daydreams. He noticed, almost immediately after taking the pills, the increase in his daymares.

In many regards, they were worse and more vivid than the nightmares. At least when he was sleeping he could awaken from the horrors to a safe place. While awake things were more...complicated.

The tolling of the school bell would become the high-pitched scream of a tortured woman, the steaming meatloaf on his plate could just as easily be a slab of throbbing human flesh, and the smiling face of a classmate with braces had once become the sneering visage of a demented demon.

His school life was trying at best.

"Daniel! Would you like to come answer this question in front of the whole class?"

He hadn't realized he'd been daydreaming again. No matter how hard he tried, his mind would always wander to other things. There was no longer anything in school that could keep his attention for more than a few moments, and so when his mercurial mind wasn't hallucinating some maniacal vision, he was excruciatingly bored.

Daniel searched around the classroom, glancing at the books open on the surrounding desks. What subject was he in again?

"Now, Daniel," his teacher repeated.

He decided to get up and go to the chalkboard before he let on that he hadn't been paying attention since the bell rang. The blackboard was empty except for three short phrases written in cursive.

All-Good, All-Knowing, All-Powerful.

"*Great. Religion.*"

Daniel stood at the forefront of the classroom, the eyes of his peers burning into him like dry ice on bare skin. He could hear the whispers winding through the room, flowing from student to student. His mere presence sparked a new level of excitement among the children. They were anxious to see if he was as smart as they had heard.

"Explain the meaning behind these phrases and their relationship with human beings," his teacher demanded.

Daniel cleared his throat before speaking. "These phrases

are often used to describe God. The *All-Good* meaning that she is good in every way and wants what's best for us. *All-Knowing* meaning she knows all that has been, is, and ever will be. And *All-Powerful* pertaining to her limitless power and ability to accomplish anything."

A hand at the front of the class shot up. "Sister Anchorage, how do we know that God is all these things? Did someone meet her and study her so that they could find all of this out?"

The teacher turned her head toward Daniel. "Why don't you answer that, Daniel?"

The boy in front of the chalkboard could feel his palms begin to moisten with sweat. He still wasn't completely used to talking out loud, so talking in front of a group of unforgiving classmates who were making up their minds about him at this very moment, was torture. He decided to take the easy way out and not let his peers think he was a pompous know-it-all.

"I don't know."

"You don't know?" Sister Anchorage looked at him with astounding disappointment. "So you were skipped forward two full grade levels to arrive at my class, and you don't *know*?"

"Is that a crime?" Daniel asked meekly.

"Well, we've all heard about how smart you're supposed to be. Some have even said *genius*. I just didn't think genius-level intelligence stopped at the seventh-grade level."

The classroom erupted with laughter. Daniel stood mentally naked before his gawking classmates as they teased him. He should have expected this. He had heard the horror stories of Sister Anchorage even before he made it to her class.

She was known for castigating students who believed themselves to be intelligent. Humiliating them, making them cry in front of the whole class. She had once made a little girl, who had been skipped forward one grade, feel so bad that her grades dropped and she had to be returned to her original grade level.

She believed herself the dictator of a small country of children, and her insecurities would not let her students feel any smarter than her, or she any less than ruler of the classroom.

"How about we get someone who knows the answer to tackle the question," she spat.

A boy at the back of the room raised his hand and shouted the answer. "Because the Bible tells us so."

"Very good, Gregory. Seems like you're a genius in the making as well."

Another wave of laughter rushed forth, aimed at Daniel's pride. He felt anger well up inside him. His intelligence was one thing he was proud of in his life. The one thing that if everything else could be taken from him, he knew his mind couldn't. Yet here he stood, beside a treacherous snake that very much intended to sully his perspicacity and ruin his chance at a comfortable social life while in her class.

He would not allow this.

"Because the Bible tells us so? That's cute. How about we take these three things and try to apply each one to God and see if it fits."

"What do you mean?" Sister Anchorage asked.

"I believe that God cannot be more than two of these things at one time."

A hush fell over the students. They couldn't believe that a student would go against what the Bible said, and in Religion class of all places.

"And how did you come up with that sparkling answer? she asked cynically.

"Let's start with, *All-Knowing*. Let's assume for the sake of argument that our God is only *All-Good* and *All-Powerful*. This would mean that she has the best intentions for us and can manipulate the elements around us, but she doesn't know what the outcome will be once she does. This could be used to explain why bad things happen to good people, wars, and even natural disasters. It's because when God does something in one place, her actions cause a chain of events she cannot foresee that may cause bad things to occur. In this case, even her lack of action can cause *evil* things to occur."

Another hand rose at the front of the classroom. "So, you're saying God isn't All-Knowing?"

Daniel smiled. "Okay, let's throw *All-Knowing* back into the mix, and let's take out *All-Powerful*. If she were *All-Good* and *All-Knowing* then that would explain a lot because then she wouldn't be All-Powerful. Meaning she would know what is going to happen to us in our lives and would want the best for us, but she lacks the power to change anything. Doesn't that make a lot of sense when you look at the world we live in?"

The room grew quiet, but he could still hear subtle murmurs of agreement from the students. He was winning them back.

"That's very cute, Daniel," Sister Anchorage interjected. "So, why don't you explain how our God isn't an *All-Good* god?"

"Can God really be *All-Good* with so much evil in the world?"

The teacher snorted haughtily. "Yes child, it's called *Necessary Evil*. We must learn *through* the bad things in life to be better people *for* God."

She wasn't going to let him have his pride if she could help it, and he wouldn't let her pry it from him without a fight.

"Ok. If our hardships are what make us better people and being better for God is the goal, then why not remove our hardships and just make us better people? An *All-Powerful* God can do that with a wave of her hand. Why make us suffer with hardships to make us better people when you have the power to instantly make us better people? An *All-Powerful* and *All-Knowing* God would do this, but not an *All-Good* one."

"That's very clever Daniel, but you're forgetting about a little thing called free will. God has granted us the will to choose our own destiny and it is this very freedom that is the cause of all of our hardships." She stood to her feet, addressing the class in boisterous fashion. "Yes, our God can be *All-Knowing, All-Powerful,* and *All-Good*, but it is our free will that is the cause of all the evil in the world, not God."

Daniel watched Sister Anchorage sit down and give him a self-satisfied grin as if to mock him further. His teeth clenched in his mouth but he decided to turn it into a wide smile.

"Ah, free will. I was wondering when this subject would come up in this classroom." Daniel cleared his throat before he began. "I know that some of you believe that an *All-Knowing* and *All-Powerful* God can simply grant her creations free will and that would make her all good. This is a fallacy. If our God is *All-Knowing*, then free will cannot exist."

Daniel began pacing back and forth down the aisle of the classroom methodically.

"Consider this. God knew what you'd do this very moment before even you did. She knew what you would do this moment before your parents were born. She knew what you would do this exact moment before your grandparents existed, before the first animal touched land, and before sunlight touched the first plant."

"Knowing what someone will do is not the same as controlling them, Daniel." Anchorage butted in abruptly. "Like how I knew you would bore my class to death with your lazy argument but I'm not *making* you do it."

Soft chuckles fell from smiling mouths around him. He decided to address his teacher's claim directly.

"No, Sister. There is a difference between *guessing* what someone will do and *knowing*. No matter how much you may claim to know what someone will do, there is always the possibility that you are wrong. That possibility vanishes with an *All-Knowing* God. She knows what choice you will make even before the option of choice has presented itself. Tell me, if a being can know what choice you'd make before the option has even appeared, how could there ever have been a choice to begin with?"

His teacher was stunned. You could hear a pin drop in the classroom. Daniel had taken her argument apart effortlessly.

She stumbled over her words. "Well...um. Yes, but—"

"It's perfectly fine if you don't know, Sister Anchorage. I'm sure our genius-in-the-making, Gregory, can help tackle it for you."

The sound of giggling children was like salt on an open wound. Her face flushed red. She stood up and slapped Daniel across the face with a wooden ruler, instantly quieting the students.

Daniel's face was stolid as if he hadn't just had his cheek viciously bruised.

"You will not mouth off to me, little boy. Now, have a seat."

For some reason, Daniel was ok with this. Probably because they both knew she had been defeated. Her lashing out was the only way to show dominance now that he had shamed her in front of the entire class. She had single-handedly helped guarantee that he would soon be the most popular kid in school. Word would spread now about how Daniel outsmarted the great and cruel Sister Anchorage and took her unfair punishment without a word of complaint.

It's not like he could feel it anyway.

The young boy smiled. "With pleasure, Sister."

The students all eyed his glowing red cheek as Daniel

strolled back toward his desk, his chest sticking out more than usual. The room suddenly began to roll. The faces of his peers became hazy and all sound became muffled. The weight of his body doubled and pulled him to the ground.

His hand slammed onto his desk before he could hit the floor. Normal sight and sound returned to him as he noticed the entire class staring wide-eyed at him. Their faces were masks of confusion.

He had almost passed out again.

The incessant rabble of schoolchildren filled the cafeteria like white noise in the background of a radio broadcast. Like a chaotic drum, the pitter-patter of tiny feet permeated and echoed. Brown, blonde, and red hair of varying lengths and textures swirled about each other in a twister of color. Light reflected from thick glasses onto a large metal table stacked with plastic trays and filled with greasy foods.

Daniel preferred not to take part in the circus that was lunchtime.

He sat outside near the football field, a half-eaten sandwich next to him. After a few bites, he had lost his appetite. That wasn't a normal side effect of the drugs, so he decided that he just wasn't that hungry. He had also decided that taking an extra pill in the morning without anyone knowing was not the best idea.

Proazin had a nasty habit of making him feel light-headed. But he needed to up the dosage after last night. As little as the medicine helped, he hoped more of it would make a difference. He couldn't go back to sleep after last night. Not if it meant more nightmares like that.

"What you eatin', Barf?"

Daniel heard the words, but they weren't directed at him. He stood up and saw four figures underneath the bleachers he sat next to. Three of them loomed over a much smaller one.

"Mommy make you a yummy snack, Barf?"

Bullies. Daniel didn't have to hear any more to know that. Probably a trio of seventh-graders picking on a sixth or fifth-grade kid.

"*Poor kid. And not a teacher in sight,*" he thought.

For a moment, Daniel toyed with the idea of helping him. He quickly dismissed the thought. If he was stronger, yes. If he was in his other body, the body he had spent years in and grown accustomed to, with its strength and speed and all the things that were now a distant vivid memory to him. If he had that now, he would be a champion for all who were too weak to defend themselves.

He felt himself shake. He could not form words for how much he desired that power again. His real power.

Anger bubbled inside him like a pot of water left on the stove for too long. He remembered again how much he hated his shell. How, in an instant, he was pulled from his strength and enmeshed in weakness. Consumed by it. Suffocated by it.

The taste of hemoglobin brought him back to reality. He had bitten down on his bottom lip and drawn blood. A hollow chuckle escaped his lips. Partly because he had lost himself in his longing for his old body again and partly because, once again, he could not feel his wound.

"Gimme that food, Barf!"

The lead boy snatched the lunch box from the smaller boy's hands. Daniel still couldn't quite make out who they were. He decided to try and ignore them.

"Oh, looks like mommy made a nice turkey and spinach sandwich for the little barf. Good thing you're not hungry huh, Barf?"

Daniel could hear the laughter rising from the other boys as the sandwich was dropped onto the ground. Suddenly his eyes shot wide open.

Sandwich. Turkey and spinach.

He looked down at the half-eaten sandwich next to him and knew who the kid was. Firstly, because this particular kid had a bad habit of shutting down when faced with antagonists, and secondly because mom had always made them matching turkey and spinach sandwiches for lunch.

Daniel was off his feet and running down to the bleachers. He had no earthly idea of what he would do, but he knew he had to protect his brother.

"The ants deserve this meal more than you don't they, Barf? Answer me!" The tall boy pushed Adam backward, almost knocking him off his feet.

"Leave him alone."

The trio turned around to see a short and skinny specimen standing behind them. Daniel instantly recognized the leader. Brett Devlin.

Brett used to be in the same grade as Daniel before he moved up. A loud and energetic child whose grip was as powerful and as inescapable as a steel trap. Daniel knew him well because Brett had been a terror in the previous grade.

After Daniel's accident, he had been put in remedial classes because he refused to speak. Once he had returned to normal(or as normal as he could be)he did so well that they moved him up two grade levels. The first-grade level was one he and Brett both occupied and where they had initially met. It was because of Brett Devlin that Daniel vowed not to remain there long.

The problem with Brett was that he was the ring leader of a group of troublemakers, outcasts by choice. That, and he was almost twice the size of a normal child his age.

"Well, look-a what we have here. Big barf came to save little barf. Ain't that sweet?"

The other boys chuckled at his taunts.

"His name isn't barf, Brett." Daniel tried to sound tough.

"Well, he certainly looks like a barf doesn't he? And so do you."

"Isn't this the one who used to be a retard?" One of the boys said.

"Yeah, he is. Those retard classes must be working out good for him. Look, he can form full sentences now."

They all laughed. Daniel glanced over at his little brother who cowered behind the three massive bodies in silence.

"Yeah, I can see you guys are still having problems in that area. I can recommend a good teacher if you like. She only teaches retards though, so you may have to take a few extra courses before you're ready for her class—"

Brett snatched Daniel onto his toes by the collar before he could finish his sentence. "You're real talkative now, big barf. You get skipped ahead a couple grades and now you think you're big shit. That brain of yours is gonna bring you more trouble than you want." A sinister smile slid across Brett's face. "In fact, let me help you make that overgrown brain of yours a little smaller."

Before Daniel knew it was happening, Brett had slammed his forehead into his.

His ears rang, his sight blurred, and his frontal lobe shook in his skull. Blood rushed from his forehead and he felt his feet become heavy. Before he could recover, a secondary head butt rocked his cranium, then a third. He felt the blood roll from his nostrils down to his lips, then he hit the ground.

"Have a nice nap, big barf."

The boys turned their attention back to Adam and cornered him against a pole under the bleachers.

Brett lowered himself to Adam's eye level and grabbed the boy by the collar."You want to feel what your brother just felt? I think I got a few more in me."

As Brett reared away, he felt a small hand push his head forward into the metal pole. The deep ring of vibrating steel doubled in intensity inside the giant boy's head.

He fell forward and rolled onto his back clutching his head in pain. "What the hell was that!?"

As his vision cleared, he could just barely make out the silhouette of a short and skinny specimen crouched over his body.

His teeth clenched tightly in his mouth, and blood still ran down his nose. "No. Not yet, Brett. I've still got plenty more left in me."

Daniel reared backward and slammed his forehead into Brett's. He didn't feel much after the initial contact and this was the only thing he knew he could beat Brett in. His former classmate was stronger than he, so there was no chance he could overpower him. Even if he could outrun him, his brother could not and so escape was not an option.

This was the only thing he could do. Outlast him. Show him that his tolerance for pain was greater than his. Greater than anybody. Show him that no matter what he did to him, he could never truly hurt him.

A second strike. The red whelps on both their heads grew brighter. A third and Daniel could feel his teeth rattle. A fourth. The wet slapping sound of blood-stained foreheads had finally arrived.

Daniel couldn't fathom why the other boys had not pulled him from their friend by now. Perhaps they were as interested in seeing the outcome of this quarrel as any other, or perhaps they were too shocked and terrified to do anything but watch.

He didn't bother himself with such trivialities. He was busy with head-butt number five.

With each blow, Daniel could feel himself slipping further and further away from his conscious mind. His vision was a splatter of red and blue static. Sound was a single uninterrupted cacophonous note. B sharp, if he wasn't mistaken.

The world around him became an opaque glass through which he could receive no information about his environment. Still, he dare not stop. He continued reigning down blow after terrible blow until he could no longer tell if it was his own blood he was tasting or Brett's.

The words '*Somebody grab him, he's gonna kill him*' finally broke through as the sweet and gentle arms of oblivion wrapped themselves around Daniel and he blacked out.

SECTION 2

He didn't exactly remember waking up, only the fact that he was awake now. The bright checkered pattern wall in the nurse's office hurt his eyes. Yellow and bright green. An ugly choice of colors for a nurse's office.

The nurse herself sat in the corner of the room, her back to her patient, her hands busily crafting his treatment. His vision was normal but still swam slightly. His nose was cleaned and stuffed with some kind of medical paper.

Oddly enough, he had the faintest remnant of a headache. He had no idea why this excited him. He could barely remember what they felt like.

The nurse whipped around and gently placed a large white bandage over his forehead. "You're a tough one aren't you? Ten stitches and not a sound."

Daniel didn't reply. His face remained stoic and uninterested.

"If it means anything to you, you're very brave to stand up to Brett Devlin like that. He's sent more battered kids to me than anyone would like to admit, but this time he won't be sweet talking his way out of it."

Daniel felt a twinge of guilt at the fact that Brett could be expelled because of him.

He was uncertain about his own fate as well. Would he face expulsion too? And what about Brett's cronies, would they be punished as well? Most importantly, what would become of his brother?

"I...didn't mean..to. I didn't want...this," Daniel stammered.

"Oh, it's not your fault, sweetie." The nurse rubbed his head softly. "Everyone knows Brett started the fight. You were just protecting your brother. It's just too bad nobody got there until Brett had already knocked you unconscious."

And there it was, truth laid bare. Everyone thought he had been rendered unconscious by Brett's hand.

He replayed what he remembered over in his head. Up until he passed out he had been on top of Brett. He couldn't remember if Brett was conscious or not at that point.

Had Devlin stood to his feet after he had blacked out? Had his friends helped him up and tried to flee the scene? Either of these scenarios happening just as a teacher arrived would paint a very different picture from the truth.

Daniel could feel his headache swell, his brain protesting against the brutalization of Brett with his skull. A moment later the pain was gone.

"From what I heard, you got in a few good shots on him yourself. He needed twenty stitches." The nurse stepped away for a moment and then handed him a slip of paper. "This is a prescription for any pain you might feel later on. Your parents are waiting outside."

Daniel slid off the nurse's table and walked toward the door. The nurse sat back in the corner of the room finishing her paperwork. As she turned her back to him, Daniel crumpled the slip of paper and threw it away.

"I heard about your altercation at school today."

Daniel kept his head down, purposefully avoiding eye contact with the woman across from him. "Yeah."

"Would you like to talk about it?"

He fumbled with the materials on the table in front of him, still not meeting her gaze. "Not really, probably should though."

"Is that why you decided to come here? You could have canceled today and picked it up again next week. Your parents said you wanted to come."

"I want to get better. I *need* to get better."

"Then let's start with how you felt during the fight. Did you feel scared, sad, maybe a little bit angry?"

Daniel finally looked up at the brown-haired woman and pointed directly to his bandaged forehead. "You tell me, Dr. Coin. You're the psychiatrist."

"I'll tell you how I *think* you felt." Dr. Coin adjusted the glasses on her face. "A bit of sadness at the fact that you were forced into a fight, and anger at yourself for hurting that boy like that. But you didn't mean to hurt him."

Daniel smiled a brief hollow smile.

"Tell me if I'm right or not," she said.

"I was angry, but not at myself. The moment I jumped on top of him I couldn't see his face anymore. I saw the face of a demon. It was grinning at me. I remember its teeth. Cracked, yellow teeth. I wanted it to die. I wanted to kill it. I wanted to make it disappear."

"You wanted...revenge?"

"Revenge?" Daniel looked as if he didn't recognize the word.

"Revenge for what they did to you. You told me you spent years with them. You were tortured for years, Daniel. You didn't want a little payback for that?"

The boy became silent. He knew the truth, but he didn't want to say it.

Revenge. A despicable word. He disliked it and everything it represented. It was an evil and selfish word and was too closely associated with the creatures in his nightmares for him to want any part of it. He could never have anything in common with those monsters.

Dr. Coin noticed his hesitation at the question. "We'll come back to that. How are your dreams?"

She was good at telling when a question made him uncomfortable. He didn't know if it was from years of giving therapy or if his inner thoughts were just an open book to her. She could read his emotions as if his head were a computer monitor with the words 'happy' or 'sad' flashing across the screen in bright bold letters. He admired that about her. She was the only adult that still retained his respect.

"Nightmares." He corrected her.

"Still bad? How have they been since beginning the medication?"

"Slightly diminished. I dream while I'm awake now."

"And how is your family taking things?"

"They're struggling. Adam acts like he believes me. I know he doesn't really understand what's happening. My mother would rather not talk about it. She likes to pretend like everything is normal as if it will slowly fade away with time." Daniel paused again.

"And your father?"

"I'm hardest on him. He tried to talk to me today and I made it impossible for him."

"Why?"

"Because, unlike the rest of the family, he thinks I'm utterly insane. He makes no active attempt to believe what I say at all. No matter how much I believe it happened to me, this world does not and cannot logically exist in his eyes, and he will not compromise his intellectual integrity for anyone. Not even his firstborn son."

Dr. Coin looked at him with a serious expression. "Do you hate him for it?"

"Yes."

It came out easier than he expected. He felt a little closer to those demons he so desperately wanted to individuate himself from.

Maybe he didn't mean it. He had a tendency to speak bluntly without giving his words much thought at times. He tried to clean it up.

"Maybe."

The woman's eyes peaked over the top of her glasses and perused Daniel's countenance. He could feel her gaze peeling away the insipid expression he held and drilling into the unfettered emotion behind his eyes. She always looked at him like this after a serious question. After all, she didn't expect the truth to come from just his lips.

This was her technique. Her simple upfront questions would hold your immediate attention. Then, she would blindside you with a question you couldn't possibly answer without your subconscious pouring to the forefront of your mind. Because that's where the truth was.

It only took moments, and that was all she needed. She didn't read the truth in your words, she read the truth behind your eyes.

"I think we should recite the words today."

Daniel's eyes rolled. "Again? Why?"

"Because you haven't been reciting them at home, have you?"

"No. It makes me sound crazy."

"To whom?"

"To myself." Daniel removed his gaze from hers as he spoke.

"Come on. I would like to hear you say it."

The boy swallowed hard before returning his eyes to hers. He felt his mouth moisten as the words came forth.

"My name is Daniel. At ten years old I was struck by a car and killed. When I died my soul went to a place called Sheol, but most know it by the moniker, Hell. I lived and was tortured in Hell for years until I was suddenly thrown back into my own ten-year-old body. I can't explain what happened, but I retain all of the memories of that place in my mind."

"You paraphrased a bit, but good enough. How do you feel now?"

He wanted to admit he felt a bit better after hearing the words out loud. Dr. Coin's presence had made it easier for him to believe himself. She was the only person who didn't make him feel completely certifiable in his beliefs.

While she never actually said that she believed him, he didn't want to ask. He wasn't even sure she would tell him, but the fear of someone he respected so much rebuking him was enough for him to remain silent.

"Crazy," he answered.

"Ok, let's try something else. Do you remember your latest dream?"

"Plumes of smoke. Talons ripping my skin open. Screams. Fire. Yeah, I remember it."

"We're going to try a new technique. This is something you

can do at home on your own as well." She leaned forward in her chair. "I want you to close your eyes and replay your dream in your mind as clearly as you can."

Daniel complied, closing his eyes and drawing himself back into the recesses of his brain. He felt goosebumps on his skin.

"What is the first thing you remember seeing?" She asked.

"Nothing. Darkness. Just the smell of something burning."

"And then?"

"Falling into a cloud of smoke. Too thick to see through. Choking me."

"What happens then?" Dr. Coin sat on the edge of her seat.

"I land in a pit. These strange shadowy creatures are all around me. At first, they don't notice me, but then one of them does. It screams at the sight of me."

"It screams?"

"Not a fearful scream, a happy one. An excited one. Like the scream a toddler makes when its parent walks through the door. Then all the others turn around. They scream too. Happy screams. They're elated that I'm here because now they get to play with me. They scream so much and so loud that I can't hear anything else. And when they finally get their hands on me, I realize that the only one screaming is me."

Daniel opened his eyes, already glossed over with tears ready to run down his cheeks.

"Is that when you wake up?" She asked.

"On a good night."

"We're going to try this again, but this time we're going to change some things as we go."

"I'm not going to pretend I understand what you're trying to accomplish with this. But I'll trust you for now." Daniel closed his eyes once more.

"What was the first sense you had in your dream?"

"Smelling something burning."

"Let's stop there. Let's replace that smell of burning with something else."

"Like what?" Daniel cracked his eyes open.

"Something better. Something you would like to smell. What's your favorite scent?"

He had no clue. He couldn't remember anyone ever asking him that. His face must've shown how puzzled he was.

"Just pick something. Something good," she added.

Daniel exhaled loudly and closed his eyes again. The scent came to him from a distant dust-covered memory. The smell of his father's shirts when he held him close as a baby. The mix of aftershave and soap on his skin. Daniel always wondered how he smelled so good.

As a child, he had tried to use his father's soap and aftershave on himself with disastrous effects. He smelled like pure aftershave for the rest of the day. His dad was tickled pink.

"Do you have it?" Dr. Coin asked.

"Yes. My father's shirts."

"What's your next sensation?"

"Falling."

"You're not going to fall this time. What can you change that to?"

Daniel could feel the metal springs inside the couch pushing back on him. He slowly imagined the springs bouncing him into the air, higher with each bounce until he was bounding through the sky.

"We used to have a trampoline before we had to move."

"Good. Now, we don't need any screaming creatures for this dream, do we? What are you going to do about them?"

"Change them."

"Into what?"

He paused momentarily, his thoughts bubbling up to the front of his mind.

"My family. We're all on the trampoline now. We're bouncing around like crazy. My dad's throwing us around trying to see how high he can make us go. I keep trying to send Adam flying over the edge of the trampoline. Mom doesn't approve, but she laughs hardest."

Dr. Coin became silent and watched Daniel. The expression on his face said it all. He was happy here.

"Daniel," she spoke gently.

His eyes slowly peeled open, bright and tear-free. It took him a moment to notice the smile on his face.

"What was that?" He asked.

"It's called IRT, Imagery Rehearsal Therapy. We take your recent nightmare and change it into something more pleasant. It may seem simple, and it is, but it is also very effective. Many patients with PTSD have overcome or lessened terrible nightmares with this technique alone."

"So, I can stop taking the pills?"

"Not quite yet. Just try it out for now, just a few times a day for a couple of minutes and we'll see how it goes. Keep at it and it may just stop your nightmares altogether."

"And this technique works?"

She gave him a playful smile. "Well, you tell me, Daniel, you're the patient."

Daniel left the room in a pleasant mood, which was usually the case after a session with Dr. Coin. His father stood in the waiting room for him. He felt his mood diminish somewhat. His brother sat in a chair swinging his feet excitedly, a blue cup of flavored ice running down his fingers as he licked.

"Take your brother to the car, Daniel. I'll be there in a minute," his father said.

Daniel took Adam by the hand and walked out as his dad approached his doctor.

"Dr. Coin, I know Daniel requested that none of his family be present during his sessions with you, but I'd like to know, is he at least getting better?"

"I think *you'd* be better suited to answer that question. You spend more time with him at home than I do here," she replied. "Have you seen any improvements?"

"No. He's pulling further away from us every day. I'm scared he's just going to up and leave one day or maybe even hurt one of us."

"I wouldn't worry too much about that. You heard about how he came to his brother's rescue today. I'd say the love he has for his family is still there."

The man rubbed his hand across his face in frustration. "Then what do you think is the problem?"

"Daniel is an interesting case. He is very unique and extremely intelligent, and I'm not talking about his test scores. I've been around my fair share of geniuses. I'm raising two incredibly bright twin boys myself, so I know how a gifted mind works. Daniel displays something more than that. It's not just book smarts with him, it's wisdom and that's something I haven't seen in a child his age."

The man stepped away from the woman for a moment. His brow was furled as if he were contemplating something important.

She could tell her words had sparked a pertinent memory. "What is it?"

"When things got really bad for us, we took Daniel to get a CAT scan. We thought that maybe they could identify if something was physically wrong with him. The doctor showed us a side-by-side comparison of Daniel's brain and the brain of a normal kid his age." He hesitated before he spoke again.

"And?" She nudged him.

"The doctor said his brain was more similar to that of a man in his 30s than an eleven-year-old boy. He said he had never seen anything like it. He was almost ready to classify it as some kind of disease." The man had an offended look on his face. "Do you believe that? Because I don't. My boy is not sick."

Dr. Coin could see that his mind was making connections he was not ready to accept.

She decided to push him. "So, what *do* you believe?"

The man looked at her awkwardly, as if she couldn't possibly be asking him this question. "You mean, do I believe my eleven-year-old son went to Hell and came back a thirty-year-old man trapped in a child's body? No, I don't and I hope you aren't spending the time I pay for in there encouraging that belief."

"My job is to provide him with the tools necessary to help him with his problems and I hope that you still respect Daniel's request that you not be made privy to the details of our discussions." Her tone showed she was about ready to end the conversation.

"Are you saying you believe him?"

"Whether I do or not is negligible. I'm going to do what is necessary to help him and you should do the same."

"So what would you have me do?" The man's voice was now one of sympathy.

"Nothing. I'm going to have someone sent to your home who can help. He has experience with this type of thing and may give your son someone he can relate to. Call me when he gets there." She turned and walked back toward her office before stopping halfway and facing him again. "If you aren't ready to consider the idea that your son may be telling the truth then there is one other thing you can do to help him."

"And what's that?"

"Buy a trampoline."

SECTION 3

His fingers traced the nape of his neck, sliding down to his slightly protrudent collar bone and then to his bony shoulders. His arms were thin and didn't have much muscle to them. He placed his hand on the bathroom mirror and wiped it across its surface. No good. He was still locked within this body.

Shouldn't he feel ashamed? The truth was that this was *his* body or at the very least his original one. How could he feel such anger toward it? He should've been happy that he had his life back and that the nightmare was finally over, but how could he go back to his life after what he had seen?

The answer was, he couldn't.

It was impossible to forget everything he had experienced. The pain was forever burned within his memory, and like a throbbing hot cattle prod pressed onto soft skin, the sights and sounds were seared into his brain and would not leave. They had become permeant scars.

A crimson hand suddenly burst through the sink and grabbed at him with clawed black fingertips.

Daniel's heart froze in his chest as he fell backward onto

the bathroom floor. Pieces of white porcelain scattered around him like broken chunks of hard chalk. His head slammed into the wall behind him. He looked up and the hand was gone.

Water sprayed into the air from exposed pipes inside the broken sink. Daniel's eyes were stretched wide as he scanned the area for his missing assailant.

The bathroom was eerily quiet. The soft splash of falling water and quick rhythm of heavy breath was all there was to be heard.

Until he heard something else.

Coming from the other side of the door. A quick and hard rapping. As if someone had placed their hand on the door and drummed the wooden surface with their fingers. The sound repeated and Daniel knew at once that no human hand had made it.

He stood up facing the door, his heart running laps inside his body. The sound continued again and again. He felt helpless, trapped by a creature he knew was not real but was powerless to control. Each thump against the door made his spine tingle until, as abruptly as it started, the drumming stopped.

That's when the blood came.

Like a gently flowing river, it streamed from underneath the door and toward Daniel's feet. He closed his eyes and felt the thickness of the liquid lap onto his toes. The drumming returned, this time much harder.

"*Do something. Think of something else. Think of the trampoline.*"

He forced his mind to his old backyard. A brown picket fence trimmed with bright yellow Daisies. The giant trampoline sat in the middle of the yard and he stood in the center of it. He started to jump.

With each bounce, he added a family member. First, his

father, then his mother, and finally his brother until they were all bouncing together. The sound of their laughter drowned out everything else. He could no longer hear the rapping of the fingers on the door. He replaced the smooth thickness of the blood under his feet with the spring of the trampoline.

As a smile slowly etched its way across his face, he opened his eyes. Everything had returned to normal. The destroyed sink had been repaired and there was no blood on the floor. He felt a swell of pride fill his chest at this latest development. This was the first time he had defeated his hallucinations with his own willpower.

"Good job, Daniel," he whispered to himself.

The sudden slap of wet flesh on tiled floor made him bite his tongue. Another echoing slap against hard tiles made his muscles tighten. It was coming from behind him. Another slap and he knew what it was.

Footsteps. Wet, barefoot steps from something much bigger than him.

He looked down and the blood had returned to his feet. This time it flowed from behind him. He jammed his eyes shut again.

"You're on the trampoline. You're on the trampoline. You're on the trampoline!"

He tried to force the image back into his mind. This time he couldn't. The sound of nearing footsteps had broken his concentration completely. The breath left his body as he heard the footsteps stop directly behind him.

He refused to open his eyes. No matter what, he would not give the creature the satisfaction. His mind was blank now, fear pushing all rational thought from him. There was no hope of getting that peaceful image back and he knew it. But he would not open his eyes.

A familiar clawed hand grabbed at his shoulder and Daniel

took off toward the door. His eyes were shut, but he knew how far he was from the exit. Two and a half strides later, Daniel reached out for the knob, and...it wasn't there.

He felt his feet touch carpet and he slammed against a warm body. This was too real. Powerful hands grabbed his arms and his eyes shot open.

"What are you doing?" His father asked.

Daniel looked up at him, puzzled. He turned and looked back at the empty and sparkling-clean bathroom and returned his gaze to the man in front of him. He must have looked a frightened mess.

"Nothing," he replied, fear still fresh on his face.

His father looked at him questioningly. "Well, someone is here to speak with you. Come to the living room when you're ready."

Daniel dragged his feet across the carpet to the living room. He wasn't in the mood to talk to anyone, he just wanted to be left alone. Between school, his parents, and the demons scrambling around in his head, that wish was rarely, if ever, granted.

He dug his feet into the carpet as he walked. For some reason, he could still feel the blood under his toes.

As he entered the living room he noticed his father and mother standing with an older man who was dressed in all black, with the exception of his sparkling white collar.

"Daniel, come and meet the father."

Upon hearing his father's words, Daniel walked toward the priest and extended his hand. The older man removed his short-brimmed hat, revealing most of his hair to be brown instead of grey, and crouched low to shake the young boy's hand.

"Daniel, I've heard so much about you. I'm Father Eric and it's nice to finally meet you."

"It's nice to meet you, too."

"Dr. Coin recommended you talk to Father Eric. She said that you two might have some things in common," his mother said.

As much as Daniel didn't want to talk to this man, he trusted his doctor's opinion. She probably knew him better than both his parents, and so her word on any subject regarding him was infallible.

His mother offered the man a refreshment. He politely declined.

"Well, if there is anything else you need we'll be in the next room. We'll let you two get to it," his mother said and left the room behind her husband.

The older man set a brown bag on the floor and took a seat, offering Daniel a chair next to him. Daniel sat down and wrung his hands together, anxious to get this visit over with.

"So, you've been having bad dreams. How are those?" The older man suddenly asked.

Daniel paused a moment wondering how he knew about his dreams. "Still bad."

"Dr. Coin recommended you use Image Rehearsal Therapy, didn't she? How is that coming? Have you seen any improvements?"

Once again Daniel silently questioned how this man knew what was supposed to be confidential. "Not yet."

"Keep at it. IRT is a fairly new method, but it seems to be promising. It will be difficult to maintain your thoughts at first, but you'll get used to it."

"Are you some kind of expert on IRT or something? Is that why she sent you?"

"I am very knowledgeable in its uses, yes, but that's not all."

The boy grew tired of the priest's mysticism and decided to cut right to the chase. "You're here to talk to me about Hell."

"I hear you've given it another moniker. Please, don't spare me the opportunity of hearing its true name. Call it what feels natural to you, what feels right."

Daniel looked at the priest in silence for a moment, then cracked his lips and let the name slide from his tongue. "Sheol."

He was even more surprised when the priest said the word in sync with him. Now the conversation had become interesting.

"So, are you going to ask me to describe my nightmares to you now?"

The man smiled. "Goodness, no. I'm sure you've had your fill of that. And I'm just as sure that day and night your thoughts are plagued with fire and torture and horrid creatures that evade description."

Daniel was stunned at the accuracy of his apparent guesses.

"I'm not here to listen, Daniel. I'm here to talk. I'm here to give you weapons to defend yourself with."

He began digging around in his bag for something. The sounds of clinking glass and rattling metal piqued Daniel's curiosity. Whatever he was looking for was lost in a sea of various materials and utensils.

"This is your first and greatest weapon."

The priest produced a solid black leather-bound book and pushed it into Daniel's hands. The only two words inscribed on the cover read 'Holy Bible'.

"I've read this one. I'm afraid this particular book isn't exactly my cup of tea," Daniel replied.

The older man held up a single index finger signaling for him to hold on a minute. The priest dove his hands back into the bag, this time he came back quickly, placing another giant book in Daniel's hands. He watched the boy look at the book cover then give him a perplexed stare.

"The Koran?"

"Yes, maybe you'd be more comfortable with this one. Unless you've read it as well?"

"I'm just...um...well, can you actually *have* both of these?"

"Why not?"

"I don't know, it's just that you're a priest. I figured you carrying around a copy of the Koran would be...you know, illegal or something."

The older man laughed out loud. "Not quite, son. You may have guessed by now that I'm not your average priest and my methods are just as unorthodox."

"Curious is the word I'd use," Daniel said with a raised eyebrow.

"I'd be lying if I said inspiring your curiosity wasn't somewhat intentional."

Daniel ran his hand across the book cover. "Is there something more here that isn't in the Bible?"

"They differ, yes, but neither story is greater than the other."

"Then why? Surely you could get in a lot of trouble for giving me this."

"I'm sure I'll be fine, Daniel. I've got a copy of the Jewish Talmud and the Tao-te-ching as well if you would like to see those." Father Eric placed his hand on Daniel's shoulder. "God is less concerned with what you call her and how you come to her and more concerned with you just calling and coming."

Daniel didn't know how to react. Here sat a man who defied his working definition of religious conviction and yet seemed steadfast in his beliefs. Most people he talked to about faith or, more accurately, his doubts about faith would respond with the old tried and true aphorism: 'Because the Bible tells us so'.

He didn't much care for the good book. He didn't hate it, but he had read it before and decided it had one too many contradictions and too much of it was open to interpretation. If man is as flawed as the good book says then how could he ever put his faith in something made by man?

"I have a question for you," Daniel said, handing the books back to him and standing up. "I'd like for you to be as honest with me as you can."

The priest nodded in agreement. "I'll try."

"Today in class we discussed whether God could be *All-Knowing*, *All-Powerful*, and *All-Good*. Most of the class believed she could be, but I listed various reasons why she could not. I stand by my theories, but I'd like to hear your opinion on the subject. Can God be *All-Good*, *All-Knowing*, and *All-Powerful*?"

The man placed the two large books he was holding in Daniel's empty seat and then clasped his hands together. Daniel eyed the priest as he took another moment to think before giving his answer.

"Yes."

Daniel stared at him in silence, waiting on his explanation.

"I suppose the simplest way to put it would be to ask what is *All-Good*? How do you define *good*? If you ask ten people to give an example of good you would probably get ten different, and probably conflicting scenarios."

"So, what's your point?" He folded his arms.

"My point is, humans lack the capacity to know what true goodness is because we have never experienced it. Even if God was all good it doesn't mean that we measure good the same way as she does. If I murdered a man I knew was going to kill someone, was my action good or bad? What if my murdering him inadvertently caused the deaths of two innocent people? Am I to be judged by the good of my initial act or the bad that came from it in the end? And when do the ripples of my actions cease? And when they do, if the final outcome is good does that make the entire spectrum of ripples I created good? Only God knows, and whether we admit it or not, we have never experienced this notion of *All-Good* and are grossly underqualified to judge its existence."

"You're speaking of the domino effect. Each action causing a series of reactions that can't be controlled beyond the initial one. But being *All-Powerful* means God would be able to dictate and control the outcome of her actions, and thusly all our actions, beyond the first."

"True enough, so let's consider another method for calculating what 'goodness' is instead of a convoluted debate on its definition. For the sake of argument, let's remove the domino effect and define 'good' by the single direct action a person takes. In this situation, a person would be judged good or bad by the single number of direct actions they took and not by the various outcomes of said action."

"Like giving a homeless man money would still be considered a good act even if he used the money you gave him to buy drugs and destroy himself," Daniel interjected

"Exactly."

"That would mean a person's intentions are all that would matter in this scenario."

"Correct. Intentions are all that would matter, and there would be no need for a being, divine or not, to consider the long-term repercussions of their actions as long as the first action isn't innately evil."

Daniel was silent as the meaning of his words began to unfold upon him.

"In this scenario, God's first action, the creation of life, is the only action we can judge her by. Regardless of the trials we go through on a daily basis, she has allowed us to exist when she could have chosen not too. That seems like a big deal for an infallible being to know the hardships a race of people will experience and still opt to create them. The real question is, if you were in the same situation would you allow the human race a shot at life or would you simply decide not to create us?" The priest leaned forward in his chair. "The real question is, with all the good and bad, do you appreciate your life, Daniel?"

The boy was silent as memories of his past came flooding into his mind. The absolute horror he faced as a captive in Sheol. The constant nightmares, the pills and passing out, the moving, and the things he put his family through. Then he thought about his family and how things used to be.

How his father and brother used to go camping. It was at a local park, but it was fun nonetheless. How his mother always tried to get him to learn to cook. She used to say 'Nothing impresses a girl more than a man who knows his way around the kitchen'. He hated doing it, but he tried sometimes just for her. She didn't even ask him to anymore.

He used to wrestle with his brother all the time. He hadn't wanted to do that in so long. And the trampoline. The thought of it brought a smile to his face.

Without any further thought, he gave his answer. "Yes."

"Yes?" The father questioned." Even after being trapped in Sheol for years? Being tortured and enslaved? You are still grateful for your life?"

"Even if things don't get better. I still have my memories of what things used to be like when I was happy. I'm grateful for that."

Father Eric smiled at the boy. "Forgive me, but it seems to me like you don't need much convincing that there is a God."

"I never said that I don't believe she exists. I've always believed in her, and it wasn't my experiences in Sheol that made me a believer if that's what you're thinking."

The old man shook his head. "Far from it actually, but please enlighten me on your take on the subject of God."

"I just don't think God has to fall into the categories we set for her. We want her to be loving and kind and all-powerful and wise, but the truth is she doesn't have to be any of those things. The only category she must fall under to be our God is, creator. Everything else is what we want her to be and is unnecessary. Whether she is good, bad, powerful or weak, wise or unwise, she just has to be our creator and that is all I ask of her."

"Well said, young man."

Daniel placed his hand to his chin in a moment of thought. "There is one thing that I need to know about, Father. How did you get all of this information about me? Did Dr. Coin tell you?"

"No, your sessions with your doctor are still confidential. I've known Dr. Coin since she was just Ms. Coin and we've worked jointly for a long time. Whenever she comes across a case that is a bit out of her reach she gives me a call."

The thought of Dr. Coin not being able to handle a patient startled Daniel. She was so intelligent and very good at her job, so it was hard to imagine her not overcoming any problem. And the thought that his case was so severe that an expert was forced to call in another expert scared him even more.

The priest sensed the boy's sudden despair. "Don't worry. Your situation is extremely severe, but it is not a hopeless case."

"How did you know about me having nightmares?"

"You have dark rings around your eyes, Daniel. You look

like you haven't slept in weeks, a symptom indicative of chronic nightmares."

"You knew about Dr. Coin suggesting IRT," Daniel said.

"It is a very effective method and many therapists are beginning to use it for patients suffering from Post Traumatic Stress Disorder. And as I said, it's obvious you're stressed, so why wouldn't I guess she recommended it?"

Daniel began to become annoyed. He knew he wasn't wrong in thinking this man had somehow gotten hold of information from Dr. Coin. He was slightly disappointed that she would share the details of his personal sessions with this man. She obviously trusted him, but that didn't matter because Daniel didn't know him and *his* trust only came with time. He was ready for the priest to fess up to his wrongdoing.

"You said you were here to talk to me about Hell. You knew about my dreams."

"Actually, *you* said I was here to talk about Hell, Daniel. We didn't start that particular thread of conversation until you began it. As for your dreams, it kind of goes without saying that a person's dreams of Hell would consist of fire, torture, and monsters."

"Sheol. You knew that I called it Sheol," Daniel spoke in an irritated tone.

Father Eric stared at Daniel blankly for a moment. "Indeed. I suppose you've got me. I'd better confess to my misdeeds before I make my situation worse than it is."

The man began gathering his things together and putting them back in his bag.

Daniel saw the man preparing to leave and became confused. "So that's it? This is all you came here to do?"

"If you're going to continue accusing me, then yes it is."

"What was your purpose here? What did you want?"

"I've confessed to your accusations, son. Now, if you will

excuse me, I have other people who are in real need of help." The man strung his bag over his shoulder and stood up to walk to the door.

"You're lying," Daniel suddenly said.

The old priest stopped and looked at the boy. "Excuse me?"

"I was wrong. Dr. Coin didn't tell you about me."

"And what makes you say that now?"

"Earlier you said that I had been enslaved in Sheol. That much is true, but I never told Dr. Coin that I was a slave."

The older man was silent.

"There are only two explanations." Daniel continued. "Either you have talked to others who have been there or you've been to Sheol yourself."

Father Eric dropped his bag and walked up to Daniel.

He took a knee in front of the boy and began rolling up his sleeves. "Let me just say that you aren't the only person to be touched by the supernatural."

Father Eric held his arms out to Daniel and slowly turned his hands. His wrists held gruesome puncture wounds as if someone had driven a stake through them both. The injuries were raw and half-healed as if they had bled out recently.

"What is this?" Daniel asked.

"A touch of the supernatural, Daniel."

The young boy looked back up at the curious man kneeling before him. "What do you want?"

"I want to offer you something, Daniel. A completely different life than the one you have now. An explanation for the things you've seen and felt. I want to help you, Daniel. I want you to come with me."

"Why?"

"Because I can make you better. I won't promise you it'll be easy, it won't. I *will* promise you an answer to most of your questions and even to questions you haven't bothered to ask yet. I can make you happy again."

Daniel pretended to think. He pretended that he had a daunting decision before him, to leave his family and travel with a man who was a stranger to him. To visit frightening places and answer questions that were even more frightening. Inside, he knew the truth and it was more immutable than the lie he tried to tell himself.

He had already decided to leave.

SECTION 4

The wooden steps bend and creak under Daniel's weight as he traversed each step carefully. Dust rattled to the basement floor with every step leaving his signature on the dirt-covered boards.

He remembered how he used to hate himself, how he hated his body and its weakness. It had been more than fifteen years since he was just a scared little boy with screams in his mind and fire in his dreams. He had grown in many ways since then.

He rarely had nightmares anymore. That was one of the first things he rid himself of. His sense of pain had returned somewhat. Though he still didn't feel pain quite like other people, he wasn't as numb as he was at eleven years old. Most importantly, at least to him, he didn't hate himself anymore.

Daniel reached the bottom of the staircase and surveyed his surroundings. The basement was even more dilapidated than the rest of the church. A cracked and split wood ceiling hung over a rough-shod cement floor with old wooden crates stacked in the corners of the room. Most were broken or rotten to the point of collapse, filled with green-packaged military rations.

Daniel stepped further into the basement and it opened to him like the maw of a man-made monster. He flicked the light switch and watched the hanging bulbs flicker to life. Inside was an aggregation of moist air and moldy wood spaces filled with pockmarks of darkness. Old dirt-covered lights hung from the ceiling and bags of sand were strewn about the floor and piled atop one another in various locations. Some were torn open, their contents spilling onto the floor, and everything was covered in a thick layer of dust and cobwebs.

The soft knock of two hard bottom shoes alerted Daniel to the presence of another. He turned around to see his demon adversary standing in the doorway at the end of the staircase. The light behind him flickered and then died.

Obsidion stood with an abstruse grin spread across his lips, slowly cracking the knuckles on his fingers.

"Curious. Now, what purpose could such a place serve?" The demon dragged his eyes across the room slowly. "Old broken crucifixes, unused war rations, heavy sandbags. Quite the motley assortment of items to keep below a church, don't you agree?"

Daniel's reply was a silent stare. Obsidion stepped further into the basement, gleaning information from the aged items all around him. He picked up a packaged military ration and looked it over in his hand.

"Perhaps this place was once a stockade during some old war or maybe one of the priests was a bit fanatical in his preparation for the coming apocalypse." Obsidion wiped his hand across the surface of a tied sandbag. "And these bags of dirt, a contingency in case of extreme flooding I presume? Something this area is perhaps prone to." Obsidion tossed the package in his hand in an arcing path over toward Daniel. "What do you think, Guardian?"

Daniel caught the ration with one hand, careful not to take his eyes off the demon in front of him.

"Forgive my assumptions, Daniel. I have always been the more curious of my brethren, but I have one more question to ask and I hope you would be so kind as to answer."

Daniel already knew what the demon's question was. It was plain as day to him as the murder in his eyes.

"Your class. You want to know how I knew your class without seeing your brand."

Curiosity lifted one of Obsidion's eyebrows. "I see. This isn't the first time you've been asked this question by a demon, is it?"

"So where is it?" Daniel ignored the demon's question. "I'm willing to bet you're second class, level three, and not much higher, but why don't you show me so that the both of us can know that I'm right."

Obsidion's face showed he was deeply offended and on the verge of wild anger.

He shot a laser-focused glare at Daniel. "You dare ask me to shame myself in front of you, human? What makes you think I would even consider it?"

Daniel cleared his throat and ran his fingers through his short black hair, needlessly combing his already perfect locks. "Whenever a demon asks me how I know their class or elemental affinity, I always ask them to show me their brand. Some of them become offended like you and most try and rip my throat out where I'm standing, but none actually show me."

Daniel still fiddled with the ration that had been thrown to him. He tossed it back and forth to each hand almost as if he wasn't aware he was doing it.

"I know it's a long shot, but I figure one day I'll come across a demon that will show me his brand."

"A foolish notion, Guardian. Why would any demon purposefully show you his brand on a whim?"

"I wondered that for a while, Obi. Then, one day, I realized something, and it was so obvious that I was amazed I didn't notice it before. There are so few first-class demons on Earth that running into one is nearly impossible, but, you see, I've been to Sheol. Every first-class apparition there has its class brand marked on a visible part of the body, the hand, the cheek, the forehead. They wear their brands with pride."

"What is your point, Guardian?"

"My point is that you're ashamed of it. There isn't shame in showing a human your brand. The shame comes from the fact that most demons on Earth have a low class. They're weak and they know it." A smile spread across the Guardian's lips as he spun the military ration on his fingertip, gleefully mocking his new acquaintance with his words. "So, now I think of demon brands a different way. Like a penis, actually. You don't show it off unless it's one you can be proud of."

Obsidion lowered a menacing glower. "So, you don't expect me to show you my brand because you think I'm weak?"

"You misunderstand me, demon. I don't think you're weak. You do."

Obsidion's oak-colored eyes meandered off into the distance. He did nothing to hide the contemplation on his face. After a moment of thought-filled silence, he grabbed his right sleeve and began rolling it to his elbow. Daniel stared at the demon in shock, he couldn't believe what he was seeing. Upon the inside of Obsidion's forearm was a crooked and twisting demonic symbol cut gruesomely into his flesh.

"Interesting," Daniel said unenthusiastically. "If you are a second-class demon, then would I be correct in assuming you were once a..." He let his voice trail off.

"A first class." Obsidion flipped his wrist to reveal a grisly scar covering the back of his hand. "Imagine, gripping a hot, blessed blade in your hand and cleaving the skin from it until the symbol that once defined your very existence is gone. Then, taking that same blade and carving a new one upon your flesh." He turned his hand again to show the crooked scar on his forearm. "Though this wasn't nearly as painful as the journey here. The horrid sensation of power you were rightfully born with being ripped from you, and the fear that you may never have it back again."

Daniel was oddly empathetic to the demon's description of power being lost. "My condolences. A former first-class demon now a second-class. If traveling here took that much power from you then perhaps you should have prepared a bit more. You might not have survived the trip at all if you were any weaker." The snide in Daniel's remark was dripping.

"Preparation is pointless. There is no way of knowing how much the journey will take from you, and I am more resilient than you give me credit for."

Daniel's pupils constricted and peered through the creature's subterfuge. He could see the demon's tail whipping behind him in anxiousness, his burnt umber skin and glistening teeth mere preludes to his true atrocity.

Obsidion began cracking the bones on his knuckles again. The sound was piercing and unnaturally loud.

"Now that you have seen my brand, Guardian, I can no longer allow you to leave this place alive."

Daniel tossed and caught the packaged food in his hand repeatedly, acting as if he weren't really paying attention to the demon in front of him. "Somehow Obi, I doubt that was ever an option."

Lightning suddenly struck.

The green ration so blithely toyed with by Daniel hurtled toward Obsidion's face. Like a hot knife through butter, Obsidion's ruby-colored claws slit the package in two and he rushed through the basement. Daniel had already fallen back, legs spread in a low fighting stance, his once empty hands now gripping tightly the plastic guards of dual silver blades. Adrenaline pumped hotly through his veins like fuel sprayed into a car engine, shocking it to life.

Like a hungry panther, Obsidion pounced on the Guardian, dragging his dagger-like claws through the air. Rather than retreat, Daniel stepped into the demon's downward swing, striking upward as he did so, and sliced into the fire demon's forearm with his blade. Green demon blood stained his weapon and points of muffled pain traced the lines on Obsidion's face as he stifled an angry roar.

The demon struck again, catching nothing but air as Daniel skirted out of his reach. A puckish smirk spread its way across his face, mocking the demon, daring him to try again. And so he did.

Obsidion lunged at the Guardian, this time burying his claws in a bag of sand half a foot from Daniel's head. He snatched his hand from the bag and the sweeping motion threw sand across the room and into Daniel's face. His eyes screamed, leaking briny tears onto his cheeks to wash the mineral-sized daggers away.

He raised his forearms in defense while trying to blink the stinging salt from his eyes. He felt his arms rock back and forth from the blows his opponent dealt his limbs. It was all he could do just to stay on his feet as his eyes adjusted to the burn of the sand.

Finally, after several seconds(a lifetime in any fight to the death)his eyes cleared enough to function. Daniel's arm shot down and tossed one of his blades into the toe of Obsidion's shoe. He heard a sharp yelp spill from his assailant's mouth, though he wasn't sure if it was from pain or knee-jerk surprise that his foot was suddenly nailed to the ground. At that moment, Daniel struck at the demon's face, the silver in his dagger reflecting the deep brown of his enemy's eye, his target.

Lightning had struck again.

Daniel eyed the sliver of green blood on the tip of his weapon. Obsidion had scrambled backward holding his palm to his face, the sting of blessed metal making a home in his nerves. The Guardian had missed his target. Merely a scratch to his demon opponent's cheek and nothing more. His adversary was nimble, maneuvering his face away from the blade so that most of the damage would be avoided.

"That was fast...for a human, that is," Obsidion spoke, wiping the green blood from his cheek. "I have never met a human who could go toe to toe with me."

Obsidion pulled the blade from his shoe and examined it methodically. He ran his fingers across the rubber handle but dare not touch the metal. By the absence of the green tint of blood, Daniel knew his thrown weapon missed its mark as well. Moreover, his hellish adversary knew the handles of his weapons were not blessed and were, thusly, safe to touch. This disturbed him more than slightly.

"Did you know, Obsidion, that most demons fight similar to wild cats; leaping and clawing wildly at their prey? You're no different. That's why this fighting style was developed." Daniel tore the shredded pieces of dangling fabric from his sleeves and revealed smooth, black, laminated vambraces covering his forearms. "It's very effective when used against demons like you." He spat 'you' from his mouth as if it were loose debris. "You may have the advantage in strength and speed, but that is all you have. My fighting style is specifically tailored to dismantling yours."

The bubbling sense of concern in Obsidion's stomach meant he knew Daniel spoke the truth. And the shallow grooves he left in the guards strapped to his opponent's forearms also meant, implicitly, his tactics had to change.

His tongue grazed the dagger-tipped canines in his mouth, testing their sharpness on the pink muscle. "Let's try something a bit different then."

The moment Obsidion completed his sentence, he tossed Daniel's weapon over his shoulder and snapped his foot forward into one of the nearby broken crates. The wooden box hurtled toward Daniel, splitting in two as it flew, throwing packaged army rations through the air.

Daniel moved as if fire was at his feet, ducking the wooden missile and swatting packs of food from his field of vision. He was quick, precise, but most importantly, too late.

By the time he heard the crash of the wooden crate upon the floor behind him, his line of sight to the demon was gone. He stood in the middle of a partially lit basement alone, the slight swing of a dangling yellow light bulb the only proof that someone else had been there.

Daniel's eyes dragged slowly across the dimly lit cave. Patches of darkness now seemed to stretch across the room, swallowing the light hungrily. The basement was deathly quiet, but his ears were abuzz with prolific sounds.

The hollow drip of nearby water. The soft hum of the incandescent bulb. Slow dragging breaths as he pulled air in through his nose. The strong rhythmic pace of his heartbeat. But he could not find the sound he was searching for. Then he heard it and like before, he was too late.

By the time the vibrations in the air gave away the location of his enemy, Daniel was lying face down on the basement floor. He recovered quickly, rolling back to his feet and spinning around to face his attacker. Cold and still darkness was the only thing there to greet him.

"So, you have more armor hidden underneath." Obsidion's voice bellowed from the blackness.

Daniel turned his head and found a tear in his coat, a black laminated strip of protection exposed where the attack had landed.

"You're just full of surprises aren't you? I wonder if I can find you under all that armor."

Obsidion's voice bounced off the basement walls, echoing deep into Daniel's bones. He couldn't tell where the voice was coming from. Worse yet, most demons had insurmountable vision. In the darkness, Daniel knew his enemy could see him clear as day.

Another strike, this time from the side, knocked the Guardian from his feet and sent him sliding across the ground. He recovered swiftly enough to see the demon melt back into the shadows. This time his enemy's assault came laced with stinging pain, and a glance at his left arm revealed thin blood rolling down his coat.

"Ahhh, there you are," Obsidion spoke before being enveloped by the dark.

Daniel retreated further into the basement, pushing into the heart of the gloomy sepulcher. His opponent held the advantage and he had to get it back. He searched the blackness of the basement, knocking over worn crates and open bags of sand, his eyes locked onto the pools of darkness that hung in the corners of the ceiling.

Daniel fumbled through the dark, taking in slow mouthfuls of air and sliding his feet across the floor as he moved because he couldn't afford to take his eyes off the ceiling. Every subtle diversionary sound produced by his surroundings mocked him and his efforts to glean truth from subterfuge.

Something slammed hard into his back. Not hard enough to knock him from his feet, but hard enough to trigger his reflexes and have him bury his weapon fiercely into it. There was a discernible sloshing of water followed by a spray of liquid onto Daniel's face. It took him a moment to realize that it was him that had backed into it and not the other way around.

His eyes strained to recognize the image of a plastic barrel set into the wall of the basement. The weapon he so vigorously attacked with was jammed deep into its center. What his eyes *did* notice immediately was the small symbol etched into the front bottom of the barrel.

A cross.

Daniel wiped the liquid from his face with a smile. Holy water. What were the odds?

Questions immediately flooded his mind. How long had it been down here? Was it still holy? Without wasting another moment, he reached inside his coat and pulled a small clear vial of green liquid from his pocket. Popping the lid, he splashed the fluid onto the barrel and watched it roll down toward the knife. Upon reaching the opening, the green liquid began to sizzle caramelizing into brown syrup around the blade.

Daniel made the sign of the cross and jerked his blade from the barrel, spraying pressurized water into the room. With a sharp intake of air, he drove his weapon back into the plastic container near the first hole. He twisted his weapon, opening the orifice wider and allowing more of the liquid to pour out before pulling it out and stabbing the barrel again.

The water ran in streams across the floor as Daniel tore more holes into the container. He had a plan, but it would require the entire amount of water in the barrel to work. His grunts of effort and the ripping sounds of tearing plastic filled the room as he worked until his arm was sore. By the time he was finished, there was a growing pain in his arm and nearly the entire basement floor was slippery with water.

"Well done, Guardian! Now I would love to know, what was the point of that little show? Had I been on the ground your trick might have offered you a slight advantage, but I no longer need to touch the floor, so your efforts are futile."

Daniel stepped into the middle of the room and spoke into the darkness. "Don't worry, you'll know soon enough."

The demon slowly emerged from the shadows on the other side of the room. "Confidence will not win you this fight, Guardian. You have needlessly spilled your best chance for survival onto the floor. The only thing you have successfully killed is time."

"Time is all I need to end this fight." Daniel locked eyes with his enemy before losing him in the darkness again.

"Ah! Hoping to buy time until your associates can kill my minions and come assist you? My dear, dear Guardian, you'll be dead long before they arrive."

Daniel was struck from behind again. The force of the blow stole the air from his lungs and pitched him forward onto his stomach. He hit the ground rolling and jumped back onto his feet, whipping his head in the direction of the attack.

Dark and silence.

"You'll have to be faster than that, Guardian." Obsidion teased.

Daniel held his weapon close and moved slowly toward the dangling light bulb at the basement entrance. He was struck down hard from the right and sent sliding back toward the interior.

"No no, let's not ruin the fun we've been having just yet. I want to see what the great *Daniel* has planned to save himself."

The Guardian got up from his back, a numbing pain setting itself in his bones. He almost missed being an eleven-year-old boy again.

"Sorry if I'm disappointing you, Obi. I'll have to try harder."

Daniel stepped backward, the whip of sharp air stung his face as clawed hands raked near his cheek. A second strike to his stomach made contact and sent him rolling to the floor. The ring of metal tapping against stone caught his attention and he realized it was the sound of his blade bouncing out of his hands and into the unknown. He would've cursed out loud if he was sure the demon wasn't in earshot.

He pulled himself to his feet and checked his body for new wounds, leaning against the broken plastic barrel for support. All of the demon's attacks had caught his armor. His last one had even pierced it. Daniel pulled a blood-red talon from the side of his laminated plating.

The demon's blows were like jackhammers. His armor protected him from being shredded by his claws, but there was little that could be done about the force of the attacks being rained down on him.

His ribs throbbed with what he could only assume was pain. Wobbly gelatin replaced the muscles attached to his bones. He was being tenderized with each successful hit to his body. As he caught his breath, his opponent stepped confidently into the light.

"What do you plan to do now, Guardian? You are tired, beaten, and now you have no weapon."

The monster was right, of course, but only somewhat. He was tired, but only of hearing him bluster. He had been beaten on, but he was not defeated. And as far as him having no weapon, in this aspect, the demon was exceptionally, irretrievably wrong.

Daniel stood up straight, cracking the bones in his neck like steel joints shaking free years of rust. He rotated his shoulders and shook his hands loose. Then, much to Obsidion's surprise, he balled his hands into fists and took a stance in front of him.

"Just needed a moment, Obi. I'm fine now."

The demon laughed heartily at the Guardian. "And just what do you intend on fighting me with? Your fists? You are weaponless."

"Just because I'm less one weapon does not mean I'm weaponless."

"And you plan to defeat me with this tactic? Show me."

"Gladly."

Daniel closed the gap between them with one step and thrust his balled hand at the demon's face. With an Impeccable smile, Obsidion caught Daniel's fist in the palm of his hand. The piercing slap of flesh upon flesh served to widen the demon's grin and suddenly, Obsidion's smile transformed into a grimace of pure agony. He pulled his hand away, the brown flesh covering each of his digits burning to nothing.

Before he could utter a scream, his face was met with a left hook, whipping his head around and searing the skin from his cheek. The blow shattered his world into splinters, spun him on his heel, and sent him stumbling backward. The Guardian struck again, but his enemy was agile. Obsidion leaped haphazardly back into the shadows before another injury could be sustained.

Daniel shook the blood and charred demon skin from his knuckles. "My clothes are soaked, Obsidion. Did you really think knocking me across the floor in a basement flooded with holy water was a good idea?"

He could hear grunts of pain echoing from the shadows,

sharp huffs of agony and rage through clinched grinding teeth. He paced the center of the basement, smug in the fact that he had hurt the demon so badly.

"You know Obsidion, I hadn't thought about it until now, but there are many interesting facts about fire demons. Some are obvious like reddish skin tone, resistance to heat, and so forth."

A clawed hand reached from the darkness and lashed at Daniel's neck, catching nothing but air as the Guardian pulled himself away and continued.

"And there are some little-known facts that even some Guardians don't know. Like the fact that second class, level two fire demons and higher can increase the temperature of a room by at least one hundred degrees just by expelling their internal body temperature."

Another stealthy attack from behind flew over Daniel's head as he ducked and rolled to the other side of the room.

"But by far the least known tidbit of information about fire demons is my favorite because even most fire demons don't know it." He inserted a pause, allowing suffocating quiet to claim the air and suspense to thicken in the demon's throat. "The fact that all fire demons have difficulty regulating their internal temperature. The more energy a fire demon uses the hotter it becomes, and if a fire demon is wounded severely, it becomes a walking oven."

The demon attacked again from Daniel's front. The Guardian parried the blow with his arm guard, catching his opponent in the chin with the heel of his hand and knocking him right back into the shadows he came from.

"Now, I wouldn't say you've been severely wounded, but you *have* been throwing more heat around since I wounded you earlier and you're only getting hotter. You can't hide from me anymore, Obsidion. I don't need my eyes to find you."

The Guardian stared into the dark corner of the room with unblinking eyes. He didn't even flinch when the demon came barreling toward him, his claws stretched for his throat. He already knew he was there.

Daniel fell backward, lifting his legs into the air, and hammered the demon in the chest with his feet. Obsidion went sailing over into the dark, his face wrapped with pain and anger.

Daniel could hear the racket made by Obsidion's falling body as it crashed through pieces of wood and bags of sand to the floor. Icy water rolled down Daniel's body, leaving trails of clear veins on his skin. A glint of reflected light caught his eye and he realized he was staring at one of his blades turned over in a puddle of brown water.

Daniel took his time gathering his weapon and getting to his feet. He was certain his last attack slowed the demon down considerably; he could still smell the stench of sizzling flesh hovering in the rank basement air. He stood in the puddle of dirty water tapping his leg impatiently with the ridiculously sharp weapon.

"I haven't got all day, demon."

.

SECTION 5

A thick silence swallowed the room for a long moment. An almost tangible silence. The kind of silence that always sounded like soft buzzing to Daniel. Almost as if his ears, with no other sounds available to them, could just barely make out the vibration of electrons whipping around atoms at near-light speed. Or maybe it was the sound of air molecules scraping past his ears as he moved through them.

Certainty was often an elusive luxury. What could he possibly be hearing behind the ruckus and racket permeating his human senses? What lie furtively between the echoing cracks of the real?

It always came in spurts. Waves, really. One moment he would be surrounded by the sounds accustomed to him and the next at the mercy of nothingness. A hollow sound he couldn't explain or describe if he wanted to. Then shortly after announcing its presence, it would be swallowed by a cascade of human tongues, barking dogs, and car horns. This time the sounds that returned to him were less comforting.

Heavy breath, dripping water, and the soft ping of his

weapon repeatedly making contact with his knee were the loudest noises to be heard. That is until Obsidion exploded from the pitch black of the basement issuing a blood-curdling howl.

Daniel stepped backward, gauging his opponent's wild posture and adjusting for the powerful swing he knew was coming. He raised his blade to his face defensively, angling its edge so the force of Obsidion's attack would cut his own hand off.

Instead of the splatter of hot blood, Daniel's face was met with a torrent of stinging salt. Before he knew what was happening, he slammed against the wall and nearly stumbled over a stack of broken crucifixes. His eyes burned and his mouth had become desert dry. He forced his eyes to focus through the ocean of needles that swam through his pupils. He had to bite his tongue to keep from cursing this time.

Instead of Obsidion's arm, Daniel's blade had bitten deeply into a bag of sand.

Struggling to keep his feet under him, he leaned backward as his opponent whipped another sand-filled bag past his face. Obsidion gripped two brown sacks in his hands, whirling them mercilessly like twin wrecking balls. The air trembled with the force of each colossal swing as they howled murderously past his face.

With shaky footing and sand-muffled vision, Daniel was able to dodge the next swing, but his luck failed him as he was struck head-on with the partially torn bag. The orifice in the weaving tore through the length of the container and spilled more sand over the Guardian, throwing him onto his back.

His mind still reeling from the 25-pound blow, Daniel was able to pull himself to his knees before Obsidion fell upon him again with another bag gripped tightly in his claws. It burst over his forearms as he raised them in defense of his head.

Through the ocean of particle-sized earth, he felt the heel of Obsidion's shoe press into his chest and kick him from his knees. The impact sent him sliding across sharp granules of sand, the dry taste of salt filling his mouth as he came to a stop.

Without taking his eyes off the demon, Daniel rose to his feet, a flowing tide of sand rolling down his body as he stood. He watched Obsidion with hot singeing eyes. His vision was still spotty, but the burn of the sand was not enough to force him to blink. He let the pain in his eyes force them to precipitate and slowly rinse them out. He could see Obsidion staring tirelessly at him.

He could swear, through his sand-stifled vision, that Obsidion was examining him, analyzing his body. Almost searching for something. Saliva coalesced inside Daniel's mouth and he spat a glob of dirt-filled mucus onto the floor. In that instant, the origin of the surreptitious smile spreading across Obsidion's face was made unmistakably clear.

It was the sand.

Initially, Daniel thought Obsidion's attack on him with sandbags was an act of senseless desperation. It was, in fact, a part of Obsidion's plan to cover him with sand and rid him of his most devastating weapon. The sand would stick to his clothes and skin, absorbing and covering the water.

Of course, the water, by now, had soaked into his clothes and no amount of sand could completely remove it. This brought Daniel a modicum of solace, but he could tell that this wasn't Obsidon's only purpose for his actions. With so much sand covering him, Obsidion had effectively cut off his use of water as a method of attack. Not only that, but the water on the floor was now rolling forward and collecting toward the center of the room, aggregating itself just behind a now effusively confident demon. In order to wash the salty detriment from his body he would have to get to it, if he could.

"It occurs to me, Guardian, the coincidental nature of you luring me down here and there being a ten-gallon barrel of pressurized holy water here."

Obsidion spoke, slowly pacing on the edge of the pool of water gathered behind him. He folded his crimson-clawed hands behind his back in a formal manner, as if there was still some sense of regality he couldn't let go of.

"A well-thought-out plan I must say, to battle me in a place where you held such a clear advantage," he spoke as if the fight was already over and their conversation was mere ceremony.

"I wish I could take credit for that Obsidion, but the truth is I have never been to this church," Daniel spoke through a mouth still peppered with sand.

"No need to lie now, Guardian. It will not lessen the bitter taste of defeat."

Daniel pulled himself from the mound of sand that surrounded him and shook the minuscule pebbles off his clothes. Even after that, most of the sand remained stuck to him.

"What point would there be in lying now? Finding that barrel was a stroke of luck and that's all."

Obsidion slid his hand across his burned chin in suspicion. "A dubious claim, but be that as it may. It's a shame that your efforts were in vain. Your water can no longer help you."

"On the contrary." Daniel slowly approached the demon while spinning his weapon in hand. "You've just given me the advantage, demon. If you haven't noticed, I have you surrounded."

Obsidion followed Daniel's meandering eyes to the pool of water lapping at the back of his shoes. "If you think your precious water will—"

Before he could finish, Daniel was already in his face, the gleam of polished steel dancing its way toward his open neck. His attack was blazingly fast as if the blade had turned itself into light, quixotic and ethereal. A flash of deadly luminescence humming toward a blood-filled and thumping jugular.

Obsidion's head flew back and his foot snapped forward instinctively, connecting with Daniel's ribcage and sending him sprawling into soggy wooden crates and wet sand. Daniel's strike had missed, but Obsidion was forced to step back into the shallows of the water behind him.

Upon hearing the splash of the liquid on his shoes the demon quickly jumped back to the edge of the waterline. Though he had not actually made physical contact with the water, he could feel the bottom of his feet tingle as if tiny molecules had permeated through the soles of his shoes. He knew it was all in his head. A warning from his brain to his feet of his close proximity to a substance that could quite effectively destroy him.

Daniel returned to his feet, his jaw tight with conviction, wet sand still clinging to his face. He looked furious as he pounced on the demon again. Obsidion would not allow himself to be pushed back into the water for a second time and so, the two collided viciously.

Obsidion's razor claws bounced from the Guardian's armor and Daniel's shining dagger swiped at the air around the demon. Their attacks so fast that they left silhouettes floating on the still air. Their movements so swift their own eyes struggled to keep pace.

His blade screamed, his claws howled, the hoard of useless and expired junk their only audience. Sandbags open like gaping mouths at the lash of the human's blade. Crates wet as perspiring foreheads at the snatch of the demon's talon. Weapons blurring vision with the movement of silver knife and red nail. The flash of metal and the streak of crimson.

Obsidion was stronger and faster than Daniel, but the Guardian had better tools and he had a tactic for defeating the beast. Patience.

Through each near hit on the creature and glancing blow to himself, he waited. Waited for the opening he knew would eventually, inevitably come. Then, as if Daniel had willed it into existence himself, lightning struck.

The hardwood bottoms of the demon's shoe gave way to the unnatural slickness of the stone floor and with one movement slightly too quick, he slipped backward toward the water he so desperately wanted to avoid. His body leaned and Daniel wasted no time, throwing his weapon with all his might at the demon's center mass.

There was no escape. He would either be skewered through the chest or plunge head-first into liquid death. Daniel knew this well.

Obsidion saw the attack coming before Daniel had even let go of the weapon. He let gravity do the work for him, pulling him down to the water head first. The dagger flew over his stomach and past his chest and head, humming with holy fervor straight into the darkness. The weapon never came close enough to touch the demon, but it didn't have to. Daniel watched as Obsidion fell backward into the pool, his plan coming to fruition before his eyes.

The demon's right hand stretched out and broke the surface of the water, catching his weight mid-fall and holding the rest of his body arm's length above the pool. He shrieked as the water bubbled and frothed around his submerged hand. Then, in an act of sheer indomitable will, the demon, with a single hand, threw himself back to the edge of the waterline.

The rising sense of assurance that was slowly making its way through Daniel's nerves stopped cold in his veins.

Obsidion dropped to one knee and issued another ear-splitting howl. Not from just pain but from relief, anger, joy, and a cocktail of other emotions too intense to describe and too complex for words. He lifted his hand and examined the damage he had wrought upon himself.

His right hand was a bloodied mess. Pieces of charred skin hung loosely from the mangled appendage. Green blood sprayed randomly from openings in his flesh. His once gorgeous brown skin was now an ugly charcoal, a mockery of its former beauty. He pulled himself to his feet and tore the wet sleeve from his right arm, tossing it back into the water.

His eyes met Daniel's and, for a moment, the Guardian could feel the hatred beaming into his soul. A moment later and the demon had blitzed him in a pain-filled rage. The claws on his left hand were digging into the lamination on Daniel's right arm guard. The boiling mass of flesh that was Obsidion's right hand slowly inched its way toward the Guardian's face as he struggled to hold it back.

Daniel's teeth clenched, his jaw wrung tight as veins stretched across his forehead like thin pulsing fingers. Obsidion was built like an ox. His demon heart pumped strength to inhuman muscles that, despite Daniel's agility or speed, left him helpless in the wake of his raw power.

The demon's sizzling hand moved nearer and just as it closed the distance, Daniel's mouth stretched open and a thick viscid fluid leaped from his tongue onto Obsidion's face. Once again the gloomy cavern was filled with screams as the substance spat from Daniel's mouth latched onto the demon's face with a sound like fresh butter on a hot pan. In that instant, Daniel broke Obsidion's hold on him and barreled toward the swirling pool of refuge.

Obsidion's shouts still rang through the basement as Daniel darted past his enemy's blind swings. Even now, feet pounding the wet rock of the basement floor, he could feel the force of the demon's claws rake the air behind him. His opponent already knew what his goal was, but there was no way he could stop him now.

Daniel dropped to the ground and slid into the swirling water like he was stealing home plate. There was nothing Obsidion could do. The mighty splash was all the confirmation he needed to know that Daniel had nearly submerged himself in the pool.

The Guardian rose from his murky salvation triumphantly. Dirt-colored water rolled down his body, peeling the layers of sand and salt away.

With an air of satisfaction, Daniel watched Obsidion tear the left sleeve of his coat off and wipe the mysterious substance from his face, a painful grimace stuck to him as he did so.

He dragged his sleeve across his face, his skin still sizzling and popping, and a flash of realization crossed his eyes. "Wet sand?"

Obsidion spoke almost as if he were in shock. His mind reeled, offering him a series of glowing mental images that even *he* had difficulty accepting. His demon pride took a stinging blow as he imagined Daniel collecting sand soaked in holy water and stuffing it into his mouth, waiting for the opportune time to launch his weaponized loogie.

But, how? When did he even put the sand into his mouth? Had he had it there the entire time?

Impossible. He wouldn't be able to speak with it in his mouth. In fact, he had abstained from speaking altogether for some time.

That's when it hit him. His mind raced through a stack of

recent memories and uncovered Daniel's last words to him. Something along the lines of 'having him surrounded', but more important than that was the surprise attack. The one quick as lightning. The one that was neatly dodged and ended with his shoe in Daniel's ribs and Daniel face down in the dirt.

He remembered that moment, not because of the satisfaction of putting the Guardian in his place but, because immediately after that he stepped backward into the edge of the pool. For a second he had taken his eyes off of the Guardian in concern for his own safety. That was the moment. That second was more than enough time for Daniel to palm a handful of wet sand into his mouth and rise to his feet under the guise that he had just fallen head-first into a pile of dirt.

Obsidion eyed the Guardian curiously, his face a bubbling mix of excitement and anger, waiting for some sort of hint or telltale sign that his mind was lying to him. Some type of confirmation that this human was not as clever as he seemed.

Daniel, almost in reply to the demon's unspoken vexation, coolly dipped his hand into the dirty pool he now stood ankle-deep in, sipped the water from his palm, swished it about vigorously in his mouth, and spat the salty substance back into the water. This time it was the demon who had to stifle a bellowing swear.

The Guardian's veneer of calm faded and his face was once again a mask of seriousness. He reached into the water, lifting the right sleeve of Obsidion's coat into his dripping-wet hands. Grabbing a torn-open sandbag, Daniel poured out its contents until there was only a corner of sand filling the bag. He tied the bag closed and roped an end of the torn sleeve around the bag tightly, letting the weighted end dangle just above the water. He began to swing the weighted end of the torn cloth like a makeshift ball and chain, spinning it around and passing it to each hand. He spun on his heel and whipped his new weapon through the surface of the water, sending a hard spray toward a scrambling demon.

Obsidion shielded his face and body with his arms, his bare limbs searing as they caught the brunt of the assault. The Guardian swung the weighted whip again through the water and sent another holy shower flying at his enemy. Water bit into his skin like hot grease, tearing past flesh into throbbing muscle. Like minuscule atom bombs, the droplets exploded on brown skin leaving it black and desolate, the smell of charring meat filling the already foul cavern air.

Obsidion shook with pain, gnashing his teeth and falling to his knees before Daniel's affront. The splash of the sandbag cutting through the pool was like a shotgun blast to his ears. The spray of dirty water was something akin to machine gun bullets to his nervous system. With each swing Daniel broke the surface of the water and with every follow through that water was delivered fervently to the demon. The Guardian would not let up.

Obsidion cowered in the basement corner, his teeth biting into his bottom lip as he endured the fusillade. The rain of liquid fire continued and it became clear that Daniel had no intention of stopping until all that remained of him was a blackened stain on the floor.

Obsidion stood to his feet, powering through the waves of pain racking his body. His brow was furrowed, his teeth bared in a grimace of madness, and anger flowed from him like the spirals of smoke fissuring from his body.

"That is...ENOUGH!"

The demon's voice reached an inhuman tone and Daniel could see his true form shine brighter than ever. His teeth were maliciously jagged and his eyes a sinister crimson. His ears, an oblong shape matching his head, and a thin forked tail rose and fell behind him.

An invisible wall of heat slammed into Daniel, nearly making him stumble in surprise. He could feel the moisture on his skin evaporate almost immediately before another wave struck him. His mouth suddenly went dry and his eyeballs burned as the water in them vanished. Daniel struggled to keep his eyes open as he watched hot air expelled from tiny holes in the demon's neck and arms. Another explosion of heat forced the Guardian to shield his face with his arms.

It wasn't until then that he noticed his sleeves were dry. A cursory inspection of the rest of his body revealed that there was no longer any moisture left in his clothes. Even his hair was now bone dry and the pool of brown water he stood shin-deep in was disappearing quickly.

A single spin of his makeshift weapon sent a splash of holy water flying to the demon. A bellowing laugh spewed from the creature and confirmed what he had already postulated.

The droplets were evaporating before they could make it to their target. Daniel launched more at him only to watch as the liquid became wisps of smoke before they could touch the demon. He gritted his teeth as another crashing wave of heat forced him into a bout of profuse sweating. A moment later and Daniel realized that his sweat was the only liquid surrounding him now. A dry mud-caked indentation was all that remained of his protective puddle of holy water.

Steam swelled throughout the entire room, turning the basement into a sweltering sauna. Daniel was defenseless as the last traces of water returned to the atmosphere and his burning enemy encroached upon him with a smile.

"This is the end, Guardian. I want you to look into my eyes and know that a slow death awaits you. I plan to make you suffer for the pain you have inflicted upon me today."

Daniel covered his face with his arms, taking a step backward with each step Obsidion took forward.

"Look at how you cower." The demon mocked. "You can't even face me without your precious wat—"

A spray of green bloodshot from the demon's mouth suddenly. Obsidion's eyes widened in surprise, a heavy cough heaved in his chest followed by more blood. A devastating second cough dragged him to a knee clutching his face in bewilderment. The air left his lungs and it became difficult to get it back. His body was heavier now than it was just a moment ago.

A piercing headache rocketed into his brain, and a third cough made its way up his throat. His hands clasped over his mouth in an attempt to stop it. The cough blasted through his hands sending emerald-colored liquid showering over the floor. He could feel his blood leaking from his eyes and nose, and the only thing greater than the confusion rising in the pit of his stomach was his fear. He looked up and, through blurred vision, set his gaze on a smiling Guardian.

"What have you done to me?"

"Actually, demon, you've done this to yourself," Daniel responded smugly. "You seem to be aware of the fact that heat evaporates water, but you forgot that this is a basement and there is nowhere for the moisture to go. And what is a fundamental rule about holy water after it evaporates?" Daniel approached the demon and stared directly into his eyes. "It stays holy."

The intense heat expelled from the demon began to subside as Obsidion fell to his hands and knees, his life pouring from the orifices on his body.

"You've been standing in a sauna of holy moisture. One of your own making," Daniel spoke dismally.

Obsidion rolled onto his back, his mind piecing together a singular undeniable truth. "This was your plan all along wasn't it?" he spoke through sputtering coughs that repeatedly racked his body.

Daniel stared at the writhing demon in stark silence, neither confirming the question nor denying it. He didn't have to. Obsidion could see the answer in his eyes. From the moment he spilled the water onto the floor, his trap was set. Soaking his clothes, spitting wet sand into his face, and cornering him with sprays of holy water were all means to an end, all used to push the demon. Daniel knew he could never kill Obsidion with the water, so he pressured him into heating the room until he turned the liquid into a deadly inescapable gas.

"Clever...for a human."

Obsidion's body began to shake uncontrollably as the holy moisture seeped into his muscles causing them to spasm. His teeth clenched, biting through his tongue and filling his mouth with blood. His back arched in a grotesque parenthesis as the pain reached its apex. His eyes stayed locked on the Guardian through it all.

Daniel looked down on Obsidion as green tinged foam frothed from his mouth and his red eyes rolled to the back of his head. He made the sign of the cross and issued a short prayer, not for the demon but for himself and all the innocent lives the creature had taken before this moment.

A thunderous jolt rocketed through the basement and shook dust from the ceiling. Daniel's comrades were still engaged with the demon's minions. The Guardian quickly recovered his weapons and left the basement, leaving the demon's twitching corpse writhing on the floor.

He leaped up the weathered steps two at a time. Another tremor rocked the entire church as he burst through the basement door to find the ogre lying recumbent across the church floor. Through the rising dust, he could make out a spry old man, his face covered in sweat, sitting atop the mountainous creature.

The priest pulled the metal flask from his bag and raised it to his lips, sucking down the liquid inside in three swift gulps. The old man's face puckered and he exhaled a hot cringe as he eyed Daniel behind his beverage.

"What kept you?"

CHAPTER
FIVE

F*amily Matters*

SECTION I

The elevator rumbled down the steel shaft with a series of stops and starts. The three men huddled together inside, jerking left and right as the metal container threw them like scattered bowling pins.

"God, I hate this elevator," Prophet snapped.

"Don't start," Daniel replied. "I hear enough complaints from Mark about this damn thing and Father's the one who refuses to get it fixed."

Another sharp drop from the elevator threw the three men to the floor.

"It's got character," Father answered snidely.

The elevator sputtered to a stop and its doors creaked open. Behind them stood a still simmering, but concerned, Adam.

"What happened? Who's hurt?"

"Prophet. Father's taking him to the infirmary now," Daniel said letting the elevator doors close behind him.

"I'm fine, I'm fine." The giant man waved them away. "Just a couple scrapes. No biggie."

Father walked with the metal-armed man past the two brothers and down the hall. Daniel and Adam stayed silent for a moment longer until they were out of earshot.

"So, what is it? Just say it already so we can get this over with," Adam spat.

"Fine. What the hell was that back at the church? Were you trying to get your ass kicked by an angel?"

"I was trying to get the truth. Why weren't any of those condescending assholes there to help Gabriel when she needed them? Yet, they talk down to us like we're not even worthy of being in their presence. I freaking hate angels."

"Be that as it may, you stepped over the line when you said that to a seraph."

"Screw him. Who cares how he feels."

Daniel grabbed Adam by the arm tightly. "You don't get it, do you? Are you so blind that you don't get that you put us all at risk? That could've ended very badly for all of us if Raphael had decided to entertain you. Like you said, they don't think very much of us."

Adam's eyes meandered off into the distance. He knew he had crossed the line.

"Sorry. That was dumb...but he deserved it." Adam snatched his arm from Daniel's grasp. "He *should* feel bad for what happened to her."

His eyes finally met Daniel's again and the older Guardian could see he meant every word.

"Maybe," Daniel admitted. "But that's not for you to decide."

"Then whose decision is it? Gabriel was our friend, Daniel. She was the only angel who didn't look down on us. The only one who treated us as equals."

Daniel could see a moment of real pain register on his brother's face. He could barely hide his feelings anymore.

"She helped us, even saved our lives. Am I the only one who thinks she deserves a little more respect than this?" Adam's voice was nearly shouting now. "Am I the only one who even cares!?"

Daniel grabbed Adam again, this time it was *his* face registering pain. "No, and don't ever assume that again."

Adam could see the emotion behind his brother's eyes. He was hurting as well.

Daniel loosened his grip and pulled Adam into a tight hug. "We're going to figure this out, but I need you to focus. I need to be able to depend on you, to trust you. You're smarter than this, Adam. I need to know you won't go flying off the handle at the mention of her name."

"Something feels wrong about all of this, Daniel. Gabriel's dead and the day her brother takes over, you guys are attacked at a meeting point specifically chosen by him. Things are changing and not for the better. Tell me I'm wrong."

Daniel exhaled deeply but remained silent in his brother's arms. Suddenly, a deep red light flashed in front of the elevator door. A moment later, several other red lights began flashing down the hall, bathing the entire area in a cherry lipstick color.

The brothers pulled away from each other and faced the elevator door. They could hear the metal box screeching to the ground and their jaws tightened in anticipation of what they were about to see.

The doors opened with a grating screech and two men appeared inside, one hanging off the shoulder of the other. His blood ran trails down his arms and legs, changing the color of his natural brown sugar skin. His long black hair dripped blood, but the moment he set eyes on the two brothers he fashioned a weak smile.

The uninjured man had his partner's blood smeared across his oak-colored and tattooed face. In fact, any part of his body that was not covered in clothing was marked with a different holy symbol. The Star of David, the Hindu Om, the Wheel of Dharma, all in different sizes and styles spread all over his body. The most prominent being a large black cross that stretched from the top of the frohawk on his head to the base of his chin. His expression was one of extreme annoyance that was matched only by the irritation in his voice.

"God, I hate this fucking elevator."

The vociferous sound of merriment filled the infirmary and spilled down the hallway. The four men occupying the room spoke loudly at one another, laughing and joking through bloodied wounds and broken bones.

"I'm serious man, I've never seen no shit like that my whole life," Prophet spoke sitting up in a hospital bed. "So, Ezekiel and The Maker are running from two badass second-class demons, and they start to climb down this fire escape on the side of the building. Well, somebody shoulda told Maker to go down first, because when I look up all I see is a yellow stream of God-knows-what running down his pants and splashing on Ezekiel."

The room rolled with laughter again. Prophet grinned mischievously at the tattooed man who checked him for injuries.

"And then Zeke slips on it and falls straight to the ground in front of me. He looks up, realizes what just happened, and goes 'did you just fucking piss on me!?'"

Another wave of laughter rolled across the room at the tattooed man's expense. If not for his oak-colored skin he would've been red with blush.

"I swear I wanted to kill his ass," Ezekiel spoke while

stroking his head. "Do you know how embarrassing it is to walk around smelling like piss all day?"

"No. But I take it The Maker knows," Adam retorted with a smirk.

"I lost what little respect I had for Theodore that day," Ezekiel said pressing his fingers into Prophet's stomach.

Adam was hunched over the long-haired man sewing stitches into his skin. "Theodore? That's his real name?"

"Yeah. He thinks 'The Maker' sounds cooler," Prophet answered with a wince as a stab of pain hit him.

"Here we go. Two broken ribs, bro," Ezekiel spoke pressing his fingers into Prophet's side. "So how many bones does that make now?"

Prophet tilted his head in a moment of thought. "Today, with two ribs and a cracked wrist makes one hundred twenty-three."

"Holy shit," Adam proclaimed.

"Don't worry about it, kid. Prophet's just clumsy. The rest of us don't have nearly as many calcium deficiencies," the long-haired man suddenly spoke, though his eyes remained closed.

"Well, well. looks like chief soaring eagle has something to say." Ezekiel turned his attention to the brown-skinned man laying opposite to Prophet. "You can talk crap when you don't have four holes in your limbs, Sadju. I tell this guy to wait for me but he goes chasing after a second-class demon by himself. The next time I see him, he looks like three-day-old hammered shit."

Saduj shrugged. "It was a second-class, level three demon. I thought that I could handle him, but he got the drop on me. Not my proudest moment, I admit."

"You goddamn right it wasn't your proudest moment," Zeke shot. "Next time you want to be a tough guy, you ain't getting normal medical treatment. We're gonna get a shaman, let him wave a magic stick over your ass and send you on your way."

The room erupted with laughter again. Even Sadju had to smile.

"Now that I think about it, I don't ever remember you spending more than an hour in the infirmary, Sadju. You must be losing your touch," Prophet said stroking his beard.

Ezekiel finished wrapping Prophet's cracked wrist in a cast before returning to the conversation. "First time for everything right?"

"And a last time," the Native American added, closing his eyes again.

"Hey, kid, I need your help here for a second," the tattooed man called.

Adam left his resting partner and joined Ezekiel at Prophet's side. The smaller man held a crowbar in his hand and motioned for Adam to stand on the opposite side of the giant.

"All I need you to do is to hold him down. Think you can manage that?"

Adam glanced over the bearded man's size and remained silent, placing his hands on Prophet's shoulders. Ezekiel wedged the small crowbar in between Prophet's metal shoulder and arm and paused, looking at them both for confirmation that they were ready. Adam nodded and Prophet stuck a plastic tube in his mouth.

"One, two, three!" Ezekiel shouted as he pressed the crowbar down and leaned his body weight against it.

Prophet's eyes jammed shut and bulbous veins raced up his skull. Adam threw all of his body weight against him but still couldn't keep the man's back pinned to the seat. Ezekiel felt his teeth grind as groaning metal pleaded against him.

Grunts of pain exhaled from Prophet's lungs. His muscles went stiff as he fought against the pressure shooting down his spine and scattering through his nerves. Then, with an abrupt and obtrusive "*pop*" the arm snapped off.

Ezekiel lifted the now-free limb and dropped it on a white dolly. "Theo's gonna have a field day fixing this. How the hell did you warp the metal like that?"

Prophet spat the red tube from his mouth with an exasperated breath. "Ogre."

Ezekiel shook his head in disappointment but said nothing, his way of teasing his older brother but also acknowledging a valid excuse. The tattooed man sprayed a clear liquid onto the area where his brother's arm used to be.

"What's that for?" Adam asked.

"This keeps away build-up between the arm and the real Prophet so they don't end up fusing together," Ezekiel explained as he continued working. "It's important that it's cleaned so that removing the arm is easy and doesn't hurt. If it ain't cleaned well, you can end up tearing off skin or breaking the arm. Not that he needs any help in that department."

"How often do you clean it?" Adam asked Prophet.

Before he could answer, Zeke's hand slapped the back of his head.

"Not often enough," Ezekiel answered for him.

Daniel sat on the edge of the bed in his room. The only light was the flicker of a wax candle on a tiny wooden desk in the far corner. He leaned forward on the bed and reached into his coat pocket pulling from it a small black feather.

He stared at the feather for what seemed like ages as images of events long past flowed through his mind.

The longer he stared the more memories flooded his head, pooling in the front of his brain and spilling from his eyes in tear form. Daniel closed his eyes and let the watery brine roll down his face, squeezing the feather tightly in his hand.

"You were right Gabriel, I was a fool."

There was a sudden knock at the door. Daniel quickly tucked the feather back into his coat pocket and wiped the tears from his face.

He cleared his throat of what felt like dry cement. "Come in." His voice still cracked.

The door slowly creaked open allowing more light to come pouring in. The sound of light footsteps entering the room caught Daniel's ear as he held his position with his back to the door. He didn't bother to turn around. He already knew who it was.

The tiny light from the candle cast dancing shadows upon the wall. Cursed souls writhing in eternal agony, praying for a respite that would not come. Ethereal demons clawing at an impenetrable field as they hungered insatiably for new flesh. He couldn't decide which they looked more like.

The door was slowly closed and the footsteps continued around the bed. He held his head down, staring at the black heels his visitor wore as they came to a stop in front of him. A hand reached out and gently took hold of his chin, lovingly lifting his head.

"Looks like you need a little light in your life."

Daniel stared up at a beautiful Latin woman, hair long and dark and in a ponytail, eyes green and piercing, and a slightly morose smile across her face. She ran her fingers through his short black hair, rubbing his scalp softly.

"Are you okay?" She asked, her voice like subtle but clear wind chimes in a gentle breeze.

"Yeah. Thanks, Emmanuelle."

"I know you were close to her. She was like a sister to you, wasn't she?"

Daniel stood up and walked over to the closed window. "Yes. She was...a friend when I needed one."

Emmanuelle followed him to the window, placing warm hands on his shoulders. "It'll be okay, you know that right?"

A sarcastic, empty laugh fell from his lips. "I don't know. I want to believe that, but the truth is I'm afraid, Elle. Things are about to change. Raphael doesn't care for us, and Gabriel isn't watching our backs anymore. I wish I could make it okay. I wish someone would come and just make things right."

Emmanuelle slid her hands across Daniel's chest and to his chin, pulling his face closer to hers. "I can't make it right but, for a while at least, I can make it okay." She held Daniel's lower jaw in her hand and began to suck on his lips.

He pulled himself away from her and put his back to the wall. "Elle...I..."

Before he could finish his words, she was back in his mouth again, this time tying her tongue into his. She managed to slide her hands under his shirt, pressing her palms against sculpted abs. As she exchanged her saliva with his, Daniel found himself kissing her back.

Her eyes fluttered as sparks ignited in her brain, rewriting synapses and turning her neuropathways into the 4th of July. Tremors from the explosion in her mind rippled down her spine, sending fireworks through her nervous system. She shuddered as her hands traveled from his stomach to his chest and back to his obliques, gliding over several bruises as her fingers mapped his frame.

He grabbed her and pushed her away from him. "Stop."

"What is it? What's wrong?"

Daniel's eyes moved to the far right corner of his sockets, refusing to make eye contact with her. "I'm injured."

"That didn't stop you last time."

"I told you that was a mistake." He turned his head away.

Emmanuelle placed her hand to his cheek and turned his head to face hers. "The night we had together. Those feelings we shared. How could that be a mistake?"

Daniel looked her straight in her eyes. "Because I don't share those feelings, Elle."

"That's not what I think. There's something you're not telling me. What's the real reason you keep pushing me away?"

Daniel could feel the cement drying in his throat again. "Adam."

Emmanuelle took her hands off of him and turned away. "How long are you going to keep using your brother as an excuse not to love me?"

"You know how he feels about you."

"That's not my problem and I can't worry about that," she snapped, whipping her neck around to glare at him.

Daniel walked calmly over to her, placing his hands on her shoulders. "You're right. It's my problem. *I* have to worry about it."

The Latin woman dropped her head. "I know."

She walked out of Daniel's grip and grabbed the door knob. Before turning it, she looked back at him.

"Te amo."

Daniel looked at Emmanuelle's face and dropped his head. A sigh, full of regret and dejection mixed with cold cement, fell from his mouth as he replied.

"I know."

She turned the knob and walked out the door, shutting it behind her. Her mind was a cocktail of weltering emotions that suddenly breached the dam she had so carefully constructed around them. Her hands latched onto her face trying, and failing miserably, to stuff the swirling feelings back. She could feel her palms moisten with tears and her breaths become deeper and more labored.

There was a monster in her chest.

A winged beast with the head of a lion and the claws of an eagle that slashed at her lungs making it nearly impossible to breathe. She sat on the floor next to Daniel's door and tucked her head into her knees, clutching the back of her head tightly. The monster had won but would not stop thrashing a wild celebratory dance inside her. Its talons rang the bones in her body in a brutal morse code only she could hear.

"*Why won't he just love me?*"

She took in a sharp breath and realized she had actually begun to sob and quickly got to her feet. Broken-hearted as she was, this was still no way for a Guardian to act. She began the slow march back to her room. At least there she could break without the threat of someone watching.

She was halfway there when the sound of another pair of footsteps began to echo off the metal walls. The steel hallways never made her feel comfortable, but their one saving grace was that no one could ever sneak up on you.

"Hey, Elle. I heard you made it back." A young vibrant voice called to her.

She quickly wiped her face of any sign of a meltdown, turned around, and saw Adam walking briskly toward her.

"I just wanted to come see how you were doing since, you know, Gabriel."

Adam stopped in front of her and placed his hands in his pockets. His face was one of deep concern.

"I'm fine. Thanks," she lied. "Just more exhausted than anything."

Adam stepped closer toward her. "I hope not too exhausted. I was hoping we could go somewhere and maybe grab a bite to eat and talk a little. There's a café not too far from here that has some incredible pumpkin pies."

He watched her closely and, before she could open her mouth to speak, her body language had already given her answer. The subtle lean away from him, the half a second pause and blank stare, the looseness in her jaw. Adam prepared himself for a punch in the gut.

"No thanks, I kinda want to be alone right now. Everybody grieves differently, right?"

The words didn't sting him as much as he thought they would.

"Right, I understand completely. You want to be alone. Do what you have to."

She turned to continue her walk and in four short steps, five disarming words blasted her eardrum.

"So, how was Daniel doing?"

She froze in her tracks, her mind spontaneously backflipping at the sudden question. Had he seen her enter his room? Was he watching as she left? How long was he there? Her mind came to a screeching and painful halt as the most important question slammed into her brain like a cognitive car crash.

"*Dear God, did he see me break down?*"

The monster was suddenly back with a vengeance. This time it threatened to eat away her insides entirely, but she forced herself not to break again.

"You know him. He acts tougher than he is," she spoke, turning to him with an innocent smile on her face.

That part was true.

"I was concerned so I just went to check on him. I think he'll be okay though, just give him some space for now."

That part was true, too. She was somehow impressed with herself because she hadn't been forced to lie to him.

"Oh, all right." Adam's eyes narrowed a bit as he scanned her for signs of falsehood.

Before he could accrue any, Emmanuelle blindsided him with a disarming question of her own.

"So, I heard Daniel sent you home today. Any truth in that?"

Adam's face immediately flushed. It was bad enough to be sent back to base but to be questioned about it by the woman he was desperately trying to impress was a visceral blow.

"Uh, yeah...I umm, I kinda lost my temper a little bit. I mean it was nothing really."

"Nothing to lose your temper over, or nothing worth being sent back to base for jeopardizing a mission over?" She asked in a mocking tone.

Adam's response deteriorated into a series of stuttering 'uh's and 'um's. She had effectively won this battle. He was too embarrassed to even give a straight answer to her question and if he couldn't think straight then he couldn't question her about her dealings with his brother. Though, if he *had* seen her crying outside Daniel's door, why he didn't bring it up was a mystery to her.

She opted to quit while she was ahead. "Don't worry about it, kid. Next time just try and keep that ego of yours in check. Catch you later."

She offered the young man another smile before continuing down the hall and out of the conversation.

"Yeah, catch you later," he mumbled to himself.

Adam was stuck, left standing in the hall flustered, head buzzing and wondering just what the hell happened here. He dragged his feet out of the hall and into the infirmary, flopping down tiredly in a chair next to his sleeping comrade. Adam covered his face with his shirt and released a muffled and waspish yell into the fabric.

The Native American man occupying the bed stirred slightly, only furrowing his eyebrows. "Shot down again?" He spoke without opening his eyes.

"Yep," Adam answered without removing his shirt from his head.

"You suck at life."

"And so life constantly reminds me."

Saduj gave a deep exhale. "Just let it go, brother. She's out of your league anyway."

"Maybe when you come down off your morphine high you can give me some real advice, chief." Adam poked uncovering his face.

"No. Morphine good," Saduj spoke in a stereotypical Indian accent.

Saduj finally opened his eyes to look at the man he was speaking to, and it hit him like a wrecking ball. The pained expression on his hollowed face. Dark circles around his eyes, and the eyes themselves, tinged with dolor.

He was in love with her.

"I don't know what to do, chief. She just...I..." Adam choked on the rising emotion in his throat. "Why won't she just love me?"

Saduj sat up in bed. He could see the redness in his eyes. "Love is...complicated, Adam. Rarely is it ever simple."

"You know what she called me in the hallway? Kid. She called me a kid. She doesn't even see me as an equal, Saduj."

"You don't necessarily make it easy."

Adam stood out of his seat and began pacing the room. "I know, I know. I've been trying to work on being more mature for her, but it's like she doesn't even notice. But of course, she notices when Daniel's in a bad mood. She goes running to him if he so much as stubs his goddamn toe."

"You think she's interested in your brother?"

Adam shot him a facetious glare that all but screamed out *'Are you kidding?'*.

"When I was coming down the hall I heard her leave his room. When I caught up to her I could tell she had been crying. She said she went to check on him to make sure he was all right."

"But *she* looked as if she had been crying?" Saduj queried.

Adam nodded. "And then she gives me some garbage line about how she wants to be alone after just leaving Daniel's room. I don't understand it. She and I shared some amazing nights together and all of a sudden she just turns it off like it didn't ever happen." Adam's eyes drifted into space, lost in a bright memory of spiraling passion. "Like it meant nothing to her."

Saduj was silent for a while. Long enough for Adam's nostalgic moment to fade into the back of his mind once again.

"If you love her, Adam you have to talk to her. You have to find out where you stand and if there is a future there. If you don't, you will regret it for the rest of your life. Trust me, you don't want to be an old man near the end of a life filled with regrets."

The young Guardian silently nodded his head.

"And keep on trying to be that mature man," Saduj continued. "Not for her, but for yourself."

SECTION 2

Daniel's footsteps resounded loudly off the hard metal floor as he walked down the hallway. He had begun to recklessly chew the inside of his cheek until now it was becoming tender and raw. His fingers twitched nervously at his sides, invisible needles pricking the very tips of his digits. He was not looking forward to this, but why was he such a wreck?

He never enjoyed chastising anyone, but he knew what his job was and what was expected of him. And the truth was, whether he liked it or not, this needed to be done. More than that, he knew Father would be disappointed if he neglected his duties, even to spare *him* a punitive tongue. Ironic, because the very person he was now headed to impugn upon was Father himself.

That still didn't quite explain his extensive jumpiness. He could more than handle issuing a couple of mean words to the old man just as Father was more than capable of taking them. He still couldn't imagine why he was so damn apprehensive.

An image, clear as an HD photo, shot into his head almost in answer to his unspoken question.

Long dark hair falling between heavenly shoulder blades. The gentle slope of a sacred lower back. The subtle bounce of holy hips. The graceful footsteps of the unequivocally graceful. Without even trying, Daniel's mind produced an image of Gabriel striding forward in front of him.

Not some random illusionary amalgamation conjured into being by the influx of images of her in his brain. This was an honest-to-goodness memory. He knew because he remembered her turning to him and after that...

"No."

He immediately shut off his mind, turning the glistening memory into static. He couldn't think about her now; he refused to think about her now. He actively stuffed the image into the far recesses of his working memory, piling countless other files stacked inside his mind on top of it.

That should hold it for now. Silently he promised her that he would come back to it, devote the proper attention to it later. Her loss was too great right now. The wound too fresh and the sting too painful.

"Focus," he whispered to the empty halls.

There were things he needed to talk to Father about. Right now those things took precedence over whatever emotions he may have been feeling. He reached the door and turned the knob, entering a sparsely furnished room. Save for a small twin-size bed and a tiny nightstand holding a clock, the room was arid and nearly devoid of furniture. The only decorative item in the room was a beautiful and meticulously designed fireplace protruding from the wall opposite the door.

Pictures of battling tigers and dragons were drawn into the frame of the piece in bright vibrant colors. The near emptiness of the room contrasted sharply with the exquisiteness of the work, making the fireplace seem like the only important thing in the room at all.

Amber flames leaped and danced, throwing shadows across the floor. The old man stood in front of the fire, peering into it pensively. He leaned against the frame of the fireplace, flicking the ashes from his cigarette into the flames. He still had not acknowledged Daniel's presence.

The young man closed the door behind him and walked halfway into the room before stopping and folding his arms in front of his chest expectantly. Father was quiet for a moment longer before speaking.

"I was beginning to wonder if you would ever show up," he said still staring into the fireplace.

"I wanted to give you some time to think things over."

Father did not reply. The room grew uncomfortably silent.

"Or at least come up with a decent excuse as to why you were drunk on a mission today." Daniel's words were biting.

Father turned toward him, revealing the open metal flask still in his right hand. He took a sip from the container, exhaling hot breath through pink cringing lips.

"Drinking," he corrected. "Not drunk."

"If you weren't still a capable fighter I would have sent you home with Adam."

Father was silent again, but Daniel could tell he was reflecting on something that happened today. His face was an ocean of calm whose surface was marked by rippling flecks of rage exploding beneath it.

"You saw something back at the church. Something's got you upset." Daniel tried to ask but stated it more as an assertion.

Father turned away, throwing his attention back into the fire. He hated being read by him, especially when he didn't want to be.

"Any other nuggets you care to share with me that I already know?" Father said sharply. "I told you how I feel about deciphering emotions through body language and then stating them out loud. It makes you look like a pretentious asshole."

"Well, maybe if you could hold your liquor without falling apart like some drunken prom date you wouldn't be an open book right now."

Daniel's words were loud and stinging, meant to cut deep into already tenuous pride. Even Father was surprised. Daniel had never shouted at him before and never spoken with such acidulous tone. The elder Guardian turned toward him with a look that screamed '*Have you lost your mind?*'.

Then he realized what was going on.

Daniel was deliberately trying to impel him into an argument. The sharp tone, the excessive loudness, the uncomfortable distance between them, all presaged a fight. A moment later and the old man was no longer surprised. impressed was more accurate. Using anger to get someone to open up was simple psychology. A little more time and a few more sips and he would've been too drunk to notice.

Now that he had indeed noticed, his surfacing anger was quelled and replaced with glowing satisfaction. The satisfaction that comes to a proud teacher when they know, undoubtedly, that their student has nearly surpassed them.

All Father could do was smile. "Impressive, Daniel. Well done."

He lifted the flask back toward his lips again but felt a hand push his forearm down. Daniel had crossed the remaining six feet of the room in the blink of an eye and was now standing face-to-face with his mentor.

"Talk to me, Father," he said, his tone now soft and pleading. "You haven't had a drink in years and you've been smoking nonstop for the past few days. What's going on?"

A breath of hot air escaped from Father's lungs. "He sent those poor rephaim to die. He knew they would be slaughtered. He knew." The old man paused, taking a drag on his cigarette. "He just threw their lives away."

"You mean the masked fighters at the church?"

"They were slaves, Daniel, not warriors. I took the mask off one and..." The priest struggled to hold back his emotion. "He had tortured them. Mutilated them. Maybe for years, God only knows how long."

"You know how cruel demons can be to half-breeds. You've seen things like that before."

"And I'm tired of seeing them!" The old man's face had flushed with anger. "I met that demon years ago and he escaped me. All this time he's been free to do that to innocent people. All this time and we couldn't stop him until today. I've been in this fight for a long time and it never gets any better. It never changes. I'm just tired of seeing the cruel nature of a world I can't change."

Daniel placed his hand on the priest's shoulder. "Someone once told me that you can't judge the world by what you can see, because your sight cannot encompass the scope of the world. All you can do is try and change the world for the better. The rest is up to God."

A plume of smoke drifted from Father's mouth as he spoke. "All of a sudden you're teaching me my own lessons. When did this happen?"

"When did you start getting so emotionally attached to rephaim?" A curt smile played on Daniel's lips as he took the metal container from the old man, closed it, and placed it on the fireplace.

"Uh oh, I know that look. It's time for inspection isn't it?" Father said half seriously.

Daniel grabbed his right forearm and pulled back the sleeve. "Damn right it is."

A black twisted scab about the size of a quarter rested

between his hand and his forearm. Daniel glanced over the old wound, checking for any sign of recent bleeding. After a second cursory look, he lifted his other arm and checked that one as well.

"All clear, doctor?" Father teased.

"These have healed pretty well. Seems like they've closed for good this time."

"Maybe." Father stared at the charcoal rivet fused into his skin. "Stigmata has a tendency of sneaking up on you when you least expect it."

"You have dark circles around your eyes."

Daniel's observation slapped him in the mouth. Stated bluntly while he was still examining his wrist as if he noticed ages ago but chose not to mention until now.

"You haven't been getting enough sleep. Something keeping you up at night? Nightmares maybe?"

Father pulled his arm from Daniel's hands and began rolling his sleeves back down. "Maybe."

"All right, keep your secrets. I know something is going on, and it's more than just what happened this morning. Something has been bothering you for a while now and it's driven you to alcohol." Daniel turned away, taking a few steps back toward the door then stopping and turning to face the man. "I've seen you you know, out of breath sometimes. Sweating profusely. Clutching at your chest. You're in pain. If I wanted to be more accurate, I'd say you're sick."

"Dilated Cardiomyopathy," Father said flatly, looking Daniel straight in the eyes. "If you want to be precise."

The air was ripped from Daniel's lungs. Father had stated the words with such dreary lassitude it seemed almost as if he wasn't serious. Daniel's voice caught at the back of his throat. He was serious and he knew it. Before his voice could return, Father had continued.

"Alcoholic Cardiomyopathy, they call it. From my years as a drunkard. The inside of my left ventricle is too thick and it won't allow my heart to contract properly. They told me it's spread to other parts of my heart now."

Daniel was still stunned. All he could manage was a simple question.

"How long have you known?"

"For some time now. I didn't want to raise a panic until you were officially captain of this team."

"That's not important. I've been leading this team unofficially for almost a year now. I'm ready to take over."

Father took another drag on his cigarette and flicked the ashes into the fire. "I have no doubts about that."

"Then give them to me. Hand me the reigns so that you can rest and receive treatment."

"I don't care about treatment!"

A volcanic eruption of sudden emotion caught Daniel off guard. Father's tone was one of aching pain spliced with furious anger and laced with reckless despair. The gruff words rattled Daniel to the core. For a moment, he nearly forgot his mentor was glowing pink with the alcohol in his veins.

He couldn't have meant those words.

"That treatment is going to save your life." Daniel rebuffed seriously. "Maybe you don't care about that, but there are people who do."

The room was silent again. Thick uncomfortable silence. Father's eyes had found the floor. Daniel stood awkwardly near the center of the room watching him.

"I need this, Daniel. Just for a bit longer, I need this."

A lump of coal slid off the back of Daniel's tongue and splashed into his belly. If Father would not cede his power then there was nothing he could do.

"It's your funeral, old man."

Quizzically, the words brought a convoluted smile to the priest's face. "There is one other thing you have to do before you are ready to take over as leader, Daniel."

"And that would be what?"

Father tossed the entire cigarette into the fire and walked over to the Guardian, placing his hands on his shoulders.

"It's time for you to meet the witch."

Raphael's pace was brisk. So was the pace of the entourage of angels trying to keep up with him. He and at least ten other angels tromped down a bustling subway station without uttering a single word. He had nothing to say to them. Though he wasn't particularly happy with so many bodyguards constantly surrounding him, he wasn't going to argue with procedure. Especially since he had helped design said procedure himself.

"*You realize that we are infinitely more powerful than any of the angels you can assign to protect us, don't you?*" Michael's words echoed in his mind.

Then Gabriel's words responded.

"*If one of us is killed, that infinite power you speak of would start to seem much more finite.*"

He backed Gabriel that time, but now that he was actually in the situation, he would not deny how ridiculous he felt at being protected by angels much weaker than him.

Raphael and his angels tore through the myriad of colorful souls packing the hall. Moving through the crowd of hundreds of faces without stopping to recognize any. They, on the other hand, were recognized by many.

Men in army fatigues with stars on their chests identifying their rank. Women with pure white togas draped across their bodies eyed them with marvel. Soldiers, covered head to toe with heavy shining armor, their breastplates covered in white cloths embroidered with crimson crosses, gave salute. Killers, dressed in the darkest black, their faces hidden behind hoods of coal, leered at them maliciously.

No one dare waylay their path.

They swept through the terminal and moved past the turnstiles to the very far end of the station into a narrow hallway lit with candles. Men and women dressed in robed garments from orange to white sat, crouched, and kneeled throughout the hall, filling the small space with their prayers. The group of angels took care not to disturb them and moved through without shattering the peace they had found.

Flung open near the end of the hall was a pair of large wooden double doors. Just as Raphael turned into the opening, he was stopped in his tracks by a trail of people from the doorway leading into the chamber.

"Of course, there is a line," Raphael huffed.

A man in front of the angel turned around, hearing the seraphim's complaint. He wore a tight powder blue suit trimmed with ruffles at the sleeves and white socks stretching from his feet to his knees. His face was powdered, giving his skin a pale and colorless look. Atop his head was a mass of fake bone white hair stretching six and a half inches off his crown and done in giant curls.

"There is always a line," the man said turning back to face the front.

The angels stepped around the line and began walking through the chamber toward the front. Past the doors was a huge inner sanctum reminiscent of the inside of a Roman chapel. Six stone columns supported the ceiling of the chamber and golden candles were hanging from the walls near giant rainbow-colored windows which poured in light. The eyes of those in line next to them stared enviously as they cut to the front importantly.

At the very front of the chamber was a man wrapped in a brown robe seated on a marble throne. The hood of the robe covered his face in darkness. His hands, however, sat outside of the garment. Large, brown, and riddled with circuitous veins, his hands were rough and powerful, yet rested gently on the face of a man wearing gold-plated armor and a helmet adorned with a red Mohawk.

The two men leaned into one another, whispering discreetly. The armored man then removed the gold helmet from his head and smiled widely at the robed figure. The seated man drew his hand across the soldier's face and a second later, the armored man exploded in bright piercing light. The inner chamber was smothered in it as the line of people shielded their eyes from the blinding flash. In the next moment, it was gone, leaving an ethereal wisp where the soldier once stood.

"That's very compassionate of you." Raphael suddenly interrupted. "Many of these ghosts would be trapped in this purgatory for a long time if you hadn't chosen to be here with them."

The shrouded figure's hood turned toward the angel, silently declaring that he now had his attention. "I help where I am needed, Raphael."

"At the cost of being trapped here yourself. Tell me, who will free *you* once your job here is done?"

The man turned his hooded face back toward the line of souls at his door. "I fear that day will never come."

"Indeed. You humans die so violently and with so much hate, sadness, and regret in your hearts. It's pathetic."

The hooded figure turned back toward the seraphim. "And when Gabriel died, what was in her heart I wonder?"

Raphael's face twisted into a mask of hate-filled anger. In a single sentence, the masked man had invited the seething pain spiraling inside the seraphim to his doorstep. The angel lifted his foot and stomped the ground devastatingly hard. The chamber rattled like a tambourine and the line in the center of the room quickly dispersed, each soul beaming out of the chamber in a series of flickering lights.

Raphael stomped toward the seated man and snatched the hood from his face, staring into his brown eyes angrily. "You dare insult *my* sister!"

The now revealed man stared into the seraphim's furious eyes calmly, stroking a long black beard. "I know the truth of you, Raphael. You have bled for us. Fought against your brothers for us. Protected us when we all but deserved protection. But make no mistake, God can see past blind action into the very heart of your beliefs, and she has spoken to me." The robed man stood to his feet to be at eye level with his addresser. "You share the same beliefs as Michael himself. You don't believe humans are worthy of God's grace, and though you fought alongside her, you never agreed with Gabriel's cause."

A palpable silence swallowed the room. The man stared unblinking into the angel's eyes.

"Now tell me, who insults her more?"

The rage on Raphael's face was now unbridled. With a bellowing grunt, his foot snapped forward and collided with the marble throne, shattering it to pieces.

Raphael growled at the robed figure. "You believe yourself special. That you are somehow better than your kin, but you are not. I am one of only five in the entire cosmos! I have built worlds, filled entire oceans. I could destroy this place with a word."

"And yet, here you are, preparing to ask me for help."

Utter surprise slapped the anger right off of Raphael's face.

The man smiled at the seraphim's stark silence. "I know what you are looking for, and I'm sorry to tell you that you have made a blank trip."

Raphael bit deeply into his bottom lip, trying to shake the last remnant of anger from him. He forced himself to speak as calmly as he could.

"I need to know where Gabriel's power will go. I need to know who will become the new angel of death."

"That, I do not know."

Raphael clenched his teeth, biting back his fury. "You're lying."

A reckless laugh escaped the robed man's lips. "No. You wish that I was lying, but you know that I am not."

As much as the angel hated to admit it, he was right. That was something he couldn't stand about this man. He had an uncanny ability to read angels as easily as they read humans. He turned around, pausing a moment before his anger got the best of him. Strong hands wrapped themselves around his shoulders and thick digits dug into them, not painfully, but shockingly gently.

"This duality is tormenting you, Raphael. Tell me, why do you fight against Michael if you agree with him?"

Raphael stepped out of his grasp. "I don't agree with him completely. His methods are destructive and cruel. Yes, I believe humans are unworthy, and yes angels should be loved above all others, but not through violence. Not by the extinction of an entire race."

Raphael turned to face the man. The anger he held was now gone, replaced with a sense of helplessness. Something an angel rarely felt.

"I need your help," the seraph pleaded. "Your people need your help."

The man stepped away from the broken fragments of his throne and placed his hands upon the angel's face. "Before this plight is over, you must recognize the strength in humans, Raphael." The man kissed the angel's forehead softly then backed away. "Until then, I cannot help you."

Raphael looked at the man, blood-red tears welling in his eyes.

"Then we are all doomed."

The cool evening air chilled the dew on the grass, making it crunch like broken shards of glass. Four tires pulled up on the frozen lawn causing a crescendo of shattering brakes under the spinning tires. Three sets of legs stepped out of the midnight blue car and began marching through the unthawed foliage, kicking molecule-sized shards of ice with each step. The air was set with moisture from the multitude of plant life in the surrounding area, one of the consequences of life near the bayou.

"Why did I have to be here again?" Adam huffed in irritation.

"Because two of us had to stay behind with Prophet and Saduj because of their injuries, and since Emmanuelle and Zeke took the job, you don't need to be there." Daniel wiped the wetness from his face as he answered.

"You should be honored, Adam. It's taken Daniel many years to finally meet this person, and because you're his brother he's decided you should tag along," Father spoke while leading the group.

"Thanks, bro." Adam slapped a mosquito from the side of his neck and replied sarcastically. "I'm honored."

As the three climbed a sloping hill, in came to view a

gorgeous white mansion. It was a three-story estate surrounded by giant twisting oak trees whose tops were covered in moss. Like the fingers of an enormous tortured hand, the branches of the trees jutted this way and that, in some cases spiraling around columns supporting the house.

As they admired the structure of the plantation, an incorrigible Irish accent grated unceremoniously into the approaching Guardian's ears.

"Welcome, gentlemen! Good evening to you all! A thousand hugs and kisses be upon you! May your grandson's grandsons have achingly large penises and so forth!"

Upon hearing the voice, Father shook his head in disapproval, Daniel covered his face in embarrassment, and Adam chuckled loudly.

"Oh, you didn't tell me *he* was going to be here," Adam said. "This should be fun."

Atop the hill stood a man with short, spiky blonde hair, a wide nose, and a thin-shaven goatee that gave away the fact that blonde was not his natural hair color. A lit cigarette dangled from his mouth as he spoke.

"About time you got here fellas. Our delicate flower over there was just about to go over the edge waiting for you."

Daniel stepped forward and greeted the loquacious man. "And I'm sure that has nothing at all to do with you, right Mark?"

A vulpine smile spread across the Irish man's face and he exhaled smoke through his teeth. "You know me. Was just doing my best to allay the boredom."

"I'm glad you could meet us here. I trust you haven't been here long?" Daniel asked.

"Not long enough to become insect fodder if that's your worry," Mark spoke as he slapped a bug dead on his wrist. "Sides, I wouldn't miss this for the world, boyo. We finally get to meet the psychic. I'm sure Zeke and Prophet are pissed they couldn't come."

"Where's Sera?" Daniel interrupted Mark's string of sentences.

Mark gestured over toward the mansion. "Our resident turtle dove is upfront. In a charming mood as usual."

The group, Mark with them, continued to the front of the plantation where a 5'5 blonde haired woman leaned against a wood column. Her long hair was done in a single French braid that fell down the front of her shoulder. Her cheekbones were strong, giving her small face a hard look, and in front of her narrow eyes sat a pair of gold-framed glasses. They were the only thing softening the glower glued to her face.

"Don't ever leave me alone with him again."

She spoke before the group could reach her, but unlike Mark's egregious accent, hers was slight. Nearly perfected from her years as an American citizen. Most times her accent only showed while pronouncing vowels like "o" or words that began with "th". Beyond that, she made it very difficult to decipher her Russian ancestry.

"I nearly put a dagger in his throat." Her stone face made her threat seem genuine.

"You would kill me, Seraphim? Your loveable, huggable Irish teddy bear?" Mark gushed.

"No. That would be just to shut you up," she remarked sharply.

Father's voice came from behind everyone suddenly. "Well, now that we've all said hello, let's not forget what we're here for."

The priest stepped through the group and toward the front doors of the plantation. On either side of the white double doors stood two women dressed in tight-fitting black business suits with skirts. They wore dark sunglasses with earpieces in their ears and pistols that were not exactly hidden from view at their waist. At first, the women's faces were hard and unnerving, but that slowly gave way to warm and inviting smiles as they recognized Father at the front of the group.

"Good to see you again, Father," one of the women spoke. "I'll let her know you've arrived."

Father nodded his head as the two women reached for the door knobs and pulled both doors open. As the cool air whipped into the Guardian's faces, the warm air rushed from their lungs in a simultaneous gasp.

A giant twin staircase accentuated by a glistening crystal chandelier greeted them in the first room of the mansion. Except for the foyer's polished black marble floor, most of the house was blanketed by a sensual bright red carpet adorned with luxurious and assiduously polished oaken furniture. All of this, though exceptionally salubrious, was not the reason four out of five of the Guardians suddenly had to fight to regain the air swept from their lungs.

Walking jauntily in six-inch heels, posing naughtily for flashing cameras, pouring spilling wine into expensive glassware, and otherwise enjoying the company of wealthy men, were alcohol-addled, half-naked women. Without even noticing their presence, the women laughed and downed entire bottles of liquor while being carried off by various men into closed rooms. Heedless merriment ruled the day as even when bottles were spilled over or glasses were broken or even when one of those wealthy men emptied the contents of his stomach onto a bare-chested girl, the partying did not stop.

Apparently, this was the norm in this household.

Once Daniel's senses had returned to him, he glanced over at his companions, who were already staring in awe and confusion at one another. Daniel began to let his mind wonder if they had come to the right house. There was more than one plantation in these parts after all.

Without warning, a topless woman whipped her head in their direction and stared for a brief moment. A fluttering expression crossed her face and Daniel could tell it was the spark of recognition.

The woman sauntered across the floor, a smile slowly spreading across her face as she closed on the group. With about three feet left to walk, she threw her arms into the air and leaped into Father's chest, wrapping her arms tightly around his neck.

"Father! Oh my God! It's so good to see you! Where have you been?"

The elder man closed his arms around her waist, a genuine smile creeping through his beard. "Glad to see you too, Missy. I've been busy. How are you?"

As the topless girl answered, other women began to notice Father's presence and made their way over to greet him as well. Within minutes, the marble floor was aflutter with the high-pitched squeals of dozens of giddy women all clamoring to be recognized by the old Guardian.

"Father, you are awesome," Mark said excitedly before a sharp elbow caught his ribs.

"Shut up," Seraphim snapped.

"Well, well, well, if it ain't old Padre come to pay us a visit." a Cajun voice cut through the prattle sharply.

The crowd of women looked up at the speaker standing at the very top of the staircase. She was a short husky woman wrapped in a silk red dress with matching lipstick and hair that sat on her head in a high bun. She made her way down the staircase, her earrings, shaped into the Star of David, bouncing loosely with each step.

"Y'all go on back to your guests now." She waved apple-colored fingernails toward the girls in the hall. "Don't go making a bahbin at me either. Go on, chat."

The eager women began to disperse and return to their business. The red-dressed woman reached ground level and crossed toward the group. Once she reached the stone floor, the Guardians could see her face was virtually glowing with makeup.

"I see you brought your clan with you this time. Nice to meet y'all. I'm Matilda. Padre's told me lots about y'all. Dis way please, to our sittin' room."

The group moved behind the red-dressed Madame through the heart of the mansion. All around them, carnal pleasures were shared unremittingly. Men in ludicrously expensive suits brandishing rolls of bills in remuneration for a job well done. Scantily clad beauties of every nationality stuffing wads of crumpled cash into dresser drawers or hidden pockets. The moans and screams of pleasure and pain or some twisted miscellany of both resounded behind locked doors.

Somewhere between the men in high-priced clothing and the screams of pain, Father chanced a thought.

"They're taking this in stride. Better than I had thought, actually."

A timid hand placed itself on the priest's shoulder. He knew he had spoken too soon.

"Father, what is all of this? What is this place?" Daniel's face was a mask of confusion.

"Surely, you didn't think you were the only one I found?" Father turned his head as he walked and glanced over his shoulder at Daniel. "There were many before you and many after you. Sadly, not everyone who falls on hard times can lift themselves out of it. These are the ones that couldn't quite make it out."

"Were these women...hurt?" Adam hesitated.

"In more ways than you can imagine. Some raped, beaten, molested. It's hard to find your footing after events like that. The ones that I can help end up putting their lives back together somewhere else. The ones I can't end up here."

Mark's upbeat Irish soprano found a level of sadness that surprised even him. "Jaysis. I'm sorry, Father."

"It's not all bad. The girls here are taken care of pretty well. They have a job, food, shelter, and even classes to help teach them a thing or two. It's better than where they came from, and sometimes a few girls can pull themselves out of here. These are the lucky ones."

"It's not all bad? Lucky?" Seraphim cut into the conversation. "Look at what these women are being reduced to. How can it get much worse than this?"

"You didn't know their conditions before this. Trust me, this is an upgrade for most of them."

The Russian women marched closer to Father's side to address him directly. "You said that these women were raped and molested. How is this any better than that? They are selling their bodies as playthings for rich men just to stay here. You could find them a church or—"

Father cut his eyes at the woman, demanding her silence. "There are no easy answers, Sera. For many of these women, this is all they know. There is no sense of inferiority in what they do because it's how they have survived for years. Besides, it's hard to argue the demerits in what they do when they make enough money here to support themselves and their families."

"The church," Seraphim continued. "If you could find these women positions at a church I'm sure—"

Father cut her off again, this time with a loud frustrated exhale. "Don't you think I've tried that, Sera? Some of these girls started off working the church, while the rest..." The old man let himself trail off into an all-eclipsing thought. "...the rest were molested by priests themselves."

The Russian woman bit her tongue in her mouth and let the man continue.

"I understand, Sera. I understand that, to you, this seems deplorable. You must understand that some women don't have the options or the talent that you had. Some don't have the drive to change. But I'd rather they be here than dying in a gutter with poison in their veins or from some drunken angry fool's fists. This is the lesser of two evils."

The Guardians continued their walk in uncomfortable silence. Mark eased himself next to Adam and leaned in so as not to be heard.

"So, what do you think about all this?"

Adam contemplated for a moment, his eyes drifting into space. "I think the problem with the lesser of two evils..." A second later and they had found Mark's eyes, brimming with affirmation. "...is that it's still evil."

CHAPTER
SIX

T he Psychic and The Deal

SECTION I

Matilda guided the small group of warriors to a small door at the end of the hallway but stopped to address them before entering.

"Father, Daniel, y'all come with me. The rest of you can enjoy the refreshments in our waiting room." She waved a palm in the direction of an open door to her right. "Don't go wandering off now. You might not like what you find."

The three uninvited Guardians adjourned to the waiting room reluctantly. The Irishman's reluctance, however, soon dissipated as he began stuffing his mouth with cupcakes and sandwiches. Adam watched his brother follow Father and Matilda through the door. Before entering, Daniel threw his sibling a thumbs-up in an attempt to allay his apprehension. Adam nodded his head, accepting the gesture and Daniel closed the door behind him.

The room was uncomfortably small. So much so that Father had to remain standing so as not to bump the round table that took up most of the space. Daniel thought it terrible irony that the woman had led them to such a tiny room in a house so enormous. Surely, this was done purposefully.

Matilda sat on the opposite end of the table and, with an outstretched hand, asked Daniel to sit.

"Glad I could finally meet you, Daniel. Been trying to get old Padre to bring you here for a while now, but he always said no. Some nonsense about waiting until you were ready or whatever." The woman reached under the table and lifted a cigar from a red box, lighting it, and placing it in her mouth. "Persistence pays off, don't it?"

Her lipstick left cherry-colored rings around the end of the cigar as she took puff after puff, filling the room with smoke.

"Let me properly introduce myself. Name's Mama Tilda, but folks round here tend to just call me Matilda. You can do the same."

"Nice to finally meet you, Matilda," Daniel replied.

"First off, don't you go judging Padre for what he done here. He saved a lot of lives by bringing girls to me and to call him anything less than a saint—"

"Matilda." Father's voice was one of censure, hinting that she had gone off-topic.

"Yes, well that's beside the point, ain't it?" She corrected herself. "Forgive me, I tend to let my emotions get the best of me at times."

"Then I'll let you two have it." Father opened the door and left the tiny room, giving Daniel a knowing stare as he exited.

The two who remained sat in silence. Matilda blew more noxious gas into the air with each breath on her cigar. Daniel could feel the smoke invade his nostrils and fill his lungs. Heavy breaths of secondhand aerobic cancer attacked his organs diaphanously.

"So, let's get to the vay ya. What would you like to discuss?" Matilda asked finally.

Daniel gave her a queer look. "You asked for me, didn't you? I think that question belongs to you."

"Weh." Matilda leaned forward in her seat. "What have you been told about me?"

"Not much. Father comes to see you from time to time. You're supposed to be some kind of psychic if I'm not mistaken."

"Ugh, I hate that term. I much prefer soothsayer. People hear the word 'psychic' and assume you're supposed to be a mind reader or know everything before it happens. All about the future and the past and all such nonsense. I tell you, if I had a nickel for every time some fool asked me for winning lottery numbers, I'd be more than well off."

Daniel was leaning forward now. "So, you do have a supernatural ability."

A hard chuckle coughed from her throat in response to Daniel's words. "No, child. This ability don't come from me. Same as any person able to see demons and angels, I've been blessed by God. Dis is a gift, honey, and it can be taken away just as easily as it's been given."

It was at that very second that it became clear to Daniel. The way her hand shook slightly while holding the cigar. The layers of makeup she rigorously applied to cover up the dark circles and crow's feet near her eyes. The stress resting in the folds of skin on her face. Her gift may have been more aptly described as a curse.

"What's it like?" He gently pressed.

"I can't choose what I'm gonna see or when I'm gonna see it. She gives me visions at her own discretion. Dey just come and go. No tutorial, no instructions."

"That must be difficult for you. I'm sorry."

Another mocking laugh spewed from the Cajun woman's mouth. "You ain't got time to be sorry for me, baby. We got more important things to talk about. Like the question dat's been burning at the front of your mind since you found out you were comin' see me. You know the one I'm talking bout."

Daniel's eyes narrowed at the woman. She had just said that she couldn't read minds and now she was claiming to know what question he wanted to ask her. Did she somehow know what he was thinking? She couldn't be that powerful, could she?

"So, go on." She nudged. "Ask me."

Daniel stared blankly at the woman, pretending not to know what question she meant until the words came spilling from his mouth suddenly.

"Did you know Gabriel was going to die?"

The question sucked the oxygen out of the room, leaving only spiraling cigar smoke left to breathe.

"Weh. Yes."

The answer didn't surprise Daniel, but her words still struck him like a battering ram. The invisible blow emptied the burning smoke from his lungs, filling his chest with something dark and cold. A slow viscid something that only comes when you fail someone in the worst way. It crawled its way from his lungs to his stomach, drinking the bile hungrily and growing until it filled his belly with thick black nothing, and through it all, he knew one thing.

He could have saved her.

"Why didn't you do something!?" The Guardian shot out of his seat.

"It ain't my business to intervene in affairs of dis magnitude. What could I do?"

"You could've told Father! You could've told *me*! If I had known I would have—"

"You woulda fought bravely and died quickly, baby." Matilda interrupted Daniel and finally put out her cigar in an ashtray. "These ain't your run-of-the-mill angels we talkin' bout here. These is salt raining, tsunami forming, tornado summoning seraphim and they *ain't* to be trifled with. Trust me when I tell you dat no demon you ever faced is gon prepare you to do battle with the hand of God herself."

Daniel's eyes and head dropped. "I should've been there. She's protected us so many times, and I wasn't there to protect her. I won't forgive myself for that."

"Dere may be something you can do to end this war, Daniel. Gabriel is da first seraphim to die in all of creation. But there has to be an angel of death whether it's Gabriel or not. Her angelic powers gon transfer to another angel and that angel will decide how dis war ends." Matilda stood to her feet and walked over to Daniel, taking his hand in hers. "We can't allow an angel on Michael's side to inherit her power and dere may be an artifact on Earth that can make sure dat don't happen. An artifact dat can decide who inherits her power."

"Where is it?"

The Creole woman turned and sat back in her seat smugly. "Imma tell you how to find it, but first I want you to tell me something. I want you to tell me bout your secrets. The secrets you keep from your teammates. The secrets you keep from Padre."

"Secrets? Why?"

"Whatever we discuss gon be between you and me, but these secrets you keep ain't healthy for you or your friends, Daniel. Dey will come to light one day, and it may not be in the way you want."

Daniel's eyes widened in shock. He knew what she wanted to talk about, or more precisely, who.

"You want to talk about *her*, don't you? You want to talk about Eve."

Matilda leaned forward in her seat again, a wicked smile

on her face. "Mais, yes, let's talk about her. But me and you both know, she ain't the only secret you keep."

Mark's pale hand swatted the nape of his neck in bored irritated fashion. He peeled the squished exoskeleton from his skin and flung it lackadaisically into the marshy grass.

"Christ, the bugs out here are the size of bleedin greyhounds. Remind me never to invest in any estates on the bayou."

The Russian woman flipped a dagger in her hand, only half listening to the Irishman. Which, in her case, was more attention than she usually gave him.

"They don't bother me." She teased. "Perhaps you should think about wearing a less flamboyant cologne."

A short burst of laughter erupted from Adam's mouth which he quickly stuffed back into his throat and swallowed. "Well, you *are* pretty fragrant."

"Glad to see he has a sense of humor," Seraphim spoke while still toying with her weapon.

"Oh, you're one to talk," Mark spat at the blonde. "Or perhaps he's trying to make an impression on you, Sera. Take it from me kid, you're barking up the wrong tree. This one would slit your throat sooner than she'd kiss ya."

Adam stuttered, red-faced and wide-eyed. "No, no. I wouldn't..I...I mean, I can't. Um, even if, like, I...I wanted to, I uh, I mean, we..."

Adam's tongue was having the equivalent of an epileptic seizure in his mouth. He wasn't sure if he could stop it himself. Which is why he was immensely happy for Seraphim's next words.

"He's joking, Adam."

A tidal wave of relief washed over him, cooling the red-hot flames making his tongue dance. "Oh. Yeah, I know. Right."

"Sides, you look like a heartbreaker, kid. That's one heart that'll break you back." Mark poked.

Seraphim leaned coolly against the front of the car they arrived in. "Isn't that what they say about angels?"

"I think it goes something like..." Mark paused, staring into space as his mind recounted an old dust-covered memory. "*Break the heart of an angel and yours will be broken in return.*"

"What's that again?" Adam tried to sound like he had at least heard the words before.

"Some ancient saying that came about way before our time. Supposed to have something to do with killing angels from what I remember. Can't recall the rest of it though." Mark slapped his open skin again.

"Why would we need to know how to kill angels? I know some of them don't like us, but they wouldn't just outright attack us, right?"

Adam asked the question in hopes of an answer. His only reply was eerily disquieting silence. Mark's fingers rapped on the hood of the car and Seraphim cleaned her nails with the tip of her dagger. Neither of them was certain enough to answer.

Daniel made his way toward the trio, the wind catching and throwing his hair from left to right. "We're done here."

Adam turned to Daniel as he walked past him and to the car door. "So, what do you think of her? What's she like?"

He thought about what he should tell them. The psychic woman's warning of secrets played in his mind like a recording stuck on repeat. She was right. They should know, just not right now.

"I don't know," he answered. Strange, I guess."

"Is she the real deal or what?" Mark asked.

The three waited with bated breath for Daniel's answer. They were more anxious about his encounter than he was.

"Don't know, but if Father trusts her then that's good enough for me for now."

The four found their eyes critiquing Matilda and Father as they stood just outside the plantation doors in deep conversation.

"It was good for my soul, seeing you again, Padre. Don't you ponder on those dreams of yours for too long now. It'll drive you mad."

The priest took a tight hold on Matilda's hand. He let her feel him shaking.

"I can feel it getting closer, Matilda. Somehow, I can feel it. It's so close...and I'm petrified."

Matilda could see the burning fear in his eyes. He was falling apart.

She took his trembling hands firmly in hers. "Ya can't fear it now. Your whole life you knew it was coming, so don't you cower before it. Embrace it and know dat it's your destiny."

The old man stood in silence, clutching her hands.

"Your worry ain't only for yourself, is it?" The question came more like a statement from her lips.

"Yes, it's Daniel. I'm worried about him the most. I fear for him."

"As do all fathers when dey set their children out into the world. Daniel gon be fine, Padre. You the only one who need worry. Your final test is coming and you need to prepare. It could very well decide your eternity."

Father released her hands and pulled her into a warm embrace. "Thank you, Matilda. Thank you for everything."

The Cajun woman patted his back and let him go. "And try not to drink and smoke so much. Not dat it matters much, but you're starting to carry a smell like a peunez."

Father smiled crookedly at her. "I'll try."

The eerie glow of moonlight cascaded through the clouds over a dark cemetery. Wily shadows flickered and danced over tombs in a macabre waltz of merriment. Fog, thick and tangible, rolled over the soft earth, covering the ground in a blanket of grey.

A man followed the fog, light and graceful, his steps making the souls trapped in sarcophagi of decaying flesh scream his name in praise. The damp air permeated with the whispers of forsaken spirits, begging for his embrace. The trees bent and creaked in the wind, stretching for a brief touch of his skin. Even the light breeze is thankful and ecstatic just to be caught in the locks of his short hair.

The man is far from human.

He stopped in front of a twisted black tree, running his hands through his thin-shaven goatee. The fog stopped with him as if it were bound to him like a shadow.

"I know you're there."

Without warning, a dark hooded figure stepped from behind the blackened tree. A mortal eye would have found it strange as the tree trunk was much too thin to hide a full-grown man behind it effectively. Yet, no trace of the figure could be seen until he moved into the open.

"Michael, as sharp as ever I see. I also notice that you've gotten used to the souls that follow you around." The man pointed to the fog swirling at Michael's feet.

"They don't bother me nearly as much as you."

The hooded man pulled a crumpled pack of cigarettes from his coat pocket and removed the final stick from the pack. He touched the tip of the cigarette to his tongue and then turned it and placed it, lit, in his mouth.

"Nevertheless, you summoned me here. If my presence disgusts you so much, then maybe I should take my leave." The hooded man turned around and strolled back toward the tree.

"You know if I summoned you here, it was for good reason."

The man hesitated at Michael's words. "Then spit it out, angel."

Michael grew silent, which only served to deepen the man's suspicions and in a moment of joyous elucidation, it struck him. His eyes widened, the edges of his mouth cracked in a villainous smile and a sinister chuckle came retching from his throat.

"So, one of the most powerful angels in heaven, maybe even the strongest being in existence, with the exception of the almighty herself, has come here to ask for my help." He tossed the crumpled cigarette pack away and a long, excessively moist, tongue lapped across his lips in anticipation. "Forgive me if I relish this moment."

"I have not come here for your taunts." Michael's demeanor was one of absolute seriousness.

"Wait, let's get a bit more comfortable."

The figure clapped his hands twice and the enveloping fog dispersed from the graveyard. The screams of hapless souls were quieted for fear of the wrath of the man. Even the wind ceased to blow.

The dark man pulled another pack of cigarettes, a fresh green pack, from his coat and methodically removed the plastic. He tapped the bottom of the box on his right hand and slid a single from the box with his teeth. Somehow, within the span of a few sentences, he had already finished the first cigarette and was now working on a new one.

He breathed in the fire of the cancer stick and breathed out the smoke in, what could only be described as complete ecstasy.

"Now, if you please, Michael."

"You know better than most how relentless angels can be when they believe they are fighting for the right cause. I have weakened them, but I have not won yet. If I don't finish this now, they will return with even greater conviction."

"Ah, so you lack the means to finish this yourself." The hood deduced. "So, in taking Gabriel down you have all but exhausted your army and your resources. Quite a quandary."

He began to pace back and forth in front of Michael, his arms tucked regally behind his back, cigarette dangling from his lips two thirds finished already.

He stopped suddenly as he realized what the angel had summoned him for. "Rather than wait for Gabriel's powers to be transferred, you plan on preemptive action to win this war." Somehow the dark man's smile grew even more wicked. "And what do I get in return?"

Michael's face distorted as if it caused him unfathomable discomfort to say the words. "Name it."

The man tossed the cigarette butt away and clasped his hands together in effusive contentment. "Oh, what a delicious moment! Let's see, should I take the region of heaven that you rule over?"

Michael shot him a stinging glare.

"No, you're right, the property tax is outrageous." The shrouded man began to walk in slow circles around the angel in a taunting gesture. "Maybe I should take that fiery sword of yours. It would make for an excellent collector's item, don't you think?"

Another acid-laced stare from the angel to the man.

"Nah." The hood mocked him. "I'd have to polish it every day, and between work and the kids I just don't think I'll have the time."

"Make your choice!" Michael's hefty voice rattled the gravestones.

The hooded man grabbed Michael from behind, pressing his lips against his ear. The seraphim could feel the thickness of his goatee scratch his neck as his arm slid over his shoulder and wrapped around his chest.

"No, no that won't do," the man spoke softly. "Perhaps I should make you human for a day?"

Immediately, he could feel the angel's body seize. Those were the only words that struck fear into him.

The dark man let his hands slip up and down his angelic associate's neck and across his chest. "Let you feel the smothering imperfection of the creatures you hate so much."

The shrouded man looked into the night sky with a sense of wonderful decadence as he pictured Michael's suffering. He grazed his lips against the seraphim's ear and whispered to him in angelic tongue and smoky breath.

"Kill the Guardians."

Michael's eyes grew wide. "They can't be that much of a problem for you. Why would you want this?"

The strange man let Michael go and stepped back in front of him, already placing a new cigarette between his teeth. "I have my reasons."

"Reasons you will not share with me."

"You will be made privy to them in due time, Michael. Just play your part for now."

What sounded like a curt laugh came from Michael's lips. "I am given a task that even you can't accomplish. Forgive me if I relish the moment."

"On the contrary, I could destroy them whenever I so choose. From the inside out."

Michael avoided the obvious question and decided to make a statement instead. "You have planted someone in their group. A traitor."

"No, a traitor would imply that they were once genuine."

"So this betrayer has always been your subordinate. Then why do you need me?"

"I don't." Fissures of smoke leaked between his teeth as he gave a smile. "But this way will be undoubtedly more entertaining."

Michael gave an expression that looked like he had caught the putrescent stench of the bodies buried beneath his feet. "If that is all, then our business is done."

"Not quite, Michael. Businessmen usually seal a newly formed partnership with a handshake." He extended his left hand.

"I am not human nor do I care for any of their futile idiosyncrasies."

"Humor me, Michael. This is one trait that you would admire in humans. It shows that, though we may not like one another, we understand the need for agreement between us."

Michael let the hooded man's hand hang in the air a bit longer, then hesitantly took it in his grasp. Instantaneous pain ripped into his body, stretching its hot fingers through his angelic system like a glowing red poker. His arm tightened, his head snatched backward as if ungodly powerful hands had taken hold of his hair. The dark man's countenance was icy cool as he flicked the cigarette butt into the wet grass.

"And there is one thing you should know by now, Michael."

He tightened his grip and a red fluorescent glow began to pulse from their hands. Michael fell to one knee, pain surging through every fiber of his being. He could feel searing hot tendrils scorching through him, burning every ounce of him into useless, charred, black, slabs. His blood boiled under his skin, forming large bulbous protrusions in his flesh that burst in a piebald smattering of black and green.

"Always expect more than you bargained for..."

His angelic grace scratched and clawed at the surface of his body, trying desperately to escape the wild and fervent darkness that bastardized his being. Worse than the pain fissuring through him was the substance now pooling at the back of his mind. A foul sickening substance produced rarely by angels and never by a seraph. Yet there it was, leeching away what dismal amount remained of his holy nature.

Fear.

And when he could bare no more, at the peak of his agony, Michael's teeth sharpened like daggers. His eyes became inky black and blood-red tears fell from them as he let out a soul-shattering scream. Gravestones burst into pebbles, the ground split open, and all the while the cloaked man stared at him, the angel's screams driving a callous smile onto his face.

"...when you make a deal with the devil."

CHAPTER
SEVEN

A ll Gone to Hell

SECTION 1

Ezekiel's fists slammed powerfully into the red punching bag that hung before him. He hopped from left to right, switching his feet as he did before hammering into the bag again. The chains supporting the heavy bag rattled and the bag itself swung out in a half circle before returning to meet the tattooed man's fist again. Sweat glistened on his forehead and his lungs swelled in his chest. Though he wished it was just him and the punching bag, something else drew his attention.

A mordant, sometimes flippant, voice was grating into his ear, begging for a reaction from him. Begging for a fist in the mouth, was a description more to his taste, but what else were brothers for if not occasional annoyances?

"What are you doin? I know you can hit harder than that. If you're not gonna hit it then quit wasting its time. If that were a demon you'd be dead already."

Ezekiel whipped his head in Prophet's direction, watching him critiquing his every move, a red apple in his single remaining hand.

"Hey, you want to take its place?" Ezekiel said in a daring tone.

Prophet smiled effervescently at his brother and held up the splint wrapped around his hand. "No strenuous activity. Doctor's orders."

Ezekiel sucked his teeth as he went back to his training. "Like that's ever stopped you before."

"So, what's the deal with the tattoos?"

A new, somewhat younger, voice interjected into what could barely be called a conversation. Both men glanced up through the training room. From the shadow of the doorway, Adam stepped onto the soft ocean-blue mattress that covered the floor, crossing over toward Ezekiel.

The young Guardian's eyes perused the dark markings etched into his teammate's skin. "They supposed to mean something?"

Ezekiel looked at Adam imperiously. "Yeah, how many nights I've spent by your mama. Getting a new one later today."

"Ouch. Low blow," Prophet said loud enough for both men to hear him.

Adam cut his eyes at Ezekiel. "Sorry, I just assumed they were targets in case Theodore felt the urge to piss again. Last time I checked, Guardians *fought* demons, they didn't run from them."

"Oh, a hit below the belt by the kid! How will Zeke respond?" Prophet played as if he were a sportscaster.

"How many demons have you fought again?" Ezekiel turned toward Adam then quickly back to the bag. "Like, one and a half? Talk to me about fighting demons when you're not getting expelled from missions okay, kid?"

"I plan to," Adam retorted. "And I'm glad you're on the

punching bag, my mama says your technique needs work anyway."

"Boom!" Prophet's voice echoed throughout the room. "Down goes Frazier! Down goes Frazier!"

Ezekiel dropped his hands and let out an exasperated breath. An irritated smirk crossed his face, an expression that said he was done with words.

"You want to know about my tattoos? All right. Beat me in a fight and I'll tell you everything you want to know."

Adam was quiet as he contemplated Ezekiel's deal. The tapestry of symbols gleamed on his sweat-covered body as if they had been laminated onto his skin.

"And the crowd goes silent." Prophet teased.

Adam caught the glimmer in Ezekiel's eyes. He was serious.

"All right then. Let's do it."

Prophet shot out of his seat and onto his feet, his arm high in the air in excitement. "It's on, ladies and gentlemen! It's on!"

Adam looked around the room at the bevy of options he had to choose from. Other than the weights and training equipment to one side of the room, there were several racks with dangerously sharp weapons located on sections of the walls that weren't padded like the floor.

"So, what do you want? Spears? Swords? Tonfa?" Ezekiel asked.

Adam grabbed a pair of red sparring gloves from the wall and put them on, indicating just what weapons he planned on using.

"Oh, I'm going to enjoy this." Ezekiel smiled nefariously.

"Me too!" Prophet shouted from his seat.

Ezekiel placed his gloves on and the two warriors squared up with each other.

The brown-skinned man beamed at Adam. "Bout time I showed you how Z gets down."

Those were his last words before throwing a light jab which bounced off Adam's glove. Adam answered with a right hook which careened by Ezekiel's jaw.

"Going hard from the start, huh? Okay." Ezekiel taunted the young man and attacked with a left jab followed closely by a right hook.

Adam slapped both attacks away and stepped forward with a wrecking ball of a left hook. He was sure he had nailed his smug, tattooed chin until he took a blow to the stomach and then another to the ribs. The combo shook his frame and made his bones sing.

"Aw, so close."

Ezekiel's gibe came from Adam's right. He wasn't sure how he had gotten there so fast.

"Those two were free, Zeke."

The fro-hawked man laughed at Adam's words and raised his guard again. Adam tossed a quick right jab at his face and found that once again he was not there. Ezekiel stepped to the left of his punch and hammered into his ribs three times. The move was like lightning. Adam wasn't sure what had happened until a throbbing pain soaked into his side. He could see the pleasure on his opponent's face.

"And those? Were they free too?"

The young man gritted his teeth. Pain was now swimming freely inside his abdomen. He rushed Ezekiel, feigning a high right hook but then dropping to a low left. Somehow, his opponent had anticipated him and dropped his elbow to absorb the hit.

Ezekiel's vision blurred red, his sight suddenly hampered by the bright color of the glove that stung him in the jaw. He fell backward, a tiny sliver of blood in his nose.

"You know a little something, I see. A double feign, nice."

The tattooed warrior readied himself again "Too bad it don't mean nothing."

Ezekiel rushed inward, dodging a jab meant to hold him at bay and pushing Adam backward with his hand. Daniel's brother toppled over the leg Ezekiel had slipped behind him and fell into a backward roll. He popped up onto his feet already dodging a flurry of punches being thrown at him. He could feel the vibrations of force left in the air with each missed attack. Shivers of energy calling his name but not quite reaching him.

Adam dashed to his left and out of the line of fire, leaping into the air and nailing Ezekiel below the temple with a sloppily thrown left. He was surprised at the strength of his attack, which sent Ezekiel into a spin on his heels. He landed with a sense of self-satisfaction which quickly dropped into his stomach and dissolved at the next thing he saw.

Ezekiel had used the force of his attack to propel him into an impossibly fast roundhouse kick that raked across Adam's chest and connected with his chin.

Adam stumbled away from his attacker and then launched himself viciously back at him, throwing wild blows madly. This time it was Ezekiel defending against a barrage of punches, yet he seemed content to let Adam pound away at his forearms.

Ezekiel's last attack must've dazed him a bit. Adam's punches were sloppily thrown and few even landed properly. All Zeke had to do was bide his time and wear him down, and he was doing just that.

The moment Adam's attack lulled, the fro-hawked man leaped out of arm's reach, accentuating his maneuver with another tag to his opponent's side.

"Those ribs of yours are starting to sing to me."

Adam leaped through the air toward him, cocking his fist

way behind him as he flew. Ezekiel readied a counter, but the foot to his face changed all that.

The younger Guardian drew the tattooed man's eyes toward his hand only to strike him off guard from below. Ezekiel's pride took the brunt of the blow while the hit itself threw him from his feet and onto his back.

"Let's change that tune then." Adam's words were like salt on an open wound.

Zeke stood up, blood boiling. "You got a mouth on you, kid. Let's see where it gets ya."

"I know what you're trying to do. You're trying to piss me off. Throw me off my game. It won't work. I've got you figured out."

Ezekiel walked within arm's reach of Adam. "Let's see about that."

Adam saw it coming. A meteor of a blow flew toward him in the form of a red-hot glove. His forearm trembled upon intercepting it. That particular meteor was meant to be a planet killer. He thanked his lucky stars he saw it coming.

He decided to put some distance between them and backed away. His body jerked forward, his leg seemingly fused to the floor, fighting him from moving from that spot. He looked down and Ezekiel's foot was planted on top of his, turning his tactical retreat into a lost dream. Before Adam could cover himself, his head was blown backward by a powerful left hook.

His world was sent spinning into an opaque blur. No colors or sound aside from the steady thrum of his heartbeat. In a single moment of clarity, he questioned why he could even hear his heartbeat at all.

There must've been a million other sounds his ears could register, but they choose his heartbeat. Not the manly grunts of his attacker or the thumping of constantly moving feet on a floor mattress, just his heart. As if it was of some great importance right now that he had one. Rhythmic, powerful, and, to his surprise, strangely slow.

He intended to wonder about the weirdness of this when a sharp strike to his left side brought him back to reality. His body lurched forward from the blow and again his face was kissed with Ezekiel's fist, knocking him to the floor.

The brown-skinned man stood over Adam triumphantly. "Finished yet? I'm sure there's someplace else you could be right now other than here, getting your ass kicked by me."

Adam struggled to his feet, shaking the static from his vision. He was still seeing red for some reason.

"Screw you, I could do this all day. No one's waiting on me."

"Oh really? You can't fool me, Adam. I've seen the way you look at her."

His vision instantly cleared, his ears burned and his heart stopped. He couldn't be saying what he knew he was saying.

"Must suck knowing she's in your brother's bed every night."

Ezekiel had barely finished the sentence when a left hook snapped his head to the right. An uppercut sliced through the air like a missile, rattling his teeth like an explosion in his mouth. The final blow hit like a meteor to his head. Hard, fast, and devastating.

The planet killer.

Spit flew from his mouth and Ezekiel hit the mat with an audible thud. It took more than a few moments for his vision to straighten itself out and for three Adams to become one again before he realized what had happened.

Adam stood above Ezekiel, not triumphantly but angrily. The words had touched a serious nerve in Adam and he had lost it in an instant. He had gone from zero to sixty in the blink of an eye and in his blind rage had knocked his sparring partner senseless.

Ezekiel wiped the blood now freely flowing from his nose and pulled himself to his feet. "That was one hell of an atom bomb you dropped there, kid. So, I'm guessing this is what you got sent home for?"

The oxygen caught in Adam's throat. He had done it again. He had lost control of his emotions. His hands went from palsied fists ready to reign destruction on his enemy to open palms pleading for forgiveness.

Ezekiel began to unstrap his gloves, he was done fighting.

"If you care *that* much about her then here's a piece of advice," he said 'that' as if referring to the punch that knocked him flat. "If you do manage to get the girl, treat her like an angel. Don't you dare break her heart." He maintained eye contact as he spoke, letting Adam feel the gravity of his words. "You know what they say, *Break an angel's heart and yours will be broken in return.*"

The tattooed man threw his gloves to the floor and walked off. Adam was silent for a moment, unsure if he was being teased again or if he had been offered genuine advice. He decided on the latter. At least it made him feel better.

"How does the rest of it go?" He shouted to Ezekiel, who was now at a distance.

The nearly bald man threw his hand into the air arbitrarily and answered without turning around. "Who the fuck cares?"

Adam smiled at the answer, shaking his head at the nebulous man. "Bastard didn't even keep his end of the bargain."

Prophet had made his way from his seat and to Adam's side nearly without being noticed. Along with Adam, he watched his brother walk out of the training room.

"They're for protection."

Adam looked up at the bearded man and then returned his eyes to the tattooed man. "Like body armor or something?"

Prophet gave Adam a cynical glare. "Haven't you learned that holy images can harm demons?"

"I know that already, but that's just a drawing. A picture. A picture of a cross can hurt a demon?"

"Not just a cross, anything holy. The Star of David, Mary Magdelene, anything. Anything used as a representation of belief in God."

Adam was quiet. Prophet's words were sinking into his mind.

"It's pretty clever really," the bearded man continued. "Guns run out of bullets, knives get rusty but Zeke is the only living holy weapon against demons. He could kill one with his bare hands if he had a mind to."

"That's all well and good, but he could have just told me that instead of being a pompous ass."

Prophet cleared his throat. "Some people see scars, and it is wounding they remember. To me, They are proof of the fact that there is healing. Linda Hogan."

"Huh?" Adam looked up at the taller man.

A soft melancholy laugh pushed through Prophet's lips and his eyes found the floor. "Ezekiel was tortured by demons once. They chained him to a wall and cut into his skin with their claws, licking the blood from his body. He got his first few to cover up the scars and after that, he just started getting them everywhere. I suppose he realized just how vulnerable he really was."

Adam stared wide-eyed at Prophet, unable to catch the words swimming freely in his mind.

"He told me one day that he had made a promise to himself." Prophet's stare finally found Adam's. "That no demon would ever touch him again."

There was a knock at the door.

"Yeah?" Daniel's voice shook, struggling to get out of his mouth.

"It's me. Can I come in?" Emmanuelle's soft peal vibrated through the wood.

"Sure. Come in." Again his voice trembled as if it took concentrated effort to speak.

Emmanuelle stepped through the door and saw Daniel upside down against the wall, supporting himself with a single arm. She could see why he sounded out of breath. He looked as if he had been there for a while. Beads of sweat began to permeate his skin, and his arm trembled as he slowly lowered himself to the floor and then back up again.

Emmanuelle cocked her head curiously. "You know we have a training facility for that, right?"

Daniel spread his legs into a perfect split and fell from the wall to the floor. "Just warming up a bit, that's all. What's up?"

"Well, I know you're leaving soon, so I was just coming by to wish you luck."

Daniel jumped expertly to his feet. He could feel her eyes scanning his shirtless features.

"Thanks, Elle. I appreciate it."

The Latin woman sauntered over toward him. He wondered if she knew she was doing it or if it was some unconscious reflex triggered by his propinquity.

He knew there was something else there. Something he caught in her eyes that filtered into her walk. Something nearly imperceptible in that slow stroll of hers that spoke volumes to him. She had something else on her mind.

"Is that all?"

She stopped about an arm's length from him. "I wanted to

apologize. I know I'm putting you in a difficult position with your brother, and I wanted to make it clear that I'm willing to slow things down if that's what you want."

He thought about speaking but decided to let her finish.

"I know when we first hooked up, it happened so fast that neither of us really knew what was going on. We were lost in a moment of passion, and I understand that. I'm willing to wait as long as it takes, so take as long as you need to. We can go catch a movie or go to a restaurant, you know...date and see where things go."

She paused and looked at him, hope in her eyes dangling from an ever-tearing rope over a hundred-foot drop into despair. Then he realized, he held the knife that would cut the rope.

He ran his hand nervously through his black locks, his eyes meandering about the floor as his lips parted.

"I'm sorry Elle, but it's time I was clear as well. You were right when you said I was hiding behind Adam, using him as a scapegoat. I can't do that anymore. It's not fair to either of you." He held his breath, looking her in those sparkling emerald pools, and cut the rope. "I don't love you, Elle. I don't care for you the way you care for me, I never have. I shouldn't have done this. It was wrong."

"Wrong?" She covered the distance between them in a step. "How could what I felt..." She stared into his eyes and started again. "How could what *you* made me feel be wrong?"

He heard the inflection. Like a punch to the gut, it stung him. All of her emotions in a single word blaming him for her feelings, and she was right. He *was* to blame. Immutably.

He kept his eyes pinned on her, not daring to look away. " Because I'm the one breaking your heart."

His words cut into her heart, pouring her love, thick and unconditional, to her feet. Her hands shook at her sides and her head lowered to where Daniel could no longer see her eyes. He wondered if she was going to slap him. Even more so, he wondered if he would let her because he deserved it.

Surprisingly, she didn't strike him.

Her voice floated from her mouth, soft and listless. "I know you don't love me, but if it's not too much to ask." She lifted her head, tears wetting the edge of her sockets, just waiting to fall. "Could you try, for me?"

Daniel took her face in his hands, gently cupping his hands around the bridge of her chin. "Do you love Adam?"

She turned her head in his hands, taking her eyes off of his. "No."

He lightly pulled her face back to his, regaining eye contact and watching her hope crash into the chasm below. "Could you try for him?"

There was a deafening silence as Daniel watched a tear tumble from her eye and cascade down her cheek into his hand. He then saw her actively force the remaining tears back into her eyes.

She pulled herself from his hands and wiped her face. There was a flash of pride and anger Daniel had seen that wouldn't let her be completely vulnerable. He moved in to try and console her when his door flung open.

"Hey bro, I know you're leaving in a sec so I—"

The air in Adam's chest flew out of the room. His jaw tightened and his heart sank into a pool of snapping piranha. He was angry at himself mostly. After all, he had made a habit out of barging into his brother's room unannounced. This time he'd witnessed something he wished he hadn't. His brother, half-naked in a room with the woman he had fallen in love with.

His mind fumbled with how to process it, and he ended up falling into a series of half-words and stutters. Daniel cleaned up the mess that was his brother's mind and asked him a straightforward question.

"You wanted to see me for something?"

The wetness returned to Adam's throat and his jaw loosened once again. He needed to speak before he made himself look like an idiot again.

"Was just coming to see you off, but if you're busy I can just come back."

"It's fine, Adam. Elle and I are done."

Daniel looked over at the woman and she stared back at him, a tinge of pink forming in her eyes.

"I guess we are," she said before walking out the door.

Adam moved out of the way and watched her walk briskly down the hall. "Is this a good time?"

"It's fine. As good a time as any."

Adam closed the door behind him and approached his brother. "I came to apologize about earlier."

Daniel cringed internally. He'd had enough apologies for one day.

"It's fine, Adam. No need to."

"No, it's not fine. It was stupid of me to assume I was the only one hurting. I know everyone here was close to Gabriel, and I shouldn't have said that. I just wanted you to know before you left."

Daniel nodded his head in agreement. "Okay. Thanks."

Even with that, he could tell Adam had more to say. Without a second thought, he knew what it was about and he didn't feel like discussing it now. He had a mission to prepare for and he didn't have time to be distracted again. He wanted to end the conversation before it started.

"If that's all, I have some things to do so, I'll see you later."

He turned around and began gathering his things without giving Adam a second look. He threw on a shirt and grabbed his bag and coat before the words slapped him in the back.

"Do you love her?"

He stopped in his tracks, his back still to his brother. His brother, still waiting for an answer.

"No," he said without turning.

"Does *she* know that?"

"Yes."

Daniel began packing again. Adam began firing off more questions.

"So, when were you going to tell me about you and her?"

"You're a smart guy, Adam. I'm sure you didn't need *me* to figure out that something was going on."

"I didn't need you to sleep with her either."

His words were callous and anger filled. Daniel could hear the bellicosity in his voice. Adam was willing to fight.

"I'm sorry." He turned to finally face his brother. "That was out of line."

"So, it's true." Adam pretended to be more shocked than he actually was.

"I was in a dark place. I needed somebody, anybody. She was there."

"So you never even cared for her!?" Adam sounded amazed at Daniel's audacity not to love her.

For the second time, Daniel found himself wondering if a punch to the face was imminent, and for the second time, he knew he would deserve it.

"I'm sorry, Adam. It was a mistake."

"You knew I cared about her! You knew we were seeing each other and you still did this!"

Daniel held his palm up in opposition. "No, Adam. She and I had spent the night together before that. Before you started seeing her."

Adam found himself in a rare moment of utter confusion. "Why would she hook up with you first, then date me only to try and get back with you? I don't understand it."

Daniel could see it happening again. A rope unraveling over a crooked chasm ready to receive another body. And Daniel, once again, had to oblige.

"Because she doesn't love you, Adam. She never did, and you didn't need me to tell you that either."

Adam wanted to speak. He wanted to argue his point and call Daniel a liar. Trouble was, Daniel knew that he knew the truth. Worse than that was the icy cold feeling at the back of his mind that told him he knew all along but was too blind to see it. Maybe he didn't want to see it.

"She needed you Adam, and you were there for her. But that's all she needed from you." Daniel's tone was apologetic as if he could somehow apologize for Emmanuelle's wrongdoings.

He grabbed the remainder of his things and opened his door. He didn't want to leave Adam like this, but he didn't see how any more good could come from his staying.

"I'm leaving. We'll talk some more when I get back if you want to."

Daniel turned to walk out the door when Adam spoke up.

"*Break an angel's heart and yours will be broken in return.* Do you know how the rest of it goes?"

Daniel smiled quietly at his brother from over his shoulder. "*Take the heart into your hands and watch an angel burn.*"

SECTION 2

Daniel stepped outside into the cool evening air. The wind whipped against his face, softly messaging his cheeks like ethereal fingers. He took a deep breath, taking in the smell of the outdoors. The smell of the long grass all around him, the thick moisture that was pushed around by quixotic gusts of wind, and the sound of nocturnal critters coming to life as the sunset.

And then the smell of smoke.

The sting of arsenic burned intrusively into his nostrils, singeing his nose hairs and sending olfactory receptors into a frenzy. He exhaled sharply, pushing the stench from his nose and then witnessing a small cloud of grey ash rise into the sky nearby.

Standing in the grass, cigarette in hand, was Father, staring into the setting sun. Daniel wondered if he was aware of his presence and walked quietly toward him.

"Still haven't cut that hair, huh?" Father asked without turning.

Daniel wasn't surprised at all. The old man had picked him out before he could come within four yards.

"Well, at least you don't need a hearing aid."

"I'm old, not ancient."

"I think most paleontologists would find an argument there."

Daniel stood beside his mentor and beheld the setting sun. The priest spoke before he could.

"I never asked you how you were doing, with Gabriel's death I mean. I never asked you if you were okay."

"And you don't need to," Daniel answered the question clearly and curtly.

Father took it as his way of telling him he did not want to discuss it. The priest quietly went back to his panoramic view.

"I'm sorry about doubting you, Father. Back at Matilda's, I didn't mean to attack you or question your work. I trust your judgment completely and I respect what you did for those girls."

Father laughed a bit, pushing smoke through his teeth. "I understand if you don't trust her yet. That's why I hesitated to introduce you. Her methods are...unorthodox, and I know your trust is not easily earned. Your relationship with her will not be an entirely pleasant one, but it will be a necessary one. Try and trust her, but if you can't seem to manage that, try and trust me."

Matilda's words thrummed harshly in Daniel's mind, her talk of secrets and consequences.

"*They will come to light one day, and it may not be in the way you want.*"

Daniel bit into the side of his mouth and twiddled his fingertips. He hated that through his mannerisms alone, he could tell he was nervous. He second-guessed for the fifth time if he should wait. Maybe a little later, after he made it back from the mission.

No. He knew if he didn't start now, he wouldn't at all.

His teeth clenched and he swallowed the stones in his mouth into his stomach, making the acid roil and pop angrily.

"Before that car hit me, before I was trapped in Hell, I had dreams every night. Dreams of these screaming things chasing me and fire all around. I thought they were nothing, but what really made me pay attention to them was the fact that I had them consecutively. Every night the same dream. Me running and those things chasing me."

Daniel had to rub his hand against his cheek to stop chewing it. He still couldn't stop his fingers from swinging madly though. He decided to let them be and continue.

"Then I was trapped in Sheol, and after a while, I realized they weren't just dreams. They were visions of the future. My future. When I made it back, the nightmares got worse. I even tried avoiding sleep altogether. Then, one night I heard a voice in my head, more vivid and real than any dream I ever had. It told me to protect Adam, to guard him with my life. It told me he would accomplish deeds of great importance, and that it was my job to prepare him for them. My job to watch over him."

Father dropped his cigarette into the grass and stomped it out. "You've never told me that, Daniel. Why?"

"I don't know. Maybe I didn't want the responsibility. I thought that if I just pretended it didn't happen, I could escape it. Today, Matilda told me otherwise."

"Why would you be afraid of protecting your brother? You've done a fine job so far. What do you think is going to happen to him?"

Daniel's brow furled and his head dropped. The stones

swishing around in his belly kicked stomach acid up his throat. He could feel the back of his tongue burn.

"One night, Adam came into my room. He was shaking. I could see in his face something had scared him badly. He actually wanted to sleep with me that night. While we were under the covers, I asked him what was wrong and he described a dream to me. A dream with fire and screams and running. He described Sheol to me."

If there was a cigarette in the priest's mouth, he would have dropped it. He stared wide-eyed and mouth agape at Daniel. "What does that mean, Daniel?"

"It means Adam is going to go to Hell one day, Father," Daniel's hands were visibly trembling now. "And that petrifies me."

Father could see that Daniel had become unnerved. Recounting these events had taken a toll on his system. There wasn't much he could do to comfort his student.

"You were right you know," the priest began. "I don't sleep much anymore."

Daniel watched the old man pull a cigarette pack from his pocket and lift a single smoke from the thin case. His hands went through the motions precisely, with the speed and grace that only comes when a series of movements have become second nature. He slapped the tail end of the pack against his hand, slipped out a cigarette, and lit it between his lips.

"The nightmares keep me up most of the night."

Father breathed the gas out into the evening sky and Daniel watched him attentively.

"I start off running, alone in the dark. I have no clue why I'm running, but then I see a door in front of me. There's light shining behind it. A flashing light that's calling to me. I open the door and there's a wall of fire behind it. A literal wall of flames that leaps over me and traps me in place. My eyes start to bleed. I try to scream, but I can't. I try to move and I can't and, just before it's over, the fire jumps to my chest and burns right through my heart."

Daniel couldn't help but feel a little small after hearing Father's story. If the priest had intended to distract him by occupying his mind with his own problems, it had worked. Daniel was feeling sorry for him.

"What do you think it means?" The young Guardian asked.

Father avoided eye contact with him. He didn't want Daniel to catch him lying.

"I don't know."

He took another drag of his cigarette. *His* hands were shaking now.

"Do you know why I chose you to lead, Daniel? It's not because you're a genius or an amazing fighter. It's not because of your resistance to pain or because you are a natural leader." He turned to Daniel and took him by the shoulders, the orange and red of the sunset beaming down the side of his face. "It's because of your courage. You have a courage in you that I have never seen before. Because of that, your team will follow you to Hell and back, and so would I. You are a braver man than I ever was, and I'm glad to be leaving them in your capable hands."

Daniel gave Father a puzzled look. "Are you saying what I think you're saying, old man?"

"I figure I could use a break from all this. About time I stop being so stubborn and let the next generation take it from here. That being said, upon your return you will officially be captain of this team. The paperwork has already been filed."

Though the tone for this moment wasn't particularly happy, Daniel was beaming inside. He put a lid on his giddiness for now. He had a few more words to share with his mentor.

"Do you remember that factory where we faced down that

first-class demon?" Daniel turned back toward the picturesque scene before them.

"How could I forget? That was one of the worst days of my life."

"I know. It's still as clear in my mind as if it happened yesterday. Prophet was down, Sera was hanging, barely awake, off my shoulder and I had blood running down my face with a broken dagger in my hand. I knew it was over. I didn't even give it a second thought. I was certain we would all die there."

Daniel's eyes made their way to Father's face, a sense of marvel embedded into his pupils.

"That's when you showed up, pulling yourself from a pile of scrap metal with two twisted hunks of steel in each hand. You stood in front of us and stared down that monster and didn't move. It was the most courageous thing I'd ever seen. There was blood all over you. It must have been agony just to stay on your feet, but you stood there, between us and certain death as if you could somehow stop it. I'll carry that image with me until the day I die, Father. The image of you staring down a monster without fear."

Father placed his hand on his pupil's shoulder and smiled at him. "Now Daniel, you should know by now that true courage isn't the absence of fear. It's—"

"The will to go on despite it." Daniel nodded with a smirk as he finished his mentor's aphorism. "I know, Father."

The old man couldn't help beaming in silent pride. Never had he trained a student he was so sure in, that was so perfectly crafted to lead this team. His pupil was ready.

"Regardless," Daniel continued, "that's where my courage comes from. Not from me, but from you. One day I hope to become as brave as you." He gave his mentor a knowing look and began to pace away from the priest, readjusting his bag as he walked.

"May the Lord be with you, Daniel," Father called, trying to catch him before he got out of earshot.

The young Guardian turned around and answered with a smile. "Where else would she be?"

Daniel spun on his heel and left the priest on the grass. The old man peered into the dusk halfheartedly. The words he couldn't say to his student slipped up his throat, over his tongue, and past his teeth through his lips.

"You're wrong, Daniel. There *was* fear present that day, just not for myself."

Adam dragged his feet down the polished metal hallway dispiritedly. His mind tumbled like a dryer on its highest setting, angry heat pulling sopping rationale from his mind the longer he pondered. He tried not to think about it. He didn't want to be upset at his brother, and he knew that was exactly where his thoughts would lead him if he let them.

But it was impossible not to let them.

Every quiet moment he found was filled with throbbing anger. He tried to sleep but couldn't. He tried music but found himself listening to tracks that only strengthened his anger and justified his rage. He tried working out his hatred on a punching bag but decided to stop when his knuckles began to bruise. He tried to forget the reason for his anger and succeeded, then he later found himself grinding his teeth and punching his pillow for reasons he could no longer fathom.

So now he was here, dragging himself down the hall, mind sorting through the events of today at mach speed, yet still finding no solution. And he was still angry.

Who did Daniel think he was anyway? To keep something like this from him was a cardinal sin among brothers. It was damn near blasphemy to sleep with a girl knowing your brother had his eye on her.

Adam was completely justified in his anger. He didn't even begin to believe that she had been with Daniel first. Not for a second.

The sound of sharply exhaled breath and slapping leather echoed down the hall, catching his ear. Apparently, he wasn't the only one who couldn't sleep. He could hear the rattle of the chains attached to the heavy bag. Upon traveling closer to the training room he recognized the higher-pitched peal of the effortful grunts made with each blow.

He peaked through the open doors and saw her, hair in a messy bun, green gloves clashing with her sky blue tank top and black yoga pants, pounding mercilessly into the white bag hanging before her.

The only sound she made was the forceful expulsion of air from her body as she made contact with the bag. Her form was sloppy and she didn't seem to be practicing any particular style or strategy. The more he watched her, the more she looked like a mad woman crassly attacking an inanimate object. Her strikes landed recklessly, either too high or too low, and with no rhythm whatsoever.

This was his chance. He could finally take this opportunity to ask about a future with her. He could finally ask her how she felt about Daniel. He could finally ask her how she felt about *him*.

He stepped onto the blue mat and began walking toward her back. He could hear in her breathing that something was wrong. There was emotion in those punches. With each step closer, he could hear it clearer. Rising from the pit of her stomach, spiraling through her arms, and blowing outward through her fists.

He wondered how he didn't see it before. It was in her

posture, the way she struck the bag, and in her breath. The very same thing that made him forego sleep and wander the halls this night. Pure, unrelenting anger.

Then it hit him like a pair of brass knuckles. A truth harder to swallow than a seven-hundred-twenty milligram placebo. He *wanted* to be angry. He wanted to stay mad at Daniel and the answer was right in front of him. Because he couldn't bear the thought that she never wanted him. He didn't want to imagine that his brother never took her from him at all, and that was because he never had her in the first place.

He listened a minute longer to her anger-filled exasperations against the punching bag and knew they were both angry at the same person. Maybe they needed to be for now. He turned around and quietly walked out of the training room. He would have to work up the nerve to talk to her another day.

Further down the hall, he saw another sleepless Guardian occupying the space near the elevator. This one's limbs were bandaged tightly and his long black hair hung loosely about his shoulders as he methodically swept the hallway floor. Adam had no problem addressing this one.

"Shouldn't you be in bed, Saduj?"

The Native American man continued sweeping without looking up at his addresser. "I needed to move around a little. I feel like I've wasted half of my life in that bed."

Adam leaned against the wall near the injured man. "You shouldn't over-exert yourself."

"I'm just sweeping the floor. If I can't do this, then I shouldn't be a Guardian at all."

Adam was quiet for a while, watching the raven-haired man work.

"Did you talk to her yet?" Saduj asked.

"No. I chickened out."

"Understandable. Disappointing, but understandable."

Adam's hands dragged across his face. "Daniel told me they were a thing before we were."

Saduj stopped sweeping and turned to him. "Do you believe him?"

"I don't want to."

"That usually means, yes. A better question would be, what do you *want* to believe?" The injured man went back to his task.

"I want to believe that I was with her first, that Daniel stole her from me, and that she wants me more than him, but she's just confused. That's what I want to believe."

Saduj leaned his body weight on the handle of the broom to help allay the aching in his limbs. After a few breaths, he addressed Adam sternly.

"Then let me tell you what you *should* believe, Adam. It's doubtful that Daniel is lying to you. You said you saw Emmanuelle leaving his room before, but it looked like she had been crying. After which you tried to reconnect with her and she turned you down, and you haven't been anywhere near her in weeks. Your answer is staring you right in the face, but you refuse to see it."

Adam pulled himself from the wall and stepped close to Saduj. "Then what is it? If you've got it all figured out then tell me. Where does that leave me?" There was a bit of desperation in Adam's voice and a fleck or two of that anger he couldn't seem to get rid of.

Saduj eyed his teammate solemnly. "You're the rebound guy my friend. She wanted your brother and when she couldn't have him, she settled for you. But she does not love you. As unpleasant as it sounds, she may not ever have."

Adam could feel his food rising in his throat. He walked past Saduj toward the elevator, trying to give his stomach time to digest the information.

"If that's true, then why doesn't Daniel want her? Why would he get with her and then kick her to the curb? It's selfish and stupid." Adam could feel that old anger rising anew again as he justified it.

Saduj continued sweeping once again after catching his breath. "It *is* selfish, and that's exactly what Emmanuelle did to you."

Saduj's words stung him, and for all the right reasons. That unreachable pedestal he had placed Emmanuelle atop was now cracking and swaying in the wind. Another word from Saduj and it would shatter. As much as Adam knew his friend was right, he couldn't let him expose her flaws. He couldn't let him tear her down.

Adam whipped around, face a disfigured mask of rage. He opened his mouth wide to give his friend a piece of his mind. That's when the hallway flashed red.

The lights in the hall showered them in raspberry, and Adam caught his words before they could leave his mouth. The red lights only came on when a Guardian was entering the base seriously injured.

The two men stared wide-eyed at each other for a split second, then immediately turned to the elevator that came tumbling downward. Adam did a quick mental head count. Saduj was here and so was Emmanuelle. Prophet was down the hall with his brother and so were Mark and Sera. The only two unaccounted for were Father and Daniel.

He didn't know where Father was, and Daniel couldn't have made it back from his mission so quickly. Perhaps things didn't go as planned.

Adam turned his head toward Saduj and mouthed his brother's name to him. Saduj shook his head in return, clarifying that he was unsure. Adam approached the elevator doors and waited for the metal box to arrive.

With a haphazard jerk and crash, the steel cube dropped to the floor and stopped. Adam leaned in toward the doors, ready to assist a, probably, gravely wounded teammate. He prepared his mind for all manner of scenarios, broken bones, bloodied limbs, impaled organs. Still, he was caught completely off guard by what emerged from the doors.

A shoe, black and heeled, sprang from the opening doors and crashed into Adam's chest, throwing him into the wall next to Saduj. When his double vision returned to single, he was able to make out what was now pouring out of the elevator and into the halls of his home.

Demons.

SECTION 3

Black and slender forms crawled out of the doorway like insects in all directions. At least ten, wriggling about on all fours, slick with a thick membrane that covered their wiry frames. Their fingernails were long and hook-shaped and their toes gripped the walls and ceiling with the help of whatever substance secreted from their skin. Large bulbous heads teetered atop gaunt bodies that were probably not as frail as they looked, but the most unsettling thing was the glaring lack of sensory organs on the creature's faces.

There were no eyes, no noses, or ears. Just a mouth, each one gaping and horrid. Perpetually open, tasting the air and filled with jagged, rotted, yellow teeth and a black moist tongue that squirmed endlessly.

Adam was disgusted but somehow found a moment to wonder how this many of even these skinny creatures managed to fit in that elevator. Then he heard the click of heeled boots and remembered it was a human-shaped foot that struck him.

Last out of the elevator stepped a viciously beautiful

woman. Long jet-black hair and blue eyes that smiled for her even though her lips refused to. She wore a long black coat over a red buttoned silk shirt and tight black pants and those boots Adam had already become acquainted with.

She stood behind her writhing demon horde without worry, her eyes beaming through the two men fumbling before her.

"Hello, Adam, Saduj. Where are the other Guardians?" The words sang from her mouth as lovely as she was but somehow edged with nefarious intent.

"Who are you? How did you find this place?" Adam demanded, climbing to his feet.

The woman stepped forward, gliding over the polished steel of the hallway with barely a sound. "You shouldn't concern yourself with petty details, Adam. You should be focusing on how you plan to survive the next few moments."

Saduj stepped in front of Adam as if to protect him. "Get out of here, Adam. Sound the alarm and rally the others. I'll hold them here."

Adam gave his teammate a twisted stare. He couldn't be serious.

"You're kidding, right? You can't stop all of them by yourself. You don't even have a weapon."

The moment Adam finished his sentence, Saduj brought his heel down on the end of the broomstick, breaking the brush from the handle. He spun the wooden stick expertly in his hands and pointed the broken end at the horde.

Without words, the demons lunged at the two men, tongues thrashing wildly in their mouths and claws raised to find blood. Saduj stepped forward and knocked the first of the attackers to the floor with the dull end of his weapon.

The next came to his right, raking its claws across the wall and slashing at his face. Pulling his head back and avoiding the lash, Saduj cracked his attacker across the cheek, throwing it into its allies. The brown-skinned man ducked as another set of serrated digits whipped the air and sliced through his hair. He spun on his heel and slammed his foot into a demon skull, then pierced its head with the broken end of his makeshift Bo. Green blood sprayed from the wound as he jerked it free.

Adam stepped forward to receive the next attacker. The demon barreled toward him and he was suddenly struck across the chest with a green-stained broomstick. Saduj crashed his knee into the barreling demon, knocking it into the wall.

"Dammit, Saduj! What was that for!?"

The Native American spun his weapon around his body, connecting it with any creature that dared to come near. "I told you, I don't need your help. Get out of here." Saduj stepped forward again, swinging his staff at blurring speed.

He could hear demon bones crack and see lemon-yellow teeth shatter under the weight of his blows. A slim creature dove at him from the ceiling, arms wide as if to tackle him. The man spun away, letting the demon land on its knees, and put his stick through its face right where its nose should have been.

Adam stepped up to assist again, bringing his heel into the chin of one of the skinny monsters that threatened to get to Saduj's side. As soon as he hit the demon, Saduj brought his stick down on Adam's toe and kicked him in the belly, throwing him further down the hall.

With his attention divided, a slender hand reached out and cut his weapon in two. Saduj fell back, holding both ends of his broomstick tight in each hand.

He looked back at Adam who had made it back to his feet. "With all the time you're wasting here, you could've sounded the alarm by now."

Adam balled his hands into angry fists. He knew what his friend was trying to do. "I can't leave you, Saduj. You won't—"

"You can and you will," he interrupted. "I'm not about to say I let Daniel's kid brother die on my watch, no way. There's still time. Go and get the others and come back and save me. I'll be waiting for you."

Adam lingered a moment longer, his comrade stared unblinking into the swarm of bloodthirsty foes.

He looked over his shoulder at the young man, a terse smile playing on his lips. "Go save us, kid."

Adam backed away from his friend, he didn't want to take his eyes off him. The fear echoing in his brain wouldn't let him mask the truth. That this might be the last time he saw Saduj alive.

"I'll be back, chief. I swear. Just hold on for a little while, okay? I'll be back." Adam had to force himself to turn around and run down the hall.

The woman laughed, her voice echoing off the steel walls. "Brave of you, Guardian, choosing to die here for your friend. You and I both know you won't survive this."

As she spoke, the demons that Saduj had beaten into bloody, puss-filled, pulps were rising back to their feet, popping displaced joints and bones back into place and smiling horrible open-mouthed smiles. Even the foes impaled by his weapon had returned for revenge against him.

"You are exhausted, your weapons are not blessed, and—" The woman pointed down toward Saduj's knees."—you're injured."

He looked down at his legs and saw that the white bandages wrapped around them were now dark red. He had reopened his wounds and blood was seeping through the fabric and onto the floor.

His lips cracked into a hopeless smile. "Maybe you're right.

Maybe this is where I die. Or perhaps this is where I hold you off just long enough for backup to arrive. I don't know. What I do know is that none of you are getting past me while I still breathe."

Saduj shut his eyes and issued a quick silent prayer. The next moment, his eyes shot open and he launched himself at his enemies.

"So come then, and bring all of Hell with you!"

Adam thundered down the hall, shame gripping his heart tightly. He could still hear Saduj's shouts and grunts of expressed pain echoing down the hallway. There was still time, but he had to hurry. He had already left Prophet's room and he was nowhere to be found. Ezekiel's room was next.

He slammed through the door and into another empty room. Cursing loudly, he took off further up the hall.

Time was short and he knew Saduj couldn't hold out for long. He'd made a promise to get back to him and he intended to keep it, but after barging into two rooms and finding no one, his stomach began to tighten. Where in God's name was everyone?

The bounding noise of harsh screams and guttural sounds clambered from the open training room doors. He remembered who was in it. Emmanuelle.

Adam struck into the room and his heart dropped. The good news was that he had found Prophet and Ezekiel. The bad news was, along with Emmanuelle, they were in a no holds barred fight for their lives against at least eight more wire-framed demons.

Adam cursed again.

Ezekiel's back slammed onto the training mat and he rolled

up onto his feet. He brandished twin steel claws strapped to both his hands and leaped back into the fray like a wild man. Adam grabbed a pair of dual six-inch scythes from a nearby weapons rack and raced into the herd. With flashing blades and flurrying moves, the four tore into the demons, cleaving through flesh and bone.

"What the hell is going on, Adam?" Emmanuelle grunted out through a dazzle of attacks.

She had a belt of small cross-shaped knives slung over her shoulder and was nailing them accurately into oily black skin.

"We have to help Saduj! He's in trouble! We have to get to him!" Adam relayed in a crazed voice.

Prophet swung a spear tucked under his arm, mostly keeping the creatures at bay since one of his hands was injured and the other was missing altogether.

"First things first, kid. We have to make it out of here, then we can go help Chief."

Ezekiel howled wildly while driving his claws into a demon's skull. "Yeah, these are third-class, level-two demons at best. Won't take long."

Adam huffed in frustration and dove into the onslaught of demons. A few precision strikes and crippling blows later, the Guardians had successfully cleared the training room of the demon horde, leaving the remnants of their enemy's demon army scattered across the floor.

Adam stepped over the mutilated corpses and green glowing blood toward the doors. "Come on, we have to go now!"

Before he could reach the exit, he was blocked by another group of black hissing beasts and a familiar figure standing between them. The beauty that stomped his chest was standing in the doorway holding red-stained bandages in her hand.

"Looking for your friend? You just missed him."

She tossed the bandages onto the floor in front of them. Her eyes remained stoic and listless as if killing a Guardian was nothing to her.

It *was* something to Adam. He watched the bandages hit the floor and froze. A mixture of fear, anger, and heartbreaking guilt welled up inside of him threatening to push out organs, muscle, and bone.

He couldn't believe it. He refused to. He couldn't face the fact he had failed his friend. His eyes shut and he bit down on his bottom lip. Not from anger but just to keep it from quivering.

He heard the clatter of wood pieces at his feet and his eyes opened. The makeshift Bo, now split into two pieces, lay at his feet. There were bloodied hand prints covering them as if they had to be pried from Saduj's grasp. As if he refused to stop fighting even when his hands were covered in his own blood.

The acrid taste of hemoglobin wet Adam's tongue and he realized his teeth had pierced his own flesh. He looked at the uncaring expression glued to the woman's face and struck out at her. He could hear his teammates shouting at him, pleading for him to stop, but it was too late for that. His emotions burst inside of him, sending him headlong into mindless fury.

He drove his weapons into her ribs with enough force to break them and growled menacingly at her expressionless gaze. She slammed her hand into his chest and sent him sliding back and eventually tumbling end over end toward his comrades. She brushed her wound with her hand and set her gaze on the rest of them.

Prophet's jaw dropped. "How in the hell did she take six inches of blessed metal and not flinch?"

"I've never heard of a demon doing that before," Emmanuelle added.

Ezekiel swallowed the lump of fear in his throat. "Somebody please tell me what kind of fucking demon we're up against here."

Adam stood to his feet, the blind fury that was pounding through him now replaced with an unmoving sense of fear.

"She's not a demon."

The Guardians looked at him in utter shock and horror as he held up his weapons, soaked in dripping black blood.

"She's an angel."

CHAPTER
EIGHT

B*etrayal*

SECTION I

"A *power* to be precise," the female angel boasted. "An angel created for battle."

Her last words were spoken in a way that implied that conflict was imminent. She stood before the baffled foursome coolly, almost lackadaisically. Her stolid face held no discernible expression for the Guardians to pick out. If there was a single word that could describe her outward appearance, it would be '*bored*'.

The Guardians stared hard at the woman, peering past her human facade and into her true angelic form. The pitch-black eyes, white immaculate wings fluttering behind her, and the halo of pure light that hung over her head were all markers indicating they were dealing with a holy being.

"What's the plan here guys? We are very unprepared to fight an angel," Emmanuelle whispered to her comrades.

The expressionless angel responded in answer to Emmanuelle's question. "Oh, you won't be fighting me, human."

Surprise shook through the ranks of the Guardians as they realized she had heard every word.

Just who would they be fighting if not her? Before the question could even be asked, the squirming cluster of demons opened and three figures stepped forth from behind her. The Guardians could feel their throats tighten.

Three more angels stood in front of them now. One with skin nearly charcoal color and thick dreadlocks falling over his face. Another, with pale skin and short, slicked-back, blonde hair. The final one was the color of tanned beach sand and was bald. They each wore long black trench coats over plain white shirts.

Their feet made no sound on the padded floor as they crossed. Their stares were unnervingly constant as if nothing else existed but the group of four that stood before them.

Ezekiel found it difficult to hold his gaze on them. He could feel their eyes reaching into him, peeling back the layers of his tattooed skin to expose soft and tender pink flesh. He suddenly felt naked in front of them.

"They're here to kill us," Adam's voice was sharp and cold.

Ezekiel watched as Adam stared back at the angels defiantly. There was no fear or anger anymore. All he could see in Adam's unmoving stare was wild conviction. A conviction that was, apparently, contagious because now he felt a swell of determination as well.

Zeke's eyes became steely. "So what are we gonna do about it?"

The threesome closed the distance between them and the Guardians in silence. Their black fingernails grew curved and long and their eyes became dark as night. Their lips cracked open and they bared pointed fangs.

Adam gripped his dual scythes tightly and readied them to spill more angelic blood. He gave the warriors behind him one final look, then turned back toward the advancing threat, his teeth bared in a mighty scowl as he answered Ezekiel.

"Make them regret ever coming into our home."

Ezekiel could see his conviction spreading through the ranks of his comrades like a fervent pathogen, infecting and destroying all fear and doubt. Now they were ready. Now they were determined, determined to fight, to survive. Determined that, if they did die, they would take as many of these heavenly bastards with them as possible.

Adam held his weapons in front of him and charged into battle, his motivated comrades by his side. Their enthusiasm was short-lived as, in an explosion of surprising speed, the bald angel shot toward Adam and hammered him in the chest with his open palm, sending him tumbling backward across the floor.

Adam tucked into a backward roll and sprang to his feet. Midnight black claws were already raking at him viciously. He swiveled in and out of the paths of the feral attacks. His heart palpitated wildly in his chest as he struggled to keep pace with his opponent, the talons of the angel coming close enough to split the minuscule hairs on his face.

He lifted his right-handed scythe over his face, impossibly sharp claws raked across the flat side of the weapon filling the air with a piercing ring. The force of the redirected attack spun him on his heels, bringing him back around in time to block another strike at his face with his other weapon.

Another ring of scratched metal ripped the air in two as calcified nails met polished steel. Adam let the angel's claws slide off his weapon and counter-attacked with a slash to the face that glided over his opponent's head as he ducked.

The bald warrior struck out hard, his claws bouncing off Adam's scythes once again. The angel pulled to the left, aptly dodging a downward thrust of Adam's blade. The Guardian swung his second weapon to the angel's midsection, biting his bottom lip as he felt the tip of his blade pass through the angel's coat. He spun away from the angel, analyzing the hole he had made in his enemy's clothing, hoping for some sign he had caused harm even though he knew he hadn't.

The bald warrior stared the young Guardian down coldly, not an ounce of worry in his face. "You Guardians are talented humans. I have never met one who could stand up to me."

Adam returned the icy glare. "Thanks."

"And I have yet to meet one." The angel held up his black talons. "Your fight is a futile one, Guardian. Unlike the rest of your kind, I have respect for you. You serve our God at the cost of your own lives. Be without doubt that this battle will surely cost you yours."

With a gentle flick of his wrist, the angel flung a tiny smattering of red blood onto the blue floor. Adam looked at the droplets in confusion and then down at himself, checking for injury. Sure enough, it was there, three small slices across his belly, glowing red with his blood.

The wound was superficial, barely breaking the skin, but when had he received it? He had no idea when the angel had gotten an attack through and couldn't recall it even if he tried. His eyes returned to his opponent's, now doused in confusion.

The angel stared him down without remorse. "I have lived battle for longer than your race has existed. There is no victory for you here, human."

Adam scowled at the creature before him and lifted his weapon high enough for the angel to see. "Catch."

Adam threw his scythe at the angel and watched it fly by his shoulder as he moved effortlessly out of its path.

The angel began walking toward him slowly. "Is that all?"

"Wasn't talking to you."

The angel stopped, and his black eyes grew wide as a

familiar pain pierced his spine. He turned his head to see the very weapon he had just dodged lodged deep within his back. Four yards away, Emmanuelle held out an empty hand, her body lurching forward at the end of a throwing stance.

She whispered, knowing the angel could hear her. "Gotcha."

The angel turned back to Adam, the expression drained from his face. He reached behind him and pulled the weapon from his back with a sickening wet pop. The blade of the scythe was painted black to match the angel's fingernails and eyes.

He thoughtlessly dropped the weapon to his feet. "Indeed."

In the next breath, the angel was running full sprint toward Emmanuelle with Adam charging behind. After four steps, a streak of blonde hair blocked his path and Adam found himself desperately trying to avoid impaling upon tar black claws again. This time he was at a distinct disadvantage. He had needed both scythes to compete with his former combatant and he had only the one now. It was only a matter of time before his new enemy took advantage and laid his entrails across the mat before him.

That's when his savior showed up. His dark tattooed body glistening with sweat from battle shoved him out of the way and took over the fight.

"I got this, kid! Go help the others." Ezekiel gave Adam a stern glare, a trickle of blood running down the side of his face from a forehead wound.

Adam didn't waste another second and took off. He could still feel the pain in his chest from the seconds he wasted arguing with Saduj. Had he just listened to him the first time, his friend might still be alive.

Following the trail of his thoughts, his eyes found themselves resting on the pale-faced female angel. She hadn't moved from her position in front of the door. Her crystal blue eyes surveyed the war-torn gymnasium listlessly. Her placid countenance made Adam's blood boil, and he soon found himself sprinting at her headlong.

He could feel his teeth grinding into powder at the back of his mouth. That empty expression of her's drove him mad. She still had his best friend's blood on her hands and he wanted to make her pay for it.

He nipped across the floor toward her unexcited form and was met by a powerful shoulder that sent him crashing into a wooden weapons rack. The rack splintered into pieces, heavy swords and spears falling all around him as he recoiled onto his hands and knees. He looked up to see the dreadlocked angel staring down at him with inky black eyes.

"You are not worthy to stand in her presence, human."

Without warning, the chaotic sound of a nearby explosion ripped through the room. The lights flickered off and then back on as the shock moved the ground under once stable feet. The Guardians looked at each other in confusion, dust rattled from the ceiling.

"Was that a...a bomb!?" Ezekiel shouted.

"Yes, it was," the female angel answered. "Our demonic lap dogs have placed them throughout your base. Shortly, your home will be a pile of stone and dirt." She offered a queer look that seemed to be a substitute for a smile. "They were ordered not to set them off until you were all dead, but who can account for the impatience of demons?"

In an instant, Adam had buried a short sword into the dreaded angel's stomach and rolled away, snatching up a curved scimitar in his hands and hopping to his feet. He made another mad dash at Saduj's killer, reaching back and thrusting the weapon's edge mightily at her face. The scimitar stopped a foot's length from her nose, its tip shaking in front of her uninterested face, quivering for a taste of her angelic blood.

Adam turned his head toward the dreaded angel that had caught his arm by the tricep, halting the movement of his thrust. The short sword the Guardian had previously used was still deep in his belly.

Adam fought against the vice-like grip his enemy had on him but to no avail. He felt like a misbehaved child flailing helplessly in an adult's grasp. The dreadlocked menace held tightly onto Adam's arm and then cruelly tightened his grip, digging the tips of his claws into his muscle. The Guardian gave a yelp of pain and grabbed the angel's hand, to which the angel responded by digging further into his arm. He dropped to a knee, thin blood running down his arm dotting the blue mat with red splashes.

Adam forced his next words through gritted teeth. "Why are you doing this? You're supposed to fight with us. You're supposed to be the good guys goddamn it!"

The female angel leaned close enough to whisper her words to the Guardian. "There is simply not enough room in this universe for angels and humans."

Adam's eyes beamed hatred and pain at the smug angel. "Well, I guess one of us has to go."

In his next breath, Adam grabbed the short sword protruding from the dreaded angel's stomach and pulled it free, swinging the blood-soaked blade at the female's neck. In a single mighty swipe, he cast a black stripe of angel's blood across the room, painting a section of the wall dark with its color. To his dismay, both angels had already retreated from the arc of his blade. The only thing he had done was paint a wet strip of her minion's blood across her neck, his intended target.

In the next moment, the heel of the dreaded angel's foot connected to Adam's chest and sent him tumbling end over end. The angel strolled confidently toward the downed

Guardian and felt the sharpened point of a thrown Japanese sai pass underneath his chin. He looked in the direction of the attack and was clocked in the temple by Prophet's calcified elbow. Rolling with the blow, the angel spun on his heel until he was facing Prophet again.

The giant man swung his arm back revealing a polished machete that arced just short enough to pass through the angel's coat but miss his flesh. The dark angel spun again in the direction of the swing, coming around and catching Prophet's forearm with his claws as the Guardian stepped in with a horizontal forehand swing. The machete fell from his hands and the angel stepped in toward Prophet, spun again, and crashed his elbow into the bearded man's face.

Prophet's world blurred, outlined with pain as he felt the cartilage in his nose break and a spray of blood hit the floor. The one-armed Guardian fell hard onto his back, his eyes watery and stinging. He could barely make out the silhouette of his attacker standing above him. He couldn't quite see what he was doing through the blue and purple dots that flashed brightly before his eyes, but he imagined he was preparing a final blow.

That's when the second explosion came. This time the concrete floor under the rubber mat splintered, tearing the mat to pieces and throwing stone debris like confetti. The second explosion was closer than the first, or perhaps it was more powerful. Prophet wasn't completely sure, but what he was absolutely certain of was that this was his moment to escape his distracted opponent.

Just as the thought came to his mind, an ear-splitting crack pierced the air and the silhouette Prophet could barely make out was pulled away from him. It took him more than a few moments to realize the sound was the crack of a whip that had wrapped itself around the angel's neck.

Ezekiel growled through clenched teeth while pulling the whip taut and hauling the angel away from Prophet. The dreaded angel snarled at the copper-skinned man and pulled against him, his eyes devoid of any light except the flicker of anger that had been ignited.

He tried to force himself free, but Ezekiel had the leverage. He pulled sharply on the whip and yanked his head backward, sending the angel tumbling onto his back.

Before Zeke could celebrate his minor victory, a sharp pain gouged viciously into his right shoulder. He screamed and blood fell from his body in streams. Points of sparkling calcium sunk deeply into his muscle, scratching at the bone beneath and forcing him to his knees. The blonde-haired angel jerked his head backward and snatched a chunk of flesh from Ezekiel's back with a grotesque ripping sound. He fell to his hands, the wet orifice on his shoulder pulsating pain through his body with each throb.

The angel remorselessly spat the hunk of meat onto the floor next to the man. "You would be a delicacy if you humans didn't taste as foul as you do."

Ezekiel gnashed his teeth at the pain. His vision hazed and he could feel pins slowly prickling down his arms, a telltale sign that they were going numb. His right side was covered in blood which seeped down to his fingertips and made his hands slide on the floor mat.

He peeked over his bitten shoulder and eyed the angelic form of his assailant, his own blood still rolling down his chin. The angel didn't concern himself with wiping it away.

"Get the hell away from my brother!"

The words came in a furious bellow that quickly snatched the angel from his moment of triumph. In the next moment, Prophet had buried a spear in the angel's stomach and pinned him to the wall, raspberry-colored liquid still leaking from his nostrils. A spray of black blood hit the bearded man's face as the angel coughed the dark fluid from his mouth. The vicious creature snarled through blackened teeth, his perfect hair now a shaggy mess from the force of Prophet's thrust.

The one-armed man knew he couldn't hold him for long. After fighting for so long with two broken ribs, it was a struggle to keep from doubling over onto his hand and knees. Even more pertinent was the problem of his fractured wrist. He had fought through the pain up until now, but it was becoming unbearable. The pinned angel was thrashing wildly on the end of his spear, slicing at the air between him and his attacker's head.

A sharp pain stabbed his hand and he almost let go of the weapon. The vibrations from his writhing enemy were jostling the bones in his wrist and amplifying his agony. Then there was his shattered nose, hampering his breathing and blurring his sight. He was hard-pressed to remember a point in time when he had so many broken bones all at once.

"Get away from *my* brother."

The words were the same as the ones the Guardian had just used only this time they were spoken in a mocking tone of voice. Prophet turned his head to his left and felt his blood go cold. The dreadlocked angel was striding toward him, his black claws dragging across the unpadded steel wall, peeling metal shavings from its surface.

He knew he couldn't defend himself in his current position. His pinned opponent knew it as well. His feral snarl was now a dripping, blood-soaked smile.

Prophet moved to throw the spear, and the angel stuck to it, into the approaching threat when another stabbing pain lanced through his wrist and ricocheted down his side. He dropped to one knee as the dreadlocked angel shot forward, closing the distance with one step. He saw the dead black claws and the flash of a sinister smile come across the angel's face and knew there was no dodging it. All he could do now was wait for the flash of memories to flood his mind and remind him of the successes and failures in his lifetime.

The familiar sound of tearing flesh blitzed Prophet's ears followed by the unmistakable smell of freshly spilled blood. To the one-armed man's surprise, it was not his own and, to his implacable horror, it was his brother's.

Prophet screamed so loud his voice became hoarse by the time he reached the second syllable in his brother's name.

Ezekiel stood with his back to Prophet, staring down the dreaded angel, claws knuckle deep inside his chest.

He forced an agonizing smile and turned his head slightly to see his brother from his peripheral. "I got this one, bro. You just take care of that other one."

The angel tilted his head in confusion. "You have *me*? You gravely misunderstand who has who, human."

The angel turned his wrist and Ezekiel coughed blood onto his hand.

"Zeke, move! Get out of the way!"

Prophet's screams fell on deaf ears as the tattooed warrior stood his ground. Meanwhile, the impaled angel had begun pulling himself further along the spear, painting it black as he pushed it through himself and moved closer to Prophet's neck.

Summoning the remainder of his fortitude and pushing the pain out of his mind, Prophet lifted the angel from the wall and tossed him from the spear. The divine creature toppled over a bench press and crashed to the floor on the other side.

A thick string of blood ran from Ezekiel's mouth and down his chin, dripping on his hands as he gripped the angel's forearm tightly.

The Guardian gave a blood-soaked smile. "Is...that the... best you got...pussy?"

"Such arrogance in the face of death. You humans are a crude lot." The angel raised his free hand to Ezekiel. "Your death will be quick, Guardian, but it will not be painless."

A black spear struck the dreaded angel's chest with enough force to rip his hand free of Ezekiel's body. The angel followed the blood-smeared spear under Ezekiel's armpit and to his brother behind him. The tattooed man grasped the weapon in his hand, and together the brothers pushed the spear through his chest and stapled him to the wall.

"Fuck...you." Ezekiel barely pushed out his words before collapsing into Prophet's arm.

"You're gonna be okay, Z. We been through worse than this, brother." The giant could feel fear filling up his throat as his brother's shirt grew damp with blood. "You're gonna be okay."

SECTION 2

Emmanuelle's blades danced through the air, nipping at their target as they flew by. Two twisted perfectly matching knives the size of meat cleavers twirling effortlessly in her expert fingers. Her dance partner was experienced as well. Countless times his dark nails came within inches of her vital points only to be deflected or dodged at the last possible moment.

She could taste the angel's murderous intent contaminating the atmosphere. His black tireless eyes examining every inch of her frame as he struck at her, forcing her to defend her organs. Her weapons squealed, her opponent's claws raking across the steel as she parried another near hit and countered with a wide backhanded strike toward his collar.

The bald angel saw it coming and fell back to avoid the blade, as she knew he would. If she was honest, that last attack wasn't thrown to connect as much as it was thrown to push the angel away and keep him on his toes. She had nothing left. All of her tactics were useless against her opponent. At best, she was merely *playing* the part of the unflappable heroine, because, in reality, she had no idea how any of them would survive this.

"You cannot win this, Guardian."

Hearing the angel's voice mid-battle came as a sudden surprise to the woman. Her divine opponent continued.

"All of your weapons have been blessed and cannot kill us. Only a cursed weapon can harm us, and Guardians don't keep cursed weapons."

The Latin woman remained silent and struck down hard and then across with her right-handed weapon as if in answer to the angel's taunts.

The divine being skirted away from the downward strike and then slapped away the horizontal slash with the tips of his claws. "How do you expect to defeat us if you can't kill us?"

She bit her bottom lip and fought harder in reply.

The angel continued his taunts. "Add to that, the difference in experience between us, and you are hopelessly outclassed."

Emmanuelle stepped in with an outward left-handed slash that the angel spun away from. Attempting to catch him mid-spin, she stepped in again with an outward right-handed slash that glanced off his left hand when he brought his claws down to defend. Emmanuelle whipped her right hand back toward the angel in a horizontal strike across the chest. To her shock, the angel stepped in and struck down hard across her weapon, causing a flash of quick light upon impact.

Pain erupted through her hand and the woman fell to the floor with a scream on her lips. Blood poured from her right hand as she clutched it to her stomach in horrid confusion. She wasn't sure what had happened, only that her opponent had, apparently, opened a wound in her hand during her attack. She hadn't been certain how he did it, but she had to get up and continue fighting, that much she knew.

Then she saw them, rolling toward the angel's boots as if

they now belonged to him. Leaving tiny droplets of her blood on the floor as they traveled and came to a stop at his feet. She didn't recognize what she was seeing at first. Her eyes squinted, trying to force the image to change. It couldn't be right.

She looked down at her right hand, and a spurt of blood hit her face, confirming a grim reality. The two digits laying at her opponent's feet were hers. The angel had cut off her middle and index fingers.

Upon seeing the gruesome stumps that were once her fingers, the pain in her hand tripled, compelling her to pull her injured hand into her chest and cradle it. She felt a devastating scream building inside her throat and lapping at the back of her mouth. Before she could release it, her two removed fingers came rolling back to her. She glanced at her twitching limbs and then back up at the one who kicked them toward her.

The bald angel stared back down at the woman, his face blank and as ambivalent as ever. He watched her stare back at him in silence before his lips cracked and a single word escaped.

"Outclassed."

Suddenly, the despair bellowing inside her became piping hot. It frothed and broiled like a bubbling pot of stew, churning inside her chest until it dropped into her stomach and exploded throughout her body. She could swear she heard the abject howls of the monster inside her crying out as it was boiled alive. The pain lessened, replaced with a hot stinging sensation akin to being stung by a bee repeatedly in the same two spots.

Thank God for adrenaline.

Emmanuelle shot to her feet, gripping the knife in her left hand and bringing it down on the angel's head with an ear-splitting howl. The angel leaned backward, avoiding the attack and snapping his foot forward, catching the dark-haired woman square in the chest with his heel. The kick tore her hair from the bun and the air from her lungs and sent her sailing clear across the room. She landed on shards of broken earth and shredded pieces of floor mat, bouncing a bit before sliding to a stop.

Her head was thumping like a second heartbeat. Her lungs burned for new oxygen as she coughed the last of it from her chest. As her brain assessed the correct amount of agony her body should be in, Emmanuelle found herself wondering if that kick was the summit of her opponent's strength.

Pain began steadily seeping into her nervous system like a slow-acting poison. The throbbing in her right hand had returned as well. She began hoping that it *was* the full strength of her attacker because she had never been hit by anything so hard in her life.

But she knew her fight wasn't over. While keeping her eyes trained on the angel, she felt around for her weapon and brushed against something hard and fleshy. She looked up and saw that she had bumped the clawed hand of a deceased demon. On the other side of the creature's limb lay her scratched and chipped weapon. Instantly, a plan of action began to form in her mind.

She grabbed the hilt of her weapon just as a black shoe came down on the bladed edge. She glared up at the bald angel that stood over her, casting her in his shadow as if he were a giant. He raised his dark nails in preparation for a lethal attack and she felt her heart stop in her chest.

That's when a twenty-pound, silver dumbbell smashed against the angel's jaw with an audible crack. The angel stumbled and Adam struck him again with a second dumbbell. He fell against the wall, his inky blood staining the numbers chiseled into the weights as Adam screamed at him.

"Don't you fucking touch her!"

Adam stepped in with another colossal blow to the holy creature's face. The divine warrior intercepted the attack and caught the weight by the handle before it could reach him. Adam's arm trembled as he tried to force his way through with the dumbbell, the angel's hand resting on top of his own.

He couldn't tell if he had actually injured the angel with his attacks or not. He had spilled blood, but he didn't know if he was hurting his opponent. The perpetual empty stare the angel wore on his face made him wonder if they even felt pain. Was he at least wearing him down? Do angels even *get* tired?

Before he could reassure himself with an answer, dark claws swiped across his face forcing him to block with the second dumbbell. The angel's nails bit into the hexagonal shape of the metal, carving into the surface of the weight and knocking it from Adam's hands. The young man pulled away, darting backward to put some distance between himself and his enemy's razor-sharp instruments. Before he could put two feet between them, the flawless being was on him, closing the gap once more.

Adam hurled the twenty-pound weapon at his pursuer and watched it fly uselessly over his shoulder. Now the Guardian found himself on the defensive and without any weapon at all, barely staving off evisceration. He dodged left and right, then rolled across the floor as the angel's talons tore through the punching bag behind him, snapping its chains and dropping it to the floor.

His attacker kicked the bag, sending it careening into Adam's head the very moment he stood to his feet. The heavy bag slammed into his temple, sending him right back to the floor along with a spray of silva dabbled with blood.

The angel moved toward the fallen warrior but felt a sharp tug on his left hand before reaching him. Upon looking down, his crow-colored eyes took in the sight of his left hand, pierced with a large knife, and stapled to a section of padded wall. Something whizzed past his head and into the sleeve on his right hand, sticking it to the wall as well. Without looking, the bald angel knew it was another knife, and, without having to guess, he knew who had thrown it.

Emmanuelle stood across the room, her bloodied right hand tucked underneath her left armpit, her left arm still extended as if she were reaching to shake an invisible hand. Her eyes glowed maliciously under the flickering lights as she stared down the pinned angel. In the very next breath, she had launched herself across the room at him. She stepped over the decaying bodies of demons and stomped across chunks of broken earth, leaving a trail of blood droplets as she ran.

With each hard step, the pain singing throughout her body hummed a new note, nearly pulling her bruised and battered body to the ground. She furled her brow and clenched her jaw tightly, forcing herself to cover the remaining distance in a hurry. She clambered across the last few feet and just as she reached the angel, he tore his sleeve free of her knife and brought his right hand down on her throat.

Her hands darted upward, catching the attack by the forearm and holding it above her face. Her arms shook as she used what little strength she had left to fight back the angel's hand. Her face turned pink, blood rushing to her head as five points of sharpened black daggers inched closer to her neck.

She gazed into his eyes, those black soulless voids. Twin opaque vacuums that were accentuated points of nothingness, yet Emmanuelle knew something was there. Some God-given gift that allowed his kind to see more than anyone or anything else. A natural talent that came as easily as the orgulous demeanor of a superior being, but that's not what pissed her off.

What pissed her off was the calm, effortless expression on the angel's face as he methodically bared down on her. As if he was hardly trying.

"An astute tactic, Guardian, attempting to pin my hands and take away my means of attack. Your only miscalculation is that you have forgotten my claws aren't my only weapon."

A new pain shot into her body, injected beneath her skin in an explosion of agony like a thousand rusty hypodermic needles. Her throat closed so tightly that she couldn't even let out a scream, just a weak halfhearted moan that was a mere fraction of the cacophony bellowing within her. She felt fresh warm blood wet her clothes and roll down her body, falling in cherry droplets underneath her. Strange as it was, she thought she could feel the angel smiling, even with a mouth full of her flesh.

The angel's teeth scraped against her collarbone as he bit deeper into the flesh near her neck. Her vision blurred as if God had taken her hand across everything she saw and smeared it like a wet painting. She felt herself go limp and her right side lost all feeling except for an occasional firework of pain that would somehow cut through the numbness. She fell against the angel for support, dropping her arms loosely to her sides.

Her fight was finally over. There was nothing more she needed to do. Her eyes shut slowly and an almost inaudible prayer came across her lips. If this was her final moment, she would make it count.

Her emerald eyes flashed open, a renewed sense of conviction glowing within them, and she jammed a sharp instrument into the angel's throat with her disfigured right hand.

The angel paused for a moment in frozen shock, then released his jaws from her skin and stared at her face. She watched her blood fall from his mouth as he stared, a sense of horrible realization unfurling across his face. For the first time, Emmanuelle registered fear in her opponent's black eyes.

She stepped back from him. Over her shoulder he could see the body of a decaying demon, the middle finger on its clawed right hand severed cleanly, missing. The fear became overwhelming terror as the angel realized that he had been stabbed with the middle finger of a deceased demon. Emmanuelle was delighted at the very next emotion her angelic opponent displayed.

Unbridled pain.

His face curled and his eyes squinted then widened, then squinted again. His mouth shuffled through a series of gestures as if he couldn't decide which was adequate. Tire-colored blood began to pour from his lips and the Guardian couldn't take her eyes off him. He looked confused. He looked like a child experiencing pain for the first time with no clue as to how he should react.

The injured woman lifted her blood-covered right hand, turned her palm to face herself, and flipped off the dying angel with the short grotesque stump that remained of her middle finger. He would get no sympathy from her today.

The angel's body lit into a flash of flames. Not auburn or white, but pure suffocating black with flashes of cerulean blue. She watched as a being older than human life shivered in the throes of death.

Oddly enough to her, the angel stayed on his feet as he burned. His arms were at his sides and his hands were shaking as the opaque flames licked the skin from his body. Her vision became hazed again, but she could still see the angel's face through the fire. It had finally settled on a single expression. A terror-stricken gaze, wide-eyed and mouth agape, black and blue tongues dancing back and forth across his face in a fiery ballet.

Her body pulled her to the ground and she landed with a hard thud on her butt. Her vision was swimming now and most of her body was numb. Her blood was all over her. She even had its bitter flavor in her mouth and its acrid aroma in her nose.

She could feel herself becoming more and more tired, exhaustion and blood loss causing her lids to droop over her eyes, calling her into a cold comforting darkness. She shook it off, tried to stand, and failed. She couldn't even make it to her knees before she plopped back down on her behind.

The exhaustion in her fought harder this time. She didn't have the strength to try and move herself anymore. A familiar overwhelming taste welled up inside her mouth again and she spat blood onto the dust-covered floor next to her. Before she could remove her eyes from the floor, she spied two, even more, familiar objects lying almost directly next to her. Her severed fingers.

She reached out, picked the digits up, and shoved them in her pocket. Maybe they were still salvageable. Not that it mattered. In a few minutes, she was going to lose consciousness and probably die of blood loss.

Just as she finished her thought, she was doused in an impeccable feminine shadow. Darkness crept up within the edges of her vision and in its center stood the blue-eyed, angelic leader. Emmanuelle could barely see her lips move, but even with her dulled senses, the angel's voice was clear as crystal.

"You've killed my lieutenant, Guardian. For that, you have won my most undivided and fervent attention."

Emmanuelle felt the palms of the angel's hands press against her ears as the holy entity lifted her from the floor by her head. She didn't thrash or fight. She didn't have the energy even if she wanted to. She just hung in the holy being's hands, staring into her empty eyes while her vision grew darker.

Finally, as her mind fell into the spiraling abyss of extinction, she felt the monster in her stomach rise from its shadowy bowels and belt a horrified scream.

SECTION 3

The ceiling caved in and the flickering lights died all at once when an explosion suddenly tore the training room apart. Humans and angels alike were tossed indiscriminately through the air like rag dolls, slamming battered limbs into unpadded walls, heavy weights, and the debris-strewn floor. The metal walls shivered and warped as powerful vibrations rang through them in a single cacophonous note of destruction.

Thick dust blanketed the area and floated through the air of the now dark and silent room. All was quiet.

Fluorescent lights dangled from the broken ceiling, swinging just above the ground. Pebbles rolled across the destroyed floor like marbles searching for an appropriate place to make a home. A spray of yellow sparks lit the room at random intervals from exposed wiring in the ceiling. The only sign of life was a lone shadow that soundlessly crept across the room, kneeling at one of the helpless bodies splayed across the battlefield.

Adam shot up in a plume of dust and jammed a jagged

piece of concrete to his would-be attacker's throat. A warm but firm hand grabbed his wrist, keeping him from pressing down, and spoke the sweetest words he could have hoped for.

"Adam, it's me, Father."

The young man squinted in the darkness of the room, his eyes straining to adjust to the lack of light. After a brief moment, the familiar square shape of the priest's head took form along with his hat, grey beard, and silver-framed glasses. Adam's tense body relaxed and he dropped his makeshift weapon. Father wrapped his arms around the young man and lifted him from the stone rubble and shivers of wood that lay around him.

His head was ringing with pain and one of his ears was dead. No trace of sound could be picked up with it while the other was filled with a deafening tone almost too loud to hear through. Even still, Father's voice was like silk in his ear.

"We have to leave, right now."

Adam looked around the dark room for a moment. "The others, we have to find them."

Father pointed his index finger through the dark at a far wall. Adam strained his eyes to see again and could barely make out a large misshapen figure near the wall that couldn't possibly be human. Another flash of hot sparks lit the room and he caught a glimpse of Prophet supporting Ezekiel on his armless shoulder. It was only a brief look before the shadows rushed in again to claim the space, but Adam could tell, Ezekiel was not okay.

The priest helped him to his feet and guided him through the maze of dross to the wall where a section of padding hung wearily from the metal. He grabbed the edge of the padding and tore it down, revealing a steel shutter door.

"What about Mark and Sera?" Prophet whispered.

Father lifted the shutter door in reply. Behind it stood both missing Guardians, each with fresh wounds of their own, standing in a partially lit tunnel. Mark stood in plaid pajama pants, flip flops, and a bright yellow t-shirt with the words 'The Man, The Legend' printed across the front with two arrows pointing up and down respectively. He had a bad gash just above his forehead that ran blood down the left side of his face.

Seraphim was dressed in the standard black long coat and pants but had a trickle of blood streaming from her mouth and a cut winding up her right tricep that tore her sleeve in two. They looked weary from battle and still held green blood-stained weapons in their hands.

"What happened to you?" Adam asked.

"Demons. They swarmed us. Must've been thirty of 'em," Mark spoke through heavy breath.

"Ten." Seraphim corrected him.

"Whatever," the Irishman snapped. "They trapped us in the kitchen. We barely made it out of there."

"We can finish this later. Right now we have to leave," Father interrupted.

"Where's Elle and Saduj? They aren't with you?" Mark queried.

Prophet handed Ezekiel over to Mark. The Irishman couldn't help but notice the hesitation on his face before he spoke.

"Emmanuelle was fighting the leader before the last explosion. She wasn't doing too good, and Saduj..." Prophet's voice trailed off, indicating what was already known.

"No! They're alive!" Adam's voice echoed sternly.

His dirt-covered face showed the same conviction he had at the start of the fight.

Prophet started in a solemn tone. "Adam, you saw the broomstick same as we did. That was *red* blood on it."

"I don't believe her. Emmanuelle is out here somewhere and Saduj is alive, and I'm going to find them."

Father placed his hand on the young man's chest, halting him before he could turn to move. "We don't have time for this, Adam. We have to go, right now."

"I'm *not* leaving them here to die." A bit of anger played on Adam's face.

"If we stay here any longer we're *all* going to die," Father shot back.

"I can save them! Just let me go."

"Now is not the time for your childish antics!"

"I need this, goddamn it!"

Father's eyes opened wide. The same words he had used on Daniel were now being thrown at him. He could see the desperation in Adam's face as he said them. His eyes begged and his voice pleaded with him to understand. At the back of his mind, the priest wondered if his face was brimming with such emotion when he had asked Daniel to take pity on him.

In his heart, he did understand. Two of the people he loved the most were dead or dying in some dark corner somewhere and he couldn't do a damn thing about it. If there was one feeling he hated more than any other, it was helplessness. Something he began to feel more and more often as he grew older. He was sick of it.

"It's my fault Saduj isn't here. He was counting on me, and I failed. I can't fail Emmanuelle too. Please, Father. Please, let me try." Adam's voice quivered under shaky breath, his eyes asking for an all too familiar pity.

The priest closed his eyes and huffed an exasperated sigh. He had made his decision.

"Okay."

The old man suddenly shoved Adam back into Prophet and through the shutter door. Before anyone could react, the steel door came down with a crash, sealing them outside of the training room. Adam and Prophet threw themselves against the door in a futile effort to bring it down. Their bodies were bounced back harmlessly from the metal frame.

"Father! What are you doing!?" Prophet shouted.

The priest's voice came muffled through the door. "Don't worry, I'll find them. I'll bring them back."

Adam placed his face to the shutter. "You don't have to do this, Father. I can help. Let me help you."

There was silence from the other side. The group of injured warriors began to fear that was the last time they would hear his voice.

"You were right, Adam." Father's voice drifted through the door. "Daniel was right about you."

They waited for him to continue, but silence once again took his place. This time they knew he was gone. Adam dropped to his knees with his head and hands against the shutter, defeated.

"It was supposed to be me. This isn't fair. It isn't right."

Seraphim placed her hand on his shoulder to assuage the momentary shock. "That door can only be opened from the other side. It's time to go. We have to trust him, Adam. He's not the leader of this team for nothing."

The Guardians slowly pulled themselves away and began their weary trek down the dark tunnel. Adam remained on his knees a moment longer, still trying to rationalize his teacher's decision. As he began to pull himself up, he stuck his right knee on something sharp and jagged. Something was sticking out from under the shutter door. Climbing down to his hands and placing his ear to the ground, he was able to see a thin piece of wood stuck underneath the door.

It only took him a second to come to his next conclusion. If the shutter couldn't reach the floor then it couldn't properly lock, which meant, with a bit of finagling, it could be opened again.

"Can't fathom what Father could be thinking," Mark said as he dragged his wounded teammate through the tunnel. "He can't be going after them alone."

"Calm down, Mark," Seraphim interjected. "It's Father we're talking about. If you know him like you should, then you know he's going to find Saduj and Emmanuelle and bring them back. Have a little faith for once."

"I know the old man's good and all, but the fact of the matter is, those were angels back there. Fucking angels!"

"It's not Father I'm worried about, it's Adam."

Ezekiel's weak voice caught everyone's ears with his cryptic words. The group immediately came to a stop. Everyone turned around expecting to see Adam behind them, but all that stared back was the empty blackness of the tunnel.

"What the hell? Where's the kid?" Prophet questioned as he searched the area nearby.

"I thought he was next to you? He's not here!?" Seraphim shouted.

"Kid's got balls," Ezekiel spoke through bloodless lips as his drained body hung from Mark's shoulder.

"Where'd he go, Zeke?" Prophet asked.

"I saw him slip back under the gate when we walked off. I think he's gonna go drop an atom bomb on that angel bitch that had Emmanuelle. For once I hope he's a better fighter than me, cuz if he ain't, he's dead."

"Shite! We have to go back for him," Mark chimed in.

"No." Seraphim shook her head in disagreement. "Now is not the time for this. We have to go."

Mark stepped forward toward the Russian woman. "What? That's Daniel's brother back there. We can't leave him." Mark handed Ezekiel carefully back to his brother. "I'll go back and you take them out."

"No. We're all injured and two of us need serious medical attention. We're not separating," she said firmly.

Mark looked over Prophet and Ezekiel curiously. "What are you on about? Zeke's the only one who needs attention."

Seraphim pulled back the long coat from her side and revealed a grievous wound between her hip and chest. The inside of her coat was thick with blood. Mark's voice left him at the sight of it. The wound was near her liver and, without words, they all knew the seriousness of the injury. She needed a doctor and soon.

"I can't protect them on my own, Mark. We need you right now."

The Irishman grumbled a curse under his breath and continued down the tunnel ahead of everyone else. He didn't say another word.

"*I guess you're on your own, Adam,*" Ezekiel smiled hopelessly, blood dripping from his lips. "Go get her, kid."

Father slinked through the fog of darkness blanketing the destroyed room. Dust particles dotted the still air and broken stones riddled the floor. Skillfully, the Guardian crept through the rubble, his eyes scanning the mounds of debris while he moved. He heard the clatter of falling rocks nearby and quickly turned to face the sound, fearing it came from an approaching enemy.

His pulse quickened when he turned to see a pale hand with only three fingers attached to it hanging over a pile of wreckage. The priest dashed over to find his Latin teammate collapsed on top of a hill of smashed plaster and broken dumb-bells. He placed his hand on her forehead and offered up a quick and silent prayer. A prayer that was just as succinct as it was hopeful and desperate.

"*Please, God...*"

He placed his index and middle fingers to her neck trepida-tiously. It was there. The faintest ghost of a heartbeat that sent his own vascular muscle throbbing wildly in his chest. She was alive, but barely. She had lost too much blood and would not likely be able to move if she regained consciousness.

Thankfully, he had an answer for that. Reaching inside his coat pocket he removed a small hypodermic needle from its packaging. Printed in small letters across the plastic packaging were the words, *Epinephrine*. Not only would it wake her, but it would also give her the energy to move. Father bit the cover from the syringe, exposing the needle.

With his free hand, he pressed his fingers into her arm, searching for a vein. His thumb grazed over a single pulsing line in her skin and a hand came down on his shoulder. Five steely digits dug into his muscle, not deep enough to break the skin but enough to be painful. He stopped dead in his tracks.

"You came to save her. You are most deserving of heaven."

A deafening curse echoed inside Father's head upon hearing the voice. He was too late. His body tensed altogether in a simultaneous muscular cringe that froze the blood in his veins. He turned his head slowly to face his addresser.

Her hair hung in front of her face in a tangled mess. Her body was layered with dust that changed the complexion of her skin. Her glimmering blue eyes were now blacker than the darkest corner of the room.

"Allow me to arrange your visit."

While she spoke, Father had dipped his free hand into the bag that hung from his shoulder and slipped a twisted dagger from its depths. The angel watched with a sense of futile humor as the priest dragged the curved weapon across the back of her hand.

The divine being's aura of invulnerability quickly turned to painful surprise, provoking her to pull away from the priest and cradle her injured hand. Father backed away from his attacker, holding his weapon at the ready between them.

The angel inspected the gold-handled weapon and the winding snake-like shape of the blade that now held her blood. Her pitch-dark eyes followed an invisible trail back to her injured hand, then finally to Father's face.

"That weapon is cursed. How curious."

"If you think this is the first time I've fought an angel, you're sadly mistaken. I have a few tricks up my sleeve to deal with you." Father took a step backward, reaching his left hand into his bag and leaving it there.

"I'm afraid you'll need more than a few."

With those words, Father felt his blood go cold. He realized that two angels now stood on either side of him, daring him to make a move. Their leader stared opaquely at him from the front. If angels were prone to wear their emotions on their faces, he suspected, her expression would be an effervescent and wicked smile right about now.

The old man glanced to his left and right, then back down at Emmanuelle's body. He felt an overflow of sadness at the realization of the horrible truth. He couldn't save her.

Even for a Guardian with his skills, he couldn't rescue her and himself from three angels. It couldn't be done. And to make matters worse, he dropped the shot of Epinephrine when he freed himself from the angelic leader.

He stared down at her unconscious form and felt a stab of guilt stake his heart. "I'm sorry, Emmanuelle."

The angels were upon him in the next breath. They hurtled themselves at the old Guardian at breakneck speed, nearly closing on him before he could remove his hand from the bag. Luckily for him, he was a bit faster, tearing his hand from the sack and smashing a clear orb onto the broken ground at his feet. A plume of red dust exploded into the air, swallowing the priest and the two angels at his sides.

Screams of pain erupted from within the cloud of crimson smoke, and Father came bolting from its center and darted out of the destroyed training room. The angels inside the dust cloud swiped and clawed at their skin, screaming and choking on the red powder that attacked them.

Their leader reached her hand into the plume of spreading dust and immediately pulled her limb back, her fingertips sizzling from contact with the substance. She was now certain of what it was.

"Crushed and dried demon skin mixed into a powder. Well done, Guardian."

Even she had to admit to the impressive ingenuity of the priest to be able to weaponize the flesh of demons for use against angels. After taking a few steps back, she took a deep breath into her body and released a stream of air that blew the cloud of red dust out and away from her comrades.

The two angels were covered in burns on every exposed part of their bodies. Charred flesh still popped and sizzled on their faces and red tears streamed down their cheeks. The closest thing to, what could only be described as anger played out on the burned angel's faces.

"Kill him."

She motioned toward the doorway and her two subordinates rocketed out after him, leaving her alone. She stood quietly for a moment, staring into the darkness of the room.

"I didn't think you would be brave enough to face me..."

She turned around and locked eyes with the youngest member of the Guardians standing in the middle of the ruined room, gripping two worn scythes in both hands.

"..or foolish enough."

SECTION 4

Her eyes narrowed as Adam stared at her intensely from across the room. The young man was eerily silent. He held her in an unmoving gaze that reeked of anger, but there was something else there. Something hidden beneath that hate-filled glower that he knowingly suppressed. Something more important to him than his seething rage and primal instinct that ached for revenge.

His eyes dropped to her feet then darted quickly back up to her face followed by a series of anxious blinks. He hadn't meant to do that; she could see it on his face. Her eyes wandered to where he had glanced and she finally knew what he was trying to hide from her. She reached down, grabbing a fist full of black hair, and lifted an unconscious Emmanuelle from the rubble near her.

Now she could place exactly what he was trying to hide from her. Now she could see it even if he still had the will to hide it. Now it unfurled upon his face in all its glory. A dreaded sense of vexation.

"You came back for her." She held the woman dangling above the ground.

Adam was silent for a moment, unsure if he should answer. "Give her to me," he finally spoke.

"She *is* still alive, though not for much longer, I gather. But I will not *give* her to you." The angel dropped Emmanuelle's body crassly to the floor. "You will have to come and take her."

He paused for a moment, mentally assessing his situation. "*Ok, Adam. You're tired, deaf in one ear, and your weapons are shit. So, what are you gonna do, kid?*" A smirk raked halfway across his face. "*Great, they've got me calling myself 'kid' now.*"

He tightened his grasp on his bent and chipped weapons and strolled unhurriedly toward the angel. "You've killed one of my friends. I won't let you have another. I'm not leaving without her."

Adam's footsteps echoed off of the broken walls as he came within striking distance. Her arms hung at her sides, not the least bit concerned about the approaching threat.

"Then we have come to an accord." Her black nails grew into two-inch dark claws and her teeth became sharp enough to rend bone. "You won't be leaving at all."

He lead with an upward slash that cleaved through her hair as she dodged it. She slid to his left in an attempt to get to his back. He countered her maneuver by stepping with her and dragging his weapon under her chin, missing her throat. She backed away as he charged ahead, bringing his scythe down for her head. In two paces she had completely sidestepped the attack and was now on Adam's right side.

He pulled his weapon from the floor in a diagonal strike from below that didn't come close to reaching its mark. She jumped away again, her clawed hands inside her coat pockets now.

"Are you tired, Adam? Somehow I expected a Guardian to be less predictable."

He scowled at her words and launched himself at her again, the flash of his blades coming nearer to her flesh but still leaving no mark. The two warriors twirled around one another in a deadly beautiful dance. The flickering of near-destroyed fluorescent lighting and the random spray of yellow and white sparks from loose wires were the only light in an otherwise dark room. They stepped into and around one another, crunching bits of gravel and wood underfoot as they continued their quick-paced waltz.

The flashing lights reflected off of his blades and revealed a glimmer of the angel's stoic face each time he struck at her. She still had yet to attack. She had ample opportunity to go on the offensive but had chosen not to. This was an unsettling fact for Adam.

He couldn't help but wonder what she was waiting for. Was she merely toying with him for fun? Was she waiting for him to tire himself out for an easy kill? Who was he kidding, he was an easy enough kill already.

She slipped behind him and he spun on his heel, swinging both weapons wildly as he turned, and was surprised when he felt himself make contact. Both blades rested deep within her chest cavity, yet she made no effort to remove them. Her arms remained in her pockets and she looked the Guardian over.

"I want you to understand the futility of your actions, Guardian," she spoke as if she knew she was answering the question burning inside his head. "I want you to know that you may have stood a chance against my subordinates, but you have effectively thrown that chance away by staying to fight me."

Adam pushed his weapons deeper into her body. She continued as if she didn't even notice.

"And for what? A woman? One of billions more on this planet that could give you the same empty shallow love you all scamper and scurry to find. You cannot save her. You have chosen to die here tonight."

"For someone who talks as much as you do, I'd think you'd be handing me my ass right now. You haven't even hit me yet and you're talking major shit like you're dominating this fight. Well, you and your high and mighty bullshit can kiss my ass cuz I ain't giving up. I'm a human being and proud of it, and we may chase love like fools and fight when we know there's no hope of winning, but guess what?" A genuine smile spread across his face as he leaned in close to hers. "Out of the two of us, which one does God love more?"

For the first time, an expression other than insipid boredom played out on her face, and it was as clear as crystal what it was.

Anger.

She grabbed his hands tightly and slowly pulled the weapons from her chest as his muscles strained fighting back.

"Make no mistake, I *am* dominating this battle. The only reason it continues is that I allow it." She pulled the blades from her body and held Adam's hands out to her sides. "You don't seem to understand what you're up against, Guardian. Allow me to educate you on the depth of your hopelessness. Lesson one."

She closed her eyes and took in a long and deep breath, filling her body with air. She dragged the oxygen through her nostrils producing a sharp whistling sound that made Adam's deaf ear tingle. Next, her eyes shot open and her lips puckered and a wave of warm air slammed into Adam like a freight train.

All he wanted to do was scream. He couldn't because the moment he was struck, all of the oxygen in his lungs leaped from his mouth as if he had been punched in the gut by a world-champion bodybuilder. He felt the ground move under him and suddenly he was tumbling through the air with no clue as to what was up or down. His back hit the wall and the force of the wind pinned him to it. He still couldn't scream.

The maelstrom she had created had him completely arrested. His arms and legs felt like they were shackled to the wall and the pressure on his face made sure that he couldn't even open his eyes. His skin rippled, typhoon winds peeling away layers of dead skin as shards of debris sliced into his flesh. She would not stop.

An impossibly long stream of breath hammered into him, turning his skin purple with bruises and his muscles into jello. He could feel the moisture from her mouth wetting his face as if mocking him, daring him to try and cease the torrent if he could. Adam knew the truth even if he refused to admit it to himself. He was as helpless as a blind newborn giraffe that hadn't yet learned to walk.

He dropped to the ground without warning, landing on a pile of broken stones and cracked weights. He coughed harshly, the air rushing back into his lungs so fast it hurt. Every exposed part of his body throbbed as if it had been tenderized by the gale-force winds. His hands and face had tiny cuts all over from the thrown pieces of rock and other materials. He even noticed that much of the chaff that littered the room had been blown over to his side.

He was lucky none of the heavier boulders flew any closer to him or else he might have more than just a few small cuts on his face. Or perhaps she didn't allow them to? He wasn't sure about that fact. He *was* sure that his fight wasn't over and that he needed to get to his feet before she decided she was done toying with him.

He forced himself upright, back on top of unsure muscles that still hadn't become solid again after being turned into useless gelatinous membranes. He felt the fluids inside his body swish back and forth like water in an oversized cup as he got to his feet.

The angel watched him stand erect in front of her, hope still burning in his eyes.

"Now do you understand what you're up against, Guardian? I am far from an ordinary angel. I am an arch. A captain in our hierarchy. Leader of choirs of divine warriors. It can take an angel eons to attain the title arch, but rest assured, we are far older and more powerful than any other angel."

Adam cut his eyes at her and huffed dismissively. "Are you done monologuing? Cuz I've been dying to shut you up all night."

The angel was almost surprised by Adam's devil-may-care attitude after such an overwhelming attack.

"So you're strong and you're old, big whoop. I haven't seen anything yet that'll make me tuck tail and run." He spat a glob of blood from his mouth at the end of his sentence to demonstrate his lack of respect for the angel.

She watched the mucus and saliva-filled bubble splatter at her feet and Adam wipe his mouth clean with the sleeve of his shirt.

"The night is still young, Adam. Here is lesson two."

For the second time, the angel filled her lungs with air, lifting her chest as she inhaled an inhuman amount through her nose. That familiar whistling sound made his hairs stand on end. Adam braced himself for another torrent of wind. Instead, she parted her lips, opened her mouth wide, and let loose an ear-splitting scream.

The vibrations hit him like a sonic boom, instantly dropping him to his knees. He covered his ears with his hands to offer some solace, but the piercing noise stabbed through his palms and gouged his eardrums. His vision danced through explosions of grey static and bright pink and yellow spots. He felt his teeth shake loose at the back of his mouth and blood rushed from his ears and nose.

The metal walls curled, popping screws from their face. The ground shook underneath him, bouncing pebbles like tiny stone basketballs. Once again, she would not cease. He knew she would not stop this time until his brain was nothing more than pink jelly leaking from his ears.

His eyes frantically searched the dark for something, anything he could use to stop her from turning his brain to mush inside his skull. Another flash of yellow sparks lit the room enough for him to see a glimmer of silver nearby. The light didn't last long enough for him to discern what it was, but he had already decided to grab it.

He girded himself and removed his right hand from his ear, reaching into the darkness. The palpable din screeched into his ear and clawed at its inner workings like a frenzied tiger. His hand scrambled around in the dark until he cut it on something sharp.

"*There!*"

Ignoring the pain and the newly opened wound, he wrapped his hand around the instrument and hurled it at her with all his strength. He watched the silver weapon fly into the distance but lost it in the shadows. It was fine though because wherever it struck was enough to cut off the angel's screaming. He could hear her blood-soaked cough after his weapon found its mark.

The soft drip of fresh blood echoed off the floor as the angel stepped close enough for Adam to see. He had hit her in the throat with one of Emmanuelle's throwing knives. He couldn't help but chuckle a bit. What were the odds, after all, that he would find one of Emmanuelle's weapons and strike the angel directly in the neck with a blind throw in the dark?

His chuckle turned into laughter which he had to pull back after it reminded him of the pain he was in. His head was throbbing, but for some reason, the hearing in his right ear had been restored. Probably an unforeseen consequence of her high-pitched shriek. Another unexplained effect was the strident taste of copper he now had in his mouth.

The angel pulled the knife from her throat, bemused by the Guardian's laughter. "Have you now sunken into mad despair? Humans find humor in awkward places when they are at death's door."

Adam's arms wrapped around his stomach, trying to hold back a fusillade of laughter. "No, it's just that I just realized something." He wiped his face with his sleeve and grinned widely at her, blood still running from his ears and nose. "I told you I would shut you up."

Adam rose to his feet, triumph permeating through the wide-mouth grin plastered to his face. As his second knee left the ground, his body weight pulled him back down and he collapsed face-first onto the broken ground. The angel watched him lie face down on the floor, carefully listening to the sound of his heartbeat slow. The Guardian had fallen unconscious before he could even get back to his feet.

The angel walked over to Adam's prone form and looked down on him imperiously. She wasn't surprised, humans were a fragile creation after all, but they were also immensely intriguing. In the same way she huffed in contempt at the idea of such a weak creature challenging her, she also held a sense of endearing respect for him. In Heaven, such nobility is worthy of praise and adulation. In Heaven, his sacrifice would garner endless reward.

Oddly, her mind began to draw parallels between herself and the unconscious man beneath her. Both warriors fighting for a righteous cause, willing to sacrifice it all for their brethren. Both prepared to walk into oblivion happily, in service to the same God. Both claiming to fight on her behalf.

That was a lie. She fought for herself and so did every one of her kin that chose to follow Michael. She shook the wild thoughts from her head before they could undermine her more. An angel does not second guess herself. An angel puts her duty before herself at all times.

She reached down for Adam and he popped up from the floor so fast that he caught her completely off guard. Before she could react, he had driven a long piece of rusty rebar into her chest, just to the right of her heart. In a second move, he grabbed a chunk of concrete and bashed her in the temple, crumbling the hunk of stone to pebbles with the blow.

He didn't even stay to watch her body fall. After the second strike, he scrambled over to Emmanuelle, preparing to lift her body to safety before the angel could recoup. As he arrived next to his teammate, a piece of lengthy rebar speared into the ground between them, black ooze dripping from the tip. Adam turned around to see his opponent still on her feet with a gaping hole in her chest. Her blood leaked like hot tar from the wound, but she didn't seem to notice or care.

"A clever ruse, Guardian. I wasn't aware you could manipulate your heartbeat so well. I should have paid more attention."

Adam backed away from Emmanuelle, realizing his plan to escape with her had failed. "I don't need any compliments from traitors," he spat.

He continued to slide backward, putting more space between them until his heel bumped into something made of metal. He looked down, and behind his feet rested an iron ball with a chain attached to it. Attached to the opposite end of the length of the chain was a gleaming sharp scythe. Without hesitation, he picked up the weapon.

He wasn't very adept with the ball and chain, but any

weapon was better than no weapon at all. Besides, he was certain of what to do with the scythe end of the chain. Before the angel could close the distance, he began to loop the ball overhead. He wasn't attacking with it yet, just using its range to give himself time to think.

It was a pretty decent tool to have at the moment. The length of the chain meant he didn't have to get close to those claws of hers and the dark polish of the ball made it difficult to see in the dull light of the room. At least it was difficult for *him* to see. He realized he had no clue what the limitations of angelic eyesight were. He would know soon enough, but for now, he just kept whipping the ball around his head.

The angel watched him quietly. If there was an ounce of emotion on her face, Adam would've sworn she seemed almost amused at his new weapon.

"Did you know that it is frowned upon for a Power to use a weapon in a fight?" She spoke while pacing the split floor. "It is a matter of extreme pride that an angel complete every kill with her bare claws or she will be deemed weak by her siblings."

She grabbed a length of rebar jutting out from the floor and ripped it free of the ground, spraying chunks of rock in every direction with the force of the pull. A basketball-sized clump of concrete still clung to its end. She held it straight up, and the twisted piece of metal was even taller than she was.

"Consider this my gift to you."

With that, she took the iron weapon in both hands and started a slow-paced stroll toward him, locking his steely gaze in her dark eyes.

Adam whipped the spinning orb at her temple with its next pass and cursed under his breath when she dropped her head and the ball sailed over. He struck again, this time aiming for her chest. Her next maneuver was a mocking one, as she turned her body, bending her knees and dropping her torso until her back was parallel to the floor and the crown of her head, pointing toward him. Her eyes met the ceiling as the softball-sized sphere arched over her chest and crashed through a pile of rubble to the left of her.

She returned to her normal posture and continued walking. Adam's throat tightened because she had barely broken stride.

He hurled the metal ball at her midsection and watched her leap into a perfectly beautiful corkscrew spin above the chains. She landed with barely a sound, her hair flailing like licorice-colored whips. His teeth pressed into his bottom lip and he realized after her next effortless dodge that she could see perfectly in the dark.

He shortened the length of the chain in his hand and circled the deadly orb over his head with even greater speed. This was meant to scare his attacker but had little effect. He knew that she could tell he was inexperienced with his weapon. He couldn't think of anything else to do but continue swiping the sphere at her as it passed, which was not working in the slightest. She still advanced on him like a slow but increasingly alarming inevitability.

Soon he would be forced into close combat with his scythe, which was a bad idea. His right arm had five holes in the tricep which made combat with it painful. If the wounds were any deeper into the muscle he wouldn't be able to use the arm at all. He could thank the dreadlocked angel for that injury.

He watched her take another slow step and his mind went to her lieutenant. The one Emmanuelle had killed. He didn't see how she had done it, but it was proof enough that they could be killed. That would be good enough for him if he had just seen how she had done it. By the time he had gotten to his feet, the angel was already burning.

He remembered the strange black flames that engulfed the angel and how he had seen nothing like them before. They flickered wildly yet didn't seem to emit any warmth. He remembered thinking he had never seen something so beautiful and macabre as he watched the angel burn.

"*That's it!*" He had made the connection so fast that he nearly dropped the spinning ball on his head. "*The poem! The poem is the key! Break an angel's heart and yours will be broken in return, take the heart in your hands and watch an angel burn.*" After seeing the bald angel swallowed in flames upon his death he knew it wasn't a coincidence. "*The heart! I have to remove her heart!*"

SECTION 5

Adam became elated upon finding a possible method of killing his opponent but felt his excitement die when he concluded that it meant getting close to her again. He cursed under his breath.

"Your heart rate just increased. Are you nervous?" She asked in a sardonic tone.

Adam replied by whipping the ball down on the top of her head, which she evaded by stepping to her left and letting the orb pile onto the floor with a reverberating crash.

"Are you afraid now, Guardian? Have you finally come to understand that you cannot possibly survive this encounter?"

She casually placed her foot atop the metal sphere as it rested inside the broken concrete, cradled by shards of upturned stone.

She leaned forward, pressing her body weight onto the ball. "Have you finally tasted despair?"

Adam shot her a seething glare that screamed he would spit on her if only he were close enough. Hell, she would probably dodge that too. The sudden thought of her gracefully avoiding one of his loogies brought an unexpected smile to his face. His unconventional smile brought confusion to her mind and before she could question it, the Guardian snatched the ball from under her with a mighty jerk that sent chunks of rock sailing through the air.

He spun the weapon over his head and whipped it around at her with all of his strength. In a maneuver possible only by a being first crafted by God, the angel placed the weighted end of the rebar weapon to the ground and vaulted over the attack using one hand. She catapulted herself in an arc that was more than perfect, keeping her body straight even at the apex of the arch when she was upside down and perpendicular to the ground.

The ball wrapped around the twisted piece of metal as it stuck into the floor. The angel flipped and came down on top of the chain, the force of her landing snatching the scythe from his hand. Adam could hear himself screaming in his mind as, with one impossible move, she took his weapon from him and closed the distance between them. He could suddenly taste the acid bubbling in his gut. With an aura of malicious glee Adam could almost feel, she swung the concrete-covered end of her makeshift weapon, iron ball and all, into his stomach.

An explosion of pain wouldn't do it justice. It was more like an atom bomb of agony that blew through his stomach and screeched into his senses, marring his nervous system like a rubber tire sliding across dry pavement at ninety miles per hour. His belly touched his spine and the bile that sat at the very bottom reached up to lick the roof of his mouth. Air flew from his body as if he had his own personal sonic boom form inside his lungs. The force of the blow sent him flying into the wall, leaving a human-sized dent in the metal.

The angel let Adam's ball and chain slide down the length of her weapon and fall to the floor before dropping her bludgeoning tool as well. She strode confidently toward his crumpled form as he lay unmoving atop a pile of stones. His eyes were still open, but she knew, without doubt, that he was unconscious from the slight trembling of his body. Between that and the slow-paced breaths he took, she knew this time it was no ruse.

She found it almost amusing how, when asleep, humans breathed like pigs. Snorting oxygen ungracefully through their nostrils as if it were actively trying to escape from them. Dragging great gulps of their precious gas into them with disgusting wheezes and grunts they couldn't possibly know they made with such limited hearing. How could anything live like that? Clamoring like a billion infant piglets for a single exposed teat that was so precious they would die if deprived of it for only a few minutes.

As far as breathing, a sleeping human and one that was awake were like night and day. Once the subconscious part of the brain released its rule over the rest of the body, a human's breathing became rhythmic and undisturbed. Effortless and almost eloquent in its pace. As a secondary impulse, It became everything and all, as if it were the single thing humans were created to do.

She stood over his splayed form, grabbing him by the hair and lifting his head to look him in his dilated eyes. Admittedly, he was a most curious mortal, but she had a job to do.

She spied the jugular vein running the length of his neck, pumping life in liquid form to his brain, and struck with her midnight talons. A spray of hot yellow sparks lit the air followed by the sound of iron-hard claws scraping the steel wall.

Adam had ducked her attack, tearing a tuft of hair from his messy pompadour when he ripped himself free. Her arm sailed overhead and raked the wall behind him as he kicked off and sent himself sliding on his side between her legs. She whipped around in disbelief at his speed just in time to feel the icy cold grip of an iron chain wrap around her neck. The Guardian had already reclaimed his weapon and was now standing away from her, spinning the ball end of the chain at his side in mocking fashion.

"Impossible. You're not conscious," she spoke, her voice riddled with stifling confusion.

Adam lifted his leg, bringing his foot down atop the taut chain links and pulling her head down in a forceful bow.

She gave the Guardian a long penetrating stare. "Who are you?"

With a soundless blank expression, Adam hurled the ball at her face, crushing it with a loud and wet crunch that seemed to echo through the dark. Then, his breath finally caught and he nearly choked on the sudden wind in his throat. His eyes blinked repeatedly as he gazed at his unfamiliar surroundings. Instantly he knew, it had happened again. His mind falling into a fog of grey and his body acting independently of him. Probably saving his life in the process.

Without warning, he felt a familiar tingle gradually dance its way up the back of his head. Warm and cool at the same time, it meandered its way to the center of his brain and a flash of memories bombarded his senses.

At that moment he could see it all. Like a flickering reel of images, the scene played out before him, an old memory suddenly turned bright.

Pulling free from her grasp, pushing from the back wall, sliding across the gravel-covered floor to retrieve his weapon, wrapping the chain around her neck with a single throw, and smashing her skull in with the iron sphere. The memories dispersed in an instant and Adam was left spewing air from his tightened lungs. He hadn't realized he'd been holding his breath the entire time.

Apprehensively, he reached up and felt at his hair. Small tufts of his black locks fell to the floor when he gently pulled at them. Now he was certain. He must have blacked out again.

No time to sit and wonder how it came to be. He had already uncovered the metal tip of a broken spear and was on his way toward the collapsed form of his enemy.

He took three steps and fell to the floor spewing chunks of turkey meat and string beans from his mouth. The aftermath of the blow to his stomach finally set in and the pain folded him like a newspaper onto the floor. He gritted his teeth and forced himself to his feet, still tasting the half-digested stew at the back of his mouth. He didn't have time to complain about possibly ruptured organs or cracked ribs. He had to get to her before she woke up.

"*The heart. The heart!*" He chanted in his head while dragging his feet across broken stone and torn plastics.

He reached her and immediately drove the spear tip into her chest. His eyes stapled themselves to her face, searching for the slightest sign of arousal in her fractured skull as he carved through soft tissue. Foreign blood wet his hands as he hacked deeper into angelic flesh, using the very wound he made with the rebar as a thoroughfare for his makeshift scalpel.

Even in poor lighting, the oily liquid had a polished shine to it. Like a soft shimmer or mild glow that made it seem to absorb the light around it. Though the remaining light in the room was dull and barely enough to see well with, he could tell the previous wounds he had given her were healing quickly. He had to hustle.

He had just peeled away a slab of membranous skin when five warm digits locked around his throat and snatched him from his feet.

"You think you can kill *me*, Guardian!?"

In a flash, he found himself pinned to the wall, hovering two feet off the ground and staring into the eyes of an extremely pissed-off angel. Black fluid leaked profusely from her forehead, nose, and mouth like a wrecked car engine. The right side of her face wore a deep depression where the weighted ball had struck her. He could see that some of her teeth were cracked and missing from the grimace she wore. She was done playing with him.

"This is the end of your life."

Adam closed his eyes and dropped his weapon, he was done fighting. "Then I'll see you on the other side."

With a mighty thrust, he punched into her mutilated chest, jamming his entire hand inside her open wound. Her eyes shot wide and the air was sucked out of the room. His fingers wrapped around a soft throbbing muscle and he heard her squeal an awful sound that let him know that she felt it.

He finally made her feel pain.

For a moment she looked at him, eyes beaming through him like clear water on a dark moonlit night. Seconds ticked by in the form of hours, time was now thick and palpable. So much so that even the fastest of movements became sluggish and heavy. Only emotion seemed to escape the weight of time.

Their eyes locked and he could feel the hurt pouring through her black orbs, begging him not to kill her. Pleading, without words, for mercy from a creature lifetimes younger and immeasurably weaker than her. She could see the sorrow in his face, the weariness on his lips. She could see compassion in his eyes.

Compassion that made him second guess himself, that made him fearful. Would God, *could* God, forgive him for destroying one of her beloved angels? She could sense the hesitation in him, his hand gripping tight his only means of survival. Without warning, his confusion and fear gave way to epiphany, which became anger and then hate.

She read through the boiling scowl seared across his face and into the heart of his rage. Something lost to him and so precious he would risk his place in heaven to have it back. Something he knew he would never have again. Something he could not forgive. He glared hatefully into her eyes and tightened his hold on her heart, making her languish in pain once again.

"This is for Saduj."

Adam tore his hand from her chest, ripping her black heart from its home. He fell to the ground and his rival burst into flames directly in front of him. Like her ancillary, she stood on her feet as she burned, her mouth and eyes wide, the flames close enough to the Guardian that he should have felt their heat. Strangely, there was none.

The black fire was barely a foot in front of him and yet there was no warmth to be felt. In fact, he had actually gotten colder all of a sudden. He pulled away from the alien flames before curiosity tempted him into touching it. Whatever it was, he was going to let it finish its job.

With the energy he had left, he scrambled across the floor toward Emmanuelle. Standing on his knees, he placed his hand to her throat and checked for a pulse. His heart sank. She was cold to the touch.

"Please, Elle. Please."

Putting his fist onto her chest with an open hand on top, he began to pump her chest. Each push sent a shock of force through her that made her body jump with every tremor, but it wasn't enough. He placed his mouth over hers and began breathing air into her lungs. It wasn't enough.

He continued, breathing his lung's capacity into her body and pressing his entire body weight into each thrust. Tears wet his eyes and sweat poured from his forehead. He wanted to scream, but fear made him put the energy into performing CPR. He laid into her until his muscles throbbed from exhaustion and his breathing was heavy. His teeth clenched, trying to fight back the tears now falling from his eyes and he collapsed over her body, a sobbing wreck.

He was out of options. He didn't know what to do at this point. The blood from her wounds was smeared across the stones surrounding her. She had lost too much blood and there was nothing he could do to keep her heart from stopping.

He rubbed her face softly with his hands, sliding the dark blood of the angel onto her pale skin. Even in death, she was beautiful to him. He kissed her forehead gently and whispered in her ear.

"I'm sorry."

Another acid-edged dagger struck his heart when he realized he had failed another one of his friends. He would never see her smile again. He would never get the chance to tell her how he felt about her. He could feel the dagger twist in his chest.

He dragged himself to his feet, kicking a pile of rocks near him as he stood. A thin syringe bounced from the pile of debris and rolled to a stop within sight. He brushed it off at first but took a second glance once his mind registered the word *epinephrine* printed on it. He reached out and picked up the syringe, his hands sticky with blood. He'd seen the word before, but for the life of him, he couldn't remember what it meant.

"Epinephrine. Epinephrine."

The word stirred his mind until he wondered if he was even pronouncing it correctly. Then it hit him and his heart leaped with excitement upon the realization that *epinephrine* was medical jargon for *adrenaline*. He dropped to his knees again, thanking God for this impossible stroke of luck. Now there was a chance to save her; a slim chance, but a chance nonetheless.

He wiped the tip of the exposed needle and rolled up her sleeve to access the veins in her arm. He slid the intravenous instrument under her skin and pressed down on the plunger, then went back to performing CPR. This time more vigorously than before.

"Come on, Emmanuelle. Come on."

Three chest pumps and two breaths later, despair had taken root again. Nothing he had done was causing any change. He stopped, staring at her still body as the sorrow of reality wrapped around him once more.

"She's gone."

As if a bolt of lightning had struck her, she sprang upright, clawing at his face and spitting Spanish from her mouth so fast that he knew most of the words had to be curses. Luckily, he was fast enough to restrain her wrists before she tore out his eyes.

"It's me, Elle! It's Adam! You're ok, you're safe!"

For a few moments, she was trapped in her last waking minutes. Still caught in the grasp of an archangel bent on ending her life. With time and a few calm words, Adam finally reached her and she settled into his arms. She wrapped herself around him like a scared child and held him.

She felt his heart pulsing between his lungs and he felt hers. They didn't say a word. All they needed now was this moment. Body to body and heart to heart they held each other, both afraid to let go.

"Adam?" She finally said. "Did you drop a pile driver on my chest?"

He smiled wide, happy her sense of humor was revived with her. "You wouldn't wake up otherwise."

A mild tremor rattled its way from under their feet and

through the room. They looked at each other in clear definition of what it was. There were still bombs in the building and they had to leave.

Adam helped her to her feet. "Can you walk?"

"Be damned if I don't try."

They started slowly, but within a few strides, Emmanuelle had recovered her balance and was able to walk on her own. Adam was impressed with her ability to move so well after sustaining so many injuries. She was tougher than she looked. Or if she wasn't, she definitely played the part to a tee.

"Where is everyone?"

Adam lifted the steel shutter in response to her question. "Let's go."

Emmanuelle stepped into the tunnel and before her eyes could adjust to the light, Adam slammed the door behind her.

"What are you doing, Adam!? We have to get out of here, now!"

His voice reverberated through the metal. "I have to find Father. He's still here. I'll get him and then we'll both meet you at the rendezvous point."

"This is stupid. Come with me! You can't stay here!

"I can't leave him, Elle. He stayed for us. For you. If it wasn't for me he wouldn't still be here."

"Adam, you have to come with me." She pressed herself against the shutter door so that he could hear her clearly. "I love you, ok? Do you hear me? I love you. Now open this door and come with me!"

There was silence from the other side.

"Adam?"

His voice came back low and serious. "You don't have to say that. I know how you really feel. It took me a while to get it, but I get it now. You love him. Daniel. Just keep at it, he'll come around eventually. I won't stand in your way anymore."

The silence had now shifted to her side of the door.

"Head down the tunnel and you'll run into the others sooner or later. I'll catch you later, Elle."

She stayed a bit longer and listened to the sound of his feet crunch over bits of wreckage as he walked away.

"Catch you later, kid."

SECTION 6

Father tore down the pitch-black hallway, his eyes scanning the dark for the familiar shape of the missing Guardian, Saduj. He trampled the bodies of decaying demons that lay scattered about the floor while his hand searched through his bag, taking mental stock of his arsenal. He was not happy with what he found. He was dangerously low on weapons.

Had he gotten to his weapons cache before the first explosion, he might have salvaged most of his items. No time to dwell on it now. Most of what he felt at the bottom of his bag were shards of broken plastic or glass and the various fluids and substances that they once held. None of it dangerous to him, of course, but damn sure useful when being hunted by relentless angels.

He needed a diversion or some way to keep them from tracking him. They were, of course, tracking him and they would catch him if he didn't do something soon. Sadly, all of the materials he would normally use to avoid detection were sloshing around freely in his sack, mingling with other compounds.

He had to find something else.

His feet beat into the floor as he ran until his nose caught wind of a stifling smell. The toxic and metallic aroma of smoke from a nearby fire rekindled his hope of escape. He followed his nose through the dark of the hallway and ran into the thickening smog. It was exactly what he needed.

He had been hunted by angels before. A token memory from his wilder days of youth. Though it was not an experience he was anxious to relive, he was grateful he had at least learned how they hunt.

They used their noses.

Once an angel had your scent, they could track you almost anywhere. That's why he needed the smoke. As long as your scent wasn't overpowered by certain smells, they could continue to pursue you. Smoke was one of those smells.

The priest continued down the hall until he came to an intersection. The source of the fire had to be nearby because the smoke was so thick he couldn't see through it. To his left and right were pitch-dark hallways leading away from the fire. He could take a chance and choose a path to his left or right, but he knew once the smoke dissipated they would be right back on his trail again. Dangerous as it was, he only had one option if he wanted to lose them.

He turned around and took a few breaths of air, each one deeper than the last. On his fifth breath, he held it, covered his nose and mouth, and ran into the billowing cloud of gas. He could see well enough to make out where he was going before, but now vision was impossible. Whatever light the darkness had left out of kindness, the thickness of the smoke had claimed for itself. There was no chance he'd be able to make out where he was, so he tucked his head and bolted through the smog.

The old man shut his eyes and ran in hopes of clearing the

gas before his breath ran out. The heat from the smoke cooked him inside his clothes, making him break into sweat instantly. He barreled through the smoke-filled hall at full speed, certain he'd reach the end well before his air ran out. The bottom of his shoes dragged atop loose rocks and pitched him forward, slamming him into, what felt like, a tall mound of stones and other debris.

His teeth clenched and his lungs tightened but not before the air they held came spewing from his mouth during the fall. If time permitted, he would be uttering all manner of expletives, but he couldn't waste the air it would take to vent his frustration. He drew his hands across the hill that now blocked his path to gauge what it was and what it was doing in the middle of the hallway. More important than that was how, if at all, he would be able to get around it.

His fingers dragged across broken steel beams and crumbled rocks that still tumbled down the slant of the hill. He followed the pile with his fingers from one side of the hall to the other. His lungs grew a tickle at the bottom of his throat to remind him that he was out of air when he finally understood what his hands were pressed against. He had run into a cave-in caused by the bombs set in the base.

Worse still, whatever was burning was on the other side of the collapsed debris, but the smoke was somehow still able to get through. His chances of running past the fire were now zero. The tickle at the bottom of his throat was now a burning sensation making its way up into his mouth. He was running out of time.

He placed his palms on the wall and followed it back down the way he came. Maybe there was another intersection he had passed when he ran down. He had run too far too fast to make it back the way he came now, but if he could find another hallway he could at least get to a section with fewer fumes. A shot in the dark, but he was desperate.

His lungs were kicking the inside of his chest like a wild mare. His hands scrambled up and down the wall, leading his blind body. Maybe his eyes could tell him some bit of information that would help him. Hoping the toxic cloud wasn't as thick here, he pulled open his eyes and chanced a look at his surroundings.

All he could see was a flowing pulsing cloud of blackness that moved as if it were alive. The only reward for his bravery was an invitation of the fumes into his sockets. His eyes slammed shut, black soot from the smoke sizzled his corneas into producing tears. In his anxiousness, all he had managed to do was burn his eyes. His mind shook with the curses that went off like bombs in his head.

He continued dragging his hands along the wall and fell to the floor when his hands came to an open section. He had found a separate junction leading away from the flames and smoke just as he had hoped. He would have been elated if the sudden fall hadn't made him take a sharp inhale of smoke.

Like a black snake made of poison, the fumes spiraled through his nostrils and coiled down into his chest. His lungs hiccuped inside him, reacting to the poison and trying to force it out.

Father struggled back to his feet and stumbled down the hall, forcing his airway closed even as it throbbed wildly for oxygen. He knew that if he allowed his organs to expel the smoke, they would immediately attempt to replace it with clean air. Right now there was no clean air to replace it with. His lungs would cough out the smoke only to inhale even more and kill him.

His face was tight and hot from holding his breath for so long. He tried to ease into a weary jog but fell to the floor. His head was pounding and his eyes were on fire, but he had to keep moving. He had to get clear of the smoke. He began a desperate crawl across the floor.

"*Don't pass out. Don't you pass out, old man.*"

He knew that if he did, it was over.

He fought to stay conscious, but he could feel the cyanide eat away at his organs, the carbon monoxide blocking fresh oxygen from his body and closing up his throat. The taste of burnt rubber and electrical wiring bastardized the air and poisoned his mind. He could feel everything slipping away.

His nose opened and his body forced him to take in the gas. He could feel the smoke searing its way past his nose hairs as he continued to struggle forward. His strong inhale was instantly followed by a roll of coughs and sputters, his body rejecting the pollution. He pulled himself across the floor on his stomach, his eyes still jammed shut. The throbbing in his head grew to a crescendo and a wave of nausea hit him as he succumbed to the smoke in his lungs and dropped his head to the floor.

When his eyes fluttered open, the first thing to meet him was the florescent glow of a yellow emergency light and a foul taste in his mouth. Next was the dull throb in his head and stabbing pain in his chest. It took him a moment to realize he had his eyes open and he wasn't surrounded by smoke. Somehow he had made it just outside the cloud and into semi-clean air before passing out. He thanked God for another moment of life and slowly made his way to his feet.

His senses came back to him and he recognized that he had been lying in something wet the entire time he was out. He rubbed his eyes and his vision cleared enough to see the pool of black tar he had been laying in. His hair stood on end when he thought the angels had caught up to him.

Calm came back to him when he wiped the side of his face and realized that he had vomited up the black soot in his lungs. He thanked the creator again and quietly gathered that he couldn't have been out for more than a few minutes.

He supported himself against the wall for a minute or two to steady his nerves and get his feet back under him. The life of a Guardian was filled with close calls, and this was nothing new to him. Though, if he was honest, it had been a while since he had come this close. It had even made him forget that he wasn't destined to die yet. That's when he saw something that swept his feet out from under him again. This time there would be no recovery.

At first, he wasn't sure it was real. He thought he was dreaming again. He wanted to just be dreaming again, but the pain in his body told him otherwise. There it was in front of him, light glimmering from underneath it just as he had imagined a thousand times.

The door from his nightmares.

He couldn't move. Not even if he wanted to. His muscles palsied, his joints were stiff, and his limbs went numb. His bottom lip quivered as fear paralyzed his mind and froze him in place. It took him a moment to recognize that his entire body was shaking, not just his lip.

The most gut-wrenching part of it all was that he knew he couldn't turn back. He could run back and die from smoke inhalation or be killed by the angels that hunted him, or he could walk through the door. In his mind, in every scenario, death was certain. A flash of grim humor lit into his brain.

"Well, at least I have options."

He didn't know where the thought came from, but it served to return a modicum of levity to his countenance. He was no longer shaking when he walked to the door. The memories of his last conversation with Matilda marched through his head.

"You can't fear it now. Your whole life you knew it was coming, so don't cower before it. Embrace it and know that it's your destiny."

The memory of her words gave him a little more courage and he wrapped his hand around the handle of the door. He could feel the handle jiggle in his palm. He was shaking again. Fear rose up and coiled around him like a snake with potent venom. His free hand clasped at his mouth, holding back the complete breakdown that rested on the cusp of his lips.

He bit down on his lip and snatched the door open before fear made him tuck tail and run. His bravery caught in his throat, blocking a helpless scream that was on its way out through his mouth.

Behind the door, the hallway was on fire. Not a single large flame, but a smattering of smaller fires. Remnants of an explosion near some accelerant that sent shards of fire down the hall, he figured.

The walkway was aglow with flickering light. The heat from the flames filled the area, making the air thick and heavy. He couldn't believe what he was seeing. The fire from his nightmares was right in front of him, throwing its heat mockingly at his body

He froze again, this time of his own volition, partly because of his hesitancy to enter the hall and partly because he was trying to remember what happened next. He knew the fire was supposed to come alive and trap him, but he couldn't remember, for the life of him, what happened after that.

It was ridiculous to him, the fact that he could have the same reoccurring dream for years and not remember aspects of it when he needed to. He grew mad with frustration.

The splash of something wet on the tip of his shoe made

him look down. A drop of blood rolled off the toe of his shoe and all at once he recalled what came next.

His eyes would pour with blood.

His hands shot up and timidly grazed the skin under his eyes. There was no blood. He breathed a sigh of relief. Before he could put his hands down, he noticed a wet red spot on the wrist of his sleeve. He peeled it back, revealing his stigmata wound open with blood flowing from it. He turned his head and looked back at the floor behind him, and he had left a trail of blood leading back into the cloud of smoke. How long had he been bleeding?

He didn't have time to wonder, because, in the next moment, his heart choked on the liquid in his chest and pulled him to his knees. His heart struggled and sputtered, unable to efficiently move the blood in his veins without sending a thrum of pain with it. He cringed and dropped his head to his knees, hurtful waves crashing through him with every thump of his muscle. He had felt this pain before, but it was always short-lived. This time it was not.

With every beat, the pain intensified and his heart tore itself apart. His chest was on fire. His heart screamed for mercy as his blood flowed into it too quickly. A hard cough escaped his throat, spewing blood onto the floor. The pain still hadn't subsided.

A side effect of inhaling too much smoke perhaps? It didn't matter now. All he could focus on was the pain. The muscle in his chest spasmed and sent jolts of agony tearing through his nervous system at bullet speed. He clawed at his chest in futility and sprayed more blood onto the floor.

There was no sound but the uneven thump of his worn heart in his ears. He could taste the blood on his tongue and still smell the awful scent of smoke trapped in his nose. If he survived this he would never touch a cigarette again. An invisible hand squeezed his heart in reply to the thought. He fell to his stomach and curled into a ball.

This was it. With soot in his lungs and blood on his teeth, he finally accepted the truth of the moment. He had been running from it forever, but he couldn't any longer.

He was going to die here.

He tried to force himself still, to get used to the pain. He tried to make his last moments on Earth as comfortable as he could. A weak moan echoed down the hall and woke him from his pain-induced trance. He immediately recognized the voice.

He was so preoccupied with himself that he hadn't noticed the blood-covered body that lay on the floor behind the fire. He peered through the flames at the figure. A man, with torn white bandages hanging loosely from open wounds, long dark hair thrown over bruised brown skin, and a small piece of a wooden broom still clutched in one of his hands.

He had found Saduj.

His body acted on its own after that, pulling him to his feet and slowly navigating him through the fire. Now he didn't have time to die. His time wasn't his own anymore. One of his men needed him and even if he had to staple his godforsaken heart together, it was going to stay in one piece until he rescued him.

He didn't care about pain. He had felt enough of it in his lifetime to know it well. He didn't care about dying. He refused to fear what he could not control. All he could think about was what he had said to Adam.

"Don't worry. I'll find them. I'll bring them back."

He had already failed Emmanuelle. He'd die a thousand times before he'd allow himself to fail Saduj. He reached the Native American and knelt beside him to assess his injuries. Saduj uttered another empty moan which Father was glad to hear. At least he was alive enough to do that.

Another deafening explosion blew smoke and debris through the hall and made the priest reconsider the amount of time they had left. He would check Saduj's wounds later, they needed to leave first. Father wrapped his arms around the man and began lifting him to his feet.

"We're getting out of here, Saduj."

A sharp pain tore through his chest and he dropped his teammate to the ground. He couldn't carry him under his own strength, not with his heart in the condition it was. He took a couple of slow breaths and tried to lift the man again.

"Come on, Saduj. I know you're hurt, but I need your help here, son. I need you to stand. We're going to get out of here, but I need your help to do it."

Saduj responded with a dreary sound from his throat that could barely pass for a moan. Father lifted him halfway up and Saduj planted his feet under himself. Before he could stand erect, the copper skin man tumbled roughly back to the floor.

"Come on, chief! You have to get up! You have to get up now!"

Father could feel his friend's legs shaking, his world probably a spinning mess of colors and sounds. The old man held him tightly and pulled him up to his feet. Saduj teetered, leaning most of his body weight on the priest, lest he fall to the floor again. Father wrapped his arms around Saduj's back and kept him upright as his head lay on his shoulder.

"Okay. We're okay. Let's get out of he—"

The sound of tearing flesh and the scent of freshly spilled blood filled the air. Pain stacked like dominoes in a crescendo that rolled from head to toe. The priest looked down only to see a long pointed knife buried through his side. The blade protruded through his back and on its hilt rested the brown hand of his comrade. Father lifted his head and Saduj was staring him straight in the eyes.

A string of blood trickled from the corner of the priest's mouth. "I knew we were betrayed by someone. I never would've imagined it was you."

"No. I'm no traitor." Saduj's voice was cold and monotone. "Because I was never one of you."

The warmth of the priest's blood ran from the blade and down his legs to the floor. Amazingly, the fire in his chest had gone quiet. All he could feel now was the cold steel of the knife through his body.

Saduj beamed at him with dead eyes, emotion drained from his face. "This blade is through your liver. Once I remove it, you're going to bleed to death."

Adam came coughing and wheezing through the door. By the grace of God, he had somehow made it through a hallway filled with smoke. After killing an arch power and rescuing Emmanuelle, this had to be the luckiest day of his life. Bar none.

He rubbed his stinging eyes and spat mucus, trying to rid himself of the taste of burnt metal. He still didn't quite understand what drew him here. Father could have taken one of the other two paths, but something pulled him down this one. A gut feeling he couldn't put into words. At this point, Adam knew better than to argue with his sixth sense.

He cleared his burning eyes and peered down the flaming hallway. His heart stopped. At the end, in a pool of ever-spreading blood, was Father. Standing over him was his best friend, gripping a knife dark with his mentor's blood.

He couldn't register it at first. His brain scrambled the image and pieced it back together a dozen times in a second. His eyes blinked, focused, and refocused, trying to force the picture to change. Saduj stared at him blankly from across the hall, flames flickering in front of him, distorting Adam's image of him.

Adam looked him directly in his eyes. His cheeks were smeared with blood and sweat from the heat of the fire, but his eyes said one thing to Adam. Unapologetic.

Saduj flung the knife down so hard its tip stuck in the metal floor. He gave Adam one last glance and walked away, turning down a separate hall. The young Guardian flew down the flaming hallway, stopping at Father's body. He knelt in his tutor's blood and lifted his body into his arms. The blood-soaked blade left as a taunt by his former friend.

Adam hugged Father tightly, his throat dry and tears running down his face. He had sent the priest to his death. He let out a hoarse scream as the final bomb went off and buried him under piles of dirt and stone.

CHAPTER
NINE

T*ruth*

SECTION I

Daniel stood outside a tall antiquated church, waiting in the darkness. One of the oldest churches in the city, it was a regular rendezvous point before and after assignments. After this particular assignment, he had a rendezvous of a more divine nature. The angel in question was late, something they were not typically famous for.

The moon shined in the night sky, casting shadows of the trees on the low and neatly cut grass. The spires atop the church reached into the still sky and disappeared into the darkness. The hour grew late. Either he had been stood up or...who was he kidding? There was no '*or*'. He had made the mistake of assuming all seraphim were like Gabriel. Clearly, this wasn't the case.

"What do you want, Guardian?"

The voice was authoritative and powerful. A voice that had commanded armies of unfathomable number into battles of immeasurable consequence. Daniel turned and looked up to see a man dressed in black perched at the very top of a spire. Raphael was at least three stories high, yet the boom of his voice made him sound as if he were no more than a few yards away.

"I have something for you," Daniel called stridently into the dark.

Even at the distance he was, Daniel could still see the cock of the seraphim's head in surprise and confusion at his words. The angel jumped from the spire and fell to the ground. He seemed to almost float instead of fall, and when he landed he didn't make a sound. Not even a thud from the impact of his shoes hitting the lawn.

"Understand this, Guardian. Whatever arrangement you had with my sister does not extend to me. I am not your friend, I am not here to coddle you, and this will not happen again."

"What if I had something that could help end this war of ours?"

Raphael eyed him blankly for a moment, pondering over his choice of words. "Ours?"

Daniel removed a black bag from his shoulder and began to reach through it. "I've always considered our issues to be the same. This war is just as much our problem as it is yours and I want to help end it before that fact becomes obvious."

The Guardian pulled an old relic from the bag, dust-covered and worn and ancient in design but still beautiful in its own right. It resembled something of a large round bowl or gourd in its shape, but not completely one or the other. Antique jewels of ruby and sapphire lined its outside and rim, giving the item an air of importance. Jewels aside, with its age alone it was worth a fortune.

"I'm not sure what it is, but my sources tell me you can use it to transfer Gabriel's power to someone of your choosing."

Daniel placed it into the angel's hands and Raphael scanned the relic, not fully recognizing its purpose as the Guardian went on.

"I believe it's some kind of channel that calls Gabriel's power into it and focuses it into—"

Daniel was cut off by the heart-wrenching sound of something as old as antiquity being shattered by something far more ancient. Raphael crushed the relic in his hands and the pieces dropped to the ground like broken glass.

Daniel's heart dropped into his stomach. "No! What have you done!"

He rushed over as if to somehow repair the lost item and Raphael stretched out his hand to stop him. And stop him it did. With Raphael's hand on his chest, Daniel felt as if he were an ant fighting against a bulldozer. Rather than let his anxiousness and confusion get the better of him, he decided to stop and wait for an explanation.

"Your quest has been one of great folly, Daniel. There is no item on Earth or in any existence that can guide Gabriel's power. It is a decision made at our Lord's discretion. Only *she* can influence it."

Daniel's world was dowsed with confusion and regret. He didn't want to believe Raphael's words, but he knew he had no reason to lie to him. Only one question remained now.

"Raphael, you're telling me that item I just risked my life for is—"

Raphael cut him off for a second time. "It is exactly what it was moments before you gave it to me and throughout its entire existence. Worthless."

Words caught in Daniel's throat. None of this made any sense to him, but he hid his anger behind an irritated smirk as Raphael continued.

"Your source has lied to you. Whatever effort you put into finding that artifact has been wasted and so has your time. Do not call on me again."

Raphael turned and walked away, crushing the broken

shards of the destroyed relic underfoot as he walked. Daniel couldn't muster another word in defense. Raphael was right, he had wasted both their time with this and now he knew he had to find out why.

"So, Matilda isn't as gifted as she seems. Father will get a kick out of this."

Before the archangel could walk out of sight, he stopped on the damp grass in front of the church. Daniel watched him hold his nose in the air and inhale the nightly breeze. Raphael took one long breath followed by many short sniffs and turned, halfway facing the Guardian. He wore a puzzled face as he extended his arm and held his palm up toward Daniel. Like before, only without touching him, the gesture made the Guardian root in place.

"Someone is coming." The angel sniffed again. "I smell blood."

Daniel turned in the direction Raphael was staring and heard the clambering of hurried footsteps in the dark. They both became silent as they waited while the sound came nearer. Daniel's hands eased to his weapons on reflex.

"No." The Seraphim's voice halted his movement. "You won't need them."

In the next moment, a group of people came stumbling through the brush and onto the church lawn. Daniel relaxed when he recognized his team, but dread quickly filled him when he saw their injuries.

Seraphim was the first to notice him. Her face flushed with relief at the sight of him approaching. Daniel watched her eyes shift toward Raphael and her body grew tight with apprehension.

She snatched a blade from her waist and pointed it at the angel. "What the hell is *he* doing here?"

Both Daniel and Raphael were confused, though the angel didn't show it at all.

Raphael stepped closer to the group of battered warriors. "What is the meaning of this?"

"Do you have any idea what we've been through tonight!? Get back! Get back!" She screamed.

"Sera, what's going on here?" Daniel questioned with his palms up.

"I'll tell ya what's going on." Mark brandished two hook-like weapons that he slid across his fingers like brass knuckles. "We were just ambushed by demons and angels, working together. We barely got out alive, so I think a bit of apprehension is reasonable."

"Right now, I don't trust any angel," Seraphim said shaking with anger, eyes locked on Raphael.

Daniel turned to look at him, taking in his calm demeanor at this new accusation. He had to admit, Raphael made it very clear he had no patience for mankind, but that was hardly enough to convince him he had betrayed them. Raphael gazed at Daniel, already sensing the hesitation in him.

"It was Michael. He has to be behind this," he said blandly.

"Why should we trust you?" Mark cut in. "Why should we trust either of you?"

Daniel gave the Irishman a puzzled look. "What are you saying, Mark?"

"I'm saying, the night we get attacked by a group of angels and demons just so happens to be the night you're away on some far-off trip, alone, I might add. And what do ya know, we find you here socializing with one of the bastards. That just don't sit right with me, boyo."

Mark circled around to Daniel's side with his weapons at the ready.

Daniel noticed a flicker of belligerence in his eyes. "Mark, I don't know what you're considering, but if I were you, I would reconsider it."

The Irishman lashed out with two strikes at Daniel's head and stomach, forcing him to leap backward.

"Mark, What are you doing!?" Prophet shouted.

"Don't you see? It's him! He's the one who betrayed us and let those sons of bitches inside!" Mark advanced again, bringing his right fist across Daniel's chest but missing as he pushed away. "We trusted you, you bastard."

Daniel dodged three more attempts at his life, narrowly avoiding attacks to his jugular. "Stop this, Mark. You know me, you know I wouldn't do this."

Daniel knew his plea was falling on deaf ears. Mark had gone blind with anger.

His eyes boiled with mad rage as they locked in on Daniel's. "You know Father's probably dead because of you?"

Daniel's brain stuttered. The words hit his senses like a neural train wreck. That's when Mark struck, slicing Daniel's forearm before he could return to himself. His quick reflexes saved him from a follow-up attack that could have gutted him had he not moved. He was still trying to swallow Mark's words.

The anger-fueled man continued. "That's right. Father, Saduj, Elle, and Adam. All dead and it's your fault!"

"Stop it, Mark! We don't know that!" Prophet's voice boomed while his brother hung off his shoulder weakly. "We don't know what's going on here."

The two Guardians circled each other, each holding the other in an unblinking steely gaze.

"Even if he's telling the truth. Even if this is all some huge misunderstanding, he's still to blame." Mark's voice had now reached a sorrowful note. "You should have fought with us. You should have been there. Our friends paid the price because you weren't, and now you have to pay something for that."

Mark stopped circling and took his fighting stance. He was out for blood.

Now Daniel could feel the anger swelling inside of him too. He had questions that needed answers and he intended to get them. Even if he had to go through an ally.

"I'm done playing with you, Mark. We don't have time for this, so stand down before I put you down."

Mark inched closer, his shoulders bounced steadily as his breath quickened. He was unflinching in his determination. Daniel could tell he would not be stopped easily. Pain and loss had mingled with the fear inside him, making him unreasonable and inconsolable. He would have to break him down and defuse his mental state if he planned to reach him at all.

Daniel dropped his arms to his sides and smiled playfully. "So, you think you're tough shit now, is that it, Mark? You couldn't hold a candle to me at your best, so how the hell do you expect to beat me like this?"

Mark turned cherry red and lunged at Daniel, swinging wildly at him and missing badly.

Daniel pulled back and put a few yards distance between them. "You're wounded and exhausted, and I'm not even trying yet." Two more rage-fueled swings flew by his head as he danced around on the church lawn. "So much for Mark the marksman, I guess."

"You think this is a fucking joke!?"

"You're the joke, Mark. Look at you, you're a wreck."

Mark could feel sweat cascade from his face as his arms began to shake.

"You know what's going to happen here." Daniel mocked him again. "Even your own body knows."

The Irishman's mouth went bone dry as if all the moisture

inside had gone streaming down his skin. The trembling of his hands had somehow spread to his knees now and he couldn't stop blinking.

Daniel glared at his teammate with a seriousness that bordered on murderous intent. "The next time you come at me will be the last time."

Daniel was motionless as he stood before the spiky-haired blonde, daring him to attack.

Mark drew a sweat-covered hand across his forehead. "You think I'm afraid?"

"I know you're afraid. That's why you're stalling because you know what I can do to you. You know what I *will* do to you."

Now there was silence. Both men stared at each other while everyone else stared at them. Even Raphael hadn't removed his eyes from the scene. Mark inched forward, pushed onward by fear more than reason. He came within striking distance and a woman fell from the bushes between them. Her hair was a shaggy mess of grey dirt and her sky-blue top was soaked through with splotches of red with a strip of torn fabric wrapped around her blood-stained right hand.

"Elle!" Mark yelled, immediately abandoning his bout against Daniel.

Both men helped her to her feet, Mark already bombarding her with questions.

"How in the hell did you make it out of there? What happened to Father? Where's Adam?"

The Latin woman was falling into an exhausted haze. The adrenaline shot given to her was winding down and she was now struggling to keep her eyes open.

"Adam saved me. He wouldn't leave. I tried to get him to come with me, but he went back for Father."

"Emmanuelle, do you know what happened to them?" Daniel asked with fear on his lips.

Her expression was as dark as the night sky when she answered.

"The building collapsed. They didn't make it out."

The truth hit him like a blow to the chest. There was nothing he could do. His brother and mentor were gone.

"Hey! We need help over here!" Prophet's voice cut through loud and panicked.

Ezekiel fell to the ground, his eyes low and sweat pouring from his body.

"Zeke!" Prophet screamed.

Seraphim placed her hand to his neck. He was cold to the touch and his heart beat weakly yet rapidly in his chest. She lifted his lids and checked his eyes. They were dilated, just as she thought.

"He's going into shock. We have to get him inside, now!"

Daniel rushed to the Russian woman's side and together they lifted Ezekiel from the wet grass. Prophet put his boot to the church doors and they flew open.

"Hey! Is anyone here?" His voice bellowed through the chamber filled with wooden pews and lit candles.

A short-statured, gerbil of a man walked from the back in a hurry. "Oh my, what has happened?"

The sudden sight of so much blood struck a nervous chord in the priest. He couldn't stop his teeth from chattering.

"Any medical supplies you have, Father, we need them right now," Prophet ordered.

"Yes. M-m-medical supplies, right," the priest stammered, unable to take his eyes off the blood leaking from Ezekiel's chest.

He was frozen in place, watching the wounded Guardian laid on top of the marble altar, his body lifeless, it seemed.

289

"Father, now!" Prophet shouted, breaking him from his daze.

"Yes! Of course!" The frightened Priest jumped and disappeared to the back of the church.

Vomit erupted from Ezekiel's mouth the moment his back touched the altar.

"Shit," Seraphim spat, turning his head to one side. "Raise his legs, we have to keep blood flow to his organs."

Mark jumped to Ezekiel's feet, eager to obey her call.

"We need pressure on this wound," she shouted.

Each Guardian slapped their hands on top of his chest, creating a fleshy mound of red-tinted blood-glossed hands.

Prophet met his brother's weary gaze and fear crept inside of him. "Fight it. You hear me, little brother? You better fight it."

Daniel noticed Raphael standing just inside the church doors, still watching events unfold. He removed his hands from the mound and rushed over to the seraphim.

"Raphael, we need your help."

The divine being's eyes grew wide, surprised that he would ask such a question. "You dare ask me that?"

"Please, I know you're the angel of healing. You can save him."

He stared daggers into the Guardian and turned away. "Seraphim do not involve themselves in human matters."

"You're already involved."

Raphael whipped around, apoplectically. "This is not my problem!"

"This became your problem a long time ago!"

They both glowered at each other in rage, speaking in forceful biting tones.

"This is a direct result of *your* war, Raphael. My men were attacked by Michael's angels collaborating with *demons*. You can't ignore this anymore."

"It is forbidden. I will not risk myself for you."

Daniel caught a flash of disgust in his eyes when the angel said '*you*'. He became hot with anger.

"What's your problem!? You're supposed to be on our side, aren't you?"

The angel turned his back to Daniel and walked toward the door without reply.

"You know, I hoped it wasn't true, but even my kid brother could see it." Daniel stepped forward. "*You* sent those demons to the abandoned church, didn't you?"

The archangel stopped before reaching the exit as if the Guardian's words stunned him. Floating in the stark silence that hung between them, Daniel found his answer. The heat of sizzling fury burned his tongue.

"At least Gabriel had the balls to—"

The Guardian was suddenly dangling off his feet, an angelic hand wrapped tightly around his neck.

"You will not speak of my sister again, human."

Raphael's eyes were black as the devil's pitch, staring into Daniel's face. He had moved so fast that Daniel's brain couldn't process it. He had cleared 3 yards faster than the mere mortal could even blink his eyes.

Daniel grabbed the angel's arm, struggling futilely in his grasp. "Please, Raphael. We can't handle this by ourselves," he choked out. "Those demons have angels on their side now. We need one on ours."

Raphael lifted him higher, slicing into his soul with his eyes.

The Guardian grunted in pain and coughed out his words. "I know you loved her. What would she think of what you're doing now?"

The dark faded from his eyes and he slowly placed Daniel back on his feet. "What I do is for my sister, not you, Guardian."

Raphael walked to the pulpit and, with a glance, each Guardian removed their hands and backed away from the altar. All but Prophet, who left his hand on the wound and stared, with frothing anger, at the angel.

Raphael eyed him carelessly. "I will heal him. Remove yourself."

"The last angel we met put a hole in his chest, so don't expect me to trust you so easily," Prophet snapped.

"Regardless, I am the only one who can save him right now. Do you want my help or not?"

Prophet wanted to bash the seraphim's head in with one of the metal candle sticks surrounding them. He knew it wasn't the brightest idea.

"Come on, Prophet. Let him."

Mark's voice had a dash of pleading to it, indicating he was willing to let Raphael try. The bearded man felt his brother's hand move to his own and slide it off his body. Even in his dying state, Ezekiel was aware of what was happening. He was also willing to let him try. Prophet gave his brother a final look and backed away from the altar.

Raphael placed his palm over the wound and closed his eyes, thick blood rolling down the crescent moon and star painted on Ezekiel's chest. When he opened them they were black again, and vomit came sloshing forth from Ezekiel's mouth. Prophet felt the throbbing need to rush back to his brother's side, but he fought it down and remained where he was.

There was no magic glow or flash of holy light that the Guardians expected, just the writhing movements of their half-dead friend spread across the marble top. Raphael lifted his hand slowly from Ezekiel's chest and the five openings began to weave closed. It looked as if the angel was speeding up his body's normal healing process. Like he had fast-forwarded time in one particular spot until the injuries were gone.

Raphael removed his hand and Ezekiel's body went limp. All that remained of the wounds were five grisly scars that easily looked over a year old. Even the wound on his shoulder had closed.

Raphael stepped down from the pulpit. "He is alive."

Prophet rushed to his brother, wiping his hand over the healed wound and checking his pulse. His heart beat slowly but his eyes remained closed.

"What's wrong with him?" Prophet demanded more than he asked.

"He's in a coma," Raphael stated flatly.

"Why?"

"The human body is a fragile thing. If I were to heal him too quickly, his brain would not be able to process it and he would seizure and die. His own body has to do the rest now. Whether he wakes up or not is entirely up to him."

SECTION 2

Daniel sat in the church doorway with his arms resting on his knees, the cold wind whistling through his crow-colored hair. He watched, in bellowing silence, the tree tops bend in the wind as if old sages bowing in reverence to a god that couldn't be seen. A god that could only be felt when caressing the branches and carrying the seeds of the next generation, or ripping them up mercilessly from the dirt.

Daniel heard footsteps approach and stop behind him and to his right in the doorway. He didn't look up.

"Don't worry about apologizing," he said. "I understand."

A sigh of relief came huffing from Irish lungs. "Thank God. I'm terrible with apologies anyway."

Daniel was quiet again.

The spiky-haired blonde looked him over. "So, what's the craic, boss?"

Daniel edged an eye over to Mark's leaning form. "Boss?"

"Yeah, I figured you'd be taking the reins from Father sooner or later. Turns out I was right."

Daniel returned his eyes to the trees, not bothering to

mention that upon his return he was due to lead them anyway. He decided to change the subject.

"Your wounds are gone." He motioned toward the seraphim inside the church. "Raphael?"

Mark tilted his body and lifted his hair back to reveal the thin scar running through his scalp. "Yeah. Lovely, isn't it? He stitched us up but decided to leave us scars as a reminder. Somethin' about angelic pride or whatnot. Personally, I think he's just being an arsehole, but don't tell him I said that."

Daniel cut his eyes at him again. "Mark, he's a seraph. I'm betting he heard you already."

Mark's face went blank for a moment. "Oh. Well, I guess the cat's out of the bag now." The Irishman took a seat next to him, flipping upward the lapels of his newly acquired black coat. "Good thing we had a store of extra clothes here. Couldn't well strike fear into the hearts of demons in a pair of slippers and pajama pants."

Quiet tension filled the space between them again. Daniel could tell Mark wanted to say something. Something in his body language told him that much, but he couldn't think of what it could be.

"So, why'd you leave?"

Mark's question was so obvious now, he wondered why he couldn't guess it in the first place. He cleared his throat of wreckage before he answered and pointed to the artifact that still lay broken across the grass.

"That."

"Tough break. What was it?"

"Worthless. I thought I was going after something that could change the tide of this war and it turned out to be a lie. I need to find out why." Daniel pulled himself up from the church steps and proceeded to walk out onto the grass.

"If it's the truth you're hunting, then I want in on it. I need to make amends for earlier."

Daniel waved him onward. "Then it'll be just you and me."

Mark stepped out onto the grass staring at Daniel's back, uncertain about everything happening except how he felt. Angry. They all had the right to be angry at him. They had the right to hate him for leaving. He wasn't there when they needed him most, and he knew that. He also knew that Daniel had just lost his brother and, because of that, he would never stop punishing himself.

"Where are we going exactly?"

Daniel strode forward without turning. "To a familiar place and, for her sake, she better *pray* she's a real psychic."

Daniel and Mark walked toward the white double doors at a quickening pace. They recognized the two women at the front as the same women from their last visit. They would be the only resistance. The women saw the two men coming and addressed them first.

"Sorry, but we're closed for the evening."

The two men continued their approach without slowing down.

"I need to speak with her," Daniel said.

Mark could hear it in his voice, a glimmer of the rage he kept in check. He didn't come here to be swept away empty-handed. He was willing to go all the way for answers. And if Daniel was going to cut loose, then this was certainly going to be an interesting night.

"She's not taking any callers right now," the second woman said, approaching.

"I'd let him through if I were you, lass."

Mark walked closely behind Daniel, who didn't bother looking at the women until one of them shoved her hand stiffly into his chest, stopping his forward momentum.

"Hey, I said we're closed!" She snapped.

Daniel's eyes met hers and, like a lit match flung into a pool of diesel fuel, he ignited.

Mark smiled grimly at the woman. "Don't say I didn't warn you, love."

The women in the mansion acted no differently than on any other night. Only this time there were no rich, pleasure-seeking, businessmen being entertained, and no one dressed overly sexual in attempt to swoon them out of their money. The women walked about in pajamas consisting of long t-shirts and panties and the occasional onesie, telling long-winded and obscene jokes without the usual gathering of horny men surrounding them.

The double doors flew off their hinges and landed with a clatter in the middle of the foyer, an unconscious woman in a blue suit laying between them. A man dressed in all black with dark hair and a long trench coat stepped into the foyer holding the second guard captive. The women peeked from their hiding places, having jumped behind sofas and tables upon hearing the racket. Daniel twisted the woman's arm behind her as she struggled in his grip and Mark stepped forward to address the crowd of frightened women.

"Easy now, ladies. We didn't come here to hurt anyone." He paused for a moment and looked down at the woman they had rendered unconscious seconds ago. "Well, anyone else. We just need to see Matilda, that's all, so if you would kindly cooperate we'll be out of your hair shortly."

As he finished his sentence, a heart-stopping sound rico-cheted into his ear. A drum roll of metallic clicks lit the air. The Irishman blinked and looked again. The once scared crowd of cowering women were now armed to the teeth with automatic and semi-automatic weapons pulled from beneath tables and under sofa cushions.

"Holy shite."

Mark glanced down and spotted a green ball rolling its way across the floor to his feet. His breath caught in the back of his mouth when he realized it was a grenade with a missing pin. Not wasting another second, he stepped forward and kicked the bomb high, bouncing it off the ceiling and causing it to land amid the scattering women. The explosion rippled through the plantation causing the foundation to shake. In the time it took for the bomb to go off, the women had taken shelter to avoid the worst of it, but Daniel and Mark had made their escape as well.

Mark dove for cover behind the hard stone of one of the twin staircases and Daniel pulled the woman back outside the mansion through the doorway. It wasn't long before the armed vixens pulled themselves together and opened fire through the smoke of the explosion.

The machines roared like thunder and spit bursts of fire from their barrels that launched metal rounds that chewed through all manner of materials. Outside, Daniel could hear the clatter of bullets fired indiscriminately into the foyer. Mark was still inside so he had to hustle.

His captive pulled out of his grip, reaching for her holster and her gun was not there. She turned around and Daniel held a black .45 caliber pistol to her head, the scent of her perfume still imprinted on the grip.

"Tell me where she is," the Guardian demanded.

The corner of her mouth lifted, producing a confident

sneer. "I know about you Guardians. You can't use guns, it would break your sacred decree." Her smile widened. "And you're not the leader."

Daniel answered her mocking smile with a hollowing scowl and pulled the trigger. She fell to the ground cater-wauling in agony, blood spitting from her left arm. Daniel stood above her with her pistol pointed down at her face, anger radiating from his own.

"If you knew about our decree then you would know it only applies to the pursuit and destruction of supernatural entities. You are not supernatural." He thumbed back the hammer on the weapon so that she could hear the sound. "And our *leader* is dead. I'm the new guy."

She clutched her bleeding arm and looked into Daniel's crimson-threaded eyes. The man was belligerent with rage.

"I won't ask again."

"Second floor. The library, if you can get that far."

Daniel pulled away from her and walked out into the damp air of the bayou, disappearing into the darkness. The wounded guard watched him pace away from the plantation, completely perplexed as to where he was going. Her mind remained a home for befuddlement until two sparkling headlights flickered on with the sound of an engine roaring to life.

Bullets hammered into stone, wood, and glass in an endless drumroll. Mark pulled himself tight to the staircase, hoping it was as sturdy as he guessed. He heard the sound of metal rounds deflecting off of the stone and knew he was safe for the moment. The problem was, he was pinned down and unable to ascend the staircase under the draw of so much fire.

Then, another explosion hit.

At least it felt like an explosion. What it sounded like was the shattering of glass, brick, and a farrago of other materials coupled with a thumping car engine and a blaring horn stuck in the on position. Mark peeked over the staircase at the wreckage. Sure enough, Daniel had driven a nineteen eighty-four Oldsmobile into the foyer, scattering the women like frightened mice.

He hopped out the passenger side door without a scratch on him. Mark eyed his newly christened leader as if he were something completely alien to him.

"You know, when we pinched the priest's car, I was under the assumption that we'd get it back to him in one piece."

Daniel moved past him, tossing him the pistol as he did. "Arms and legs only. At least until I find Matilda."

The marksman glossed over the weapon like a lost idol of infinite value. "I'm beginning to like you as the new captain."

The two Guardians moved quietly up the stairs and through a series of interconnected rooms. A huge living room, an adequately sized game room equipped with pool tables and miniature basketball arcade games, and a small lounge with a bar stocked with alcohol.

The mansion was indeed resplendent, but there was no time to admire any details. Stealth was the name of the game. Now that they had been lost, the trick was to find Matilda before her army of killers found them.

The two warriors eased silently past the lounge, turning a corner down a hall with six doors on each side and giant full-length mirrors between each door. At the end of the hall rested two oak double doors. Daniel's senses lit up. Without a doubt, this was the entrance to the library.

They picked up the pace, moving in fast step down the hall when a door to the right opened and Daniel found himself staring down the double barrel of a sawed-off shotgun.

The blast shattered the mirror across from them and would have done the same to his head had he not pulled himself out of the doorway in time.

"They're here! They're here!"

The cries came from back down the hall. No doubt a nearby soldier just so happened to be close enough to hear the shot.

"Take that corner and keep them from coming down this hall. I'll handle this," Daniel ordered Mark, pointing to the end of the hallway.

"What am I supposed to do, keep a whole army at bay with a pistol?"

"Yes. They're not soldiers, Mark." Daniel turned his attention back to the open doorway with the shotgun-wielding minx inside it.

She sprang from the room, already swinging the boom stick in his direction. His left hand grabbed the nearest doorknob and pulled open the door, shielding himself from view. Daniel ducked behind the door as the crack of thunder and a flash of light signaled another shot. Splinters of wood rained on his head as a hole was blown through the door just above him.

Even with the two glances he got earlier, he knew her weapon of choice would only allow her two shots in succession. Now that she had missed, he could finally make his move.

He leaped from behind the door to the sight of the blonde bombshell frantically trying to reload her shotgun and the sound of another door swinging open. Two muscular arms tied around his waist and tackled him into a mirror, cracking it with his back.

In the next instant, his body was hammered with a dozen megaton blows in the guise of a human fist. His attacker stood at full height and towered above the average-sized man. She was at least six foot two with a stone face and a shock of platinum hair styled into a mohawk. Her only armor was her black push-up bra and matching panties. As for the rest of her uncovered body, she was a specimen of ripped anatomical perfection.

Daniel lifted himself from the floor, rising with his fist, rotating his body, and striking her in the abdomen. The half-naked giant flew backward, almost to the door she came rushing out of, before regaining her balance and squaring up. Her left foot arced low under the Guardian and she followed up with a high right that was blocked by his forearm.

Daniel fell back, shaking the stinging pain from his wrist. She was a kickboxer, and an experienced one if the force of her blows was any indication. He had to hurry. The bombshell had already reloaded her gun and was about to take aim.

The stoned-faced fighter moved in, raising her right knee and pushing forward. His throat seized, anticipating another forceful kick. Her knee arced in a semicircle and snapped back down to the floor and, in a flash of tan-colored flesh, her foot struck the left side of his jaw.

Spit flew from his mouth. The equine strength kick sent him stumbling down the hallway. She squared up to him again, her back to the double-barrel shotgun. She stepped in throwing a left jab followed by a right cross, both of which were effectively parried. But they were too lightly thrown, and Daniel could tell that there was no commitment behind them.

She raised her left knee and moved toward him again. He was ready for the fake this time. Her knee moved in a half circle again and stomped back down to the floor. She snapped her right leg up and slammed it down to the floor in a second feign. Daniel reacted too quickly, barely blocking a flying knee to the temple that threw his back into a door.

The shotgun-wielding blonde anxiously aimed the weapon at him. She didn't fire. There still wasn't enough room between him and the female Adonis that attacked him. Daniel threw two halfhearted kicks to her torso and face, both of which were blocked with her knee and hand. She answered with two mountainous kicks to his face that, even when blocked by his forearm, still pushed him further along the wall to the next door.

He needed to calm down. He had let his emotions turn him up high and now his technique was becoming sloppy. He was reacting too quickly, his body still moving as if he was engaging a ferocious demon and not a much slower, much more precise, human.

He took a deep breath, breathing the thrashing fury from his chest, and watched his opponent. She moved forward again, her left foot rising. He knew it was coming before she even started the half-circle with her knee again. He stood motionless as the left foot came down again and her right fired up in a stomping motion toward his gut. His body shifted to his right and her entire leg went crashing painfully into the hole in the door made by her ally's shotgun.

She roared. Tiny barbs of splintered wood nestled into her skin as she stuck her foot through the door up to her thigh. Daniel grabbed the inside knob and pushed the door into her face, then leaped into the air with a tight spin and slammed her in the gut with a powerful jumping back kick. The kick snatched her wedged thigh from the door, goring her with even more shards of wood, and sent her sprawling onto her back.

Daniel dove into the room as two more shots sounded off. The first tearing the top half of the door to splinters and the second following him through the opening and landing in the wall.

Daniel hopped back to his feet the moment he hit the room floor. Now was the time to attack the armed woman, before she could reload. He struck out into the hall again, expecting to see the blonde struggling to reload her weapon. He was only half right because in front of her stood the mohawked warrior, her right leg trembling under her and leaking blood onto the floor.

There was no way she could continue, she knew it and so did Daniel. What she was doing was buying time for her friend to reload her weapon and take another shot at him. Daniel blitzed her, throwing a stream of flowing attacks at her. She kept pace, defending with her hands and keeping that right leg behind her so as not to be an easy target. He pushed her back until she had to start attacking for fear of losing too much ground.

She assaulted him with strikes with her fist. This time they were totally committed. While she attacked, he maneuvered his back toward an open door and backed halfway through the doorway.

He scanned her intently. He knew it was coming. He had read her without fail and knew that she couldn't help it even if she wanted to.

It had been ingrained into her through years of repetitive drills and competitive training, so he no longer had to guess. Like a beaming sunrise in the morning, he knew it was coming. Even with an injured leg, a kickboxer can't help but kick. And kick she did, her left leg aiming for his throat.

Daniel caught her attack by the foot and twisted it in his hand, forcing her to about-face. Cruelly, he grabbed the door-knob and slammed the door closed on her ankle, hearing the snap of bone under her skin. Her proud roar became a horrible shriek and Daniel stomped into the center of her back just to add insult to her injury.

He turned just in time to catch the blonde raising her shotgun to his face.

He was too close and too deadly quick to be stopped from reaching her now. In the blink of an eye, he had moved to her side, pressing his left hand down into the fulcrum of her arm and pushing her hand up with his right. The length of the barrel crashed into her face with a wet-sounding crack and fired into the ceiling.

She fell clumsily to the floor and he stripped the gun from her hands. She looked up at him through blurred stinging vision from her broken nose, and the anger he held in check was back on his face now.

"Stay down."

His words were sharp and cold. He wanted her to know he wasn't joking. To his surprise and bewilderment, she stood to her feet and raised her fists to him. For whatever reason, she was willing to die for this. Willing to sacrifice herself for a woman he was sure didn't deserve it.

"Stay down," he repeated.

She threw a weak punch and then another. Daniel slapped them both away with one hand, still wondering why she was willing to go so far for nothing. She swung a wide kick at his head which he blocked by jamming the barrel of the sawed-off into her calf. She howled, the hot metal burning into her flesh as he pinned her leg against a mirror. He pulled the trigger, shattering the glass with the sound of Thor's hammer and blowing her foot halfway off.

Mark came thumping over, eyes wide as he surveyed the destruction of broken bones and shattered glass his new captain had left in his wake.

"Jaysis, Daniel. Maybe you should take it easy."

Daniel turned and glared at Mark with crimson-threaded eyes and blood on his face. Mark immediately knew he was talking to a brick wall. The pain and anguish in him had become a mortar-lined blockade that shut out all reason and sympathy. No one could stop him or get through to him now. The worst part of it all was that the one man who actually could stop him was the very man they were here to avenge.

Daniel wiped his face, only smearing the blood more. "Come on."

The two pushed the doors open slowly and stepped into the library. The walls were lined with books, and shelves assembled in rows were filled almost to the point of clutter.

Mark closed the doors behind him and pushed a heavy desk in front of them to buy more time. When he turned, a line of women armed with melee weapons was there to greet him.

They filled the spaces between the shelves, swinging their chains and tightening their grips around baseball bats.

Daniel stepped forward to the center of the room. "Where is Matilda?"

It was quiet enough to hear sweat drop to the floor. His eyes cruised the faces of the women who stood before him. Hard and unnerving stares were his only reply. His rage became frothing once again.

"Then I will break every one of you until I find her." Those were his last words before pouncing into the line of women, Mark following recklessly behind.

The women swarmed around the Guardians like hungry ants battling for the next meal for their queen. Squeezing so close until even light was hard pressed to get through. Daniel flipped the sawed-off in his hand and used the grip as a blunt weapon against encroaching women.

The aroma of sweat-mixed perfume assailed his nostrils as he broke a woman's nose. Brunette, blonde and pink hair whipped wildly as he slung them into bookshelves. The flash of brass knuckles and knives caught his eye as he snapped dainty wrists like twigs and buried blades into womanly limbs.

Still, they pressed, coming one after the other toward him and the man at his back.

The air was filled with the ring of pain when an attack was lucky enough to get through to him and the cries of women when they thought he would be an easy kill. His anger drove him on, his mind swallowing him now and replacing him with the little boy so filled with hate and fear. He was numb to the pain again. Numb to everything but the drive to find her, and God willing, make her pay.

"Stop! Dat's enough!"

The words cut through the action like a shark's fin through water. The women stopped and looked back toward the chubby cajun madam who had stolen their attention. Daniel saw her face and struck out for her in the frozen moment. He blew past two women and jumped over a table, sliding under a second, and popped up with the sawed-off inches from her lips.

The women rushed to her side, pressing sharp and blunt weapons to Daniel's body. That's when the doors blew open and a wave of women came pouring into the library with guns, shoving their weapons into both Guardian's faces.

"Good seeing you again, Daniel," Matilda said with an almost cynical expression.

Daniel thumbed back both hammers on his weapon. "Like-wise." His tone was malicious, his eyes beaming bubbling hatred into her relaxed countenance.

"You shoulda called first, instead of just dropping by unan-nounced like dis."

"That gift of yours not working too well for you these days? I thought you would've been able to see this coming after sending me on that wild goose chase."

She flipped a strand of loose hair from her face. "Well, I ain't think you'd be quite so livid about it. Does Padre know you down here bludgeoning his acquaintances in the middle of da night?"

Daniel glared at her painfully. "Father is dead."

He watched the new information play out on her face like an emotional crescendo. Shock became disbelief which became fear and then sorrow. He saw her facetious stare erode into stark funereal eyes. Suddenly she was just as hurt as he was, though she collected herself quickly, not wanting to show such strong emotion in front of her warrior women. Or perhaps just in front of Daniel.

Her gaze found his again, steely and stronger than before. "So what you gon do with that shotgun, boy? You came here to claim your revenge against me? And den what? You kill me and my girls here, they gon fill you up with more lead than a number two pencil, and we all gon die right in this here library. Is dat what you want?"

"My friend, my mentor, and my brother are dead. And because of you, I wasn't there to protect them. So right now, I don't give a shit."

Daniel's voice was so harsh that an echo of clicks flew around the room from the women cocking their weapons. A shotgun-wielding beauty stepped to Mark's front and shoved the barrel into his crotch and racked the pump.

Mark clenched his teeth, his lone pistol pointed at a single redhead and dozens more pointed back at him.

Matilda's eyes brimmed with conviction. "Is that so?" She turned toward her Amazonian women. "Put dem guns down, ladies."

Bewilderment spread through their ranks as the women glanced at each other, unsure of the sanity of the order given.

"Right now, damn it! Put 'em down!"

She roared at them like a general giving inescapable orders and, reluctantly, they followed, lowering their weapons to the floor. She turned back to the furious Guardian.

"Now, whatever you decide to do, dey won't harm you. You can blow my brains all over the floor and walk straight out da front doors, and ain't no one gon lay a finger on you. I promise."

Daniel felt the confusion infect him now as well.

Matilda folded her hands in front of her and stared intensely at Daniel's face. "You could pull dat trigger and send me on my way and I'd be okay with that. It just means that God's finally ready for me, but me and you both know you ain't come here for no revenge. There's another question runnin round in dat labyrinth mind of yours. It's burning on your lips, so why don't you be the man that Father made you to be and ask me."

Daniel's eyes stayed locked on her, anger swelling at her mention of his teacher. His face was pink with the blood that rushed to his head.

His lips trembled as he spoke. "As much as I want to blow your face through the back of your head right now, if God really wanted you tonight—" He squeezed the trigger and the hammer on the gun snapped forward with an echoing metal twang. "—she wouldn't have had me use my last round in that hallway."

Daniel could hear the simultaneous breaths taken by the women surrounding him as if they hadn't been breathing the entire time. He lowered the gun and let it drop to the floor. Once it settled, his empty hand snapped upward, slapping across Matilda's face deafeningly hard. The whole room exhaled a grunt as her head whipped backward. The vixens gripped their weapons tightly, aching to unleash punishment on both men.

Matilda gathered herself, brushing the mess Daniel's slap

had made of her hair from her red pulsating cheek. When she met Daniel's gaze again he was no longer the same man. The anger in his eyes was drowned by brimming tears and sadness. His fury had died and he was now vulnerable. His once harsh commanding voice was laced with shame and pleading.

He looked at the woman and let his tears fall. "Why did you do this to me?"

She looked him over, then past him, at the destruction he had wrought just to get to her.

"Come on, think we both could use a drink."

SECTION 3

The three, Daniel, Mark, and Matilda, sat around a small wooden table while the Madam poured three shots of Whiskey. She slid two glasses a short distance across the table to her weary guests. Dust and flecks of red carpet spotted the table surface. Mark snatched up his drink and downed it in one swallow. Daniel didn't touch his.

He watched Matilda anxiously as she finished her drink, the toe of his shoe digging into the char black orifice in the carpet where the grenade had gone off. She looked at his full glass, then back at him, expectantly. He half rolled his eyes and exhaled irritably before knocking the shot back and slamming the empty glass back onto the table. She nodded satisfactorily and filled the three glasses again.

A rarefied chill winded up his leg from the wide opening in the wall. He looked over at the Oldsmobile haphazardly parked in the foyer and wondered why she decided to have a drink here. There had to be at least a dozen other rooms that she could have chosen that were not shot to utter hell.

She slid the refilled glasses back toward them and slammed hers back without waiting. She hadn't said a word yet, but it was obvious to Daniel that she was unraveling. Something about tonight had her on edge. Her hands were shaking more noticeably now, and she was spilling whisky over the table whenever she went to pour.

He began to wonder if she was deserving of the pity he was currently feeling for her. She had already looked weary and apathetic when he initially met her and now she looked worse somehow.

"Maybe you should slow down," Daniel suggested, watching her fill her glass a third time.

She looked at him and gave an empty smile. "You should know better than to tell an old lady how she should grieve. I been here before, child. I know exactly what to do when I'm en d'oeuil."

That was all he needed to hear to understand that news of Father's death had hit her just as hard as anyone else. She drank her glass again and removed a gold-plated cigar case from her bra, moving to light one. Daniel could tell from how quickly she imbibed and how easily it led her to smoke that this style of mourning had become routine to her. She breathed in the toxic chemicals and exhaled a plume of poison into the chill of the air.

"Here's da truth." Her shaking had stopped. "When...*She* gives me a vision it's never whole. It's always broke and incomplete. Some time ago I had a vision that Michael was in cahoots with a powerful demon, but I ain't know for what purpose. Until tonight. You told me Father wasn't the only one dead. Any of their deaths have somethin' ta do with angels?"

Daniel nodded slowly.

Matilda's eyes dropped in dissatisfaction. "I was afraid of

dat. I believe Michael made a deal with a demon ta get rid of y'all. Tonight was his attempt at fulfilling his part of the deal."

"What kind of demon would consort with an angel?" Mark asked.

Matilda shook the ash from the tip of the cigar. "Not just any demon. I'm talking bout the first demon."

"Lucifer." Daniel's tongue retreated to the back of his throat at the mention of his name.

"There's only one question left." The inebriated woman poured herself another glass. "What did Michael ask for as part of the deal?"

"Whatever it was, maybe he didn't get it?" Mark speculated. "We're still livin' and breathin' aren't we? He couldn't keep up his end of the bargain."

Matilda shook her head. "No, he gon get it, or he got it already. I know dat much." Matilda leaned forward placing her arms on the table. "But enough about that for right now. What you gonna do bout your brother, Daniel?"

Daniel looked at the woman in suspicious confusion. She spoke as if she knew something he didn't.

"Why do I get the feeling ya aren't speaking of funeral arrangements?" Mark queried in an Irish peal.

"Cause Adam is still alive," she finished.

Daniel looked at her nervously, excitement making his heart flutter in his chest but reason and logic keeping him grounded.

"How do you know? How *could* you know? A moment ago you didn't even know about Father."

"I think me and you both know dat Adam is a special case, now don't we, Daniel?" A furtive smile crept across her face.

Mark's gaze shifted from Matilda to Daniel and back again trying to decipher her arcane words.

"My brother's dead, Matilda." Daniel's voice was flat and emotionless.

"Alohrs pas." She took a sip from her glass. "Surely, you got a little more faith den dat. Your brother is alive, Daniel, and you need to save him. Or did you think that voice you heard didn't mean nothing?"

Daniel was quiet as a graveyard after a funeral. His face was stark, outlined with worry and confusion. His mind receded to his childhood days post his journey to Hell. Laying in bed, sleepless, when a sonorous voice awoke within his mind. 'Awoke' was the perfect word because upon hearing it he felt as if it had always been there. Like a far-off siren constantly blaring but your mind doesn't recognize it until, suddenly it does, and then you realize you've been hearing it all along.

He remembered that night perfectly, every detail. The soft rain that fell against the window. The wind that howled outside, whipping the trees back and forth. The voice telling him to guard Adam with his life.

He was completely alone that night and he didn't tell a soul about it until he told Father. How in the hell did she know about it?

Smoke plumed from her mouth as she spoke. "He destined for great things, Daniel. His life ain't ending here."

His stomach swirled and his heart thumped in fast step. Her words were like honey to him, but they were far too sweet to be true.

His eyes narrowed at her assertion. "What if I don't believe you?"

The husky woman emptied her glass and puffed her cigar. "You ain't got ta believe me, but you can't lie to yourself, child. You know he's alive." She filled her glass once more. "You just afraid to admit it, ain't ya?"

"Shut up, that's not true," Daniel spat sharply.

"Uh-huh. You afraid, because you know what it mean if he *is* alive."

"Damn it, Matilda I said be quiet."

"What's she talkin about, Daniel?" Mark jumped in.

"Gon head and tell him, Daniel." Another ruthless smirk made its way across her face. "Tell him where Adam really is. Tell him, he trapped just like you was."

"Matilda..." Daniel's hands curled into rage-filled fists.

"Trapped in da one place you can't protect him. In Sheol."

Daniel shot to his feet, flipping the table and throwing it out of the room. "I said, shut the hell up!"

"You knew dis day was coming, Daniel. Sure as the sun was gonna rise, you knew. Now, if dat day is here, what you gonna do about it?"

The short woman was undaunted by his display and sat with her cigar and drink still in hand. Nearby women patrolling the manor peaked into the area to assess what damage the ruckus had caused. The madam waved them away with one hand and continued her conversation.

"You gonna leave yo brother buried underneath your former home or you gonna do what you supposed to do? What you were chosen to do."

Silence passed between them. A silence filled with biting glares and scowling faces.

Matilda's face suddenly became pleading. "Adam can't do dis alone. He's gon need his brother's help now more den ever."

Daniel glowered at her in anger. For the second time, she had manipulated his rage to the forefront. He swallowed hard and took his seat again, deciding that there wouldn't be a third time.

"I don't mean to butt in here, but what the hell is going

on?" Mark raised his hand timidly. "How do you know so much about him?"

"I had many a vision bout him." She shifted her gaze back to Daniel. "Before I even knew yo name, you was in my dreams." She took a moderate drag on her stick and blew a halo of smoke. "Who you think convinced Father to visit your house dat day?"

Daniel sat back in his seat. The full meaning of her words unfolded upon him like a dull pain in his stomach. The space between them filled by a cloud of smoke, yet her eyes cut through the smog to claim him.

"I know everything bout you, Daniel."

He gave her a cold look. "Then you know I'm about to leave."

She lifted her beverage to her lips and stopped just short of her mouth. "Not before you hear what I have ta say."

"I think I've heard enough out of you." Daniel stood to his feet and motioned to Mark to do the same. "You knew Gabriel was going to die and you chose to do nothing, you try and intimidate me with knowledge of my past and you convince my mentor to send me on a wild goose chase that costs him his life. I don't know how you ever got Father to trust you, but I'm done here."

The duo walked out into the decimated foyer and headed toward the opening that had previously been the front doors.

"Mais, I ain't want you to leave, Daniel." Matilda voiced trenchantly from behind. "But, Padre insisted."

He stopped mid-step, halfway from the door. Mark looked him in the face and knew he didn't want to address her. He wanted to keep walking right out that hole in the wall, but he wouldn't. Just as she knew he wouldn't.

He turned to face her and stared at her lackadaisical expression and waited for an explanation. She made him wait a moment longer and avoided eye contact, swirling the last swallow of whisky around in her glass.

"You ain't know him well as you think you did. We all got our secrets and he wasn't no different. His most important secret though was his dreams." She finally decided to look Daniel's way. "Did he tell you bout his dreams, Daniel? Bout the flaming door?"

Daniel nodded quickly, anxious for her to continue.

"Truthfully, he been having dat dream for years, even before you was born. The first time I met him, I was a fortune teller and he asked me to tell him his future. I wasn't really telling people's fortune, but I made a decent living faking it. Soon as I touched his hands I saw dat door, light flickering from its edges. Right dere I knew it was real, and I saw what was behind it."

"What was it? What was behind the door?" Without realizing it Daniel had found himself right back on the carpeted floor in front of Matilda, practically begging for answers.

She swallowed the last in the glass and set it on the floor before answering.

"His death."

Daniel's brow furled at the answer. Already his ears had deemed it unsatisfactory. Matilda could see his body lean away from her distastefully.

"After he told me bout the dreams he'd been having, we both was certain. I told him if he ever saw dat door in any place besides his dreams, to run from it as fast as his feet could carry him, cause once he crossed through it his life would be over."

A modicum of Daniel's anger had returned and, to his surprise, it was aimed at his mentor. How could he not tell him about this? Why would he keep something so important hidden away? The hypocrite in him slapped the back of his head. How dare he judge Father when he still had secrets of his own.

"After dat, he went on to become one of the greatest Guardians. There wasn't ever a mission too dangerous for him or too difficult to complete. Dat's where the problem started. See, Padre had a manner of pride about him, and no matter how much he was praised or how many accolades was thrown his way, he knew da truth. And da truth was dat he was a capon. A coward."

Daniel felt himself lunge at Matilda and wrap his hands around her neck. The disrespect in her voice lit flames in his chest. He swallowed the urge to strangle her and remained stoic, letting her continue.

"Padre knew dat he was only great cause he knew he wouldn't be killed. He ain't have no fear, but ta him it was the same as being spineless."

"He saved hundreds, maybe thousands, of lives." Mark leaped into the thread again. "I mean, the man was fearless. He saved our arses plenty of times. How can you call that spineless?"

"Because he knew courage isn't the absence of fear," Daniel answered Mark.

"That's right." Matilda smiled at the Guardian's words. "It's the will to go on despite it. Dat's why Father wanted you to lead them. You the bravest man he ever known, and in his mind, way more courageous den he could ever be."

Daniel felt nauseous all of a sudden. Dizziness hit him and made his knees weak. He recoiled and leaned against the wall, staring at the ceiling in a daze. Everything made sense to him now and it made him sick. Father's sudden increase in drinking and smoking, his lack of sleep, his decision to introduce Matilda, and his final words to him about courage. He could feel his throat tighten with his next words.

"He knew he was going to die."

Matilda nodded her head slowly. "Mais, weh. If Padre had one flaw, it surely was his pride. His pride ain't let him tell you da truth bout his dreams, and dat same pride fo sho couldn't let you see him die." She dragged on her cigar and flicked the ashes onto the burned part of the carpet. "So, I came up with a little white lie for him ta get you outta town for awhile. Gabriel's death just so happened to be the perfect catalyst for dat. I knew you was gonna be ornery when ya got back so I figured it be better if you thought it was all my idea. At least dat way I was sure you'd come back to me for some answers. Tomorrow morning's security detail was under direction to let you straight in but, I didn't think you'd be back so soon and in *dis* bad a mood." She motioned to the car resting inside her home.

"So what now, boss?" Mark looked at the mentally atrophied man. "What's the plan?"

"You know what ta do now," the Cajun Madam answered for him. "Go and get yo brother before it's too late."

Daniel knew she was right. There was no more time for questions. His job was to protect his brother and, no matter what, he had to see it through. He girded himself and stood ramrod from the wall.

"Let's go."

"One more thing." Matilda stood to her feet. "You can't let Raphael fight Michael."

Daniel's puzzled gaze shifted from Matilda to Mark and back. "I don't think we can influence that, and how would we even stop him if we could?"

"I know it ain't yo place, and I'm asking more than I should, but I'm asking for a reason. Somehow you gonna be able to affect his decision. I don't know how or when but you can't let him fight Michael."

"Why not?"

"Cause Michael will win." Her face was grim when she spoke. "I seen it. A battle that will light da sky and shake da heavens, but when the smoke clears, Michael descends from the sky and..."

Daniel could see the intensity in her eyes. The image had been burned into her retinas and had become unseeable.

"...and Raphael falls."

CHAPTER
TEN

F aith and Fate

SECTION I

"So, that's all that happened?" The Russian woman leaned against the church wall with her feet crossed.

Mark sat sideways on a wood dresser, one of his legs dangling off. "Yeah. Long story short, I don't think we'll be welcomed back any time soon."

"How'd he handle it?" Emmanuelle asked, resting in a pew.

Mark's eyes lifted to the left corner of their sockets, mimicking deep thought. "Well, after the initial drunken blood-lust-of-rage." He looked at Emmanuelle with a touch of remorse in his eyes. "Well, you know him, love. Silent, stoic, lost in that mind of his. He went straight into that back room when we got back and hasn't come out since." Mark ran his fingers through his wild hair. "I don't know, maybe he's given up on us."

"No." Prophet's garrulous baritone grasped everyone's attention.

He sat in the front pew directly across from the altar which held his brother atop it.

"Not yet. Not him. He just needs some time, that's all. Just give him a little bit of time."

Daniel leaned over a small ivory-colored sink in the tiny room. His face was a mess of tears that fell from his cheeks into the drain. He had finally let it all out. The barricade carefully crafted over tender areas of his conscious mind had been torn down. The talcum-white bowl swallowed the briny stream of sorrow that flowed from his face.

He lifted his head and looked into the mirror above the sink, hairline fractures wending up from its base and through its center. The faces of loved ones flashed over his reflection, eyes empty, lips slightly parted as if beckoning words lay just beyond their tongue. Gabriel, Saduj, Adam, and Father.

His name was on their lips.

He shot away from the sink and moved to the closet, snatching the door open in a jerking motion. His hands rummaged through the silk and cotton garments until coming across a black priest's cassock. He took it from its hanger and threw it to the bed. From the corner of his eye, he saw something fall to the floor inside the closet.

A wide brim, black and wool hat. Strikingly similar to the one Father used to wear with the exception that its crown was creased. It was old and dust-covered, so Daniel guessed it hadn't been worn in some time. He bent down and grabbed it, his foot bumping into a dark blue box he hadn't noticed was there.

While picking up the hat he pushed back the lid on the box revealing a pair of red clippers. His eyes moved from the trimmers to the hat in his hand and he couldn't hold back a wet-faced laugh. If nothing else, God had a sense of humor.

He threw the hat on the bed as well and went back to the sink, wiping the mirror's face with his hand. He plugged the clippers into a nearby outlet and clicked them on.

"This is for you, Father."

Mark paced back and forth across the church floor, a stressful bundle of nerves. The rubber soles of his shoes were beginning to wear from the way he dragged his feet.

In his steady Irish gait, he strolled from wall to wall with his arms folded into his chest. The timed tap of his shoes echoed throughout the empty church as he reached the wall again, whipped around, and bumped into a priest he didn't realize was there.

"Sorry, Father. Didn't realize someone else was here and—"

The remainder of his words dissipated within his mouth. Daniel stood before him wrapped in an ankle-length priest's cassock and black hat on his head.

"Daniel?"

"I guess I should lose this." He pulled the piece of white cardboard from the collar and set it on the pew next to him.

Seraphim came over, taking in this new image of him from head to toe. "You look good, Daniel."

He removed his hat and wiped his hand across almost nonexistent hair. "Thank you."

"I filled them in on everything," Mark said. "So, what's the move, boss?"

"I'm going to get my brother. This isn't an official mission, so none of you have to come."

"You're not going alone," Seraphim spoke as if she were a mother warning a child.

"That's right. It's my fault he's there in the first place. If I had kept an eye on him, he wouldn't have—"

"It's not your fault, Mark." Daniel placed a soothing hand

on his shoulder. "I'm not going to fight you on this. If you want to help, then come, but we're a little short on weaponry."

"Will this help?"

The sound of Prophet's voice made Daniel look up in time to catch a weapon in his hand. His fingers glided over its dark surface and he admired it with gleaming eyes. A beautifully designed katana with a black hilt and sheath. He pressed his thumb into the hand guard, made into the shape of a large cross, and slid it from its scabbard. It shone in the light of the church, a tiny cross engraved into the very tip of the blade.

Daniel returned his gaze to Prophet. The giant man now stood broad-chested, his right hand methodically polishing the steel surface of his left. He raised his mechanical arm and turned his wrist with a whirring, humming sound. The new armament was even bigger than his original, metallic silver in color with joints trimmed in grey.

Not only was it new to his body, but it seemed to glimmer with an unused glow. The telltale glow that marked something as not only newly applied but newly crafted as well. The hand on this model arm was twice the size of a normal human hand and its knuckles were reinforced with four metallic silver rivets branded with crosses.

"How did you—" Daniel started.

"I believe that's my queue."

Out from behind the metal-armed giant stepped a short pudgy figure with shaggy brown hair. His right hand gripped the handle of a brown bag and his left moved to adjust the horn-rimmed glasses that sat on his chubby face.

"Hello, Theodore," Daniel said, extending his hand.

"Please, you know I prefer '*The Maker*'."

The pudgy man shook Daniel's hand and sat his bag on a nearby tabletop. He opened the bag and began digging through its contents.

"I was on my way to your base when Seraphim called me. Luckily for you, I was in the neighborhood with your weapons." He began pulling various bladed utensils from the bag and laying them across the table. "Unluckily for you, my weapons cache is lighter than usual today. You'll just have to make due."

The Guardians came to the table, picking their weapons. There wasn't much to choose from besides curved daggers and twisted knives either shaped in the form of crosses or with crosses engraved into them.

"You wouldn't happen to have any unholy or cursed weaponry, would you, Maker?" Mark asked examining the handle of a weapon.

The Maker gave him a puzzled stare. "Usually, only Father asks for that kind of thing."

"Yeah, and now we know why," Prophet said, still admiring his new arm.

"Well, sadly, I don't at the moment. But I do have a few new items that might be of interest." He dug through the bag again and placed four black orbs the size of softballs on the table. "My latest experiment. They haven't been field tested yet, so I thought you guys could give them a try and let me know what you think."

Emmanuelle lifted one from the group and examined it closely. The ball was almost perfectly smooth except for a few grooves made for holding it.

"What does it do?" The Russian asked.

"It's pretty simple to operate." The Maker took one in his hands and demonstrated. "You just twist it and toss it into a hole or wherever a demon may be hiding and let it work its magic." The short man went through the pretend motions of twisting and throwing the ball. "It's pretty ingenious if I do say so myself."

"Good. We'll take them," Daniel said curtly, stuffing one in his pocket.

Emmanuelle, Prophet, and Seraphim snatched the others off the table.

Mark fumed when he saw that all of the black spheres were gone. "Feck it anyway."

The Maker snapped his fingers as a thought came to mind. "That reminds me, I've got something you may enjoy, Mark."

The pudgy man reached back into his bag and pulled from it two gold-colored contraptions.

He wore a giddy grin as he handed them to Mark. "Put them on."

Mark slid the items onto his fingers. They fit like brass knuckles but with the difference of having three four-inch blades protruding from between each knuckle. Mark swung them through the air, listening to the sound of them cutting through the wind. They were remarkably light, but he could tell they were deadly sharp.

"So, I'm the Wolverine now, aye? Thanks, Maker. You always know how to cheer me up."

The short man gave a silent stare at the men and women perusing his small armory. "So." He cleared his throat nervously. "You guys going to war or something?"

"Hopefully not." Daniel tapped a button on the sheathe and a pyramid-shaped black blade with serrated edges flipped onto its round end. "You can never be too careful though."

He pushed the hidden weapon back into the sheath and moved in closer to the man. Close enough to be personal.

"I need you to do me a favor."

The Maker almost immediately started shaking his head. "No, no, no, no. You know I don't get involved with the field. Not after the 'incident'. No, no. I'm done being the laughing stock."

Daniel held his hand up to silence the man. "I need you to watch Ezekiel." He looked over toward the tattooed man resting on the altar. "Just keep an eye on him while we're gone. Check his pulse every once in a while, make sure he doesn't pass in his sleep."

The pudge-faced man was still shaking his head in disagreement. Daniel could tell he was uncomfortable with the idea.

"Please, Theo. My brother is lost out there somewhere. I don't want Prophet to lose his."

The Maker seemed to cringe at Daniel's words. "All right."

"Thank you."

Daniel motioned toward the exit and the Guardians moved to the door. The Maker watched them head through the doors in uneasy silence.

Daniel stepped out into the cold late-night air, his team preceding him. He turned around and looked up to the roof of the church. To his surprise, Raphael was sitting atop the entrance, his feet hanging just above the doorway.

"What makes you think your brother still lives?" He asked, voice near monotone.

Daniel watched the heavenly being, letting an empty silence pass between them. "I wanted to thank you for helping us earlier. I was out of line for asking you and I know that."

As he spoke, Raphael pushed from the roof and fell to the grass. Once again he was like a feather on the wind, more floating or gliding than falling.

"If Michael does want you dead, you might be doing him a favor by returning."

"We don't plan to engage in a fight. We're going to get my brother, and we're going to get the hell out." Daniel turned around and followed his allies.

In four steps, Raphael addressed him again. "Do you think

Michael is there? That would be reason enough for me to join you."

Daniel stopped in his tracks. Raphael's words bore into him like a drill, striking a tender nerve that played Matilda's words over in his mind like a scratched record.

"*You can't let Raphael fight Michael.*"

Daniel turned, facing the angel. "No, I don't."

"And if Michael *is* there, you won't have much choice in the matter of engaging in a fight."

Daniel wracked his brain for an excuse to deter the angel from following. He could feel Raphael's eyes scanning him in ways he could only imagine.

The seraphim leaned in closer toward him. "You are apprehensive. Why?"

The Guardian tried to loosen up. "*Keep eye contact, don't stutter and, for God's sake, don't chew on your gums.*" He stepped closer to Raphael to further show he had nothing to hide. "I wanted to ask you, why you told those demons about our meeting. Why did you send them to attack us?" Daniel stared accusingly at Raphael.

"I was testing you, to see if my sister was right to offer so much time to you. I wanted to see if you were worthy of her love."

Daniel's anger was rising again. "Any one of us could have died."

"I left an entire container of holy water for you to find."

"That doesn't matter, you treated us like disposable pawns in a chess game. And all because you didn't have faith in Gabriel."

"I trust my sister, Daniel. Whom I have little faith in is humans."

Daniel stared fiercely at a being infinitely more powerful

than he. "If that's true, then maybe you're on the wrong side of this war."

Daniel turned to walk away and Raphael caught him by the shoulder.

"You haven't answered my question yet. How do you know your brother still lives?"

The Guardian gave him a cutting glare.

"Because I have faith."

The sound of hard, uncompromising footsteps over broken stone and shivered metal carried endlessly on the early morning wind.

Michael walked atop the mound of rubble, surveying the remnants of the guardian's home. All that remained was a pile of wreckage. A small mountain of plaster, steel, and wood with giant stone slabs jutting outward from the mound.

Michael looked across acres of land at the sun peaking into existence.

"We need to speak with you."

The words came from behind him. He turned to a group of five of his siblings. Their faces were bleak.

"Then speak, my brothers."

A feminine figure stepped forward, her hair red and curly and falling past her shoulders. Her eyes, fog grey.

"When we joined you, we agreed that this war would be between angels, not mankind. Why, then, have you made unsanctioned attacks against humans?"

"Your naïveté surprises me. Did you really think this war would end without a drop of human blood being spilled?"

"You're the naive one here, Michael." A bald angel with

eyes of deep purple stepped up. "Did you honestly believe you could kill Guardians without suffering any casualties?"

"You're right. I should have made my intentions clear before now." Michael turned around and went back to star gazing. "I will make a formal apology to the council, until then, return home and await my orders."

"The council has convened and we have already discussed your affront thoroughly," the purple-eyed angel snapped.

Michael turned slowly back toward him, suspicion permeating his voice. "Have you?"

"We have decided to individuate ourselves from you. You are no longer commander of this army."

His siblings could sense his anger before it even showed on his face.

"I thought I smelled the stench of betrayal," Michael's words spat from his lips in disgust.

"We don't believe your interests, and your siblings' interests, converge any longer. Your actions have directly caused the deaths of two of our own. One of which being an arch, a captain of her fold. That said, the council does not wish to take further action against any human sect. Did you think these acts would come without consequence?"

"How dare you speak to me as if you were my equal." Michael stepped up to his brother, his voice low yet holding an irate flicker. "*I* began this rebellion. *I* am the reason we have come this far and *I* will win it. This is *my war!*"

Michael doubled over in sudden agony. His arms wrapped around his stomach as he hunched over. His eyes widened and thin green veins meandered circuitously from his belly, past his shoulders, up his neck, and to his face. His eyes flashed bright green.

"You have the tinge of a demon about you," his brother said with caution lacing his words.

His grey-eyed sister asked, nearly knowing, and all the while fearing the answer. "My God, Michael, what have you done?"

The Seraph pulled his head from his knees as the tint in his eyes faded. "Yet another sacrifice I've made for my family. I've brokered a deal with The Morning Star." He could hear them gasp as he said his name. "I will end this war."

His brothers and sisters watched him in dreaded amazement. The words had been sucked out of their mouths. His eyes lit green again. He didn't bother to hide it.

"Abomination." The bald angel finally found the words.

His siblings gasped again.

"You're mad, Michael. This curse has corrupted you. You cannot maintain your existence like this. A single body can't play host to demonic and angelic power simultaneously. It will destroy you!"

Michael smiled grimly, black blood on his lips. "Then so be it."

"Then our decision to extricate you was the correct one."

The gathering of divine hosts turned away from him and walked out of his presence. His sister, the misty-eyed redhead, was all that remained. She watched pain, the color of jungle vines, invade his body. She was sure it was agonizing, but he didn't show it.

"He is wrong," she started and left the words hanging in the air. "You were corrupt before you had this power." She turned and followed her brethren out of sight.

"Angels. Yeesh."

Michael whipped around and cast his eyes on a hooded man sitting on an outcropping of stone with his back to him. He held a pack of cigarettes in his right hand and tapped the case lightly against his left palm.

"One day they're smothering you in divine kisses, and the

next..." The man got up and walked past Michael, barely acknowledging his presence. "...well, and the next they're not." He turned to face him, still tapping the pack of smokes. "Don't worry. I've been in a similar situation, so you're in good company."

"Don't ever liken your selfish, prideful war with my cause. Your lust for power was the driving force behind your rebellion. I fight for my brothers and sisters, not for myself."

The hooded man slid a cigarette into his mouth. Its tip ignited the moment it touched his lips. "You may be right. I lost fair and square to you, Michael." He took a single puff on the white stick and took it halfway down. "But, at least I didn't get kicked out of the fight by my own army." He smiled mockingly, smoke fissuring through his teeth. "It's kinda pathetic, don't you think?"

His wide grin grew into rolling laughter and Michael snatched him off his feet by the collar.

"Don't you mock me! I should tear that flapping tongue of yours from your—"

The seraph dropped his captive and fell to his knees in pain for a second time. The hooded man fixed his ruffled clothing and finished his cigarette with a second puff.

"Calm down, Michael." He placed a second stick in his mouth. "You'll raise your blood pressure." He took another impossible drag on it. "I have to say I'm disappointed in you, Michael. I mean, I give you demonic powers like you asked, and you don't deliver on your end. The Guardians are still alive, so I feel like I'm being cheated here. You wouldn't be trying to cheat me, would you, Michael?"

The writhing angel gave an intense stare, his eyes flashing bright green again. He didn't respond.

"No, of course not. You're an arch of your word." The hooded figure finished his cigarette in a second drag and flicked it away. "There is, however, the matter of the debt I'm owed since you couldn't keep to our bargain. Don't get me wrong, I would normally let it slide since we're family and all, but I *am* running a business here. And if I cut you a break I have to cut everyone else a break. Next will come wage increases, equal pay, unions, and honestly, do I look like a Socialist to you?" He removed a third stick from the pack and lit it in his mouth. "So, here's what I purpose, you do an odd job here and there for me until your debt is paid. I could use someone of your caliber working for me."

Michael showed his teeth in a bloodied and malicious smile. "Sheol would freeze over first."

"Defiant to the end. But, you're in no position to argue. We had a deal, Michael and you still owe me."

Michael tried to straighten himself, but the pain wouldn't allow it. The best he could do was to place one foot down and rest on his knee.

"And if I returned your powers to you? What then?"

The man took a tremendous breath on the cigarette, finishing it in record time and flinging it away.

"Let's explore your options here." He took a seat on an outcropping of stone next to Michael, resting his arms on his knees. "You could keep the gift I gave you, find Raphael, kill him, and win this war. After that, you could hunt down the remaining Guardians at your leisure and finish our deal. Hell, I'm even willing to let you keep the powers to help you do it. Free of charge, of course. Or..." He extended his palm to Michael. "...you can take my hand and return them to me, and lose this war."

Michael's eyes hovered over his outstretched hand as he contemplated. The hooded man gave an eerie stare as if he already knew what Michael's decision would be. The seraph stood to his feet, the pain finally subsiding.

The nefarious man tucked his hand into his pocket upon realizing Michael's choice. "I knew you'd make the right choice, so I've brought you a gift."

He motioned to the edge of the tree line at the bottom of the mountain of debris. A plainclothes man stood near the rubble looking up at them, his face devoid of emotion. A woman stepped next to him holding the same expression on her face. They were joined by two others, then five, then ten, and more. In a short while, the entire area was surrounded by men and women of various shapes, sizes, and age. They were silent, their faces expressionless, their eyes flickered green.

"Since you no longer have an army, I figured I'd offer you mine. They're class three, pushovers, I know, but until I feel I can trust you, they're all you'll be getting for now."

"You don't trust *me*? That's hysterical," Michael said without an ounce of humor in his voice.

"Even demons need trust, Michael." He climbed to his feet and stuck another cigarette between his teeth. "What do you think we are, monsters?"

The white stick lit itself in his mouth as a stentorian screech pierced the air before being abruptly silenced. They both looked up in the direction of the rising sun and a soft chuckle fell from Michael's lips.

"It seems I may be settling my debt with you sooner than expected."

SECTION 2

"This is a bad idea," Mark said, wringing the chill from his hands.

"Yeah, you said that already," Prophet remarked, irritatedly.

"Well, obviously I haven't said it enough cuz we're still fucking here."

"Nobody forced you to come. You could've stayed at the church."

Mark paced back and forth over the wet grass, rubbing his palms together for warmth. "Now there's a brilliant idea. Yeah, while my mates go on a suicide mission to rescue a team member, I'll just sit this one out at the church, right."

"Regardless, you chose to be here. Besides, weren't you there when the witch told Daniel to come?"

Mark stopped and leaned against a tree. "That don't make it any less suicidal, does it?"

"Quiet, back there. You're making it hard to focus."

The Russian woman chastised the two men from atop an outcropping of earth. A telescopic lens in her hands, she lay prone across a mound of dirt above marshy grassland so wet that it was nearly a swamp.

"Michael's meeting with other angels. Five, by my count." She turned a dial on the scope and zoomed in. "Can't tell what they're discussing, but it must be important."

"Great, more angels," Mark complained. "We still don't have anything to deal with them."

"We're not here to fight, we're here for Adam. Maybe they'll leave," the bald man suggested.

"Hold on." Seraphim sat up. "Something's wrong with Michael."

"What is it?" Mark asked.

"He fell. He looks like...he looks like he's in pain."

Expressions of bewilderment were passed through their ranks.

"What the hell is going on up there?" Prophet questioned.

"Wait a minute. It looks like they're leaving. Yes, the other angels are leaving. I don't think they're coming back."

Prophet smirked at his Irish friend. "See that? The woman upstairs has got our backs."

"What about Michael?" Mark ignored Prophet's smug positivity.

"Still there." Seraphim wiped her eye with her hand and placed it back onto the scope. "Someone else is there. Can't make his face because of the hood, but he isn't an angel."

Prophet's eyebrow climbed his forehead. "Demon, maybe?"

"No. I think this one is human."

More confused looks were switched.

Mark's forehead creased in confusion. "What the hell is Michael doing conversing with a human?"

"Get ready." Daniel cut in, taking everyone's attention. "As soon as they leave, we're moving in." He turned away from them and walked up behind Emmanuelle, standing alone amidst the trees. "It's almost time."

She nodded her head without meeting his gaze. Daniel watched her habitually rub her fingers and approached nearer.

"How's the hand?"

She looked at him and held up her palm, her injured hand now fully intact. "They don't call him the angel of healing for nothing." She dropped her hand and began rubbing her fingers profusely again. "Still hurts though, and he left scars." She showed him the flesh-colored rings that circled her index and middle finger.

"He intentionally left the scars."

"Oh. I guess even when he's being nice he's still an asshole."

Daniel smiled. "Just be glad you don't have to have surgery now. Anyway, I don't think this will happen again, so try not to lose any more limbs."

She gave a hollow laugh that dripped with sadness. He could tell that pain wasn't the only reason she rubbed furiously at her hand. She needed to get something off her chest, and this time he waited for her to speak.

"I'm sorry for putting you in this position. I know we only spent one night together and I made it more than what it was. I just felt so close to you, I thought...I *wanted* you to feel the same way. I'm sorry I put so much pressure on you."

"You don't have anything to apologize for, Emmanuelle. *I* caused this. I was hurt and angry and...I used you. That was wrong. I'm sorry."

She laughed again. This time a genuine one.

"So, it *is* possible."

"What?"

"To steal your heart."

Daniel watched as she turned to look at him. Her eyes

bored like chlorophyll-colored lasers into his and he realized that she knew his secret. Somehow, through her own deductive reasoning or perhaps merely woman's intuition, she had uncovered what he thought he had carefully hidden.

Tearing away the shadow of such a meaningful lie, Daniel suddenly felt vulnerable in front of her. Naked in a way he had never been before and was not comfortable with.

"Daniel, something is happening!"

Seraphim's voice came through excitedly and both guardians dropped the conversation and headed to her. She remained perched on the crop of earth, still peering through the scope in her hands.

"There are demons out there. There must be at least fifty of them, coming from all directions. They've surrounded the base."

"Shit," Prophet growled. "Don't even say it."

Mark held his arms in the air helplessly as Prophet stared daggers into him.

"This was a bad idea," Daniel spoke Mark's words for him.

"What about Adam? If he's alive, he may not survive much longer down there," Emmanuelle said.

"Yeah, boss. I'm not one to throw my life away on a whim, but you say the word and we're with ya."

Prophet nodded in agreement. "It's your call, D."

Daniel was already chewing on the inside of his mouth. His mind racked itself with the possible outcomes of his next action. He was Captain now, just like he wanted to be, and the lives of four people, his friends, were now in his hands. He felt their eyes on him, tracing the lines of indecision on his face. He trusted every one of them with his life, and they trusted him in return. They would follow him into war if he asked.

"We're leaving."

There was a moment of shocked silence as they waited for his explanation. Even Seraphim turned to face him.

"I won't risk your lives against impossible odds. My brother means the world to me, but I have a responsibility to you all now."

Silence soaked the air.

"This mission is over."

Seraphim squinted as if forcing an image into focus. She raised the scope back to her eye and looked into the nearby trees. Her face had gone slack.

"Cover, now!"

Her words were almost whispered but were spoken with such intensity that they knew she was serious. That, and the fact that instantly after her warning she was rolling down off her perch and into a swampy mire.

The others followed suit, ducking behind overgrown vegetation and scurrying up trees in a flash. A few minutes of ubiquitous silence later, they found out why they were hiding.

Trudging through the foliage came a pride of demons camouflaged in human skin. Though they wore human guises, the Guardians could see past the subterfuge of earthly tissue. They were actually slender pale creatures. Their skin stretched tightly around their bones giving them a skeletal appearance. Their heads were elongated versions of human skulls with razor-sharp teeth and bulging grey eyes that never blinked. The length and curve of their spines gave them an animalistic look as if they belonged hunched down on all fours, though they stood and walked upright.

Their feet stamped ungracefully through the grass and their faces were fixed in a single direction. They marched toward the gathering of their kind single-minded as if they were being pulled by an invisible force and nothing else existed. The group of ten moved past the guardian's hiding places and onto their former base. The Guardians remained still a few minutes after the group had gone just to be sure they hadn't been discovered.

Seraphim rose slowly from the mire and crawled onto the shore. The other Guardians began to move from their respective hiding spots when the unceremonious plodding of more footsteps came near. They all froze again and the blonde woman dropped to the ground, hoping the muck on her body would blend her in with the rest of the foliage. The group was a trio this time, two of them leading a third that was dragging behind them.

They walked through the shallow mire directly past where Seraphim lay. She shoved her face into the mud and took shallow breaths. She knew they had but only to look down and she would be discovered.

The first two moved past without issue, sloshing their way through the thick water. The third strode past her head and into the swamp where his foot kicked into hers, jerking him into a stumble.

The demon regained his balance and looked accusingly into the filth-ridden waters. The sound of sloshing footsteps through liquid returned, but they were slower than before and going in the wrong direction. Seraphim held her breath when she realized the footsteps were coming toward her.

The demon moved slowly to her and her hand inched closer to her waist where a curved dagger waited. The creature leaned over her, perpetually sniffing her mud and grass-covered form as if recognizing the scent but being unable to place it.

He moved up her body, his legs on either side of her, his nose inches from her head. A deep growl gurgled forth and she knew she had been made.

The next sound she heard was of punctured flesh and a

BETWEEN HEAVEN & HELL

short grunt of pain as the demon that bestrode her fell on top of her with a trio of four-inch blades through its temple.

The demon's face lay beside hers, stapled to the ground, and above it was her Irish comrade with an index finger to his lips. The two lay atop one another, a slain demon between them, listening for the return of the two that had already passed.

A moment of quiet passed, then more. Finally, Mark guessed the others had wandered far enough off where they couldn't hear his stealthy attack. He lifted his head only to find himself staring into the boiling eyes and snarling face of the very demon he was trying to avoid.

The creature dove into him, snatching him off of Seraphim and splashing into the water. The demon held his face under and let him thrash wildly for air.

Mark could hear the maniacal howling of the beast that denied him oxygen even from the bottom of the murky pool. Suddenly, the beast's weight was pulled off him all at once. He returned to the surface in time to see Prophet swing his attacker into a tree and hear its spine break in two places.

The final demon leaped through the air, falling toward the metal man. In a flash, Daniel was in front of him, sliding free his sword with the ease of undoing a zipper. His blade flashed once as he stepped past the pouncing monster and when its feet returned to the ground the demon had fallen into two halves.

Prophet walked to the demon he had crippled and watched him let out an ear-piercing warble. His face twisted at the sound, it was so loud and incomprehensible. The Guardian's metal fist crashed into his face, reducing the scream to a whimper. He tapped a switch on his arm and from his elbow sprang a long steel piston. A second tap and the cylinder plummeted down with so much force, the creature's head seemed to explode.

"Where in the hell can I get me one of those?" Mark wiped the slime from his face.

"No time for small talk." Seraphim was already back on her patch of earth with scope in hand. "If we're going to leave we'd better do it now because that option is closing fast." She looked at Daniel grimly. "That thing just alerted its friends. They're coming for us."

"How many?"

"All of them."

Daniel felt his body go cold. There was only one other place he had faced so many demons at once. The one place that made his eidetic memory a curse, because he would never rid his mind of it.

"So, what do we do, Daniel?"

Emmanuelle's voice brought him back to present time. His friends and teammates looked to him again waiting for his decision.

"Run."

As he spoke he moved through the men and women and beat a hasty retreat. Without another word or second thought, the Guardians followed. The five ran toward the light of the rising sun, weaving past tall thin Cypress trees and twisted oaks with the fading moon on their backs. Quick and sharp breaths were smothered by the sound of their pounding feet on the grass.

A new sound joined the chorus that made Daniel's blood freeze. A sound similar to a stampede of horses, closing in from behind them. Daniel ventured a glance and saw the ten demons that had trotted past them earlier were now barreling down at them on all fours. Saliva leaked from their mouths as they moved, cat-like in the dark, jumping from trees and flipping over wet patches of swamp water.

They closed the distance frighteningly fast.

Daniel and Seraphim lead the group while Mark and Emmanuelle filled the middle and Prophet was last. The chocolate giant would be their first victim. The weight of his new metallic appendage was hindering his mobility. He could go no faster.

Prophet heard the growls of the beasts that chased him and could almost feel their jaws on the back of his neck. He had to make a decision and he wasn't the type to go down without a fight.

Daniel turned his head again and met the giant's gaze as if he knew what he was thinking. Prophet gave a slight nod of his head and slid to a stop, whipped around, and knocked the first demon out of the air with his steel fist.

Daniel screamed Prophet's name and reversed course, flinging himself headlong into battle. He flashed his sword, cleaving through the skull of the first demon that tried to take Prophet from behind. A second landed in muddy grass next to him and swung ivory claws past his face. He spun away from the attack into a low arching strike that opened the beast's stomach. Before he could scream, Daniel had buried his blade into his chest.

Two more sprang up in front of him before he had time to remove his weapon from his previous opponent's body. They struck like lightning, but three small knives flew past Daniel's head and caught them in the chest. They fell back in pain and Daniel's Latin savior stepped beside him, brandishing four more knives. She gave him a playful wink and began hurling more into the cluster of demons.

"Save some for me." Mark joked while sliding the Maker's

latest gifts onto his knuckles. "Let's see what these things can do."

One of the monsters walked toward the Irish man, a wicked grimace across the demon's face. Mark blew a kiss at the creature and ducked her wild swing. He danced around each blow, making them miss widely as he bounced on his toes. The demon struck down with her right and Mark eased past the attack, landing a right hook to her left ribcage. The demon's skin opened like wrapping paper on Christmas day, green blood spraying from her side.

She yelped at the sudden pain and retreated from Mark in fear. He charged in after her, unwilling to let her escape and landing two more blows to her sternum and ending with an uppercut to her chin. Her mouth filled with blood, and a second later the demon was on her back in the mud.

Mark brought both blood-covered weapons to his puckered lips. "Maker, I love ya."

A hand grabbed him by the collar, pulling him toward the other Guardians.

"Let's get back to the life-or-death battle, please."

Seraphim threw the man back into the fray and followed, dragging twin daggers through soft flesh with practiced speed. One of the demons lunged at her and she cut him down before his feet returned to the ground. Another swiped its talons at her and she covered with her left blade while slipping the right between his ribs, then into the side of his neck, kicking his feet out from under him and dropping him to the ground.

As the final demon was crushed under Prophet's arm, Daniel pointed the green-hued tip of his sword into the distance.

"It's too late."

Rolling like an avalanche, came the thunderous sound of

fifty demons, each drooling for a chance to kill a Guardian. Each wanting to lay claim to a piece of them.

"I think it's time to see what The Maker's toys can do."

Daniel lifted a softball-sized black orb from his coat pocket and twisted it. A ticking noise, not unlike the sound an old stopwatch would make, came from the ball. He threw the orb out into the coming fusillade and watched them scatter with screams of pain and cries of agony on their lips.

His brow furled in confusion because he didn't see the ball do anything. No explosion or anything noticeable, yet the demons were hurrying away from the sphere as if it were killing them.

"What the hell?" Prophet started.

"I don't know," Daniel answered. "Throw another one."

Prophet twisted his, filling the air with more chattering ticks, and rolled it hard into the fleeing crowd. This time they could hear a distant but audible 'click' before the demons scattered again, clawing at their bodies as if they were on fire. This time Daniel noticed the burns on their skin and finally pieced together what was happening to them.

"Holy gas," he said under his breath.

"What?" Prophet asked.

"Vapors. It's like condensation in a can. It's spraying blessed water moisture into the air."

Daniel couldn't hold back a smirk at the thought that he had used a similar tactic not long ago to defeat a powerful fire demon. They had successfully defeated a portion of the army that came down on them, but they knew there weren't enough bombs left to defeat them all. The horde still closed on them.

Daniel moved to Seraphim's side. "When I tell you, Sera, drop that bomb."

Seraphim raised a Russian eyebrow. "Right here?"

"Yes."

Daniel returned to Prophet's side at the forefront of the group.

"Hope you got a plan, D."

"We'll see, Superman."

The crowd of snapping monsters closed in on the warriors and just as they came within striking distance, Daniel shouted.

"Now!"

Seraphim twisted the device and dropped it amid the Guardians. After the incessant ticking, a loud 'click' erupted from the ball and five small openings appeared to release the gas with a soft hiss.

The first wave of demons toppled, falling to the ground as they crashed into an invisible wall of acid. They clawed at their blackened skin, their screams pierced the sky and the Guardians took advantage. Daniel cut down three in a single sword swing while Prophet cracked the skulls of two more with his jackhammer of an arm.

The second wave fell as easily as the first and the third lost half of their rank before pulling back. The Guardians gave chase, murdering them as they fled, but pulling back as they moved out of range of the vapor bomb. The hiss from the ball dissipated until it ceased altogether and the Guardian's sense of rabid invulnerability was gone. All that was left of their misty protection was hanging in the cool morning air.

They were nearly defenseless now.

A strong enough breeze would eliminate the remaining wall of protection around them and they would be forced to contend with the remaining horde. They stood back to back, forming a defensive circle, waiting for the monsters to enter. The demons surrounded the huddled group of five, waiting just outside the invisible wall that defended them.

"Well done."

A calm voice amid such turmoil surprised the warriors.

They were all out of breath, their lungs filling and contracting rapidly to feed their hungry muscles. Their bodies tensed when Michael came strolling between the demonic ranks and up to them.

"I didn't think you'd come back after losing your home. I'm not sure why you would but to make my job easier. For that, I thank you."

"This is insane, Michael," Daniel shouted. "You've collaborated with demons and you've attacked Guardians. You're going to start a war between humans and angels. Is that what you want?"

"Why not? You know, I always knew it would come to this. Since the moment you were declared best-loved, I knew it would come down to angels or humans. I just never thought *I* would be the one to ignite the flames of war...but I'm glad I am."

Daniel stepped out of formation and walked closer to the archangel. "I only have one question. Did you kill Gabriel?"

Michael's face was the picture of befuddlement which slowly gave way to a glare of recognition. "You all loved her, didn't you?" He scanned the rest of the fatigued humans. "All of you."

He gave a slight, almost sorrowful, smile.

"How insignificant. Your love is meaningless in the stretch of an angel's time. Interesting and entertaining, but ultimately futile. Like the love between a dog and his master. The master cares for the dog, pets him, and plays with him. He even allows the mutt to believe it's part of the family. He may even dress it up like a human and give it a human name. But the truth is something the dog can never know or understand." The angel came within arm's distance of Daniel. "That at the slightest hint of belligerence or disobedience, the master will drag him into the backyard and put a bullet through his head without a second thought." Michael's face was one of repugnance. "Human love. Frail, infinitesimal love."

"You didn't answer my question," Daniel replied ignoring everything Michael had said.

"Yes, I killed her. So what now, Daniel? Will you swear to avenge my sister? Promise on your life, or your very soul, that you will kill me?"

The Guardian let a cold silence pass between them, his eyes bloodshot at the thought of the corrupted angel murdering Gabriel.

"You're goddamned right." Daniel walked slowly toward the seraph. "I don't care how long it takes, how many of your damn demons I have to cut down, or even if I have to make a deal with the devil to do it." He lifted his sword and pointed it at Michael, the sun reflecting off the blade. "Mark my words, you *are* going to die here."

Michael smiled and held open his hand as if offering something. "Please, you first."

He walked away and the skeleton creatures began moving in. The holy mist was long gone and now the Guardians would have to fight the remainder of the demons without any protection. This would be their last stand.

"That's enough, Michael."

The voice traveled on the air loud and gruff but was sweet as a mother's lullaby to the fatigued warriors. The demons parted like the Red Sea as Raphael walked from the opposite direction as Michael, the yellow disc in the sky lighting his back.

SECTION 3

The beasts screeched and bucked as if the seraph being in their presence was enough to cause them searing agony. They backed away from him and hissed like cornered snakes wanting to strike but too fearful of the outcome. A lump of stone fell into Daniel's stomach at Raphael's sudden appearance.

"Raphael, what are you—"

The angel held his hand up and silenced the Guardian. "I think you've lied to me enough for one day, Daniel. Did you really think I couldn't see through your intentions? You suspected Michael might be here, yet you didn't want me to come. Do you not have faith that I can best him in single combat?"

"No, it's not that—" Daniel started.

"Well, why don't you show them otherwise brother?" Michael interrupted. "Show *me* otherwise."

Raphael's eyes grew black. "I intend to."

Daniel stepped in front of the dark-eyed arch. "Raphael, you can't do this. You can't fight him. You'll die if you do."

Raphael looked at him. He could feel his dark eyes moving through him as if he were made of glass.

"You cannot stop this, Daniel. This moment is beyond your control. This battle is preordained, destined to happen."

A single demon, either from bloodlust or fear, lunged at Raphael. Without turning his head, he snatched the demon by the throat, bending him backward until his body curved into a grotesque 'L' shape. While staring at Daniel, Raphael snapped the demon's neck and dropped him to the ground, steam wafting from his black claws after touching the creature.

"You should leave here," Raphael warned. "Right now."

Daniel backed away from the angel, sensing he was beyond coercion. Before he left earshot, Raphael called out to him.

"Don't forget what you came here to do, Daniel."

Adam's face flashed into the forefront of Daniel's mind. He nodded his head. Raphael's intervention reaffirmed that they may be able to do what they came here for. Daniel rejoined his team, and that's when the unbelievable happened.

The black trench coat that hung to Raphael's knees rose as if lifted by a swirling wind. As it rose it underwent a starling transformation, brightening into a glowing green color and growing tiny sparkling divots. Even his body hummed a soft glow, producing a pure white light that stood out from the sun's yellow rays and grew brighter until it was piercing. The form of his coat began to reshape itself, detaching from around his body and hovering above him as miraculous green wings.

Anarchy erupted among the demons. They bellowed and screeched raucously, dispersing from the angel in terror. They clawed and snapped at each other in their escape as if the light from his body burned them like flames from the sun. The Guardians were rooted to the ground, eyes wide with astonishment.

The bright light dimmed and the reddish-brown color of

his skin could be seen, as well as his naked form. His body was similar to that of a muscular human only at least nine feet tall and with a twisting black tattoo that moved as if it were alive, winding around his limbs and up his neck. His elbows, knuckles, and knees were dotted with sharp bony protrusions of ivory color and his teeth were razor sharp.

His wings were the masterpiece of his physical canvas, glistening beautifully in the light with thousands of, what could only be described as emeralds, embedded within each feather.

The human men and women watched with gaping mouths at what stood before them. *Stood*, was a stretch because, though his legs were fully extended, since his transformation, his feet never touched the ground. They were in awe at the impossible being that lofted silently on the chill air. Graceful without effort, terrifying and gorgeous simultaneously.

Another piercing light, not of the sun, enveloped the area. This time it was Michael who was undergoing the change.

It was the same ordeal. Giant naked form, sharp teeth, and black undulating markings. All the same except for his wings. Michael's wings were deep, blood-red, and reflected light like they were polished steel.

They were segmented vertically from the bottom up, coming together just before reaching the top. They moved like wind chimes in the breeze, but it was obvious they moved of their own accord. At some moments they would close altogether, fusing into complete, unseparated wings before suddenly breaking again and swaying as if caught by a gust of wind.

The Guardians still hadn't moved. The sight of two seraphim in natural form had paralyzed them. If they had been asked to choose whose wings were most beautiful, it would be a fool's game.

"Are you ready?" Michael asked.

"Inexorably," Raphael replied.

In an explosion of light and sound, the archangels had vanished, tossing the awestruck Guardians into the earth with their departure.

Daniel sat up Immediately and wiped the sweat from his face. "Back to the base. This is our chance to rescue Adam."

"What about what Matilda said?" Mark asked, still trying to compose himself. "Raphael won't win this fight."

"We'll have to deal with that later. Right now, we finish our mission."

An echoing screech carried on the wind and with a quick glance they realized that all the demons hadn't taken flight. Some were returning to finish the job their new master had given them.

At once they fired through the trees, racing back toward their destroyed sanctuary, the sun lifting into the sky behind them. The creatures pursued, handfuls of them closing in from the left and right sides. The Guardians ran faster, brandishing their weapons and cutting through the demons as they came upon them.

With deft skill, they cleaved through the horde as they ran, dispatching many as they pounced through the air at them.

"Don't stop until we make it there!" Daniel commanded through pounding breaths.

"Is it me, or is it getting darker out?" Mark queried.

The others looked at the sky. He was right, a blanket of dark clouds was spreading, threatening to blot out the sun. In eerie quiet, the black pillows rolled across the bright sky and swallowed the sun, returning the world to pitch black. Flashes of light hidden within the clouds lit the dark sporadically like distant explosions. The vibrations of the aerial bombs made human bones tremble.

Next, the bursts of light became arching bolts of purple-hued lightning. The veins of neon color streaked horizontally across the sky, meandering in quixotic fashion. The crack of thunder was deafening. The sound rattled teeth and shook through bone as if it were completely hollow. Still, the Guardians dashed through the swamp, the flashes from the electric storm overhead their only guiding light.

They finally arrived at the hill of shattered materials they once called home. More demons came out of the woodworks to hunt them and they cautiously began to climb the rubble.

"Elle, do you have a bomb?" Daniel asked.

"Yeah, it's the last one."

"Set it off and carry it to the top."

Without protest, the Latin woman twisted the orb until it clicked and gave the signature hiss that she was waiting for. She held it tucked under her arm as she climbed, the vapors spraying onto her clothes and wetting the material. She was unsure what Daniel had in mind until she turned her head and saw that the demons who tried to follow them up the mound were caught in the trail of vapor she left behind. They made it halfway up the side when Daniel stopped on an open patch of stone.

"We'll start here."

Seraphim exhaled heavily, readying her blades at the sight of scattering demons.

Daniel held his hand up, halting her. "Catch your breath. They won't follow."

True to his word, the beasts could only come as far as the edge of the debris without leaping backward in stunned pain. Most gave up without trying, scurrying off into the bushes to survive another day.

"The air is still, the vapors will sit for a while." Daniel looked around at the tired faces of his warriors. "Three minutes, then we search for my brother."

As the weary fighters recuperated, they watched the brilliant show above their heads. A dazzling display of purple and sometimes searing white cut through the clouds, taking away what little breath they had.

"So, this is what a fight between seraphim looks like," Emmanuelle said. "As frightening as it is, it's beautiful."

"Yeah, I've never seen anything like it," Prophet added.

Elle tipped her head at the man. "Hopefully, you never will again."

Mark moved to Daniel's side. "How do you think our boy is doing up there?"

"I don't know." Daniel shook his head. "I think It'd be best if we get Adam and get the hell out of here before we find out."

The Guardians were quiet for the remainder of their time. Reflecting on the events thus far or the upcoming task.

"Time to work," Daniel said stretching his neck.

He spoke as if the three-minute reprieve had exhilarated him.

"Prophet and Sera, you..." Daniel trailed off, his eyes glued to the sky.

The others turned their attention to whatever had caught their leader's gaze. It was the clouds, but this time they were receding from the sky. All at once the grey billowing nimbus that shielded the sun was vanishing, revealing the bright yellow star hanging in the sky in all its glory.

Something was at its center. A small black spot that grew larger as its wings carried it closer. The Guardians squinted and covered their eyes at the sudden change in lighting. Whoever approached them flew with the sun at his back, preventing any human from identifying him.

"Hate to say it, but I think we're about to find out right now, boss." Mark squinted with sweat on his brow.

Daniel gripped his sword tightly as the winged being landed softly before them.

"You look nervous. You should have more faith in me."

A wave of relief rolled through the Guardians when they realized it was the archangel of healing speaking to them.

Mark flopped down on a piece of rock jutting out from the mound. "Oh, thank God. We thought you were done for."

Raphael's head tilted at Mark's relief. "For humans working so closely with angels, I would think you'd have more faith than that."

Daniel looked over the bleeding and battered angel with suspicion in his glare. "What happened up there?"

Raphael held up the throbbing black heart in his left hand as an answer. "Do you mean before or after I ripped out his heart?"

A puckish smile slid across the arch's face and Daniel couldn't help but smile back this time. He extended his open palm toward the angel and Raphael took it in his hand.

"Thank you."

Daniel could see the angel's internal struggle to find a reply. Perhaps he wasn't used to being thanked by humans. His eyes quickly cut to the right corner of their sockets and he turned his head as if hearing something he knew was impossible. Daniel furrowed his brow in confusion and that's when Raphael put his hand to his chest and threw him off of his feet.

"Get down!" Raphael screamed with the motion.

In the next moment, a flash of white lightning struck him with phenomenal force. The entire mound was rocked and chunks of building parts were flung in all directions. The Guardians were thrown like porcelain dolls, pain unfolding on their faces as they flew.

Emmanuelle felt her mouth fill with blood as she slammed into a huge stone slab at the top of the mound. Prophet bounced across the base remnants, catching Seraphim by the collar as he skirted, digging steel fingers into the rock to stop his momentum. Mark was thrown clear from the center of the mound back to the ground and Daniel arched harmlessly to the top of the wreckage.

He landed hard but sustained no real injury as Raphael threw him before the explosion hit. He gathered himself quickly and helped Emmanuelle to her feet.

"I'm fine. I'm okay," she said with thin blood dripping from her lips. "What the hell *was* that?"

Daniel made his way to the edge and looked down at what collided with them and felt his heart stop. He looked at the scene below him and saw Raphael face down on a flat granite surface. Michael stood over him with his foot on his back and his hands gripping his emerald green wings.

Daniel wasn't sure what was most terrifying, the sinister smile on the archangel's face, the green glow in his eyes, or the gaping hole in his chest where his black heart used to be.

Black blood dripped from the orifice onto Raphael's back and the demented seraph smiled wickedly through it all.

"You cannot kill me so easily anymore. I have become more than an angel, more than a demon. I am abomination."

Green veins, thousands in number, wended from Michael's limbs to his face. The crimson wings on his back began to shed their lustrous steel feathers. They dropped all around Raphael as he lay pinned and with a single mighty flap, Michael flung the shining feathers from him and revealed his new wings.

Larger than his glowing red ones, these were like giant, webbed, human, hands. Leather and brown in color, these wings were grotesque and slick with a translucent membranous substance.

Michael looked up at Daniel and Emmanuelle. "Guardians, do you know how to turn an angel human? It's quite simple really. All you have to do is..." He looked down at Raphael. "...remove their wings."

Daniel leaped from his high ground, his sword drawn, aiming for Michael's head. "No!"

With a single flap of his monstrous wings, Michael conjured a gale-force wind and blew Daniel back up the mound and on top of Emmanuelle.

"Brother, please." Raphael reached his hand toward Michael, pleading. "Don't take my grace away."

Michael's grin grew wider at the sight of his begging sibling. "You are no brother of mine."

With a quick and powerful jerk, he tore Raphael's wings from his back, holding them high as if they were trophies.

Raphael screamed, his voice shaking the mountain of wreckage they all stood on. The heavens wept, the earth shuddered, and the deepest pits of hell cried out in joy. His pain was palpable, his blood a fountain. The emerald wings shattered into pieces, the twinkling light cast by them disappearing forever.

Michael saw the black heart Raphael still clutched in his left hand. "Oh, and the heart?" He placed his foot over Raphael's hand and slowly crushed it under his toes. "You can keep it."

Raphael groaned painfully as his hand was crushed underfoot. Michael kicked him in the stomach and sent him careening from the pile of rubble and onto the ground.

The corrupted angel floated through the air, following his broken sibling to the ground and kicking him more, taunting him as he did.

"How does it feel, Raphael? How does it feel to be one of them? Imperfect, dirty, weak. You could've joined me. You *should've* joined me. You don't even care about these damn humans." Michael kicked his back into a tree. "And now you're going to die as one of them."

"No, he's not."

Michael turned to see five battered warriors standing in front of him, limping, bleeding, and ready to fight. They were frightened, some were even shaking, but none of them were running.

Daniel stood in their center, his sword glistening in the sunlight. Fear ate away at his insides, but he refused to show it. He refused to let it slow him down.

He pictured Father standing in front of him, two pieces of twisted scrap metal in his hands, odds stacked against him, unwilling to give up. He would make him proud today.

"Guardians, this very well may be our last moments." His eyes were steely and focused entirely on Michael. "I don't know why we're here. Maybe it's to save my brother, or maybe it's to save the world. It doesn't matter now because we're here and we're not running. It's been a pleasure serving with you and if I could be anywhere else in the world, I would still be here with all of you."

A ripple of smiles spread through their ranks.

"Same here, mate."

"Damn right."

"You got it, D."

"I could think of a few things I could be doing."

They all looked over at Seraphim.

"But this is much more fun."

She laughed and so did everyone else.

Daniel pointed his blade at Michael. "He's missing his heart, which means he's a demon now. Take his head and this fight is over." He gave the bearded black man a glance and a nod. "Prophet."

The metal man stepped forward. "The Lord is my light and

my salvation; whom shall I fear? The Lord is the stronghold of my life; of whom shall I be afraid?"

Michael turned and began walking slowly toward the battered group.

Prophet's voice resounded. "Therefore, my beloved brothers, be steadfast, immovable, always abounding in the work of the Lord, knowing that in the Lord your labor is not in vain."

They all took fighting stances, bruised fists tightening around blunt blades, trembling knees pressing worn heels into soft mud. Burning fear veiled by friable courage.

Prophet's voice boomed, carrying his prayer across the battlefield. "Be strong and courageous! Do not be afraid or terrified because of them, for the Lord your God goes with you and he will never leave you nor forsake you!"

Daniel bellowed forcefully, "Saint Thomas!"

His warriors replied, "Pray for us!"

"Saint Sebastian!"

"Fight for us!"

"Saint Monica!"

"Wait for us!"

"Saint Jude!"

"Believe in us!"

"May the Lord make our days long..." Daniel lowered a menacing glower at Michael. "...and our end swift."

Nefarious laughter filled Michael's mouth as he stared down the group of warriors. "Come, I'll play with you for a while."

SECTION 4

The Guardians exploded toward Michael, bellowing a war cry in unison and leaving their pain and fatigue behind them. Their leader was the first to reach him, swinging his sword underhand across Michael's chest. The attack caught the air as the archangel jumped over Daniel's head and landed in the midst of his attackers. Prophet slid on his heels and raised his left arm just as Michael's bone-tipped knuckles reached him. Though the hit was blocked, the force of the punch sent him sliding on his feet into the rubble behind him.

Before the others could process what happened, Michael whipped around and pressed his attack. With his right wing, he knocked Emmanuelle's feet out from under her and slapped her rolling across the grass with the leathery appendage. At the same time, he booted Mark in the chest and sent him tumbling away. Daniel and Seraphim stayed on him, attacking rigorously as their teammates went down.

Michael dodged each blade as if they were moving in slow motion, a cruel smile fixed to his face. With a single flap of his wings, he whipped up a gale that swept both Guardians off their feet and sent them sprawling.

A piece of stone rubble broke against his left shoulder. He turned and saw Prophet pulling chunks of debris from the mound and hurling them at him. The metal man threw a slab of rock with his steel arm and Michael swatted it away with the back of his hand-shaped wing. As soon as he completed the motion, Mark was on top of him, throwing a barrage of punches with his lethal weaponry.

Michael inched backward then shot out with a wickedly accurate right hook to the gut that left the Irishman breathless. He fell to his knees choking on the air.

Michael stood above him with clenched fists. "Is *that* what you were trying to do?"

With a wild growl, Prophet fell on Michael, his metal fist barreling past his face by inches. Prophet swung the back of his left hand over the angel's head then stepped in and brought it down to his face leaving a crater in the ground where he missed again. Before he could recover, a green veined hand wrapped around his face, snatching him from the earth and slamming the back of his head into a nearby tree. As he stood there stunned, Michael grabbed Mark's exhausted form with his right wing and swung him into his partner, toppling them both.

The twinkle of polished steel caught Michael's eye and three knives flew by him. Glossy sweat wet Emmanuelle's forehead as she whipped more blades at the angel. Michael swayed in and out of the projectile's pathways, dodging her missiles, purposely it seemed, by inches.

The archangel jammed his hand into the base of a nearby Cypress tree, lifting it from the ground. Patches of dirt clung fervently to its tangled roots as Michael tore it from its home with a single hand. He saw Emmanuelle's eyes widen in fear when her mind made the connection of what was to come.

"Catch."

The seraph hurled the tree at her, forcing her into a rolling dive as it crashed behind.

Michael's shoulders bounced with laughter. "This is more fun than it should be."

A bolt of lightning shot through his body and pulled the angel to his knee. His eyes lit with the color of emeralds and he coughed blood that glowed a swampy green. His angelic aura was still fighting the demonic poison within him. He could feel the unnatural power tearing his body apart.

He clenched his teeth and swallowed down the rising tsunami of agony. He wouldn't let something so human as pain defeat him.

His eyes cut to the right corners of his sockets at the sound of rustling leaves behind him. Seraphim leaped from a tree branch, both daggers drawn and aimed for the back of his neck. The arch raised his hands and caught her by the wrists, her weapons trembling in her hands, a hair's breadth from their target.

"Clever, attacking my blind spot. Although, my back is not the safest place for you."

With a smile gracing his face, Michael's moist wings shot open and, in an instant, he had taken to the clouds carrying the woman on his back. He gripped her wrists tightly and cut through the air picking up more speed. Her eyes leaked tears and her skin became dry and cold and flapped loosely on her face. Michael took them higher, arching in wild spirals and twists, refusing to slow. She wanted to scream but couldn't find the air in her lungs.

Michael suddenly whipped into a spinning dive. Seraphim could feel the wind tearing at her face as they fell hundreds of feet per second. Her brain pushed up against the back of her skull and she could feel the blood leave her face. Her world spun topsy-turvy, curving away until it was swallowed by darkness.

Michael landed softly back on solid earth, gripping Seraphim by the collar in his right hand. He dangled her slack body in front of her comrades like a steak in front of a pack of hungry dogs.

"This one is a bit tuckered out."

He dropped her body harshly to the grass, daring anyone to approach her. Prophet took a step forward, eager to accept the challenge.

Daniel pressed the back of his hand into the giant's chest before he could take a second step. "Don't rush. Elle will get Sera. You, Mark, and I will go after him."

Prophet moved his eyes curiously over to Daniel. "Gamma maneuver?"

Daniel nodded his head and moved next to Mark.

Prophet readied himself and approached Michael again with a steady cocky stroll. "You think you're strong, huh, Mikey? Let's see how strong you really are."

A mocking scoff fell from Michael's lips and he strolled out to meet the Guardian. The two brutes squared off, eyes meeting in the sunlight, the silver steel of Prophet's arm reflecting the yellow disc's rays. Prophet walked a few steps further to his right, drawing Michael further away from Seraphim.

The dark-skinned man circled the angel, tapping the switch near his elbow and priming the steel piston inside. Once the cylinder rose from his arm he charged like a raging bull at a taunting matador.

Michael planted his feet, preparing to accept the man's blitz head-on. Prophet closed the distance and, with a gallant howl, thrust his metal fist at Michael's head. The angel lifted his right hand and caught Prophet's blow in his palm, sliding back a few feet as he did. The piston fired, hammering back into the elbow with a forceful kick that rippled through Michael's body and cracked the ground beneath his heel.

Prophet growled at Michael's sneering face as he held his strongest attack at bay. He could see the angel's hand begin to sizzle upon contact with his blessed armor. The borrowed demon power was making him weaker against holy and blessed materials.

Michael smiled through the pain. "Is that the best you can do?"

"Not quite."

The voice came from behind Prophet and above him. Mark had leaped from the ground, onto Prophet's back, his newly crafted weapons careening straight at Michael's open face. The angel had been duped, lulled into giving his full attention to Prophet, when a second attack from above was always intended to land.

Mark's fist had covered half the distance to its target when Michael's wings swung closed on either side of him. The thick veiny appendages clapped him in between them like slick cymbals, producing a sharp sound akin to slapping leather. Mark could only wail in shock and pain as he was smashed in the air by his opponent's wings.

"A valiant effort, but your simple tactics will not—"

Before he could finish, the grinding sound of shoes skidding across rock caught his attention and made him look down. Amid his bragging, Daniel had slid underneath Prophet's legs, his sword drawn and pointed at Michael's throat.

Faster than the blink of a human eye, Michael pieced it all together. It was called *Gamma* maneuver because it was a three-pronged attack. Center, high, and low. He couldn't help but be impressed. Prophet's attack had occupied his arms and Mark's had taken his wings, this left him open for Daniel's lower and final attack.

Michael exhaled a gust of wind from his mouth before the tip of Daniel's sword could reach him. The stream of air effectively halted Daniel's blade and swooped him and his subordinates away with a single breath.

They landed hard back in front of the mound, disappointed that they couldn't finish Michael with the assault, but not completely dissatisfied. Emmanuelle stood just a few feet off, a weary, yet conscious, Seraphim hung off her shoulder.

Michael's wings flapped happily behind him as if waving at the group. "I must admit that was an impressive tactic. I can see why you Guardians have no trouble dispatching demons." His green eyes floated over their beaten faces. "Don't stop now. Show me more."

Daniel pulled himself to his feet. His body throbbing with cuts from being thrown like a leaf on the wind. He was in pain, but not nearly enough to quit. He began to remember that his time in Sheol made him somewhat numb to pain and if *he* was feeling it then his warriors must be in twice as much agony.

He looked at their faces and the wounds covering their bodies. There was no time for sympathy. The entire human race was at stake and if they had to go through a little pain to save it, then, goddamn it, that's what they'd do.

"Sera, can you stand?" He addressed her without taking his eyes off Michael.

She closed her eyes and took a breath. "Yes."

"Then get up. We don't have time to babysit you."

The Guardians looked at Daniel, a perplexed gaze falling onto their faces. They had never heard him so stern before.

"This is what we train for. To fight harder, and longer than anyone else. We're not quitting. You hear me?" He was addressing all of them now. "We're not leaving until he's dead, or we are."

His warriors stood tall again. Even Seraphim had pushed off of Emmanuelle's shoulder and onto her own two feet.

Mark cracked the knuckles in his hands and shook out his arms. " Whoever said we was giving up? We're still with ya, boss." His teeth cracked over bruised lips.

Daniel glanced around at the men and women at his side and felt hope renew in himself as well. "Okay then, I think we've been going about this wrong. We've been attacking his body when we really need to cut his legs out from under him."

"Huh?" Mark questioned.

"We need to take his maneuverability," Seraphim explained.

Daniel nodded and looked at the Latin woman to his right. "Elle."

The dark-haired woman stepped to the front of the group, six knives protruding from between her fingers on each hand. Her stare beamed into her targets and her arms snapped up. Gleaming blades flung through the air and bulls-eyed their marks.

Michael grunted in surprise pain as three knives sank into the palm of his right wing. Green blood trickled down onto the grass and three more blades darted by, two of them finding homes in his left wing.

The green-eyed woman loaded more throwing knives into her hands and took aim again as the rest of her team charged at the wounded arch. Michael gave a solemn nod to the woman as if to say 'well played' and folded his wings behind him so that they would not be targets again.

The other four descended on him with weapons drawn. Prophet lead the pack, his metal arm clenched and dragging behind him as if his first attack would be a rising uppercut. Just as they arrived, Daniel leaped over Prophet, pushing off his back just as Mark had done earlier and throwing himself at Michael. Daniel's sword struck from left to right at his enemy's head, going for the instant kill.

On divine instinct, Michael fell backward onto his wings, allowing Daniel's sword to overswing him. The Guardian watched, awestruck, as he nearly cleared the angel's horizontal body. As Daniel flew overhead, Michael shot a blast of air from his mouth and blew the leader of the Guardians two hundred feet into the air.

Mark watched Daniel fly spinning into the sky and disappear in the light of the sun. He pounced angrily at Michael, thrusting his weapons with vigorous fury, fully believing that it was the last time he would see his friend alive.

The angel flipped backward from his wings to his feet and ducked a wicked right hook from the spiky-haired blonde. Michael's left-wing flashed out low and Mark shot up and over before it could trip him. He came down with a hard left but felt the familiar sting of leathery flesh on his backside as Michael slapped him across the grass with his right wing.

In the next breath Seraphim and Prophet were in front of him, revenge for their lost leader boiling under every swing. Michael fell back, their attacks increased in intensity. Prophet stepped forward, pushing his gigantic metal fist past Michael's head as he leaned to the left. Seraphim swung her right-handed dagger down at the angel with brutal force.

Michael caught Seraphim's wrist as she came down and redirected her blade into Prophet's right leg. The bearded man screamed as the weapon sank into his thigh and stuck out the other side. Michael leaned forward and slammed his forehead into Seraphim's nose. The crunch of snapping cartilage and the spray of blood was enough to know it had been shattered like glass.

While the two reeled in pain, Michael fell back onto his outstretched wings again and kicked out with both legs, blasting them away like spinning cannonballs. He returned to his feet and flapped his wings in a single powerful motion and whipped the five knives embedded in them back to their owner. Emmanuelle could barely catch the blades with her eyes as they streamed like bullets past her, one catching her in the right shoulder, coaxing a scream from her mouth.

The archangel laughed a vicious laugh at her pain then suddenly looked up as if he had just remembered something of minor importance. Daniel fell from the sky like a wounded bird, tumbling end over end. Michael walked toward his point of impact, an eyebrow raised in curiosity.

Any normal human would be screaming at the top of their lungs. Most would have even released their bowels at the possibility of imminent death. This man fell in utter silence, even attempting to control his fall as if it could do him any good.

Michael smiled and sent a blast of wind with his wings just before Daniel hit the ground, stopping his fall and throwing him spinning horizontally instead of vertically.

"I won't let you die yet, Daniel. You are far more entertaining alive."

Daniel spun away from the angel, whipping into a wild corkscrew before crashing to the ground.

Michael spun on his heel, surprising the two Guardians jumping him from behind with his quickness. He swatted Mark away with his right-wing as he turned and grabbed Seraphim by the throat with his left hand. He snatched her by the neck so hard that the force stunned her, making her drop her weapons.

Michael lifted her to his eyes, her face flushing red as she struggled for air. "I wonder how long it would take to peel away all of the skin on your face if I blew on it at this range."

Seraphim gritted her teeth and kicked wildly, a devilish glare shining in Michael's eyes. He puckered his lips and released a steady stream of air into her face that blew the blood from her nose and made water leak from her eyes. Her skin rippled and grew dry under the increasing force and she started to feel her flesh tear.

Five cold, mechanical digits wrapped around Michael's face, covering his mouth and burning his skin. The blast of air stopped and the blonde woman could see Prophet behind Michael, his giant metal palm covering his mouth tightly.

The angel jammed his elbow into soft human tissue, feeling the warmth of blood as he punctured it. Prophet groaned and Michael reached over his shoulder and grabbed the top of his bald head, yanking him over and slamming him on top of the Russian.

His foot came down on Prophet's stomach and the Guardian felt two of his ribs crack. Michael pressed down harder, slowly pushing Prophet's stomach to his back and at the same time crushing Seraphim, who was trapped under him.

Prophet's face flew through a series of agonizing grimaces. Pain lanced through his body and he felt the two cracked ribs break altogether and blood pour from his side wound. He shouted and grabbed Michael's leg with the metal hand.

The angel could feel the blessed material lightly singe his flesh. "Do you really think that arm of yours can move me?"

A trickle of blood ran from Prophet's mouth to the ground as he choked out his words. "No, but I think *this* one can."

He lifted his right arm and dropped a ticking black orb at Michael's feet. The arch instantly recognized the mist-spewing orb that decimated half his demon army. He immediately threw himself backward with a strenuous flap of his wings, putting several yards distance between himself and the sphere.

After that, he waited and watched. The ball rolled harmlessly back and forth on the ground, then, with a '*click*', it opened. Michael waited for it to begin spraying the area with holy vapors, but this time it didn't. The orb sputtered and went silent as if all of its contents had already been spilled. That's when he realized that this ball had already been used and was virtually empty.

The metal man was bluffing.

Another dagger of acid pain rocketed through the angel's body and drove him to the ground again. He could taste foreign blood at the back of his mouth and feel fire in his veins.

Before he could recover, the sound of hurried footsteps bombarded his ears from behind. He stepped to his right to avoid whomever it was but didn't step far enough. With a leaping downward strike, Daniel had sliced through his left wing, severing it from his back.

The giant webbed hand hit the ground with a moist flop as if the entirety of it had been slick with wetness. Daniel slid to a stop in front of his teammates, his sword covered with green blood.

"Gotcha," he whispered but knew the angel could hear him.

Michael's face was a knot of folds and furrows. His pain had subsided and was replaced with malice. Random spurts of green bloodshot from the stump that remained attached to his back. The severed wing writhed on the ground as if it were a separate living entity on its own.

Michael stared green-tinted laser beams at Daniel. "You actually believe you can win, don't you? Well, let me show you otherwise."

SECTION 5

Raphael opened his eyes to an unfamiliar world full of human trials and terrors.

His back was the first human pain he felt, throbbing as if whipped by a cat-of-nine-tails. He sat up, taking stock of his naked condition. His senses had dulled dramatically. He could no longer hear the sound of plants growing or the constant ramble of communicating insects. The sunlight was blinding and hurt his eyes. Strangely, he found that he could not look at it directly anymore. His sense of smell was almost nonexistent, and did everything look bigger all of a sudden?

The only sense that seemed to be working far too well was his sense of pain. His entire body ached. With every breath and movement came the shock of pain, as if his whole body was one giant bruise. His new existence was a tapestry of agony of different types and intensities. The flashes of pain trapped in his crushed hand, the stinging pain attached to his back, and the burning pain locked inside his eyes.

He examined his broken hand, it was wet with blood. Red blood. Another pain tore through his body, leaping from his stomach to his chest. The mysterious pain squeezed his heart and left him gasping for air. He wasn't sure what this new pain was except that it was worse than the others. His lungs filled and released air more rapidly the longer he stared at the blood on his hands. Foreign, crimson, human blood. Not his own.

He raised his head and his brown eyes focused in the light. Far-off sounds began to filter through his ears, familiar yet unrecognizable. In the distance, he caught sight of the battle between Michael and the Guardians. Michael's left wing had been removed and he was making the Guardians pay for it, trouncing each one harshly as they stepped up to him. Yet each time, they returned to their feet. Broken and against impossible odds, they pressed on only to be thrown back into the dirt.

A new pain exploded inside Raphael. This one he could place immediately. The pain of anger.

His face scowled as Mark slammed into the side of a tree. His teeth gnashed when Emmanuelle was thrown, head first, into the ground. His working hand curled into a shaking fist at the sight of Prophet kicked across the field of battle.

He couldn't fathom how they had the strength to continue fighting. It was remarkable to him. But more than the awe he felt toward the Guardians, he felt hatred toward Michael. He was torturing them, dangling the hope of victory in front of them and then dashing that hope with a single blow. Like a child poking and prodding a trapped butterfly, tearing its wings off just to watch it die slowly.

The former angel had had enough and found himself on his feet and walking toward Michael. There was no chance of victory for him, but his rage carried him to the battlefield. More than fear or hopelessness he felt the urge to fight. Not to save the Guardians or for revenge, but because he knew that if they didn't fight, Michael would win. He went from a steady walk, to a jog, and then a mad dash at the angel's back. He'd be dammed to hell long before he'd let Michael win.

Michael turned around just in time to receive a drilling blow to the cheek from Raphael. Michael stood, unimpressed, with his hands to his sides, his eyes peeking over the fist in his face. Without words, he grabbed Raphael's wrist and squeezed, dropping the former angel to his knees. Michael looked into his brother's face. Anger filled Raphael's eyes, so passionate that transparent tears leaked from them.

The angel leaned forward and stared Raphael down with acid-green glowing eyes. "You are nothing."

With a turn of his wrist, he snapped the bones in Raphael's arm and with a blast of air, sent him bouncing across the battlefield.

Raphael slid to a stop ten yards from Michael, a new and vicious agony eating away at him. He watched the Guardians continue their futile struggle, frozen in pain and amazement. How could they go on? A few minutes inside a human body and he had experienced enough pain to make him surrender into despair, yet these humans would not quit, despite their injuries.

Maybe it was the limitations of his human brain, but he couldn't comprehend it. He just couldn't make sense of it.

As he lay on his belly in the mud, he watched with a starry-eyed gaze at the impossible humans before him.

"I understand why you chose them now. I understand why you love them. They are ignorant to their brilliance, weak yet unfathomably strong and filled with fear but, somehow, the bravest creatures I've ever seen." His vision became fuzzy and dark suddenly. "These humans...they are impossible."

The world fell into darkness and Raphael's head dropped to the ground.

"God, help them."

Daniel crashed into a mound of dirt and sprawled painfully onto his back.

Michael stared down at his twisted form. "Aren't you tired of this yet?"

"I'll tell ya what *I'm* tired of."

Mark limped toward the angel, thin blood ran from his forehead, covering the left side of his face. His arms swung loosely at his sides and his eyes burned into Michael's face.

"I'm tired of losing. I'm tired of angels and demons. I'm tired of my mates dying and I'm tired of being helpless to do anything about it. But most of all...I'm tired of hearing your fucking lips flap." Mark stopped five feet from the angel. "All you talk about is how great you are and how pathetic we are. Well, I'm gonna show ya what humans can do, ya bastard."

Michael stepped forward until he was arm's distance from Mark. "Show me."

A swirl of wind blew a nerve-racking silence between the two. Sweat poured from the Irishman's face and mingled with the blood before falling. The droplet hit the ground and Mark struck out, the fastest punch he could throw tore through the air like a spinning cannonball. The flesh missile flew, drilling through the atmosphere with deadly accuracy and comet-like force. The perfect blow covered half its distance before Michael jammed his fingers into Mark's throat.

The marksman paused, his brain struggling to process what was happening. His fist hovered in the air between them and two of Michael's fingers were lodged within his neck. He dropped his hand, backing away from the angel and pulling the sharp digits from his body. Blood immediately began to leak from the aperture, spraying over the ground.

His eyes grew wide. His lips began to quiver uncontrollably. He turned and walked stumbling away from Michael, life pouring from his body with every step. His hands dowsed in red as they tried to cover his wound. He got five feet from the angel before collapsing to the ground.

Michael watched with pleasure until the flash of reflected light caught his eye. Prophet's fist dug into his right cheek and snapped his head to the left. His arm swung back and knocked his head to the right with a vibrating twang. Prophet struck again and this time his heavy arm was redirected to the ground where it pressed deep into soft mud.

Michael grabbed Prophet by the mouth and looked him in the face. His beard was a mess of mud and blood and his left eye was swollen shut. His breaths were short and shallow as his ribs echoed with pain after each one. The archangel smiled at his handy work and nailed the giant man in the stomach with his bony fist.

Prophet leaned over, coughing air and blood from his mouth. Michael then snatched him up and held him over his head with both hands, slamming him into the ground until his body was broken and limp in his hands. The seraph tossed him aside as if he were a bag of garbage, mud covering the left side of his body.

Michael turned and caught Emmanuelle in his sights. She had long since run out of throwing knives and held only a curved dagger in her left hand. Her right arm hung at her side, rivulets of blood streamed down to her hand from her shoulder. One of her knives was buried deep inside her bone. She couldn't remove it. There was too much pain, not to mention the knife was now keeping most of the blood inside her body. Removing it now would surely be more trouble than it was worth.

He walked toward her, strolling through a knee-high mire that sloshed between them, a wicked smile on his face. An eruption of water shot to the sky as he neared its center and a blonde woman with a single french braid in her hair stabbed at his head with a gleaming dagger. Michael caught her attack by the wrist, as unsurprised as if God had told him she was there.

Covered in wetness and muck, her arms trembled, trying with all her might to push through to his neck. Her eyes were twin points of rage, her nose misshapen and leaking blood into the water.

He could see it in her stare, how much she wanted to kill him. Her bloodless glower wished more than anything to split his head from his neck. She lusted for his blood, to bathe her hands in it, to taste its salt on her lips when it sprayed from his body onto her face. Her eyes begged for his demise.

Staring her down, he turned her wrist slowly and shaking back toward her. He wrapped his hand around hers, keeping her from letting go as he pushed her weapon back toward her chest. Her eyes stayed on him, this time a glaze of fear had replaced the bloodlust. Her arms shook as he inched her blade to her chest, one hand on the hilt and the other around the back of her neck.

The tip of the dagger struck flesh and inched deeper into her body. Her jaw tightened and tears wet her eyes. He moved the blade slowly, deliberately so that she could feel every centimeter of the steel pass into her.

"I could make this end, Sera. Just tell me you are undeserving. Tell me you're unworthy of her love. I promise you will feel no more pain."

Her teeth were red with blood and her entire body was shaking now. She stared at Michael in silence before a flash of desperate anger lit in her eyes. She spat crimson into his face.

"I'd rather die slow."

Michael took his hand from the weapon and slapped her hard across the face. Her hair flew wildly, the single french braid undoing as she fell and splashed into the shallow bog face down.

He looked back up to where Emmanuelle had been standing and she was gone. Lightly falling leaves and floating insects had taken her place. He scanned the area with his eyes, looking left to right meticulously.

In a blinding burst of speed, he dashed to his right and snapped an ancient oak in half with his hand. Behind it hid the woman he searched for, panicked she had been discovered. She backed away, a dagger in her left hand held out in front of her.

The angel towered over her, staring into her bloodshot eyes without remorse.

"Do you think you can hide from me, Emmanuelle? I am seraphim, you couldn't hide from just *one* of my senses. I can *see* your sins. I can *smell* your fear, *taste* your sweat on the air. I can *feel* your heartbeat sending vibrations through the atmosphere. I can *hear* you, human." He crept up on her like a tiger stalking wounded prey. "I can hear you breathing. The swelling sound your lungs make when you inhale. The constriction of your blood vessels as I approach you and the sound of your beating heart crashing against your chest plate."

The fearful woman fell to the ground and crawled on her back trying to escape but unable to keep her eyes off him.

"I can hear you blink and the wet sliding sound your eyeballs make when they shift. I can even hear the friction you make on the wind."

The panicked woman backed herself into a tree and stared, horrified, at the menacing beast above her.

"I can hear the very sound of your existence, child. You can never hide from me."

In that instant, Emmanuelle's mind flashed back to a single moment inside the training room. A moment filled with pain and blood. Her last waking moment, dangling in the grasp of a killer angel. With a terrified shriek, she clawed the dirt around her and scrambled to her feet, abandoning her beaten comrades and running for her life.

Michael watched her run, not bothering to give chase. He lifted his head to the glowing orb in the sky and stretched out his veined arms, bathing in its light.

"Is *this* what you chose over me!? These rodents? These monkeys? These are the best they have and I have laid waste to them and still, you do not recognize me."

A weary expression washed across his face. One that was mixed with confusion, frustration, and pleading.

"Then I will destroy them. I will destroy your favorite creation and then...then you will have no choice but to recognize me."

"Hey!"

Michael looked back to the earth and saw a figure standing in front of him. His clothes were tattered and his body was covered in bruises and cuts, but his sword still glistened in the sunlight.

"I'm the best, and I'm still standing."

Michael scowled at Daniel's optimistic words.

"A problem I will soon rectify."

A pale, pasty arm broke through a crack in the mound of wreckage that was the Guardian's home base. Digging its fingers into the soft earth, the arm pulled a disheveled figure from the debris. Covered in white powder with patches of red where blood had dried, Adam fell into the light of the sun, gasping for air.

He lay on his stomach a moment to get his bearings and peered across the destroyed landscape. He tried to stand but a sharp pain in his right leg made him reconsider. The stain of blood around his calf forced him to conclude that it was broken.

No matter. He would not let it stop him from moving. The Guardian began a slow crawl on his forearms and knees out toward the battlefield. His body was in terrible shape, but that would not stop him. Nothing would stop him from reaching his goal.

Daniel slammed into the ground and slid on his side to a stop. Bracing himself against his sword, he rose to his feet again as determined as ever. He found himself on his back once more before he could even get into his fighting stance. He got up, resting on one knee, with sword in hand and blood dripping from his teeth. He could hear Michael's footsteps growing ever closer and stopping barely a foot from where he rested.

The angel went to speak and Daniel shot to his feet with a rising strike before he could. Michael moved to his left and let the blade pass by, then backward as Daniel followed through with a downward swing that arced across his chest. The seraph spun low and swept his remaining wing at Daniel's feet and was surprised when he jumped it.

The Guardian came down with a mighty horse chop that ended in catastrophe when Michael stepped forward and plowed his fist into his stomach. Daniel fell to his knees, stabbing the tip of his sword into the ground to keep from keeling over. His vision blurred dark, but he willed himself to stay conscious. This pain was nothing. He had felt worse, far worse.

He spat blood and rose steadily to his feet, gripping his weapon tightly in hand. He remembered the obscene tortures he had been subjected to in Sheol. Being burned, cut, crushed, and maimed in the most brutal of ways for days, weeks, months on end. This was nothing.

Daniel met his opponent again, a flurry of dazzling sword-play flashing past Michael as he dodged. He came down with a mighty overhead swing that Michael caught by the wrist before it could connect. He released his grip on the sword, dropping it from his right hand and catching it again with his left, and striking again.

The angel kicked into Daniel's left hand and sent the weapon bouncing from his grip. Without giving his lost weapon a second glance, a small dagger slid from the sleeve of his cassock into his right hand. Michael watched closely as Daniel stepped forward, swung his arm around, and tossed his remaining weapon into the air high above their heads.

Confusion spread like wildfire on Michael's face and his eyes followed the thrown weapon into the sky. The moment he took his green eyes from him, Daniel clicked the toes of his shoes together and two blades slid from the front and rear of his right shoe. The clicking sound alerted the angel and gave him more than enough time to block the high kick aimed at his face.

The pointed tip of the hidden weapon stopped near his cheek, but Daniel followed through by dropping into a low leg sweep that slid under Michael's feet. Pressing forward, Daniel leaped high, bringing that same leg back around into a spin-ning axe kick that flashed in the sun.

Stepping forward again, Michael caught Daniel's foot over his head just above the thicker blade that stuck out from the heel. Grabbing at his heel, the angel pulled Daniel's entire shoe from his foot.

While his hands were busy, Daniel grabbed the empty sheath that still hung from his waist and thrust its round end at Michael's chest. With another audible '*click*' a thick serrated pyramid sprang from the end and stabbed past the archangel's chest as the shoe fell to the ground.

In an instant, Daniel was on him with a barrage of stabbing strikes in French fencing form. The corrupted angel fell backward, dodging each thrust swiftly and precisely then knocked the Guardian onto his butt with a well-timed sweep of his foot.

The man still would not be stopped, falling and immediately flowing into a series of low whipping swipes now in the style of Chinese swordplay. Michael backed away again, each swing coming closer than the last until he jumped and brought his foot down on the sheathe, breaking it with a loud crack.

Without pause, Daniel threw the splintered piece left in his hand at Michael's face and charged forward. The seraph shifted his head and dodged the projectile and as if on reflex, grabbed Daniel's wrist as it came down to his throat.

A small, sharp metallic protrusion scraped at his neck from the shoe he had removed from Daniel's foot. That shoe was now in Daniel's hands and pressing toward his flesh.

Michael was loathed to admit that even *he* was impressed with this Guardian's tenacity and tactical thinking. First, making him take his eyes off of him by throwing, what he thought, was his last weapon into the air and surprise attacking from below. Then, waiting until both of his hands were preoccupied before launching another surprise attack with a weapon hidden in his sheathe. Finally, there was his last attack with his own shoe as a weapon which normally wouldn't have been much, but if he were being honest, though he heard the attack coming, he never actually saw Daniel pick up the shoe.

A flash of anger sparked inside of him and he kicked the Guardian across the ruined lawn and back toward the mound. How dare this man have the audacity to impress him.

Daniel looked up and threw himself to the right as his

sword landed like a spear in the ground where he lay. He looked up at the angel standing over him, rage blistering through his perfect face.

"This place will be your grave, Guardian."

Raphael awoke to the sound of his name being called. The amorphous haze slowly began to take shape as his eyes adjusted. Adam was above him, his face a chalky white and a trail of dry blood traveling from his ears to his neck.

"Raphael, you must get up. We need you now."

The young man's voice was calm and somehow soothing. He didn't know why but he felt an air of familiarity at seeing his face. Raphael rose to his knees, sparks of pain lighting his nerves as he remembered his arm had been broken.

"You've done well, Raphael. Your siblings would be proud of you."

Adam spoke again but sounded far off as if he were not right in front of him. Raphael assumed his human body had some getting used to. His vision was still lackluster, or was this the extent of normal human vision?

"Your reward will be given to you now."

Raphael could barely make out the words, his hearing seemed to echo a high-pitched squeal into his brain. He resorted to trying to read Adam's lips instead. It was then that he got his first good look at the Guardian's face.

Aside from his matted hair and bone-white cheeks, there was something amiss about him. Something obvious even without noticing it.

The former angel focused his weak eyes and felt the breath leave his lungs. Adam's eyes were white.

They were a wet-talcum color that could only mean that

they had rolled to the back of his head upon losing conscious-ness. But how could he be moving and speaking so clearly if he hadn't truly regained consciousness? A slew of questions flooded his mind, but the most pertinent one escaped his mouth.

"Who are you?"

Adam gave the smile a father would give a confused child and cupped Raphael's cheeks in his hands. "I told you, you must recognize the strength of humans before I would help you. And now She is here to give you your reward."

Grey clouds blanketed the sky for a second time. The sunlight grew dim as swirling pillows of grey cotton candy spiraled around one another, leaving a small opening in their center. Veins of lightning began to swim through the sky trav-eling from cloud to cloud and closing on the hole in their midst. The sky glowed with electric energy that lit the heavens like the sun they were blocking. Raphael tilted his head to the sky and watched the display above him in wondrous and frightening glee.

"Dear God..."

CHAPTER
ELEVEN

T*he Beginning's End*

SECTION 1

Michael slammed the back of Daniel's head against the stone pieces of the mound behind him. The Guardian almost fell to his knees, stabbing his sword into the ground and bracing himself on its grip before hitting the earth. Blood flowed endlessly from his nose, pooling with the estuary of hemoglobin in his mouth and falling in a steady stream to the dirt. Both his eyes were black and the left was swelling closed quickly. For the first time in years, he felt more pain than he was comfortable with.

Oddly enough, a cold sense of nostalgia whirred his senses, taking him back to his childhood and the horrid things no ten-year-old should ever experience. Ironic, that of all the demons he had fought from then until now, it would be an angel, a seraph, to end his life.

Michael opened his mouth to speak and Daniel kicked the buried end of his sword with his one remaining shoe and jerked the blade from the ground. He ripped the weapon up, sending a spray of brown earth and patches of grass into

Michael's eyes. As Michael covered his face, Daniel swung his sword around and back down on top of the angel.

This was his final counter and his last-ditch effort to kill the demented angel. He put the very last ounce of fight in him into it, whipping up a cloud of dirt and striking down with a burst of speed that surprised even himself.

He felt the blade connect and send a wave of vibrations through his arms. He had struck something hard, calcified. The snap of broken metal made his heart sink to his stomach when he realized he had struck the bone-like protrusion on the angel's elbow and split his sword. The business end of the weapon spun out of sight and Michael grabbed Daniel's forearm before he could strike again.

The seraph forced Daniel to his knees, squeezing the bones in his arm together, a look on his face that was half-smile and half-scowl.

"I must admit, I thought I understood you creatures. I had spent so much time observing you that I believed there was nothing left to see. You have opened my eyes to the perplexing nature of humans because I truly do not understand your motivation." He squeezed Daniel's arm harder, forcing a groan of protest from him and making him drop the broken sword. "Why do you continue, Daniel? Your friends are dead or dying, scattered across the battlefield, your weapons are gone and you are alone. Do you honestly think you can win after all you have seen?"

Michael crouched down to Daniel's eye level and released his iron grasp on him. The divine being reached out and brushed the Guardian's bruised cheek with the back of his hand. Daniel flinched, uneasy about the angel's show of mock tenderness.

"I am older than anything you will ever see in a thousand lifetimes. I could clap my hands and destroy a mountain. I have built galaxies and wiped out entire species, held newborn stars in my hand, and blown out old ones with a single breath." He leaned in close to Daniel's face. "The entire time your team has fought me I haven't even used a fraction of my true power, and you still think you stand a chance?"

Daniel dropped his head, a hollow laugh bouncing his shoulders. "It all makes sense. I didn't understand why any of this was happening until now. It can't be coincidence, it all just makes too much sense."

Michael's face wrinkled at the battered man's rambling. He couldn't understand what he was saying.

Daniel lifted his head and gave Michael a crazed stare. "There was a plan all along. Every step led to this. This very moment."

Michael grabbed him by the throat and lifted him to his feet. "What plan, human? Speak!"

Daniel grabbed at the tree trunk of an arm at his neck and began spilling everything. "I thought it was just random events, but it's not. One thing caused another and then another...like dominoes." Daniel started rattling off events as they came to his mind. "First your deal with Lucifer and attacking our home. I thought I needed to be there, but I wasn't because I was *supposed* to go to see Matilda. She had to send me here to face you."

Daniel looked off into the distance as if some hidden piece of the puzzle in his mind had just been found.

His eyes burned with conviction. "Even Raphael. She told me not to let him fight you because he would lose. She was *supposed* to tell me that so when he asked me if you were here I would lie to him...and he would know."

Michael pulled him from his feet by the collar, his voice echoing in rage. "What are you talking about? What was planned?"

"Everything! Us coming here for Adam, you discovering us, Raphael showing up and fighting you. Even him tearing your heart out and you ripping his wings off. All of it lead to this. Even the Guardians fighting you. Even me, you, this moment. All of it's connected, all of it makes sense. I know my role now. I know my purpose. We were never supposed to win. *I* was never supposed to beat you." Daniel ceased his rambling and stared intently into Michael's glowing green eyes. "I'm the distraction."

The archangel's head tilted in utter bewilderment when a giant shadow crept over them both. He looked to the sky and saw the darkening clouds fill the air, spiraling like a giant whirlpool. He dropped the Guardian to the ground at the sight of glistening electricity leaping through the clouds. The color drained from his face.

A wet cackling sound intruded into his ears and his eyes returned to the broken Guardian at his feet. Daniel shook with maniacal laughter. Pain rolled like a perpetual tsunami over his body, making him cringe through each chuckling cough.

Michael could see it, the agony he was in. The broken bones scratching against swollen muscle tissue with every inhale. The bruised organs shivering in his body with every exhale. He laughed through the pain. Crazed, wet laughter aimed at Michael's pride. Piercing, mocking laughter.

Michael looked into the distance and saw Raphael and Adam kneeling under the eye of the storm. "No."

Michael lunged across the destroyed expanse leaving the mad Guardian behind. With a single thrust, Michael covered the fifteen-yard gap between them and was blown backward when a huge bolt of lightning flashed from the eye and struck the two kneeling men.

An explosion of blinding light and dust swallowed the area, sending Michael flying into the mound of debris. Had he been human, the force of the impact would have crushed all of his bones.

Recovering quickly, he opened his eyes to see Raphael kneeling over Adam's slumped and sizzling body. The former angel's head was bowed and his eyes were shut as if trapped in a trance. Wisps of steam wafted from his skin and other burning materials inside the smoking crater.

Michael climbed to his feet as Raphael raised his head, his eyes still closed, and the blood rolling down his back turned from red to black. His body steadily grew, returning him to the towering nine-foot giant he once was. The tears wetting his face turned from transparent to blood red and two great shadows sprang from his back.

At least, Daniel *thought* they were shadows but after staring for a while he realized they were wings. Darker than black, wings.

They flickered on his back like fire, constantly undulating as if a dancing flame had been fixed to him. The Guardian was startled by how unnaturally black they were. Like twin gashes in reality through which he could see into the depths of space.

A long, writhing, black, tattoo appeared on his skin and Raphael's eyes shot open, the deep brown corrupted by stifling black. The angel of death had been reborn.

In an explosion of godly speed, Raphael slammed into Michael, covering his mouth with his left hand and grabbing him by the arm with his right. Looking into his corrupt brother"s eyes, Raphael sank his claws into Michael's bicep and ripped his arm from the shoulder.

Michael screamed, his blood painting the ground neon green as Raphael threw his arm over his shoulder. Michael leaped to his left, putting some space between himself and his newly powered brother. A sharp jerk pulled him to a stop. Raphael had caught him by one of the thick fingers in his wing and had no intention of letting him escape. He swung him by the wing, in a semicircle, back into the Guardian's destroyed base with a crash.

Michael pulled himself to his knee with his remaining arm and felt a sharp pull on his wing again. Raphael tucked his brother's wing under his arm and stomped onto the back of his neck. With one quick tug, he tore the leathery hand from Michael's back.

The now wingless angel howled in pain and pushed from the ground, swinging a backhand swipe at Raphael. He watched Raphael dodge the backhand and stepped forward with a forehand slice with his claws. There was a flash of color and movement and Michael's right hand fell to the ground.

Raphael stood behind Michael with green blood wetting his wings. Apparently, he had severed Michael's hand with his raven-colored wings, but it was impossible to know for certain. He had moved too fast for either Daniel or Michael to see.

The dismembered angel turned and Raphael plunged his hand into his throat. There was a pause in the action as Michael's brain took a moment to register what had happened. He looked down at his sibling's knuckles sticking out from under his chin, blood leaking from his mouth.

Raphael ripped his hand from Michael's neck and shook the blood from his claws. His fingers sizzled from the contact he had made with Michael's body. He was more demon than angel now.

Michael's eyes bulged. He stumbled away from Raphael, blood pouring from his shoulder, wrist, and throat. Anger bubbled inside him, but more than that, Raphael could see the fear in him. The uncertainty in his stare was enough to make the former angel of healing swell with satisfaction. He had finally brought terror to those green eyes.

Michael turned and beat a hasty retreat, surprising

Raphael almost to the point of humor. Another flash of nearly undetectable movement and both Michael's legs fell off at the knee, dropping him like a pull-apart doll.

The broken angel growled from pain and anger as he lay helplessly on his back. Raphael watched his bloodied stump of a brother shuffle across the ground and prop himself up against the mound of debris behind him. They glared at each other in silence, beaming pure hate through their eyes.

"It's over," Raphael finally said.

"I couldn't agree more."

Whipping his head up in recognition of the voice, Raphael set his eyes on a hooded figure standing next to him.

His beam of hatred intensified. "Lucifer."

The hooded man smiled. "Nice to see you, too."

"What do you want here?" Raphael's gaze was slicing.

Lucifer stepped closer to Michael and slid a cigarette between his fingers, lighting it with the touch of his tongue. "I came to intervene before you further involve yourself in something that's none of your concern."

Raphael's face folded in suspicion but he let the former angel go on.

"You see, Michael and I have made an arrangement, and your actions have already drastically altered our deal. So, I figured I'd step in before you do something that I'd deeply regret."

"This is a family matter, and is none of *your* concern." Raphael stepped closer to Lucifer, his wings blazing behind him, ready to remove his head in a second.

"Correct again, Raph. This *is* a family matter, so let me disclose the logistics of our deal." He drew his tongue wetly across his lips. "We agreed that he would kill the Guardians in exchange for demonic power, hence the drastic change in his appearance." Lucifer motioned toward Michael's veined skin and green eyes. "The amount of demonic power I gave to him was only enough to barely contend with his divine side, but when you removed his heart, all of that changed. You and I know that an angel's heart is the source of his strength and once removed, that angel is no more." Lucifer huffed a mist of smoke into Raphael's face. "When you removed that heart it only gave my powers more room to grow. And grow they did."

"What are you saying, Lucifer?"

The hooded man left a suspenseful pause before answering. "I'm saying that your brother is nearly a full-fledged demon, Raphael, and that makes him my property." A cloud of ash blew through his teeth as he smiled. "You're out of your jurisdiction."

"I can still kill him," Raphael said, countering the man's words.

"True, but if you really wanted to kill him I think you would have done it already." Lucifer walked over to where Michael writhed and grasped a fistful of his hair. "He is a seraph after all. One of only five in creation, so I can't blame you. Though, he did kill your sister didn't he?"

Raphael shot him a glare so cold that even Daniel could feel it. "Tread lightly, Little Horn."

"Take it easy, Raphael." His smile grew wider. "You always were a big softy when it came to family matters."

"We...had...a deal." Michael's words came gurgling through the hole in his throat, spraying more blood as he coughed out each vowel.

Lucifer crouched down to eye level with Michael. "Yes we did, and you couldn't keep your end of the bargain."

He pointed with the two fingers trapping his cigarette at Daniel's beaten and broken form. "Correct me if I'm wrong, but that doesn't qualify as dead does it?"

"Just one. Just...one." Michael repeated, spitting his green liquid as he talked.

"Just one, huh? Well, I could be persuaded to be lenient if you only missed the mark by one Guardian, so let's check the status of the others first." Lucifer turned his head toward Raphael. "Would you be so kind as to take a glance at who's alive out there?"

Raphael scowled at the request.

Lucifer pressed his hands together and made a groveling face. "Pretty please, with sugar on top?"

This made the angel's face crumple even more somehow, yet he gave in and cast his sight over the battlefield. His eyes immediately grew wide with surprise, darting from one blood-soaked body to the next.

"They live!" His voice was a mixture of shock and excitement. "I can see their heartbeats. All of them." He looked at Daniel and could see the relief wash over him. "They're all alive."

"Impossible," Michael coughed.

"I don't think so. He may be new to the job, but that's the angel of death over there. If anyone knows who's dead and who's not it's him. So that means you couldn't kill one Guardian, Michael. Not one. If that ain't a breach of contract then I don't know what is."

Michael started thrashing wildly, spitting and snarling as he tried to scoot away from Lucifer. "No. You cannot take me! I am seraphim! I am the right hand of God. Mother of mothers, save your child!"

Lucifer grabbed Michael's head with both hands and held him still. "Come now, Michael, it won't be so bad. And you know what they say..." He kissed his middle and index digits and then snapped his fingers, lighting Michael's body in bright red flames. "...once you're in Hell..."

Michael screamed long and loud, thrashing even more wildly as the fire consumed him.

Raphael watched his brother burn in front of him and finished Lucifer's axiom. "Only the devil can help you."

In seconds, Michael's body was burned char-black, his limbless form wafting in a plume of smoke.

Lucifer stood erect and dusted off his pants before turning to Raphael. "Well, now that we've all gotten what we wanted, I think I'll be leaving now."

"You tricked him." Daniel surprised the remaining two by speaking so bluntly out of turn. "You didn't want us dead. This was never about us. It was about Michael. It was always about him, wasn't it? You wanted him from the beginning."

The fallen angel looked Daniel over in amusement. "Really? And how is that?"

"You saved them. Somehow you saved them and kept them from dying so you could have Michael when it was all said and done."

The Guardian's mind produced the image of Lucifer strolling about the battlefield, placing his hands on each of his teammates and using his dark power to keep them from the verge of death.

Lucifer walked over to where Daniel lay, eyeing him curiously. "Oh come now, Daniel you give me far too much credit. After all, cheating is a sin." The hooded man winked at him. "How we ever let you escape is a quandary, but I'll have you back, Daniel. I guarantee it."

The man flicked the end of a cigarette onto the ground. He had finished six of them in the time he had arrived from out of nowhere.

He smiled darkly at the injured man. "See you soon." He grabbed Michael's smoking body by the face, turned, and walked away, dragging the seared torso across the battlefield. "Oh, and feel free to drop by Sheol sometime, Raphael."

As he walked, he stepped into the shadow of an uprooted oak and disappeared, leaving his words hanging in the air.

"We'll have a...family reunion."

Adam moved as fast as he could down the hall, hurrying toward the hospital room. The crutches didn't help with his speed much, but he was glad to have them. While moving, a man in a wheelchair flew past, almost knocking him down. The speedster spun the chair to a stop in front of the doorway that just so happened to be the young Guardian's destination.

Adam straightened himself and looked at the man covered in bandages and wearing a neck brace, still recognizing the crooked Irish smile in front of him.

"Mark? What the hell are you doing in a wheelchair?"

"They're free, aren't they? Can't expect a fella to heal if he's dragging himself around on his feet all day, now can ya?"

"You almost knocked me over."

Mark shrugged lazily. "Have to be faster if ya want to be first."

"My sentiments exactly." Seraphim spoke from a seat inside the room next to the wheelchair she rolled in on.

She wore many bandages as well, one in particular wrapping and straightening her nose. The look on her face said that she had been there for a while.

"Son of a bitch." Mark rolled his eyes at the Russian woman.

"Mark, get your Irish ass in here," a deep baritone called.

Mark followed the voice inside the room and found

Prophet laying on a hospital bed, his metal arm removed but the rest of his limbs wrapped in casts.

"Jaysis, you look...great," he lied.

Prophet burst into laughter and then cringed when the pain reminded him of his broken ribs. "Yeah. Well, you can kiss my ass, Marksman. And if I still had my other arm you'd be spitting teeth and shitting metal."

Adam finally made it down the hall and leaned against the doorway. "Something tells me that if you still had your metal arm *it* would be in a cast too."

The room erupted in laughter. Adam looked over to the far side of the room at Emmanuelle who sat by the window. Her entire right arm was cast up to her shoulder. She stared out the window quietly, a somber look encapsulating her face. Adam moved over to her, the noise from his crutches alerting her to his presence.

"Hey, how you holding up?" He asked as sincerely as possible.

She gave a curt, fake smile. "Fine. Just thinking."

"About what?"

"Father and Saduj."

She said what was in the back of everyone's mind and could practically hear the joy sucked out of the room. They all dropped their heads, the smiles fading from their faces.

"It's hard to believe that they're gone," Seraphim said.

"Yeah, they were...good men," Adam replied, his mind flashing back to that fiery hallway, the blood-drenched knife in Saduj's hand and Father's body on the cold floor.

"None better," Mark added.

"I'm sure neither of them would want us sulking around on account of them."

The new voice made the injured group look up at the man in the doorway. Daniel sat in a wheelchair with casts up to his neck, being pushed by a woman covered from neck to knee in a thick brown coat. Half her face was hidden, revealing only the top of her head and her long black hair.

"How's my brother, D? I heard you checked up on him," Prophet said.

"He's fine. His condition hasn't improved, but he's stable. In fact, with him out of commission for a while and Father and Saduj..." His voice cut off and he took a moment to compose himself. "Anyway, I figured that we needed an extra hand for a while so..."

On queue, the woman stepped into the room and dropped the coat from her shoulders. The men and woman got their first full look at the silent figure as her body came into view. She was tall, almost six-foot with pale skin and a stone-cold expression on her face. She wore a black, tight-fitting body suit over a slender yet fit frame.

Mark's eyes nearly jumped out of his head at the sight of her. "Well, hello gorgeous."

"Who is this, Daniel?" Seraphim asked from her seat.

"Aye, and does she enjoy long strolls across the beach?" The Irishman added with a grin.

Daniel cleared his throat, trepidation clinging to the inside of his mouth like static electricity. "This is Eve. She's the newest member of our team."

They all exchanged glances. None of them had met her before.

Emmanuelle stood to her feet, giving the woman a disconcerting look. "This is highly irregular, Daniel. We usually know in advance when someone new is added to our team. What's going on?"

"Since we've taken such a grievous blow to our manpower, let's just say she was rushed through."

Mark leaned over toward Prophet. "She certainly passes *my* background check."

"But there's more. There are things you should all know about her first," Daniel said, nervousness returning to his chest like lumps of coal in his lungs.

His eyes glanced to the floor for a while, searching for the words. When he found them, he returned his gaze to the men and women before him, brimming with affirmation.

"She's a demon..."

Daniel saw each of his warriors jump with unease, their mouths opening to object to her presence. He finished before they could answer.

"...and...she's my daughter."

His words stole the breath from everyone in the room. Even the loquacious Mark was at a loss for words. They all looked over the steely-eyed woman standing before them, her face pale and emotionless. Adam looked at her and back at Daniel then at her again, his mind swirling into a mess of cognitive flashes that could only sum up his emotions in two words.

"Holy shit..."

ABOUT THE AUTHOR

Brandon M Davis is an emerging author of Urban Dark Fantasy. This is Brandon's first published book, but he has been writing since elementary school. As a novelist, and avid anime enthusiast, Brandon seeks to combine his favorite aspects of compelling storytelling to give his readers a world they can truly lose themselves inside. He hopes you laughed, cried, lost it and threw the book a few times(not too hard hopefully)and turned the last page satisfied yet eager for the next volume. If you'd like to learn more about Brandon, follow him on Instagram @bdavis_author, on Twitter @BDavis_Author, and on Facebook. You can also listen to him on his YouTube podcast Final Thoughts.

facebook.com/tefus2004

twitter.com/BDavis_Author

instagram.com/bdavis_author

Also by Brandon M Davis

Be prepared for Book 2 arriving soon titled:

Between Heaven & Hell

The Nephilim

If you enjoyed Between Heaven & Hell Genesis please consider
leaving a review via the link below

https://tinyurl.com/BHHG-Amazon-Review-Page

(Note: In order to leave a review on an Amazon product you must
have spent at least $50. Only leave a review if it is convenient for you.
Thanks again!)

Milton Keynes UK
Ingram Content Group UK Ltd.
UKHW010839271023
431440UK00004B/275